Rhilander drew on his cigar only to discover it had gone out. Outside in the night sky he spied a shooting star. No, shooting stars weren't orange. Another. Another. Rifles cracked.

Rhilander opened the door and shouted the building awake. "Get your clothes on quick! You wanted action, it's here. . . ."

Fire arrows streaked the sky, thudded against the building. Men were running back and forth with sloshing water buckets. Yelling, confused, frightened. A sergeant came rushing up saluting. "Indians, sir, attacking."

"Bastards," muttered Rhilander.

Lieutenant Consolo came beside Rhilander. "I guess this means you're not going to get to talk to Crazy Horse after all," he said, grinning. "Looks like he's not in the mood."

"Me either," said Rhilander. . . .

CHEYENNE

The second saga in a blazing new trail of adventure—

FORTUNES WEST

FORTUNES WEST

CHEYENNE

FORT RUSSELL

A.R. RIEFE

A SIGNET BOOK

NEW AMERICAN LIBRARY

PUBLISHER'S NOTE

This book is a work of fiction. Names, characters, places, and incidents either are the product of the author's imagination or are used fictitiously, and any resemblance to actual persons, living or dead, events, or locales is entirely coincidental.

SIGNET TRADEMARK REG. U.S. PAT. OFF. AND FOREIGN COUNTRIES
REGISTERED TRADEMARK—MARCA REGISTRADA
HECHO EN CHICAGO, U.S.A.

SIGNET, SIGNET CLASSIC, MENTOR, ONYX, PLUME, MERIDIAN and NAL BOOKS are published by NAL PENGUIN INC., 1633 Broadway, New York, New York 10019

First Printing, January, 1989

1 2 3 4 5 6 7 8 9

PRINTED IN THE UNITED STATES OF AMERICA

July 1868

The tail end of Cow Creek was as dry and dusty as Lincoln Rhilander's throat. It was the most unbearable heat he had ever experienced. Lieutenant Colonel Rhilander, commandant of Fort D. A. Russell, halted the column of six hundred men with an upraised arm. The horses—fewer than a hundred thirty—were all double-ridden, but the soldiers appeared to be even more exhausted than the animals. They staggered to a jangling halt and dropped on their backsides.

"On your feet!" Rhilander snapped as they began pulling off their boots to examine their blisters. "And stay up."

The order was repeated and the men grudgingly complied. Rhilander studied the hill rising above the opposite bank. It was carved with ledges, studded with boulders, and laced with ravines, designed by nature as an ideal ambush spot. Rhilander shaded his eyes from the glare and squinted, but he couldn't see a single feather anywhere on the slope, though he knew hundreds of them were there: Sioux, Cheyenne, armed to the eyes. Their enemy had arrived, completely exposed, obligingly moving into range.

"Mario," Rhilander burst. Lieutenant Mario Consolo, his adjutant, came running up. "They're up there, have the men fall back."

Rhilander took off his hat and wiped his brow with his sleeve. The breeze snatched at his reddish-blonde hair, mussing and tangling it. His handsome, sharply defined features were deeply bronzed, and the corners of his dark blue eyes were prematurely crow-footed from squinting against the brutal glare. He was thirty-three and had been in command at Fort Russell since it was completed two years before. A seasoned Indian fighter, he had been handed command of a force comprised of elements from Fort Fred Steele, Fort Bridger, Fort Fetterman, and other posts. Riding out of Fetterman in pursuit of Crazy Horse, his Oglala Sioux, and their Cheyenne allies, the troopers had headed north-northeast to this point. They were woefully short of horses because the hostiles had broken into the Fetterman corral the previous night and nearly emptied it.

The men fell back about two hundred yards from the creek bank, dragging their horses with them. Rhilander had dismounted. He walked back pondering, weighing his options. The pursuers had come so close that the waiting and watching Crazy Horse was easily able to see Rhilander's strength, not to mention the men's state of exhaustion. The colonel thought about circling the hill and inching up to it to within decent range for the men's Spencers, but spreading out only to spread the Indians out would gain him no advantage. Darkness was still at least ten hours away. And what good could he make of it if he did wait for it? If he was able to gain the edge under cover of darkness, the savages would only sneak away.

He put himself in Crazy Horse's moccasins: he was entrenched in the hillside for one purpose only, to stand and make a fight of it. Crazy Horse was clever as hell; he knew that Rhilander had to suspect an ambush. His retreating the two hundred yards testified to that. And the chief also had to assume that sooner or later his pursuers would have to attack. You don't chase somebody this far and not at least attempt to finish them off when they stop.

Rhilander's suppositions and conjectures, his unfinished plan of attack were blown away in the next instant, dispelled by sporadic firing from the few ancient rifles the Indians had and a volley of arrows that set the troopers scurrying for the meager cover offered by the creekside terrain.

The colonel himself hit the ground, as did Colonel Rudolph Schwimmer beside him.

"Spread out, but hold your fire!" boomed Rhilander to Consolo. The order echoed left and right of where they lay. "All horses to the rear, watch me for hand signals."

A single shot punctuated the silence that followed the firing. Blood and brains spattered Rhilander, and the corporal lying beside him stiffened in death. Confusion triggered and spread.

"Fire at will!" bellowed Rhilander.

Somebody on the colonel's right fired at the corporal's killer. The target screamed, rose from behind his concealment, dropped his rifle clattering, and grabbed his throat as his knees gave way. Blood spilled through the fingers clenched around his windpipe and glistened in the sunlight. The retaliation set off the attack. To Rhilander's surprise, in their haste to do battle the Indians popped up into the troopers' sights like corn breaking ground. The troopers attacked, pounding across the dried-up creek and starting up the slope, firing as they ran, ducking and weaving, dodging arrows and lances. Rhilander watched one man stumble and fall running through the creekbed, right himself cursing, and from a sitting position blast away with two revolvers. Carbine fire rattled up the slope. The *thwunk* of creaking old Henrys sounded. A hail of arrows and a score of lances rained down. The noise was deafening. The dust rose in furry yellow clouds interspersed with blue wisps escaping rifle and pistol muzzles. Most of the men who had started up the slope were already retreating. Some crouched under the low wall of the creekbed, popping up to fire. The savages, having taken a withering fire when they had shown from behind their cover, were now warier.

In the midst of the din and destruction—flying arrows and bullets, blue powder smoke blowing until the men's eyes smarted, men firing, shouting, cursing—Rhilander took quick stock. He decided that if the Indians weren't drawn out from behind their cover, the troopers with their comparably poor cover would gradually be picked off and diminished in number until the odds were so inflated in the savages' favor, Crazy Horse would send them running down the slope to wipe out the few survivors.

Consolo was eyeing Rhilander questioningly. The colonel responded.

"They'll be running out of cartridges soon. Let's give them a little more time."

"Bloody time, Lincoln," shouted Consolo above the din.

"Join the Army and see hell."

Men's eyes stung with sweat and smoke and fear. Their Spencers, heating up, began fouling. The pieces were so hot, the soft copper shells expanded, and ejectors cut through cartridge rims and locked them in place. Men had to hunker down and work the cartridges out with their knives while arrows sang over their heads, thudding into the ground behind them. When the cartridge was finally extracted, they'd slip in another and fire again. Up on the slope the war flutes answered the lone bugle, sounding high, thin, cutting through the noise of battle.

Chief Dull Knife sat scrunched between two flat-faced rocks, locking his forearm to his biceps to stanch the blood surfacing the flesh wound just above his wrist. He peered around the rock in front of him. From his position halfway up the slope he could not see the majority of the bluecoats crouching under the near bank, but in the creek itself a few bent low behind cover too meager to completely conceal them and sent up a steady fire. Behind them, well away from the opposite bank, nearly two hundred officers and men stayed out of accurate arrow range and fired over the heads of their fellows in the creek.

Dull Knife was a realist. He had allied his Cheyenne warriors with the Sioux and subordinated his authority to the blue-eyed, blond-haired Crazy Horse's, deciding that the Plains tribes could only succeed in driving out the invading whites by joining forces. Dull Knife spat angrily as he lowered his forearm, remembering Six Foxes, chief of the Gros Ventre and the Arapaho leader Black Moon.

CHEYENNE

Crazy Horse had invited them to join the campaign. Both had declined. Dull Knife had sat silently watching Crazy Horse upbraid them, accuse them of cowardice and stupidity, and warn that if later their bellies grew wolf guts in place of the sheep guts they carried, it would be too late for them. Roaring at them, he'd sent them hurrying away. His last word was to tell them to send their women to do their talking next time.

Crazy Horse contended and Dull Knife agreed that the settlers would let the Army do their fighting for them and that the tribes should take the fight to the soldiers, harass them, pick away at their numbers, seize their weapons, wear them down and discourage them, rather than pick on the settlers. Make war on Indian terms, not on the Army's; they had too many guns, howitzers, mortars, Gatling guns. Surprise attacks on their outposts, ambushes, traps, hit-and-run tactics would be the strategy and Crazy Horse the master strategist. He had given the order, and the Sioux and Cheyenne warriors had stripped off their buckskin shirts and leggings, leaving only their breechclouts, had knelt on their buffalo robes, untied their war bundles, and laid out their paint. That night they had attacked Fort Fetterman.

Now the *wasichus* had come chasing after them. Now they fought.

Crazy Horse had told him of a dream he'd had in the spring before the first attack on the railroad. He dreamt that he was attending the sun dance and the great medicine man had offered a painful sacrifice. He had cut fifty bits of skin from each arm, then danced for two days staring at the sun, until his sight turned black and he fell down exhausted. When he awoke, his sight returned, and he told of a vision he'd had. Many soldiers would attack a hill in which warriors had lodged themselves. The troopers would fight fiercely with many guns, but the warriors' superior position and numbers would prevail. Every bluecoat would die and there would be many guns to steal.

This was the hill and the battle. Was the dream being fulfilled? Once more Dull Knife looked out, then picked up his rifle and shouted.

A. R. Riefe

"Hoka hey, Lakotas!"

"Hoka hey, Lakotas!" came the answering war cry from all around him. *It's a good day to die!*

The unseasonably brutal heat had reduced the heavily silted Little Blue River to a slender, sluggish brook. The wagon train forded it, sloshing through and up the opposite side. The largest of the twenty-nine wagons was a ten-bow Gingrich Conestoga pulled by three pairs of long-legged Lancaster draft horses. It looked startlingly out of place in the line, since such vehicles were rarely seen west of the Alleghenies. The Conestoga was twenty-two years old; its original wheel and axle assemblies had been replaced before starting out. The Luback canvas bonnet was new as well, tied taut to its bows and bone white in the sun's glare. A custom-built driver's seat extended uncovered from the bonnet. The wagon's box, actually more of a basket on wheels, was part of the original equipment. The box rested on the axles at only three points, two at the rear, one in front, permitting the wagon, even heavily loaded as it was, to yield like a ship to the waves without damaging it or badly disturbing its contents when the front wheels rode over a rock or dropped into a hole.

"Pull boys, pull with your hearts," sang Jubal, tightening his grip on the single jerk line attached to the leader.

The horses responded, straining against their collars, slowly ascending the steep grade that rose from the opposite bank. Jubal could not hold back a grin of satisfaction. Before he'd joined, the others in the train had advised him that a smaller wagon would be better suited to the long journey. But the Hunnicutts had brought all their belongings from their home near tiny Palmyra, east of Harrisburg, Pennsylvania. Jubal hadn't the heart to dispose of a single thing; any impulsive inclination to do so was dampened by the prices offered by the scavengers in Sapling Grove, the point of departure about twenty miles west of Independence, Missouri. Husband and wife, son and daughter had discussed lightening the load, but it was unanimously decided that every single possession

10

was a stitch in the fabric of the family's past. "Dropping a stitch" was unthinkable. Abandoning the farm and the house Jubal had built entirely by himself and in which both son Jeptha and daughter Lorna had been born had been a sad and somewhat trying experience for all four of them. Leaving behind precious bits and pieces of their life was out of the question.

So Jubal had put his faith in the skill of the wagon builder, his six horses, and God, and started west.

He gripped the jerk line, a raw-boned, swarthy, intense man of forty-two, his railroad hat set squarely on his shaggy head, the wide brim shading his eyes from the glare. Jeptha sat in lean likeness to his father beside him. Jubal glanced sidelong at the boy; at eighteen he was already taller than his father's six-foot-two, but not nearly as broad or as muscular.

"This grade must be a quarter of a mile or more," commented Jeptha, looking up from his book.

"And steep as a barn roof."

Jeptha glanced back down at the brown rope of river. The last three wagons in the train forded and started up the hill in turn. His eyes returned to their horses. They were beginning to struggle, the deadweight of the wagon load combining with the poor footing to push them to the brink of exhaustion. Again and again one or another would slip on the rock-hard ground. Jeptha closed his book and jumped down to walk alongside the leader.

"You think they'll make it, Pa?" he asked anxiously.

Jubal frowned. Jeptha did not share his faith in the strength and work capacity of the Lancaster draft horse— because he did not know horses like his father did. The boy had no real heart for farming. His dream was to become a lawyer. He read voraciously in preparation for college. Whether he would ever find one or whether one would ever find him in Oregon was questionable, but his slender chances of realizing his ambition failed to discourage him.

The struggling horses made it to the top, standing, blowing hard, gleaming with sweat. Jubal gave a number of short, quick tugs on the line, tightening the off branch

11

so the lead horse's mate could feel the bit jerking to his right. He turned to that side, leading the others, pulling the wagon out of the line of traffic. Jubal pulled the brake with both hands, turning the rocker bar, thereby pulling the transverse brake beam to the rear so the brake shoe mounted on the bar made contact with the rear tire.

Jeptha emitted a low whistle of surprise.

"Will you look at that, it's even steeper going down."

Ahead of them one by one wagons were being skidded down, their bonnets shuddering, the drivers yelling at their animals. Jubal got down and stretched.

"Everything all right?" called his wife Hannah from the rear of the wagon, where she and Lorna sat talking and darning by the end gate.

"Anything loose back there, snug it down, we're going to be skidding down," said Jubal. "Hang onto the end gate when I tell you to." He grinned at Jeptha. "I'll try not to tip us over. Give me a hand with the chains and drag shoes, son."

Jeptha was already at the tool box with its wrought iron straps and fittings hanging at the middle of the wagon. He got out a number of lengths of chain.

"Chain the back wheels," said Jubal, "and when you're done, fasten the short chains around all four tires—"

"Around the fellies, I know, I know. Every time we do this you explain all over again. It's not the most complicated job in the world."

"Just don't want you to mess up," said Jubal.

"Have I yet?"

He was treating an eighteen-year-old like a seven-year-old, and really shouldn't, thought Jubal. But the boy was a dreamer like his mother, and sometimes didn't concentrate on what his hands were doing.

"You're getting your education in pioneering, son. You won't find that in one of your books."

"I'm not really looking for it," responded Jeptha.

While Jeptha set about chaining the rear wheels to the wagon box, Jubal slipped the drag shoes—fourteen-inch-long iron channels—under the wheels, and fastened them securely.

"What's that book you're reading today?" asked Jubal.

"Same as yesterday, *Pilgrim's Progress.*"

"About us pilgrims?"

"About all." Jeptha pinched his index finger slightly on a chain, flinched, grimaced, and waggled away the pain. "The full title is *The Pilgrim's Progress From This World To That Which Is To Come: Delivered under the Similitude Of A Dream, Wherein is Discovered The Manner of His Setting out on His Dangerous Journey, And Safe Arrival at the Desired Country.*"

"Oregon. What's sim—sim—?" Jubal asked.

"Similitude. Something that's like something else. A thing, a person. In this case his dream is like his life."

"Do tell. I'm glad some of mine aren't," said Jubal.

Oregon, he thought as he worked, the "New Country," was claimed to be an earthly paradise where the sun always shone, where the grass never lost its greenness, and fruit grew wild. A limitless supply of furs, wood, water, opportunity; rivers teeming with fish, miles upon miles of prime valley land. The Indians' claim to the land they had lived on for a thousand years had been officially declared false, for they had neither tilled it nor built permanently on it. Neither the Indians nor anyone else could stand in the way of the destiny that decreed the nation's sweep across the continent. The Willamette Valley toward which they were heading was an area too rich and enticing to be ignored.

Jubal looked up at Hannah and Lorna and winked and smiled, finished securing one drag shoe, and moved around to the other side, joining Jeptha, who was slipping back into deep thought. The past two years' crops on the Hunnicutts' thirty-acre farm had been bountiful, enabling them to raise and save the money to fund the move. But the preceding ten years had ranged from bountiful to disastrous, and in Jubal's opinion the soil was exhausting itself. Besides, in Oregon there would be no taxes, no need for a loan from the bank, no limit on available land.

Air to breathe!

He often complained to Hannah that people were settling in their shadows, even though their nearest neighbor was seven miles away. But there was more to his desire for change. What he craved more than anything was a government policy that would permit a farmer to squat on a piece of land, build a house, clear the trees and stumps, and after the region had been surveyed, to purchase his land at the minimum auction price without being outbid by a speculator. And he wanted not thirty acres, but three hundred.

Huggins came along at the right time. So right it seemed like fate was intervening in their lives. Jubal and Jeptha had driven into Palmyra two years before on a brisk February day to buy grain and replace the worn-out hay rake. A man named Huggins had assembled a large crowd in front of the drugstore. He mounted a Pears soapbox and addressed the gathering.

"Neighbors, I'm here today to tell you about paradise. It's a long ways from here, a long and difficult, dangerous trek, but if you've got the spleen for it, and the willingness to face the challenge of your lives, you'll be well rewarded.

"Where is this paradise, this land flowing with milk and honey? It borders the mighty Pacific Ocean. It is Oregon. Say the name and you say paradise. There so bountiful is the land immense crops of wheat can be raised; so rich the soil, so mild the climate, so plentiful the rainfall, a man need only turn the land with the blade of his plow, plant his seed, and turn his back to raise crops the like of which no eye in Pennsylvania or anywhere else in this blessed nation has ever seen."

So moved had Jubal been by his words, he had driven straight home, forgetting about the grain and the hay rake. He'd sat the family down and all but repeated Huggins's speech word for word. He compared Pennsylvania to Oregon, and the Keystone State suffered grievously in contrast.

"Winters it's frost and snow to freeze your bones to

rattling inside you. Springs it rains so there are times it drowns a good half of our acres. Summers it's so hot and dry the crop withers. Taxes take the yield of what's left. It's work, work, work, often for next to naught. Nothing sets a body to suffering so much as discouragement. And that's our most successful crop, no matter what we plant.

"We've had two good years running. Which means the next two will almost certainly be poor. What say, Mother, good-bye to Pennsylvania, hello to Oregon. Hello to God's country!"

Despite his enthusiasm, neither Hannah nor Lorna had sparked to the idea, but he worked at persuading them with the zeal and passion of a fire-and-brimstone preacher, and in time they had come around.

Jeptha fastened on the next-to-last chain. Lorna had gotten down to watch.

"You be careful taking us down, Jeptha Hunnicutt," she warned.

"Talk to the horses, don't talk to me."

"Don't be flip, little brother."

Jeptha laughed and his thoughts whirled back to the farm and that fateful late afternoon in February two years earlier when Jubal had proposed they emigrate to Oregon. His father would not have groused or sulked if the vote had gone against him; he wasn't one to demand that others agree with him, or criticize others for their failure to see what appealed to him in an idea. Everyone's opinion held as much weight as everyone else's and no more—not like some families where the father was God Almighty, the wife did as she was ordered by her lord and master, and the children, whatever their ages, bowed their heads and meekly submitted.

Jubal's courage did match his zeal, Jeptha thought. His father would have braved the wilds of the Amazon to build their future if he had envisioned one there. Mother had the courage if not the zeal, and she realized from the first that she would be essential to the success of the enterprise, and therefore would have to be as whole-heartedly committed to it as he. Bless Mother, she did have a clear sense of her own worth, and he and Lorna being grown also helped her to decide in favor of going.

Mother strove to be equal to the grueling demands of the day; she asked no special treatment or help. She prepared their meals and washed and mended their clothes and cared for them. Out of the disorder of traveling she held to some routine.

With Lorna and the other wives and daughters she collected buffalo chips for the fires when there was no wood. When there were no buffalo chips, they walked in clouds of dust behind the wagons, collecting weeds. Mother searched for wild blueberries and managed to roll dough on the top of the dutch oven in spite of the wagon's incessant rocking, and bake a pie over hot rocks so the family supper would be lifted above beans and coffee.

And in spite of her fears and lingering reservations over leaving home, she never complained; she always had a smile and a pleasant word, and husband and children thrived within the golden circle of her love.

The chains in place, Jubal released the brake and started slowly, carefully down the grade. The load was heavy, perhaps twice the weight of any one of the smaller wagons. The bed was snugly packed with bedding, cooking utensils—including the dutch oven and a reflector oven—food staples, clothing, liniment, camphor, tallow, candle molds, sewing necessities, two clocks, and a chamber pot. There were also tools, spare parts for the wagon, weapons and luxuries: plant cuttings, an iron stove, family albums, furniture, china, silverware, books, and Jubal's joy, his harmonium that, unable to read music, he played by ear.

"Careful, dear!" shrilled Hannah.

He turned to look back. She and Lorna hung onto the rear-end gate, both already white-faced in dread and anticipation.

"We'll be just fine, Mother," called Jubal. "Just hang on."

The look on Jeptha's face said all too eloquently that he didn't agree. His book closed beside him, he too hung on with both hands. Jubal kept their progress down the

hill as straight as he could, making good use of the
jockey stick, which afforded him more direct control of
the horses. It was a light, firm rod, one end fastened to
the leader's collar, the other hanging loosely from the off
side of his right-hand mate's bit. To keep the jockey line
from drooping to the ground, it was passed through three
large rings, one attached to the leader's hip, the second
attached to the swing leader's hame, and the third attached to the swing leader's hip.

Down slid the Conestoga, swaying precariously, jolt-
ing, lurching, following the wagon ahead of it. It was like
trying to maneuver a sleigh over ice. If the horses turned,
the wagon would skid sideways and tip over, possibly
breaking all their necks. Jubal shoved the jerk line into
Jeptha's hands and seized the brake as the wagon accel-
erated. The brake shoe combined with the rock chains to
slow the ponderous weight and maintain precious distance between the front-end panel and the horses' rumps,
the tongue running forward out of the front hounds pushing like a battering ram. But the strong-legged horses
were braking powerfully, fighting gravity and the load,
keeping the downward slide straight and controlled.

All six were holding up well in the heat wave. So far
on the journey, grass had been plentiful and Jubal saw to
it that their diet was supplemented with oats that he
doled out sparingly after breakfast each day. And they
were given frequent small portions of water, both Jubal
and Jeptha careful not to let them gulp it down and bind
their stomachs with cramps that, if severe enough, could
kill them.

But as the long, arduous days slipped behind the emigrants, water was becoming more and more precious.
Most of the supply brought along was saved for drinking
for men and beasts, including the Tucker's cow, trailing
that family's conventional wagon behind the Hunnicutts'
Conestoga. The Tuckers generously shared her milk with
their neighbors ahead and behind, and milk poured into
a bucket suspended from the rear bolster alongside the
tar bucket, jiggled, and jounced all day until by sundown
it had turned to butter.

A. R. Riefe

They slid to a stop at the bottom of the hill. Jubal braked and father and son got down to take off the ice cutters and rock chains. Hannah's relief at reaching the bottom of the hill without incident prompted her to begin singing. She had a sweet voice and "Evalina Mine" never sounded more beautiful to Jubal than when Hannah sang it. But her doing so made him slip into worry about her. He loved his Hannah dearly; she was the sun of his life. Like her son, she had a fine mind, but over the past eight years there were times when her mind tended to drift. She claimed to hear voices and insisted that she was visited by apparitions in the night.

Her problems had begun after the loss of their second son. He had been born dead, and she blamed herself for losing him. She locked her guilt in her conscience and there kept and nurtured it. As with the births of Lorna and Jeptha earlier, she had not been attended by a doctor. Jubal had helped to deliver all three children. Had there been a doctor for their second son, perhaps he would have been able to convince her that she was blameless. Jubal could not seem to. He had given up trying. It was too much like opening an old wound to try to cure it, enable it to heal; all he seemed to do was restore the pain with no cure.

Mercifully, her mental ramblings were few and weeks between. She had been stricken a month earlier on the night before the train was to set out. She had awakened from a sound sleep insisting she had seen her lost babe, that he was alive, a handsome little boy with curly brown hair like her brother Edward's. They had talked; it was all quite pleasant, not at all frightening. Then, promising to visit her again, he withdrew. Since then she had waited on tenterhooks for him to reappear.

It was the only time she'd *seen* him. Other previous apparitions had been strangers and relatives who had passed on. Her sister Samantha, who had drowned when she was twelve, had visited her a number of times. Jubal thanked the Lord that the visitations were restricted to her dreams.

Three days after starting out, the train had stopped for

18

CHEYENNE

the night on the banks of Big Stranger Creek in eastern
Kansas. Hannah had gone for a walk by herself and when
she came back to the camp an hour later, she was adorned
with wildflowers: garlands of butter yellow eriogonums
intertwined with white and purple cinquefoil around her
neck and waist; a crown fashioned of groundsels, blue
violets, and golden partridge pea blossoms. She had not
behaved at all strangely; indeed her getup was all a bit of
a lighthearted joke to her, but some of their fellow emigrants had burst out laughing at the sight of her. Some
even made the crazy sign around their temples. It was
not a reaction she'd expected. She had reddened in embarrassment, rushed to the wagon, climbed in, and did
not reappear for two whole days.

Jubal had been incensed at the others' cruelty, their
sarcasm, and ridicule. He had confronted Ogden Fletcher,
the leader of the train, who had been the loudest and
most obvious in poking fun; he threatened to beat him
"bloody numb." Jeptha and Mr. Tucker had had to intervene. Fletcher had apologized to Hannah, others had
also, and that seemed to settle matters as best they could
be.

The New World they were journeying to would be
vastly different from home in many ways. The farm in
Pennsylvania had been a safe haven for her. She did not
feel menaced. In fact, she felt secure. Would she come to
feel the same out there? She was trying to cope along the
way and doing a good job so far, but he could not help
but wonder how she would stand up under the rigors
ahead. Kansas and now Nebraska were strange, threatening, even frightening to her, sensitive soul that she was.
Starting out, she had seen an Indian behind every tree
and rock.

Jubal had heard that life on the trail affected everyone,
bringing out the best in some and the worst in others. It
was claimed that in some cases hardship and misfortune
served to hone people's characters, firm their resolve,
and strengthen their ability to adapt and their resourcefulness.

Jubal had no worries about his own ability to meet the

19

test, or Jeptha's or Lorna's. They were true pioneer stock. Hannah was not. She wasn't frail or sickly, just not as robust as Iola Tucker and many of the other women. Many were as strong as their men and did men's work. Iola could jack up their wagon, remove a wheel, and tar it as well as her husband.

Shortly before they left home, second thoughts had swarmed in to assail Jubal over Hannah's making the trip despite her willingness. He had discussed it with Jeptha and Lorna. Lorna raised a point that had not occurred to him; if at this late stage he did call it off, Hannah would know why. She already bore the burden of guilt for the baby's death; she wouldn't hesitate to assume a second and equally heavy burden if he changed his mind about their going. She'd know it would be on her account.

Perhaps, he recalled thinking at the time, he'd let his enthusiasm run away with him, running home with Huggins's words mesmerizing, captivating him, setting his heart singing with expectation that grew and grew as the months winged by. Still, had Hannah been Iola Tucker, no second thoughts would have come to mind. Then, too, when they did reach their destination, knowing Hannah, she would take to Oregon like green to grass, and in the long run it would be the best for her in mind and body. Lorna and Jeptha agreed wholeheartedly.

Chains and ice cutters restored to the tool box, they continued on their way. In the heat the interior of the wagon became insufferable, the air all but unbreathable. All the wagon bonnets were taken down. Jubal pulled his hat brim lower over his eyes, and surveyed the dusty line of wagons crawling the rocky road as straight as a wire fence in a northwesterly direction toward the Nebraska City road north of the distant Platte River. The first stop of importance, with a day's layover for celebration, would be Fort Kearney. Later in turn would come such landmarks as Independence Rock, Soda Springs, and Courthouse Rock. In time the way would lead by easy grades up to the eight-thousand-foot summit of the Rockies to South Pass. From the South Pass to Fort Bridger, and from Fort Bridger to Fort Hall would be the second major leg of the journey: five hundred and thirty-five miles altogether. By then the emigrants would have traveled twelve hundred miles from Sapling Grove.

Halfway to Oregon.

It was mid-afternoon. Tiny Hebron, sister site to the same named city of Palestine, lay beyond view ahead—Abraham's "city of refuge" rising in the Great Plains. How far ahead Jubal had no way of estimating, but likely too far to reach before the sun vanished behind the distant Sand Hills.

The train was nearing the three-hundred-mile mark. At between fifteen and twenty miles a day from shortly after sunrise to before sundown (less than half that when sizable rivers had to be forded or extended delays were encountered) the emigrants had already closed out their first month on the trail. If all continued to go reasonably well, if their water held out, if fresh water were found, if it rained—unlikely at that time of the year—and three or four of the interior bows of each wagon were removed, sagging the bonnet to trap water, if the horses, mules, and oxen survived in appreciable numbers, if the Indians let the intruders pass through their territories unmolested, if cholera, smallpox, dysentary, or some other pestilence did not strike, if a tornado did not find them, if the hailstorms were not too destructive, they would reach Fort Laramie, Wyoming, in a month.

They had started out in early May, nearly three weeks late, but it was either that or wait until the following year. Some of the emigrants were concerned lest they run into winter before reaching their destination, which at the tail end of such an exhausting trek could prove disastrous. It was reckoned that the latest they would reach the Willamette Valley in Oregon would be the end of October. A vote had been taken. The decision to start out won by a wide margin. Early or late, it was no trip for the timid. Jubal, having already driven his family across four states, was all for leaving as soon as possible. He despised Sapling Grove. Conditions there had become so bad that heads of families had to take turns staying awake nights to guard the wagons.

But all that was behind them now. Endless yellow Nebraska lay ahead, and half a world away was the valley of all their dreams.

The wagon ahead slowed and stopped. Jubal halted his horses and Ephraim Tucker behind him stopped his wagon in turn. He came forward, shading his eyes from the sun, looking ahead.

"Appears another ox has given out. The third wagon behind Fletcher's," said Jubal.

Alison Cooper, at the reins of the wagon in front of the Hunnicutts', came back to join them. He was visibly upset, grinding his chaw of tobacco, glaring, spitting, a bull-chested man with a full fundamentalist beard and a temper that could strike like lightning. Easy going Ephraim Tucker had such a firm rein on his temper Jubal was beginning to doubt if he even had one. Nothing seemed to upset him; everything, even the most trivial, upset Cooper.

"They's no cause, jest none! Everyday since the second week, we get held up by a ox droppin' out. Nary a mule, not your horses, Hunnicutt, always the danged oxen. Moss Larribee and me both told Fletcher back in Saplin' Grove them whose wagons was gonna be ox pulled oughta take every yoke out and march it ten mile. Five out, five back, without stoppin'. Find out afore they start if the critters is fit for such a trek. Onliest way."

"Ox is the strongest beast there is," said Tucker.

"May be, but that don't mean that underneath all the sinew they can't be a weak heart or lungs. You can't tell by lookin' in its eye if it got the consumption or not. Ox can get black-leg same as a steer. Rinderpest. They's a dozen 'flictions they can have without 'em showin' up till they put to the test. It's just unnecessary, bone stupid. Wagons headin' out this fur should be mule-hauled anyways." He stopped and eyed Jubal. "Oh, nothin' wrong with horseflesh. You're smart, Hunnicutt, feedin' yours oats. Feedin' a horse on grass only day in day out is like a human eatin' nothin' but sody crackers. Keep him alive, maybe, but cain't give him no salt, no energy.

Lookee that, not one but two of the critters. Has to be one in each yoke, of course. That's our luck every time."

A pistol was fired twice. The sounds drifted back to them; a double wisp of smoke rose lazily.

"Put them out of their misery," observed Tucker.

"Somebody oughta put us out'n ourn," fumed Cooper. "Delay, delay, delay. We ain't been on the road but a month an' already we're better'n a week behind."

"Tell Fletcher," said Tucker, "he's in charge."

"Tell Fletcher," repeated Jubal sarcastically. "It isn't dying oxen that's putting us behind, it's stopping before sundown when we could go on for at least two, three more hours."

"You talk to him about that?" Tucker asked.

"Till I get a cramp in my tongue. I give up. You know what his trouble is? He's got to do everything his way. Never mind whether it's right or wrong, it's got to be his way."

"Man's got the experience," said Tucker. "He's been out to Utah and back twice. He's the only one among us who's been west."

"Then he should know better than to stop so early in the day."

Anger's standard raised by Alison Cooper, Jubal took it over.

"At the rate we're going we'll be slogging through snow from the Rockies all the way to the Oregon border. What riles me is his high-and-mighty ways, the way he talks down his nose at everybody. Like we were children."

Cooper snickered. "Fact is, you two jest sour each other worse'n cider in the sun."

"That's so, Jubal," said Tucker.

Jeptha and Salita Jane Tucker had been wandering about hand in hand during the stop, and were standing about twenty feet away. When Jubal and the others noticed them, their hands parted and the girl flushed and turned away. Jubal suppressed a smile, which would only have added to her embarrassment. He eyed Jeptha as he half listened to Cooper and Tucker talk further about the trip. Jubal loved and admired his son and wanted only the best for him. It did not matter that he had no love for farming, that he preferred brain to brawn. Jubal had never thought of himself as stupid; he could read and cipher and did not grunt his way through conversation, but his formal education had ended in the fifth grade and rarely did he open any book other than the family Bible. Jeptha was smarter, and determined to reach the stars.

Jeptha had completed high school, cramming to finish the work and earn his diploma before they left Pennsylvania. What he had been taught would hold him in good stead in his future studies for the law, so he contended.

What he had yet to learn about life was another matter. Like his mother, he was a dreamer: impressionable, even naive, too trusting in Jubal's view. He was one of those individuals who consciously overlooked life's burrs and thorns, and like his mother, saw beauty in everything. He fancied he was in love with Salita Jane Tucker.

Salita Jane was good enough for his parents, if not his sister. She was sweet and pretty, with lovely ash-blonde hair, but no match for Jeptha's intelligence. But Jubal was sure their hearts had little patience for profound conversation. They did not ride together; with eleven children there was no room in the Tucker's wagon for Jeptha. And with eleven children there was too much for Salita Jane to do to leave their wagon. But at every stop, every evening they would meet and walk or sit by the cook fire in silence looking longingly at each other, rarely saying anything, but thinking the deep and amorous glowing thoughts of every young couple in love. To Salita Jane, Jeptha was another Abe Lincoln with the Great Emancipator's fine mind and immense potential. To Jeptha, Salita Jane was an angel.

Ephraim Tucker had stopped talking and was looking forward. "They're starting up again. You boys think we'll make Hebron by sundown?"

"Not now," said Cooper.

The wagons rolled on. Lorna came forward, squeezing between her father and brother. They passed the two dead oxen, eyeing them pityingly.

"Poor dumb creatures."

24

Jeptha put his book away and relieved Jubal at the reins.

"The trouble is," he said, "it puts that much more strain on the survivors in the team. Folks should test their animals before they put them through an ordeal like this."

Jubal shrugged. Lorna slipped an arm around each of them. Her beautiful face was clouded with concern. She was fair, blessed with striking green eyes, capable of absorbing the attention of anyone who looked upon her. Her cheekbones were unusually high, and so prominent they shadowed the perfectly flat planes of her cheeks angling down from them. They framed an exquisite nose, which she complained was too large but was not. Her lips were full—overly so, she insisted—with the merest suggestion of defiance in them that, when her temper was up, could be matched by her magnificent eyes.

She was small-busted, slender, and tall—within two inches of six feet—and would have been ungainly but for her constant attention to her posture. There was a regal look about her; at first glance one could not be forgiven presuming she'd been magically whisked from her throne somewhere in Europe, divested of crown and jewels, arrayed in cotton and calico, and installed in the Conestoga.

"Father," she began in a tone that matched her somber look.

Jubal sighed. He knew what was coming. He lowered his head and voice.

"How is she doing?" he asked.

"Not making much sense. These past two days have been babble and babble. It's the strain. We have to face up to it, we've no choice—"

"I don't want to talk about it, girl."

"We have to," said Lorna.

"Why? We don't agree, never will."

"Because you don't want to, you refuse to admit it."

Jeptha nodded. "She's right, Pa, you do refuse."

"Don't you start."

"We're all guilty," Jeptha continued. "We say she's

wandering off, she's not herself, she's overstrained. What we're really saying is she's touched."

Jubal flared. "You shut your mouth, boy, else I'll shut it for you!"

"What's the matter?" called Hannah from the back.

"Nothing, Mother," said Jubal, glaring at his son.

Lorna lowered her head and said nothing. But her father read her thoughts and lashed out at them.

"You, too, missy," he growled.

"I don't want to argue," she persisted, "but we have to talk. She was napping about an hour ago and when she woke up she said Samantha had come to her in a dream and told her we'd find gold in Oregon, we'd become rich as Croesus. She said—"

"Don't you understand English, Lorna Hunnicutt?"

He glared fiercely at her, got up unsteadily, and made his way back through the cargo to where Hannah sat on a cushion on the dutch oven, her mending put to one side, her hand on the end gate. Lorna and Jeptha exchanged looks.

"She's getting worse fast, Jep. I see it, but he just won't."

"He sees it. And admits it. To himself. Can't you see the reason he doesn't want to talk about it is because he's helpless to do anything? We all are. What can we do, turn back? We're three hundred miles from Sapling Grove, a thousand more from home. All we can do is hope and pray she doesn't fall apart completely. She's hanging on by her fingertips. She wants to and will if we help hold her up. He is."

"So am I!"

"Sssssh. I know you are, Lorry. The biggest thing we can do is protect her from the others. You know there's whispering going around—"

"What have you heard?" she asked.

"Sssssh. Nothing. I don't have to. I know what they're thinking. You can see it in their faces when they look at her. Don't you recognize pity when you see it? And the way he blew up when she came back all decked out in wildflowers and Fletcher and some of the others made fun of her. Anybody could see he was being overly protective. Like she was a child. He would have broken Fletcher's jaw if Salita Jane's father and I hadn't stepped between them."

"She's dotty, Jep."

"Perhaps." He shrugged.

"She is."

"Well, there's dotty and there's *dotty*. She's sure not about to take a butcher knife to somebody," he said.

"She wouldn't hurt a fly."

"She's no trouble to anybody but us," said Jeptha.

"She's no trouble!" snapped Lorna defensively.

Jeptha silenced her again. "You know what I mean. We're the ones who should be worrying about her—and we are. We just have to go on taking the best care of her we can."

Lorna nodded. Her helplessness in the face of her mother's condition was evident in her expression.

"We sure can't let her go walking by herself anymore," she murmured.

"No, we can't." He shook his head to add finality to his words.

"Only she'll want to. Everybody wants to be by himself once in a while."

"We can't let her. Either that or one of us will have to follow her."

"That'd be horribly deceitful. If she ever saw—" She sighed. "It's so sad. She's so sweet and caring. Why does *she* have to be sick in the head?"

"Ssssh, damn!" rasped Jeptha.

"Don't swear."

"Then stop carrying on so about it."

"Poor, poor mother." Lorna shook her head resignedly.

They looked back. Jubal and Hannah were holding hands. She was smiling. He kissed her forehead. She blushed and laughed gaily. They glanced back at Ephraim and Iola Tucker, who waved from their wagon ten yards back.

* * *

A. R. Riefe

Jubal lay beside Hannah, holding her, kissing her tenderly, reveling in his love for her.

"Hannah, Hannah—"

"Is something wrong?" she asked.

"No. What could be?"

"You seem distracted." She studied him worriedly.

"I'm not," he lied. "Perhaps a little tired."

They kissed again. The soft meeting of their lips set his heart beating wildly. He buried his face between her neck and shoulder and slid his hand over her smooth stomach to cup her breast. She gasped silently and arched her back, pressing herself against him.

"We're so lucky," she murmured. "So blessed we're a family and have this chance. It's like claiming a star for your own, reaching up and taking it. With God's blessing."

"I wish taking Oregon was so easy," he said.

"We do it day by day. It's not so hard. We're doing nobly."

"You are."

"Why shouldn't I? Does it surprise you that I'm up to it?" She smiled.

"That's not what I mean, I mean you take the rain in your face and smile. Every day. All Alison Cooper's Leah does is groan and complain."

"Everybody's different, Jubal." She searched his eyes and found his love. "You're so tender." The change of subject surprised him. "When you touch me," she went on, "it's like you're building a house of cards and you're afraid it'll topple, so every one you add, you're more patient and gentle than the one before. I'm not fragile, darling, I won't break."

She was right, he thought, he *was* overly careful, as if afraid she would shatter. He had lived in grinding fear of losing her throughout her three pregnancies, worrying she was too delicate for the rigors of childbirth. He often carried his solicitude to such extremes, she laughed good-naturedly at him. When she had been pregnant he practically carried her in and out of carriages, wouldn't let her lift anything heavier than a dish, and sprang to her side when the baby kicked, as if his nearness would lessen the

28

impact or intimidate the little thing into behaving itself. Even when she wasn't pregnant he didn't want her working in the fields at anything other than seeding and weeding. He had run to help her carry wood and water from the well, anything at all heavy. And when she took sick with even something as mild as a cold, he would baby her mercilessly.

She loved the pedestal he had fashioned for her with his constant attention, loved the love in his eyes when he turned them on her, the warmth of his touch, his sensitivity, his patience and discipline in their lovemaking. There were times when she wanted to shake him and demand that he lose all control, but that wasn't his way. His way was to elevate her to a plane higher than his, and look up to her as a loyal subject looks up to his queen. Not once in twenty-two years of marriage had he ever demeaned her or spoken disparagingly, even in anger. Not once did he set himself above her.

They made love with a quiet passion, fire blazing within them, its presence unbetrayed by violent movement. By glorious stages he sent her soaring into a state of consciousness that stripped her of self-awareness. They became one person: mind, heart, and rapture. She rose so fast and so far that presently, eyes closed, she could look down at the stars.

The blistering hot days and bitter cold nights crawled by as the wagon train passed the division of the North and South Platte rivers and neared the Wyoming border. Hannah's lamentable condition neither improved nor worsened, but for Jubal and the children, the tension was gradually becoming unbearable.

One evening, shortly after the emigrants had stopped for the night, Jubal jacked up the left rear of the wagon, and with Jeptha's help, removed the wheel. Like the other wagons in the train, their Conestoga carried a pot of tar composed of a sticky mixture of pine and lard. The night before both front wheels had been lubricated; tonight it was the rear wheels' turn. Jeptha was preparing to apply the tar to the exposed axle when the paddle slipped from his hand and fell in the dust.

"Clumsy clod!" burst Jubal.

"I'm sorry, Pa, it slipped."

"Give it here!"

Jeptha had retrieved the paddle. Jubal snatched it from him and proceeded to wipe it clean on the axle.

"That's no good," burst Jeptha. "You're getting sand on there. It'll grate it like a grindstone when the wheel turns."

Jubal snarled, and deliberately ignored his blunder. He shoved the pot and paddle into the boy's hands and stomped off.

"Clean it up! Tar it proper! And the other wheel!"

Shortly after breakfast one morning, the emigrants were taking down their tents, scattering the cook fires, and preparing to leave when three Indians came walking boldly into camp. They were the first to come into direct contact with the emigrants, although a Pawnee hunting party had been spotted in the distance some days earlier. Three warriors, all wearing their hair shaved well back on their heads with eagle feathers at the rear knots. One displayed an arrow with dried blood on the head shoved through his hair knot. He wore a metal chain around his right ear and a number of necklaces, one with a heavy silver disk depending from it. He was naked to the waist and his body was painted a bright red with black imprints of hands just below his shoulders. His face was deeply pitted as were his companions. They carried lances, bows, and arrows.

"Smallpox," murmured Jeptha.

"How could Indians get smallpox?" asked Lorna, coming up behind him and Jubal.

"From white men," said Jeptha. "They dig up their corpses to get their clothes and get smallpox to boot. I read about it."

"Wonder what they want?" asked Jubal.

Fletcher and a number of others gestured wary greeting. Conversation was not easy; the Indians understood no English, the emigrants knew no sign language, but the gesturing that ensued, punctuated by repeated demands for *uiska, uiska* made clear what the visitors were seeking. They went away with a jug of Alison Cooper's homemade sourmash whiskey. The appreciation of his fellow emigrants did not ease Cooper's annoyance, but to Jubal, Jeptha, and Lorna, the tribute seemed a trifling price to pay to avert trouble, even possible bloodshed.

At two o'clock that afternoon the train stopped again. A white man coming down from the north waved the lead wagon to a halt and began talking to Fletcher. While the emigrants waited patiently, the stranger—sitting a fine looking sorrel, wearing two guns stuck in his belt, and carrying a rifle tied under the cantle of his saddle—launched into what appeared to be a lecture. The others got down from their wagons and stood in a circle listening.

"Waste of time to go through Fort Laramie if you're headin' for the Willamette Valley. Better off takin' the next fork up the road north about thirty mile up to the Albin Trail. Better road, easier travelin', shorter by fifty mile in the long run, and safer from the injuns. Got any 'backy you can spare?"

The man was old, bearded to his eyes, attired in badly stained deerskins. He told them he was a trapper and claimed to know the northern Rockies like any one of them knew his right hand. He knew the Indians' ways, was a blood brother to the Sioux, and could speak six tribal tongues. He proceeded to do so, culminating his performance with

"Any 'backy you can spare?"

Fletcher pressed him for more information. He was quick to oblige.

"Brother, I just come from near Laramie. Trail from here to thar is so clogged with wagons you won't make ten mile a day. So clogged it looks like the rebels retreatin' from Atlanta in front of Sherman's march. Got any 'backy?"

Fletcher glanced about. One of the men offered a half-used packet of shag chewing tobacco. The trapper crammed every bit of it into his mouth.

He wound on windily, tirelessly. Fletcher and the others listened and nodded. Jubal could see the leader turning the advice over and over in his mind, examining it as a jeweler studies a fine gem. The stranger sounded as if he knew what he was talking about. He reeled off place names and landmarks with the ease of an auctioneer spouting about his wares and their worth. His name was Cabel Masefield, but he was known as Dancer "from the Platte River fork to the Canadian border to The Dalles," the gateway to the New Land on the Columbia River.

He sold the Albin route as an alternative and went on his way chewing. Fletcher assembled everyone.

"You heard what he said. We take the north fork up ahead, up thirty miles where it bends west again."

"It's takin' a chance, ain't it?" asked one man.

Jubal nodded unconscious agreement. Fletcher saw him and frowned. Ephraim Tucker noticed and grinned.

"This whole trek is taking a chance," said Fletcher tightly. "My impression is Mr. Masefield knows what he's talking about. Chance brought him to us and we'd be shortsighted, if not downright foolish, not to take advantage of his expertise. We'll go on. When we get to the fork we'll head north."

Not a single voice raised objection. Jubal wanted to, but hesitated. It did strike him, however, that if the change in route did turn out a mistake, thirty miles north and thirty more returning to the Fort Laramie trail would mean nearly four full days lost. He screwed up his gumption and calmly, quietly pointed this out.

"I don't agree at all," said Fletcher. "Mr. Masefield said we can't miss the westbound Albin route. You all heard, plain as a pan was the way he put it. Weren't you listening, Hunnicutt?"

"I heard him. It just seems to me—"

"Seems to me you're a minority of one. Any other objections?"

Jubal looked at Ephraim Tucker. Tucker looked at the ground. No other objections were raised so they boarded their wagons and pressed on. They reached the fork in the road shortly and started up the north branch.

CHEYENNE

Three days later they were hopelessly lost. At sundown Fletcher called the men together. He was patently embarrassed by his failure to find the Albin route. From all appearances Albin itself seemed to have vanished into the earth.

"As I see it," he said, "we have a choice. We can continue searching or give it up and head southwest. And eventually pick up the old road." He eyed Jubal as if expecting criticism. "No need to head back the way we came as some have suggested. I'm sure we'll have no trouble finding the Fort Laramie road. It's big enough, we'll know it when we see it."

"How?" asked Alison Cooper. "If we do like you say, even if we do come 'cross it, it'll be a further piece on than we saw afore we headed north."

"We'll find it," said Fletcher.

His tone had a flat finality to it.

"We'd better," persisted Cooper. "Else we'll be wanderin' 'round till the redskins find us."

This observation was hooted down. Jubal held his tongue. Fletcher disbanded the meeting and approached Jubal.

"Masefield was full of hot air, it appears," he said.

"Just because we can't find Albin doesn't mean it's not there," said Jubal.

"Shall we keep looking, say for another month?" He was eyeing Jubal accusingly. "You don't like me, do you, Hunnicutt?"

"Do I have to?"

Fletcher smirked. "No. But I'm entitled to the same privilege. You don't like our stopping before sunset."

"I don't understand it. Every day goes by we slip three more hours behind schedule."

They were walking slowly away from the camp out of earshot of the others. They came to an outcropping. Fletcher sat. He patted the rock beside him.

"No thanks," murmured Jubal.

"You prefer not to share the same rock with me."

"I've got no personal gripe against you, Fletcher."

"I've been to Utah and back twice safely. One thing

33

I've learned, you don't roll after dark and you don't pitch camp while it's getting dark. Let me see if I can explain so you'll understand. When a train stops rolling to make camp, that half hour or so it takes is when it's at its most vulnerable. Tents being unpacked, animals fed, tended to, fires started, weapons laid aside, children running around, women getting together gossiping, men relaxing. No sir, my train stops well before sundown and camp is set up while it's still light out. I've told you that five or six times, why can't you get it through your head?"

"Just thick, I guess."

Fletcher's face was upraised. His eyes glinted.

"I think I understand. You want to get there Fourth of July if you can. It's your missus."

"Never mind her," said Jubal.

"You want to get her to a doctor." Fletcher nodded knowingly.

"I'm warning you—"

"Only why bother? No doctor can cure what ails her. Let me ask you a personal question, and you don't have to answer if you don't want: brother, in the name of all that's good and holy, why did you bring her along? If you had to come yourself, you and the children, couldn't you have left her in the care of relatives in Vermont or wherever you come from? Didn't you even stop and think what a journey as rugged as this might do to her?"

"Shut your mouth, Fletcher!"

"If she were my wife—"

Rapidly building rage fired Jubal's conscience. He exploded, seized Fletcher by the shirt front, and jerked him to his feet.

"I said shut up!" he roared.

Fletcher's knee smashed into Jubal's groin. A great, ringing pain flared through his loins. He let go and danced from one foot to the other.

"Don't you ever lay hands on me again!" burst Fletcher.

Jubal groaned, steadied himself, gritted his teeth against his excruciating suffering, and punched Fletcher in the face, knocking him to his knees. The others had come running, and before Fletcher could retaliate they were separated. As quickly as it had started, it was over. Jubal made his way back to the wagon, helped by Cooper and Ephraim Tucker.

"What happened?" Tucker asked.

"Nothing."

His groin felt as if a flaming torch was being held to it. He was sweating furiously, it was all he could do to keep from screaming.

"You're white as a sheet," said Cooper.

They eased him down, sitting with his back against the right front wheel.

"I'll get you a snort," said Cooper.

"Never mind, I'm all right."

"What started it?" persisted Tucker.

"What does it matter? We can't stand the sight of each other. It was bound to happen sooner or later. Thanks for helping me. Did you see? He kneed me, the yellow-bellied pig."

"*Who* started it?" Tucker asked.

"Don't matter," snapped Cooper. "Forget it."

Hannah had been sitting in the back of the wagon. Jeptha helped her down. Neither he nor Lorna approached their father. Hannah hurried up to him.

"Jubal!"

"It's all right, Mother, little misunderstanding. It's all over."

Tucker obligingly told her what he'd seen. She was clearly appalled.

"You should apologize, dear."

"Me?" Jubal looked astonished.

Quarreling could be heard. About twenty yards from where Jubal sat nursing his discomfort, Fletcher stood in full view of the entire camp berating his wife. A short, stout woman with a perpetual sad face and impression of unhappiness about her, Elvira Fletcher stood stiffly and wordlessly taking his abuse. Alison Cooper snorted and strode over to them. Jubal watched as he attempted to intervene and calm Fletcher down. At that distance Jubal could not make out what either man was saying when they lowered their voices, but whatever Cooper had to say appeared to take effect. The left side of Fletcher's jaw was discolored and already looked swollen.

Cooper came back with Fletcher in tow. Ephraim and Jeptha helped Jubal to his feet. He stood leaning against the wheel.

"We'd all be obliged if you two would shake hands," announced Cooper.

Jubal started his right hand forward. Fletcher scowled and sneered.

"I demand an apology! Here and now. You attacked me out of the blue, you filthy coward!"

"I—"

"Never mind," interposed Cooper. Others had gathered to stare curiously. "I seen, didn't hear but seen; you was both at fault. Jest shake hands now and get it all over."

They shook hands—too hastily. There was no hint of forgiveness from either of them. Nevertheless, the matter ended.

2

U. S. Cavalry troopers had thrown up Fort D.A. Russell on the north bank of Crow Creek in the southeast corner of Wyoming Territory. The installation's neatly positioned collection of plank and log buildings intruded upon the serene, ochre-hued landscape like a scarecrow upon a cornfield. It did not belong.

Private Ernest Wheelwright did not feel that he belonged either. He was sitting on a crudely-fashioned, spindle-legged wooden horse, wearing a field pack filled with one hundred pounds of rocks, and holding a seven-foot wooden sword spattered with red paint over his right shoulder. This was his punishment for swearing at the first sergeant. Corporal Salme was no more comfortable marching up and down the unusual diamond-shaped parade ground dragging a twenty-eight pound cannonball attached to his leg by a two-foot chain. His punishment for filching another man's wallet.

Like Fort Fetterman, recently built on the south side of the North Platte, Fort Russell and its occupants signaled a warning to the hostiles of the region—a warning that went unheeded with discouraging regularity.

Like most western outposts, Fort Russell boasted no outer wall, the majority of frontier commanders believing it better for troop morale to depend upon vigilance and breechloaders for protection than to hide behind palisades. Crow Creek provided ample drinking water, there was sufficient grass for animals and timber for fuel, and the level terrain was spacious enough to encompass out-buildings: quarters, storehouses, stables, wagon sheds, and other structures surrounding the parade ground.

Officers occupied private quarters in fifteen cramped houses, where a lieutenant or captain and his family shared two to four rooms. Married enlisted men also qualified for houses, but whenever a new officer arrived, an enlisted man or lower ranking officer could be evicted in a maneuver known as "ranking out." The houses saddled the top and top sides of the diamond to the north. The lower sides were flanked by eleven wooden barracks, six to the west, five to the east. Between them at the bottom tip of the diamond was the guardhouse. East of it stood the carpenter's shop, and below it, so close to the creek it appeared in danger of sliding into it, was the bakery. East of the bakery, following the south-easterly course of the creek, was ordnance and beyond it, stretching in a row, the nine buildings comprising the laundry.

Unmarried enlisted men and those who had not brought wives and families west with them were crammed in the eleven barracks, where rows of cots stood headed into the walls. Ranking noncoms enjoyed the luxury of small rooms next to the barrack rooms. A luxury they were. Privacy was as rare as decent whiskey in the hard life on the frontier post.

Privies stood outside. Bathhouses, although stipulated by the War Department, were nonexistent at Russell with the result that everyone came to smell the same, and all got used to one another, save for the conscientious few who bathed regularly in the creek.

Reveille rang across the empty parade ground at 5:30. First drill followed at 6:15, falling out for fatigue duty was signaled at 7:30, guard mount took place at 8:30, afternoon fatigue commenced at 1:00, drill at 4:30, and taps sounded at 8:15.

The sun hung like a gleaming gold liberty dollar in a sky stuffed with fat clouds over the fort. On rode Private Wheelwright, on marched Corporal Salme, and the bugler had just finished blowing afternoon fatigue call when

CHEYENNE

General Grenville M. Dodge, commander of the District of the Platte, and his entourage came dusting onto the parade ground. The general's visit was wholly unexpected, and Lieutenant Colonel Lincoln Rhilander, fort commander, his second, Major Harvey Philips, and adjutant, Lieutenant Mario Consolo, were ill-prepared. All wore their light blue cavalry pants with the yellow stripes down the seams thrust into regulation Jefferson boots squared off below the knees, but only Rhilander had his shirt on, and it was unbuttoned to his belt buckle with the sleeves rolled up. Philips and Consolo fumbled into their shirts. All spruced up hastily, passing Rhilander's comb among them as he led them outside to greet the arrivals, hastily buckling on his saber as he did so. Dodge appeared amused at catching them unawares. Salutes were exchanged, the general dismounted, came forward, offered his hand, and apologized for suddenly descending upon the post.

"Quite all right, sir," rejoined Rhilander.

"We won't be staying."

He had pulled his glove off to shake Rhilander's hand. He swung about in quick appraisal of the post. Enlisted men and junior officers stood gawking. Wheelwright and Salme tried to look as if they were taking their punishment contritely, Wheelwright urging his wooden steed to giddy-yap as Rhilander escorted Dodge and the others into his office. It was fashioned of cottonwood logs chinked with clay, one of four log structures on the post. The ceiling was low, the office small, and by the time the last man to enter closed the door behind him, absurdly crowded, prompting the general to rescue the colonel.

"Levi," he said, addressing a young giant wearing captain's bars and a chest emblazoned with decorations. "You stay. The rest of you boys wait outside."

Lieutenant Consolo produced glasses and a decanter of Madeira. Rhilander poured. Dodge was a bearded, handsome man in his early thirties, though he was obviously as careless about his appearance as General Sherman and others of the old guard. His top button was undone, the third button down absent, one cuff badly frayed, and his

39

entire uniform dreadfully rumpled. He held his glass to the light and raised it.

"To the confusion of our enemies."

He explained the reason for his visit. Rhilander knew it was Dodge to whom the Union Pacific high executives listened when it came to deciding the route of the line through the territory. He had directed that the tracks through Laramie County should pass by Crow Creek. So highly did his employers think of him they had recently appointed him chief engineer, seemingly ignoring the fact that he was still serving in the Army. Among his other duties, he saw to it that the four forts along the rail line's right-of-way—Russell, Sanders, Steele, and Bridger—kept the Indians in check.

"Fort Russell's been doing yeoman service," said Dodge. "You and your men are to be commended, Colonel. Sam Reed, our superintendant of construction, and the Casement brothers, Jack and Dan, the tracklaying contractors, are most grateful. But trouble's cropped up. Two survey crew chiefs were killed day before yesterday. L. L. Hills a couple miles east of Cheyenne, and an old and dear friend, Percy Browne, over on Bitter Creek."

"Sioux, Cheyenne, Arapaho?" asked Rhilander.

"Not a clue in either case," replied Dodge. "One of the three, you can be sure. Both were good men, dedicated, able, been with the company since it started; not easy to replace. Word is that Browne's surveying party was attacked three times and lost two other men before he was killed. Now, unfortunately, much of the surveying he and his crew did in west-central Wyoming will have to be done over again, which means delay and money down the privy hole. As you might expect, we're on a devil of a tight schedule. But that's not your problem.

"Colonel—Lincoln, I'm here hat in hand. I want you to send a company out to the Bitter Creek construction site to protect the tracklayers."

Rhilander only half listened as Dodge rambled on. Why couldn't men be dispatched from Fort Fred Steele, much closer to Bitter Creek? Lincoln hesitated to question the general on it. Since the U.P. had come snaking across the border into Wyoming from the east, the Army was under orders to protect the workers from marauding hostiles in addition to protecting the settlers pouring into the territory. Recently Rhilander had been ordered to send troops out to demolish shanties put up by squatters on railroad lots in the vicinity. And when graders east of Bitter Creek had gone on strike, troopers from Fort Fred Steele had backed up Superintendent Sam Reed's threat to starve them out, and the walkout collapsed.

In effect, this meant the Army was protecting whites from whites as well as from the Indians. This did not sit comfortably with Rhilander. He had ridden out to the demolished shanties and seen the squatters' faces, their bitterness at the Army's siding against them. It was as if the railroad with all its millions had hired the Army as its private security force.

The further Dodge elaborated on the situation, the clearer it became that the general was now a civilian in blue. Rhilander had no qualms about taking orders from a man with one foot in a field boot and the other in railroading, but the possible consequences of the arrangement and their effect upon him and the other three post commanders along the route worried him. There appeared no limit to the demands Dodge could put on the men of Fort Russell, even to drafting them to set ties and lay track should the civilian workers decide to strike again.

The tail was clearly wagging the hound. Since the end of the war the Union Pacific had amassed tremendous power, demanding and obtaining from states and the federal government hundreds of thousands of acres of land for its right of ways. More than sixty millions in bonds had already been advanced the line. The U.P. cajoled presidents, purchased congressmen, bent and broke laws, and bled the taxpayers—all in the name of progress. Rhilander's private opinion of the railroad moguls coincided with that of many newspaper reporters: they were a pack of overly ambitious, avaricious opportunists. Profit, not progress, motivated them.

But the transcontinental railroad was an absolute necessity. It would bind east and west, and solidify the nation. Nevertheless, it was a pity that so much rascality readied the rails.

One had to admire Dodge's foresight. He had been one of the railroad's earliest private investors In 1864, transferred by the Army to the western Plains, he promptly attracted national attention as a savage exponent of search-and-destroy tactics against the Indians. Even then he was thinking of the railroad, recognizing that tracklaying would be severely hampered as long as the Indians posed a menace on the Plains. As he gained an increasing reputation for attacking the tribes, the U.P. bosses and other railroad promoters pulled strings to get the area encompassed by Kansas, Colorado, Utah, Nebraska, Wyoming, and Montana put under his command.

In the bitter winter of 1865, before ground was broken for Fort Russell, Arapaho and Cheyenne began cutting telegraph lines and attacking isolated forts. Without waiting for orders, Dodge collected every available soldier to sweep the Platte Valley clear of Indians. When his 11th Cavalry refused to ride because of sub-zero weather, he arrested its officers, replaced them, and had the regiment on the road by the following morning. On the trip to Nebraska Territory, thirteen men froze to death.

But two weeks afterward not an Indian could be found within one hundred miles of the communication line. When General Grant wired the Western Union manager in Omaha asking for Dodge's whereabouts, the answer came: "Nobody knows where he is, but everybody knows where he's been."

Rhilander had no intention of crossing Dodge; he had enough to contend with trying to stem a recent epidemic of desertions, wangling supplies, and other problems. But he could not ignore the nagging feeling that sooner or later he and Dodge, sitting across from him sipping his wine and smiling, the soul of friendliness, would lock horns. Rhilander and every man under him had enlisted or was drafted to fight the rebels and now the Indians. Doing the U.P.'s work, dirty or clean, was not to his liking. Acknowledging this to himself, he unconsciously let his expression mirror his feelings.

"Something wrong, Lincoln?" Dodge asked.

"No, sir," he replied.

And inwardly chided himself for being so obliging, for not pointing out the assignment Dodge had just dumped in his lap was out of Fort Russell's jurisdiction and in that of Fort Fred Steele. Still, why tell the general something he already knew?

"I'd like the men on the road in an hour if you can," Dodge went on. "Two hundred rounds, two weeks' rations, half a pup tent, extra clothes, footwear, the usual. And an experienced officer in charge."

"Yes, sir."

With little else to occupy his thoughts, Jubal nursed his grudge against Fletcher. He had no shortage of reasons for disliking the man, quite apart from their brief scuffle and Fletcher's cowardly tactic. Jubal read his Bible, valued its guidance, and tried to live by its instructions. Fletcher continually quoted the Bible, talking as if his listener, whoever he might be, was unfamiliar with it and the Lord had ordained him to enlighten him. The Bible held the answer to every question for him, so he used it to solve every problem. Jubal could find no scriptural solutions to problems like replacing a broken axle, curing raging dysentery, and countless other difficulties that cropped up along the way. When he pointed this out, Fletcher gave him a long-winded lecture on the value of faith and importance of trust. "The good Lord will find a way" was always the answer when no other answer could be found.

Jubal's groin ached, reminding him that Fletcher was a coward; nobody but a coward knees his adversary in a fair fight. Jeptha mentioned this the next day. The train had come upon a sign indicating the original trail directly below, so they stopped an hour early to permit the emigrants to savor their relief. Fletcher assembled them and assured one and all that they'd really lost very little time and would be back on the track before sundown the next day.

Jubal listened along with the others and was quietly incensed. Before starting out from Sapling Grove, Fletcher had shown all the men his copy of the 1846 map of the Overland Trail. It clearly indicated Fort Kearney and Courthouse Rock, which they had already passed. Directly ahead stood Chimney Rock. Why Fletcher would deliberately abandon the map to risk finding a shortcut by way of Albin made no sense. Or did it? Had Dancer Masefield's route proven worthwhile, had they eventually succeeded in shortening the miles, Fletcher would have been able to claim the shortcut as his own discovery. Could that be why he was so insistent on looking for it?

The more Jubal thought about it, the more sense it made. And if it turned out to be true, it was something else he could hold against the man.

Father and son turned to lubricating the front axle after Fletcher's speech, working shoulder to shoulder.

"You all right?" asked Jeptha. "I mean, where he kneed you?"

"I'm black and blue, but I'll be all right," his father replied.

"Best just stay away from him, Pa."

"I do. He walked *me* off to talk, not the other way. And talking to him is like talking to a dead tree. I've given up. I'll stay away from him till we get there, then . . ."

"What?" Jeptha asked.

"We'll see. Only thing I worry about is if we do tangle again, I'm liable to kill him," said Jubal grimly.

"Pa!"

"Let's stop talking about it. Fetch the tar bucket."

Jubal applied tar with the paddle. They talked about the increasing number of abandoned wagons, jettisoned goods, and dead draft animals. And graves—some with wooden markers, others just piles of stones, graves mostly of infants and children.

"Folks are foolish to bury their loved ones in plain sight," remarked Jeptha. "The Indians just dig up the bodies for the clothes. I read that the smartest thing is to bury your dead in the middle of the road so that the grave gets trampled on by teams and can't be seen."

"May be practical, son, but there's something sad about an unmarked grave, even sadder than a marked one. Big trouble is that the road is hard as a rock. You could break a shovel before you break the ground."

"We've only lost four people so far."

"We're still not halfway yet. But we'll make it, all of us," said Jubal.

"Yes."

Jubal could have wished for more conviction in Jeptha's tone, but knowing that the boy's heart wasn't in the journey as firmly as his own, he refrained from commenting.

Hannah joined them. She looked unusually well, her cheeks shining, eyes bright, and the omnipresent smile on her face. She seemed to Jubal to have more energy that day than she'd had in weeks. Why, he could only wonder. She read his thoughts.

"I feel so good. I had such a good night's sleep last night. End of the day and I still feel fresh. I think I'll go for a walk."

Jubal felt Jeptha staring at him in reaction. He avoided his eyes.

"If you wait a bit, I'll go with you."

"I can finish up," offered Jeptha.

"You despise walking, Jubal Hunnicutt. Besides, I want to go alone. You don't mind. That brook we passed last hour isn't far. I want to sit beside it and listen to the music and be by myself with my thoughts. You needn't worry, I promise not to wander and get lost."

"You never have. Why should I worry about that?"

"And no wildflowers."

"You pick all the wildflowers you like, Mother."

It was spoken like a direct order. Jeptha was standing facing the head of the train. His face darkened. Jubal noticed and turned. Fletcher was only a few steps away, coming toward them. From the way he was looking at Hannah, he had overheard every word. His face softened into a pitying expression. He started to shake his head, but caught himself.

"Evening, Hunnicutt, Mrs. Hunnicutt, boy; lovely evening, isn't it?"

"Beautiful," murmured Hannah. "I was just about to go for a stroll."

Fletcher had stopped. He stood too close to Jubal and with his hands clasped behind his back. He furrowed his brow and pursed his lips.

"Not by yourself, I hope. See here, we wouldn't want you to get lost."

"I won't," said Hannah quietly.

"Perhaps you could ask Mrs. Tucker to go along, or your daughter."

"She prefers to go by herself," interposed Jubal.

Fletcher chuckled. "Well," he drawled, "far be it for me to tell you what to do."

Jubal frowned. "Then don't."

Fletcher touched the brim of his hat to Hannah, forced a smile, and went on.

"You were rude, Jubal," said Hannah.

"I'm sorry, Mother, I'm afraid he brings out the worst in me."

"You shouldn't let him. I'm sure he means well." She smiled warmly and turned away. "I'll be back in a little bit."

Jubal looked anxiously after her.

"Son, go tell your sister to follow her without being seen."

The evening the train crossed into Wyoming, Ephraim Tucker and Alison Cooper prevailed upon Jubal to accompany the celebration songfest on his harmonium. A number of the old favorites of the war years were still popular despite the heartache some of the lyrics recalled. "The Girl I Left Behind Me" and "Tenting on the Old Camp Ground" joined "Lilly Dale," "Sweet Evalina," and "Listen to the Mocking Bird."

Then Jubal was besieged with requests for some of the grand old hymns, which reaffirmed the travelers' faith in the God who had brought them this far safely. And as if to confirm that the war was over in everyone's hearts as well as in fact, there were requests for Southern songs, among them "Bonny Blue Flag" and the sweet and plaintive "Lorena."

Jubal did not know the last two songs, but was able to play both flawlessly when their tunes were hummed for him. For upward of three hours he was the center of attention. The finale of the evening was the saddest selection of all, but a nearly unanimous choice: "Home Sweet Home." Eyes glistened with tears in the firelight, every woman got out her hanky, every man looked somber and saddened. "Home is where the heart is" had little meaning for any of them. Home sweet home was where they had come from to head into the unknown. Home was the island of safety they had left. None seemed to have any second thoughts about leaving, but distance did lend nostalgia and stirred sentimental feelings. The tug of home sweet home was stronger in this alien place than it would have been standing in one's parlor.

Lorna cried openly, Hannah comforted her. Watching them as he played, Jubal sensed that Hannah was holding back tears of her own. Fletcher sat opposite them on the far side of the fire with his wife and three grown daughters. Mrs. Fletcher clung to his arm and stared into space, seemingly unmoved by the sadness of the song. The leaping flames blocked out the sight of the two of them to Jubal, but when the men stopped feeding the fire and it began to die, Jubal could clearly see his nemesis in its glow. Fletcher's look could have been envy at the attention Jubal's playing attracted; it could have been boredom, even though he sang along spiritedly with the others; it could have been smoldering resentment. Perhaps, thought Jubal, it was a little of all three, but mostly disapproval—of Jubal Hunnicutt.

Jubal did his best to keep his own face from reflecting the man's. He was enjoying himself too much to let his simmering annoyance with Fletcher prey on his thoughts.

Even though he could still feel the man's knee.

An hour later the fires were reduced to embers, and all were asleep except for the four men whose turn it was to stand guard over the train. It was Jubal's turn. One of his three companions was Ephraim Tucker, but the two neighbors had no chance to get together to relieve their boredom. When the postings were decided, Tucker found himself two hundred yards east of the camp, Jubal two hundred yards west. He checked his Springfield and propped it against the rock he was sitting on, then examined his .32-caliber Smith & Wesson. The ivory grips were discolored with age and the barrel slightly pitted on the outside, but down its interior length it was as smooth and unblemished as new. He had not fired it in three weeks; the last time he had missed a rabbit.

The stars twinkled prettily against the blackness of the firmament for a while before it began clouding over. The quarter moon sliced through the overcast until eventually it too was obscured. But before the night lost its light, Jubal had taken note of the endless sea of tall grasses crowding the border, mostly needlegrass and bluestem. To the north Lodgepole Creek spilled and splashed down out of the Laramie Range toward Nebraska. Available water for crops. His first step into Wyoming persuaded him that it held marvelous potential for wheat. He had never raised wheat, never tried to. It *was* grown in Pennsylvania, up near Lewisburg and down south near Lancaster by the Amish, but he preferred vegetables. The little he had been able to find out about the Willamette Valley made it sound ideal for both root and aboveground vegetables. Best of all, everyone seemed to agree that the weather was tamer and followed the seasonal changes more predictably than back home. Rain fell in the spring and sufficiently throughout the growing season; in Pennsylvania too often it fell in early spring and in the months that followed there was little or none.

He set his Springfield across his knees, resting his elbows on it and thinking about Hannah. If only she could have more days like the past five. She had been her old self—no strange, haunted look in her eyes, no drifting, no quiet babbling. And she seemed to have regained her old zest. She had gone walking, Lorna had followed her watching, and reported nothing out of the ordinary, nothing that might lead anyone to question the balance of her mother's mind.

He glanced at the camp. The fires were reduced to glowing coals. The tents stood stark and lightless in spaces between the wagons drawn up in a circle around them. A lantern gleamed and came bobbing toward him. He squinted, but could not make out who it was, only that it was two people.

Jeptha and Salita Jane dropped their hands and looked self-consciously at each other when he smiled and greeted them.

"Aren't you two out strolling a bit late?"

"Best time, Pa, it's quiet, private."

"Aren't you afraid of redskins?" Jubal asked. Salita Jane looked startled and stiffened. "Oh, I haven't seen any. You'll hear if I do."

They were a picture, he and Hannah at that age, hand in hand, enduring the jibes of their elders, yearning, aching for privacy, blushing too easily, overly sensitive, with eyes only for each other. When they got to the valley, and settled in, they would be married. He had married Hannah when he was eighteen and she sixteen. He didn't know how old Salita Jane was, but she looked a full-grown woman.

So Tucker and Hunnicutt would come together in the sight of God in holy matrimony. He liked the Tuckers, and especially enjoyed Ephraim's company. One bright and beautiful Oregon day, they would become grandparents. Images galloped across the screen of his mind. The two houses side by side and acres upon acres of crops. The Lord was good to give to the world Edens like the Willamette Valley!

Salita Jane hung onto Jeptha, looking soulfully into his eyes. Would she, Jubal wondered, one day be a lawyer's wife? She broke into his musings.

"I should get back. Ma'll be worried."

Jeptha nodded. "Sure, hon—Sal."

They said goodnight and started away. He was very good to her, Jubal thought, a gentleman; they were so in love it obviously dizzied them both. It made them awkward and blundering, blind to everyone and everything except each other. Sitting beside the boy on the wagon seat when Jeptha was staring into space, he daydreamed not about his future, but theirs. He wondered if they were talking about marriage, and concluded that they must be.

He tightened his grip on the rifle.

Jeptha and Salita Jane had vanished into the circle of wagons. Another lantern was approaching. The moon and stars still hidden, and he could not recognize the figure. He waited. It was Fletcher, making the rounds, checking on his outguard. Giving the devil his due, he took his job seriously; no one could accuse him of loafing. He lowered the lantern, setting it down by his side. He paused and lit a stogie.

"Hunnicutt . . ."

"Fletcher."

"All quiet?"

"As fog," said Jubal.

"Moss Larribee'll be relieving you at one o'clock." He paused, tilting his head and looking down. "You all right?" Fletcher looked suddenly concerned.

"All right, why?"

"Just thought you might be tuckered out after your performance tonight. You sure can play that thing. I can barely carry a tune. How's the missus?"

"Fine. How's Mrs. Fletcher?"

"Head cold. Nothing. I've been meaning to tell you, there's a doctor at Fort Laramie. Simpson or Simpkins. Army doctor. Perhaps he could have a look at your wife."

"Did you come out here to talk about her?" Jubal asked.

"Of course not."

"Then don't."

"I'm sorry. Believe me, I can understand why it's a sore spot with you. My wife had a maiden aunt, dead now, who was touched in the head."

"Shut up!" snapped Jubal.

Fletcher's hands came up defensively. "All right, no

offense intended." He paused as if to give time for a response. Jubal said nothing; his eyes narrowed and his jaw tightened.

"But I must say, if she was my wife I'd put her where she could get proper treatment. You know, when a person begins to show the signs she shows, it's time to take matters in hand, get 'em tended to soon as possible, before—"

Jubal's rocketing anger did not affect his thinking. It drummed in his brain. Clearly Fletcher cared nothing for her welfare. The man was a sadist and Jubal despised him. But he broke off his needling when Jubal jumped up. The rifle clattered to the ground. He swung. Fletcher ducked, and took a glancing blow off the side of the head, but up came Jubal's left, fired by his fury, sledging him in the short ribs. He went down gasping, eyes rolling wildly, pain twisting his mouth.

"Get up, you bastard."

Fletcher's eyes danced, gleaming devilishly. Knees bent, he scurried like a crab to one side before rising. He swayed slightly as he did, his hand going to his ribs. He sucked air to ease the pain. Jubal closed on him, readying his right to smash his jaw, but Fletcher's hand snaked behind him. When it reappeared, the steel in it caught the velvet glow of the circle of light cast by the lantern. A rasping rumble rose from his throat; he lifted the knife and lunged. Down it arced. Jubal shifted sharply right. Fletcher swept by. Jubal had turned; he shoved his leg out. Fletcher tripped and fell heavily. He lay facedown.

"Get up, you bastard!"

He did not stir. Jubal leaned over him. Fletcher lay on his right cheek, one eye agape, staring at the ground.

"Dear God, no . . ."

He knelt and eased the man slowly over on his back. The knife was plunged hilt deep into his belly. Blood glistened. Jubal got some on his hand and wiped it off on his trousers. He leaned over and listened for his heart. He placed a finger to Fletcher's jugular.

No pulse. None. Dead. The moon slid from behind its cover, bathing the area in feeble, gray-white light, the color of death. Fletcher stared unseeing upward at it.

"Dear God," Jubal whispered.

3

Even before the last board was nailed into place at Fort Russell, the first of what threatened to be many hog ranches was already three-quarters completed. Every time a new fort went up in the territories, no sooner was it finished than hog ranches popped up like toadstools after a rain in a ring around it.

This one was two miles from the fort, cleverly named Two Mile Ranch. It was intended to be a combination saloon, trading post, and hotel in the tradition of the road ranches. What it was intended to be and what it actually was were in sharp contrast. The main building was built of hewn logs, fifty feet square with loopholes on each side to be used to repel Indians. East of this fortress lay a saloon, large storehouse, bunkhouse, ice house, blacksmith shop, billiard hall and sod corral. The most imposing structure in the complex if not the largest was a long, low building with four doors and four windows constructed of grout, an early form of cement in which coarse gravel was used instead of sand.

Two Mile Ranch was hastily completed. The following morning an expensively overdressed, meticulously barbered, perfumed, powdered, and manicured stranger rode up to the place leading three wagons loaded with saloon furnishings, including a fourteen-foot mirror, roulette wheels, and cases of liquor. Bringing up the rear of the caravan was a Concord coach crammed with befrilled and beruffled *filles de joie*.

A. R. Riefe

The liquor offered by hog ranches, particularly the whiskey, was of dubious quality, but fell short of being lethal. Before the arrival of the railroad, Fort Russell, and Two Mile Ranch, before the fledgling town of Cheyenne began to attract residents, the only liquor available to the area trappers was raw alcohol. Mellow liquor was too bulky to pack from St. Louis on mules. The scalding, wretched, raw rotgut the trappers drank was bought in Missouri for ten cents a gallon and sold in Wyoming for sixty-four dollars a gallon.

As to the coach full of soiled doves, of all the women who worked in western saloons hog ranch hostesses were by reputation the worst. Only the lowest of their sex could be induced to work in such loathsome surroundings, but along with the liquor and opportunity to relieve the boredom of life at the fort, the women provided a powerful attraction to the soldiers. Colonel Rhilander had no authority to close the hog ranch. Even if he had, sending the owner and his ladies packing would not solve the problem. The soldiers would only drift into Cheyenne to raise their hell, squander their pay, and get into trouble.

The colonel thought about Cheyenne as he rode in company with Philips and Consolo toward Two Mile Ranch. General Dodge had named the budding town after the tribe he had so hated and hunted. As the railhead inched westward and word leaked out that the U.P. had selected Cheyenne as a division point, an army of prairie flotsam and jetsam started to drift into town, even though the end of the track still lay four hundred miles southeast at Julesburg, Colorado. Among the arrivals were real estate speculators, saloon keepers, gamblers, freighters, whores, and representatives of the U.P. So large was their influx that even before the official survey was completed on July 19, 1867, a number of permanent buildings had gone up. Within two weeks more than three hundred businesses were in operation. So pressing was the demand for housing, anything capable of shedding sun or rain served the purpose. People lodged in covered wagons, in caves along the banks of

CHEYENNE

Crow Creek, pinned up makeshift tents, or pieced-together leanto shacks.

When the first smoke-belching locomotive came chugging and puffing into town in place of the usual cargo of passengers and freight, it carried a whole town, most of the visible remains of the previous terminus, Julesburg. Flatcars were piled high with knockdown shacks, stripped-down saloons, furniture, lumber, poles; less sturdy materials such as tents, personal belongings, drugs, drygoods, and all the other rubbish of a mushroom city crammed the boxcars to bursting.

On the train, along with the physical remains of Julesburg, was a new-style saloon for Cheyenne. Collectively it was called "Hell on Wheels." It was a city within a city, a portable town of saloons—dance hall saloons, drinking saloons, gambling saloons, and of course cribs. Hell on Wheels was freighted westward with each twenty-five-to-fifty-mile leap made by the railhead. Every establishment in Hell on Wheels could be easily dismantled, placed in crates, loaded on flatcars, shipped upline, and upon arrival, reassembled. Barrels full of potent whiskey and beer also rode these trains westward while armed men stood guard over them and the rest of the valuable cargo.

The Hell on Wheels that was unpacked in Cheyenne had operated for over a year, and its workers—from carpenters to bartenders—were seasoned veterans.

Cheyenne felt the change immediately. The earth gave birth to a town. In one afternoon twenty-three saloons, dance halls, and cribs were set up. Until Julesburg and Hell on Wheels arrived, the few permanent buildings featured nothing more elegant than clapboard siding. But within a week the U.P.'s newest metropolis boasted business blocks that, at first glance, appeared to be built of substantial brick and marble. Only the "bricks" and "marble" were actually hand-tinted wood stamped out in prefabricated sections in Chicago mills and shipped by rail with do-it-yourself instructions Prefabricated saloons, stores, hotels, even houses were available. In one prefab saloon a patron was killed in a brawl before the roof was set in place.

One highly popular style of section saloon was a building that featured satin-draped front parlors and a bar in the left rear corner. Light flickered from mineral lamps through red bull's-eye shades. Behind the parlor stretched an unlighted canvas corridor with curtained cubicles, five feet wide, opening off both sides. Each compartment featured the identical furnishings—a straw mattress, a rocking chair, a commode, and a young woman.

Rhilander had no desire to inspect such establishments, but the enlisted men flocked to them, and many officers, including some married ones. Even though the fort was situated only a mile from Cheyenne, Two Mile Ranch was destined to be the more popular place to visit on a night out, offering as it did a private club for the men in blue.

"You remember to bring the dynamite?" Rhilander asked Consolo.

The lieutenant grinned and patted the canvas pouch riding his right hip, its strap slung over his shoulder.

"Two sticks."

"Rough night, Lincoln?" asked Philips, riding on the colonel's right. "You look loaded for grief. Somebody else's."

"Just thinking about Dodge and Captain Stoddard and his men over by Bitter Creek, working their way back with the tracklayers."

Philips clucked and frowned. "Stoddard's wife was furious when she found out he'd be away for at least two weeks."

"I hope you told her we can't play favorites," said Rhilander. "Everybody has to take his turn in the barrel, married or single."

Philips grinned thinly. "The conversation didn't get that far. She was too upset."

They came within sight of the hog ranch, reined up in front of the saloon, and strode in. The owner-manager, O. K. Freeling, commanded the bar sporting a sight-stinging brocade vest, garter-sleeved silk shirt, and jet-black mustachios flowing from his upper lip. His hair was plastered down on both sides of the part centering his pate and resembled patent leather. It was nearing 10 A.M. and only two customers were present, both civilians. A number of hostesses lounged about sipping and gossiping. Sharing a table and breakfast at the far end by the escape door were two men. Rhilander assumed they were bouncers. Each one looked as if he'd been carved out of a sequoia, with two muscles where every normal individual had one. Both looked fully capable of dismantling a Baldwin locomotive with their bare hands. A sign above the gossamer-clad odalisque reclining above the bar mirror proclaimed: "We never close."

Freeling greeted them effusively, producing a bottle of bourbon. He set it and three gleaming glasses on the mahogany.

"Colonel, Major, Lieutenant, welcome to our humble establishment. This is an honor. Permit me to introduce you to John Quigley's bourbon, the finest, most expensive, most delectable bourbon available in the territory. My pleasure to serve you, gentlemen. Ahem, my name is—"

"Oscar Freeling," interposed Consolo.

"Ah, news does travel fast. O. K. Freeling in the flesh, gentlemen, all the way from Kansas City. Any of you boys happen to hail from Kansas City?"

Nobody did. Freeling was a well-filled bag of wind. Not the least bit nervous at their appearance, seemingly as if his life depended on it, he could not stop talking. He cited the durability and appointments of the place, the quality of his liquor, the merits of his gambling equipment. He emphasized that every wheel, every faro game, every die, every card was strictly legitimate. He fancied the phrase, so he repeated it several times.

"I gather this is a social call," he said to Rhilander, beaming his most benevolent smile.

"You could say that."

"Fine, excellent. Allow me to introduce you to some of my fair business associates. Lena, Lena Dawkings. . . ."

A. R. Riefe

Rhilander held up his hand. "Make that a business call. *Your* business."

"So be it. What can I do for you? Name it. By the way, you boys smoke? Just yesterday I got in a shipment of Cuban panatelas. Finest tobacco leaf, finest cigars money can buy. Try the bourbon. Ambrosia. Nectar of the gods. Questions, Colonel? Fire away. I've nothing to hide. Everything's strictly legitimate here. Say the word and I'll give you a guided tour. Let you see with your own eyes what we have, how we operate. Legitimate, all strictly legitimate. Our hostesses provide companionship in plain sight. Preachers, deacons, princes of the church need have no qualms about stepping in here. Anybody looking for mattress action will have to take their pick in town, not here. I run a clean operation. No hanky, no panky. Tell you something else, my liquor prices are on the square. No gouging, watering, little something slipped into the glass. Try the bourbon, plenty more where that came from. Nine cases. Yes, sir—"

Without looking at him, Rhilander held up his hand, stopping his mouth. Eyeing the brass rail at his feet, he waved the two bouncers over to join them. Freeling glanced their way and nodded. They came swaggering over.

"I'm Colonel Rhilander," said the colonel to Freeling.

"Pleased to—"

"Post commander, Fort Russell. My second in command, Major Philips. Adjutant, Lieutenant Consolo."

"O. K. Freeling. Everybody calls me—"

"Listen, don't talk. Let me tell you about me. I'm realistic. Boys will be boys and I can't keep mine from flocking here on their time off. I wouldn't want to. They're human, they're entitled to let off steam."

"That they can do—" Freeling started.

"Shut up. They can spend their money here, enjoy themselves, only I want to be sure they get a fair shake. Ladies, will you kindly leave us alone?"

"Go on out, girls. Move it, move it!" boomed Freeling.

They cleared out. Meanwhile Rhilander had wandered over to a bird cage. He thumbed two bars farther apart

58

and took out one of the three dice. He held it up for all to examine.

"Dice," he said in a voice like velvet. "Not shaved, but what are they loaded with, lead or mercury?"

Without waiting for an answer, he placed the die on the nearest table and shattered it with his revolver butt. "Lead. Roulette—"

Moving to the nearest roulette table, he picked up the ball and held it as he had the die.

"Heavy for ivory."

He upended the table with a crash. Freeling jumped. The wheel flipped over, revealing a concealed magnet. Wheel and magnet Rhilander proceeded to stomp to pieces. He moved back to the bar, the others following.

"Deck of cards," he murmured, staring fixedly at the two bouncers. "Sealed."

Freeling hesitated, then produced a deck with black and white spotted backs. Rhilander undid the cellophane wrapping, shuffled dexterously, and handed Freeling the deck.

"Hold one up with the back to me," he ordered.

By now O. K. Freeling was beginning to unravel. Sweat gleamed across his ample brow. His eyes looked like a frightened rabbit's. He shrugged and held up the top card.

"Nine," said Rhilander. He spread the pack face down on the bar. "The key," he explained to Philips and Consolo, "is a dotted seven. It revolves clockwise through eight positions from the seven to the ace. Let's see your decks, Oscar. All of them."

"What are you talking about, I got three gross!"

"The whole crate."

Freeling nodded sullenly to one of the bouncers. He went out the rear door and came back in seconds lugging an opened wooden crate. Only two decks were missing. Stenciled on one side were the words: GRANDINE SPORTING EQUIPMENT, NEW YORK, N.Y. THREE GROSS PLAYING CARDS. CUSTOM DESIGN.

Rhilander smiled broadly. "Custom design. I like that. Lieutenant—"

"Sir?"

"Take these cards out back and shuffle them. Permanently."

He added the deck Freeling had given him earlier to the contents of the crate. Consolo nodded to the nearest bouncer. He picked up the crate and led the lieutenant toward the rear and outside.

"Oscar," said Rhilander. "Consider this your first and last warning. Clean up your house. Clean up your games. Top to bottom. Clean up or close up."

"You've got no authority—"

"Minor technical detail. I never let details stand in my way. Fair warning: if one of my men, just one, comes in here and goes out drugged, cheated, rolled, or with his crotch full of clap, I'll haul a couple twelve-pounders over here, set them up, blow this pigsty into one big pile and torch it."

"You wouldn't dare," rasped Freeling.

"Try me."

A muffled explosion sounded out back. Freeling and the bouncer gaped.

"What the hell . . ."

"Better order some new cards," muttered Rhilander. "Legitimate."

Consolo reappeared with the man. The lieutenant nodded.

"All done," he said, unable to suppress a grin.

"We heard," said Rhilander.

They downed their drinks and left. Outside, Consolo looked admiringly at the colonel. "How'd you know we'd need dynamite?"

"I didn't. Just figured it'd come in handy for something. Touch of the dramatic never hurts when you're out to make an impression."

"You should have seen those cards. Like a blizzard."

"Good bourbon," murmured Philips. "Real good."

⦿◀4▶⦿

A fire had been kindled. The flames leaped crackling into the night, breaking the silence pocketing the wagon circle. There was no breeze, no coyote's mournful song, no katydid's sharp chirrup. Fletcher's body had been wrapped in a piece of canvas to be buried in the morning. When awakened and told that her husband had been killed, Mrs. Fletcher had gone into hysterics. Now she and the couple's three grown daughters sat sobbing in their tent, consumed by shock and grief, heedless of the comforting words of those trying to console them.

Jubal had gone to Moss Larribee, Fletcher's second in command. He had shown him the body and explained what had happened. Larribee and two others woke all the men; they were holding a meeting close by the scene of the tragedy. Jubal stood watching, waiting patiently for them to decide his fate, feeling naked not to his enemies but his friends. He did not wake Hannah or the children; they needed their sleep and he could tell them in the morning.

He stood watching the men talking in low tones, shaking their heads, eyeing the ground, one and another occasionally looking his way. Larribee had retrieved the knife, wiping it clean. He was a large, awkward man whose hands and feet seemed too big for his limbs. He beckoned Jubal to join them.

"We've decided. This is a terrible thing. He wasn't just

another of us, he was the leader. Who's to lead us now? Who can? None of us got his experience."

"We've got the map," interposed Ephraim.

When he looked Jubal's way his expression said he was on his side.

"Paper ain't like a flesh and blood leader, Ephraim," countered Larribee, his tone implying that Tucker should realize that without being reminded. "And we got his widder and the three girls our responsibility now, too." He eyed Jubal accusingly. "Yes, sirree, this is a terrible thing you've did us all."

"I keep telling you, I didn't kill him! It happened like I said, it was his knife, I never touched it. He came at *me*!"

"You saying *he* was trying to kill *you*?" Disbelief stamped Larribee's eyes. "Why would he?"

Other eyes, all, even Ephraim's, questioned. Larribee's dark, tight look demanded explanation. They were angry, he could see that, and could feel the fear that pervaded the gathering at being left leaderless to wander in the wilderness.

"I don't know," murmured Jubal.

"You say you argued. About what that he'd want to kill you for?"

"Or you him," interjected a voice, a man out of Jubal's sight behind Alison Cooper.

"He said things about my wife. I got mad and hit him. He pulled the knife."

"And killed himself," said Larribee.

"By accident. I keep telling you: he fell on it. You saw how he was lying."

"You tripped him," said another. "You admitted you did."

"He explained all that," said Ephraim. "I believe him. Like he says, it was an accident."

Cooper nodded his great bear head in agreement.

"Accident or deliberate, he's dead and we're stuck at the end of nowhere," said another man. "Thanks to you, Hunnicutt."

"Everybody knowed you had it in for him," said the man beside him. "We all got eyes and ears."

"I didn't!" burst Jubal. "Sure, we disagreed on some things. I had a right to speak my mind."

"We want to be fair about this," Larribee went on. "We're none of us peace officers, or judges, only plain folk and can only think and figger like what we be, but we've talked it over and decided what's best for all is for you to separate from the train. When we start out in the mornin', you can lay back a time till we're outta sight, turn 'round and go back, or settle somewheres 'round here. Whatever you decide, we're separate from now on."

"We don't want you with us no more," said another.

Jubal's eyes drifted from one to the next. "You'd cut us adrift? You'd punish my wife and children for what I did, an accident?"

"It's the way it's got to be," said Larribee solemnly. "That's how the vote came out."

"Dammit to hell, how many times do I have to tell you I was defending myself!"

"Whatever you was doing, he's dead, and that's our decision. Can't see as there's any more to say about it. Let's all turn back in. We'll bury him decent and proper in the morning, and get back on the road. If the weather holds, we could make twenty miles toward Fort Laramie tomorrow. Be there before the end of the week. Relax, rest, catch our breath."

He paused and studied Jubal as the others began to drift toward the wagons and their tents within the circle.

"It ain't for me to tell you what to do, Jubal, but 'fore we split up, maybe you oughta have a word with his missus."

"Tell her I'm sorry? For what? I didn't kill him."

"Do what you like, it's your conscience."

Jubal shook his head, by now frustrated with Larribee's refusal to understand. He headed back to the wagon circle alone. He stopped by the tent where Hannah and Lorna lay sleeping. Next to it he and Jeptha slept. He stood at the open flap watching his son sleeping, smiling, no doubt dreaming about Salita Jane. Before the train started out in the morning he would have a word with Ephraim, ask him to take Jeptha aboard their wagon. Salita Jane would appreciate it, Jeptha too. Only where would the boy find room with them? Husband, wife, and eleven children were already crammed like sheep in a pen.

But he would still suggest it to Ephraim. Maybe they could squeeze him in.

When he told Hannah what had happened, her reaction surprised and relieved him. She didn't come apart, wail, and wring her hands. Her first thought was that she should go to Mrs. Fletcher and do what she could to comfort her and the girls. Other women in the train had already tried, with little success. He resolved not to dissuade Hannah. Lorna went along with her mother. Jeptha was still asleep when they walked off. Jubal went to talk to Ephraim. He found him brushing down his mules.

"Jubal, Alison Cooper and I both believe it happened like you said," said Ephraim. "So do others. We both stuck up for you."

"I wanted to thank you. You're a true friend, Ephraim."

"If the lot of them cooled down long enough to think clearly about it, they'd realize it happened exactly the way you described it."

"It did, I swear."

Jubal somewhat hesitantly turned the subject to Jeptha and Salita Jane.

"It'd break both their hearts to have to separate, Ephraim. And on my account. It just doesn't seem fair."

"It's not. Jeptha's welcome to ride with us. We can make room."

"Appreciate it. He's a good boy, he'll earn his way. I'll give him his share of our food and he'll shoot you an antelope or rabbit or two. He can drive, service your wagon, he's strong and healthy. He can help you lots of ways. You can work him till he drops and he won't bridle."

CHEYENNE

Ephraim smiled and winked. "Wouldn't want my future son-in-law dropping dead on me, would I?"

"I do appreciate your taking him."

"Ha. Salita Jane'd never let up on me if I didn't. They do make a handsome couple." He paused, bent over for a blade of grass, and began chewing, deliberately avoiding Jubal's eyes. "We'll miss you folks. Iola will miss Hannah. Who'll we share our milk with every morning? The Coopers, I guess. When we get to the valley we'll look for each other, okay? Get back together."

"That'd be great. There's nobody we'd rather have for next-door neighbors."

"Shake on it," said Ephraim.

They shook hands. Jeptha had gotten up. He came over to them, stretching and covering a yawn self-consciously as Salita Jane appeared from the opposite direction. She had finished milking, carrying the heavy bucket with both hands. Jubal saw her eyes sparkle at the sight of the boy. Jeptha relieved her of the bucket. He started away toward the Tuckers' tents.

"Wait, son," called Jubal.

He gestured him to put down the bucket and told him what had happened. Salita Jane listened wide-eyed.

"Mr. Tucker and I've been talking. He's kindly agreed to take you on their wagon."

"What about you and Ma and Lorna?" asked Jeptha.

"We'll be following at a distance, two or three miles. Out of sight. That's what the others voted we should do, and we'll do it."

"No."

"It's what they decided, Jeptha. I can't go against the majority. They blame me and that's the punishment."

"That's not what I'm talking about, Pa. I mean I'm sticking with you."

"Oh, Jeptha!" Salita Jane's eyes glistened. She bit her lower lip lightly. "You heard what he said, you can ride with us. There's room. Please, Jeptha—"

"I'm grateful to you, Mr. Tucker, but I really should stay with my family."

A. R. Riefe

Salita Jane showed signs of becoming frantic. "Jeptha . . ."

Jubal glanced Ephraim's way, then at her. He set his arm around Jeptha's shoulders and walked him away a few paces out of earshot.

"Son, you know you want to be with her."

"I do, but I can't desert you," said Jeptha.

"You wouldn't be. We'll be right behind all the way. You won't see us, but you'll know we're there."

"It's not the same as being with you, helping, holding up my end. No, I'm staying. Don't try to talk me out of it. Besides, you need me more than Mr. Tucker. Especially the way Ma is. We're a family." He held up a tight fist. "Whatever happens, we stick together. I can say good-bye to Sal. She'll understand. We won't be split up forever. And you know what they say about absence and the heart. So let's let that be the end of it, okay, Pa?"

He had turned to face Jubal, his eyes brimming with seriousness.

"Jubal," said Jubal. "Boys call their fathers pa. You're not a boy, anymore. You're a man. Jubal."

"Jubal."

They hugged.

Salita Jane and Jeptha's parting was tearful for one, gloomy for the other. Watching them say their good-byes, Jubal felt another weight piling itself upon his already heavily burdened conscience. He stood holding the water bucket for the lead horse in the team, continuing to wonder why Fletcher had come at him with a knife. They disliked each other, perhaps couldn't stand the sight of each other, but he would never dream of attacking the man intending to kill him. Why was Fletcher so determined to kill him? What demon goaded him to such an extreme?

Mrs. Fletcher was a permanently cowed and subservient wife, and the couple's three daughters had lived in constant fear of their father's tyranny. Why did he behave so toward them? Was the well of his frustration so deep that his only recourse was to lash out at those closest to him?

Fletcher wouldn't have tried to kill him out of mere jealousy, for all the attention the others paid him as the center of the songfest. Perhaps it was Jeptha. A man blessed with daughters only often envies the father of a son. Some people fancied that unlike daughters, a son testified to a father's manhood. Then, too, anyone could see that he and Jeptha got along well, that they were friends as well as blood.

Could Jeptha be the reason Fletcher had attacked him?

Whatever his reason, he'd come out to the guard post prepared for trouble—and started it.

Moss Larribee showed Jubal the map of the Overland Trail taken from Fletcher's body before the train started out, giving him time to make a crude copy. From where they were, the trail headed northwest toward Fort Laramie. It continued beyond Laramie up to the center of the territory to Emigrant's Gap, moving west of it, then curving southwest toward Independence Rock, and beyond it, Devil's Gate. Circling the Rattlesnake Range, it followed Sage Hen Creek down to the Sweetwater River, up into the mountains, through the South Pass, and three day's journey beyond it to Sublette's Cutoff.

At the cutoff emigrants generally headed either south for Fort Bridger and the overland route to California or northwest to Fort Hall, Idaho, and eventually over the Cascade Mountains to the Willamette Valley.

They waited in the Conestoga until nine before starting out. By that time the train was long vanished in the distant mists. Endless stretches of waving grass spread as far as they could see to either side of the trail. Jubal read regret in Jeptha's eyes when the boy took his seat alongside him. The sun had come up blazing, setting the sky glaring so it hurt the eyes to scan it, but by ten, sullen clouds had come tumbling in from the east, buffeting and bullying each other, their bellies bloated with rain. It had not rained a drop for nearly two weeks; now it appeared that all the storms locked in the clouds were conspiring to strike as one, a tremendous deluge, an ocean bowl tipped upside down to submerge the territory.

Thunder pealed, boulders the size of planets rumbling

across the heavens. A lightning bolt as white as dead eyes
jagged the heavens. In minutes the sky ran through the
full range of its many shades of blue. The rains came with
a vengeance that frightened Lorna so she cried out. It
battered the bonnet, drummed the horses' rumps, and
set Jeptha choking when, glancing upward, he swallowed
some. Jubal pounded his upper back.

"Get back inside, I can handle things."

"Get back yourself, Jubal." Jeptha peered through the
gray scrim slashing down between them. "No point in
trying to go on in this. It'll be like driving through a lake.
You can't see a foot in front of the leaders."

"I can barely see them," rejoined Jubal loudly.

One, then the other climbed inside. Water dripped
down through three small holes, and between the hickory
bows the canvas sagged heavily. Hannah was looking at it
with worried eyes. Lorna sat with her straw hat pulled
down over her ears, shutting out the bully's voice.

"You think it'll rip from the weight?" Jeptha asked his
father.

"Never."

Jubal looked toward the standing horses. All six heads
were bowed, the downpour flogging them from muzzles
to tails. The road was already reduced to a quagmire.

"Wonder how the Tuckers are doing," mused Jeptha
aloud.

Jubal smiled. "Your little girl, you mean." He sobered, clearing his throat self-consciously. "I want to say
something I've been meaning to. To all three of you. I'm
. . . sorry this happened. You'll never know how sorry."

"It wasn't your fault," said Hannah.

"It wasn't, but I was a part of it and now we've got to
do this by ourselves. What I feel bad about is putting that
extra burden on all of us. We do have the map, we'll just
follow it. We've already covered better than a third of
the distance. It'll be harder ahead, but not as dusty and
easier in other ways, I'm sure."

"We'll run into Indians, won't we?" asked Lorna.

Jubal shrugged. "We could. I'd be lying if I said otherwise, but those that came into camp before turned out

friendly. Everybody says most don't go looking for trouble. It's not as if we were a threat to them like soldiers, they know that. We're just passing through."

"We'll make it," said Hannah reassuringly and set her hand over his.

"With God's help. No real reason why we shouldn't. Thousands of others have, thousands more will. We're lucky in some ways. There *is* the trail, we stick to it and we won't get lost. The time of year's in our favor, the weather." Jeptha snickered. "You know what I'm saying, son. This is a good sturdy wagon, we've enough food—"

"Water." Again Jeptha snickered.

"Weapons. Everything we really need. And most important of all, each other."

Jeptha made a fist and held it up triumphantly.

"Jubal," he began.

Both Hannah and Lorna eyed him questioningly.

"That's me," explained Jubal. "What *men* call me. What is it, Jeptha?"

"Why don't you get out the harmonium and we'll have a song."

"Good idea!" burst Hannah. "And start with 'Golden Hair.' "

Jubal uncovered the harmonium and played "And Her Golden Hair Was Hanging Down Her Back." They all sang it through twice, then "Rock of Ages," ignoring the rain-battered world outside. But in the middle of "Ole Black Joe" the thought sneaked into Jubal's mind that they were sitting in their Conestoga at the mercy of the elements alone. Every other living thing had been washed away by the downpour, and the wagon was an island that they'd been marooned on, a tiny, lonely piece of the world. To his mind's eye came the image of the candle of hope. It glowed and suddenly flickered, threatening to go out, but it resumed more brightly than before.

The roof of the verandah attached to headquarters leaked badly. The rain hammered its way through it, splattering on the unpainted floor. Like the verandah itself, headquarters—every other building from the hospital to the north to the detached stable complex to the southeast—the roof was brand-new. Who had built it, how drunk they had been at the time, Colonel Rhilander had no way of knowing. All he did know was that he couldn't step onto the verandah for a breath of air without getting soaked. He stood in the narrow doorway with Major Philips looking upward at the wooden shake sieve.

"You can actually see the holes," said Rhilander.

"I'll see that it's repaired soon as it's over."

"Better install a whole new roof." The colonel sighed. "Will you look at it come down . . ."

Down it came in thick gray sheets as straight as a plumb line, turning the concrete-hard, sun-baked parade ground into a vast bog. Through the downpour Rhilander could dimly make out the blurred silhouette of Private Wheelwright astride the wooden horse, his ridiculous, paint-stained sword resting on his shoulder. There was no sign of Corporal Salme with ball and chain attached. Shading his eyes for no earthly reason, Rhilander scanned the heavens and wondered if the deluge was some sort of freak of nature. In any given time span, hundreds of storms drenched the world in various places. Were all of them concentrating their combined wrath upon Laramie County? It looked so. One couldn't see individual drops; it was all one enormous spilling from the bucket of the black heavens.

"I hope Captain Stoddard and his boys aren't catching this."

Captain Stoddard and his men were catching rain of a lethal sort. Under a pulsing ball of fire hanging straight overhead, whitening the heavens as far as its rays could reach, Stoddard and C Company crouched behind packing crates, tool boxes, tie piles, equipment, and whatever else they could find for cover against a rain of missiles: lances, arrows, fire arrows, and lead coming at them from all sides. Nearly three hundred whooping, wild-eyed warriors, had surprise attacked the railhead, sending the tracklayers and other workers scurrying to hide, and the soldiers into defensive action.

CHEYENNE

His grim and stubble-studded round, red face smeared with dust and sweat, Corporal Crowder elbowed his bulk closer to Private Hannigan on his left. Crowder was a veteran of both Bull Runs and so many other battles they blended together as one in the corporal's memory. Hannigan, also well seasoned and bearing the scars to prove it, clucked in annoyance, cursed in his brogue, and let fly a glistening brown strool of tobacco juice.

"Jazus, they got us better'n three to one and they're raising so much doost you can't see to shoot atall, atall."

"Mike," called the man lying belly down a few feet away to his left. "You hear?"

"Hear what, for chrissakes?" asked Hannigan.

"Stoddard catched it."

"The captain?"

"How many fuckin' Stoddards we got in this outfit?" Crowder rasped irritably.

"Blessed lamb of Jazus," muttered Hannigan. "And him only married a few months. His poor wife—"

"Lieutenant Wojack's taken over," continued their informant. "Captain caught one clean through the eye."

Hannigan grunted. "Where in the name of sweet Jazus did the red bastards get all the damned rifles, I wonder? I ain't seen so many rifles one-eyeing me since Shiloh, Jazus. And they don't sound like no Henrys, they snap like Spencers."

"That's what they are," said Crowder. "Some thievin' bastard supplied 'em, you betcha. They was probably on their way to us at the fort when they got sidetracked."

"Which," responded Hannigan, "is soomthing I never could fathom. What in the name of Jazus the red heathens got to trade for arms, except beads, blankets, or baskets and sooch shit."

"And gold, silver. Look at 'em: Foxes, Elk soldiers, Red Shields, Dogs, Bow Strings, Crazies, every damn soldier old Roman Nose got to throw at us—"

"And Sioux," murmured Hannigan.

"What Sioux? They's no Sioux out there. You're seein' things."

"Oh yeah? Look at that trooper down the line there,

the one rolled over by the wagon wheel. Look at the
arrow stickin' in his liver. Sioux arrows are different from
Cheyenne, from any of the tribes; different from Cheyenne as night froom day. Faith, don't you know anything?
See how long it is: measured from a man's elbow to the
tip of the little finger ploos the length of the finger again.
And pulled through a sandstone hole to smooth it clean
as a baby's arse. See the way it shines in the sun? And
with them zigzag lightning lines down the shaft. Sioux,
bet your boots."

"Sioux *and* Cheyenne, Jesus Christ!"

"Wurra wurra. As me sainted mother used to say,
being in the wrong place at the wrong time may turn out
the last place you're in."

Bullets slammed into the packing cases in front of
them.

"Sweet Jazus," burst Hannigan worriedly. "They get
any closer they'll shoot clean through."

Crowder was looking around as he got out a tube of
cartridges, preparatory to reloading his carbine.

"Where the hell did all them Mick tracklayers disap-
pear to? Dived into the nearest wash and cowerin',
coverin' their heads like women in a hailstorm, the yellow Irish bastards."

Hannigan reddened and bristled. "Who you callin' bastards, you bastard? What the hell you expect? They're
not soldiers, they wasn't hired to shoot, don't know weapons. Paid to lay track is what they are, and a damn grand
job they do of it."

"Shit, bears and monkeys can lay track for all the
brains it takes. What the hell they doin' out here without
guns anyhow? What would they do if we wasn't here to
protect their pink asses, lay down and die, for chrissakes?
You don't got to be a professional to defend yourself.
Man's a man or he's not whatever he's wearin'. Goddamn fish eaters; all mush bellies and glass balls, that's
the Irish for ya."

"Why don't you shut your big fuckin' mouth!" burst
Hannigan.

"Why don't you shut it for me, fish eater!"

"Why don't you both shut up," bawled the sergeant two men over on Crowder's right.

Hannigan glared fiercely at his antagonist and resumed firing. Lead slammed his crate, arrows struck, twanging to rest. A fire arrow came arcing in, dropping, lodging in the ground inches from his heels.

"Heathen bastards!"

His anger erupted; he raised on one knee, aimed, tracked a Cheyenne clad in breechclout and moccasins only sprinting by on his pony, and dropped him screaming from its back with one shot. He roared victoriously, unconsciously exposing himself as he raised his arms. Out of the welter of shots fired by the circling savages one found his throat. His eyes popped in astonishment, he dropped his rifle, his hand started toward his throat and down he went. Positioned beside him as he was, Crowder saw him hit, but could not see where. Hannigan rolled over, blood spurting from his throat, glistening in the sunlight.

"Mike!" shouted Crowder. "Mike! Oh God, oh no . . . Mike, Mike."

He dragged closer to him and lay a hand on his unmoving chest, then reached slowly upward to shutter his staring eyes. He grit his teeth, shook it off, died a little himself, fought back the surge of regret twisting his heart, and resumed firing. Far down the line to his left a couple of workers lay with rumps high, their upper bodies hidden under overturned wheelbarrows. As he watched a fire arrow came blazing down, hitting the one closest to him in the left cheek. Up flew the wheelbarrow as he reacted wildly, tugging the arrow, freeing it from his rear, scrambling about yelling, screaming. A shot hit him in the chest, and his song of agony died on his lips as he fell.

"Dumb bastard," growled Crowder to himself.

The sun was starting down the sky. He drank from his canteen; a stray bullet passed through it, setting it leaking out both sides. He flung it away, cursing. The battle had been going on for close to three hours. He wondered how many casualties besides the captain, Mike, and the few he could see, the company had suffered. A flock, he decided ruefully. Blue and white smoke rose from the barrier ring. Roman Nose wanted the railroad out of the Cheyenne hunting grounds, and was willing to throw every man he could muster into the effort. When, Crowder wondered, had he struck his deal with the Sioux? Historically, they allied with no one. No tribe wanted to fight with them; still, these were desperate times for all the Plains tribes. It wasn't just the railroad snaking through their lands, it was what it brought along with it: emigrants, tradesmen, gamblers, bodies, and guns in ever increasing numbers. The red man was doomed, however hard he fought to forestall it. Crowder wondered if the wiser heads realized it. Washakie did; he refused to take up arms against the invaders. Sky Chief, the Pawnee, also refused, as did Plenty Coups of the Crow and Chief Guadalupe of the Caddo. But with the exception of the Pawnee, nearly every other tribe siding with the whites was peaceful.

The Cheyenne under Roman Nose were the big threat, the Sioux under Red Cloud even bigger. Both tribes had the numbers; they had been implacable enemies before the white man, but resentment loves sharing and desperation can spawn the unlikeliest alliances, so here was C Company facing their combined firepower.

"And takin' a fuckin' whippin' like to strip the hide off a man's back," muttered Crowder.

Again he reloaded, licked his fingertips, and tested the barrel of the Spencer. And seared the flesh as any halfwit might expect, yelling, cursing vilely.

The rain had not let up throughout the afternoon, into evening, into the gray dark of night. If anything, as the hours rolled by it increased in ferocity. It was nearing four when Rhilander's striker jiggled him awake.

"Colonel, sir, sorry, it's Sergeant Olson come in from the railhead."

Rhilander eyed him sleepily, his head fuzzy with whiskey and sleep. He managed a grunt of acknowledgment.

"C Company," continued his striker. "They're being wiped out. May already be."

Olson looked as if he'd ridden through Lake Absarraca. The downpour had washed the lather from his horse's neck. He had come upwards of 170 miles, changing horses a dozen times. He was so exhausted he couldn't stand. But neither his heroics nor his exhaustion were any defense against the colonel's anger when he spilled forth his story.

"Why in the name of Christ did you ride all the way back here for!"

"Lieutenant Wojack's orders, sir."

"Stupid Polack! Didn't either of you stop to think? You could have stopped off at Fred Steele. It's less than two hours ride from there. Explained, demanded reinforcements, gotten back there with a couple hundred men—"

"Lieutenant Wojack said—" Olson began.

"I heard you!" Rhilander threw up his hands. "Christ, is everybody in this army stupid! What are you, stone between the ears? You know what you've done? You've guaranteed a massacre!"

"I was just following—"

"Shut up!"

Rhilander groaned, drooped his shoulders, dropped into a chair, slumped, stretched his long legs, and seethed. Olson eyed him and swallowed. When the colonel resumed speaking, his tone had softened noticeably. He lifted his head and fastened sympathetic eyes on the sergeant.

"I'm sorry, son. You're not to blame. How bad was it when you left?"

"Terrible. They were throwing lead at us like no injuns I ever seen. At least four hundred, Cheyenne *and* Sioux, three out of every four armed with a rifle or pistol. And ammunition. They musta raided a depot. Was a miracle I got away. It's a blood bath, sir."

"You got away and rode right by Fred Steele. Never mind. Reach over, there's a bottle in the bottom drawer there. Take a good stiff slug."

Rhilander watched the liquor jolt the floor of Olson's belly as it hit. He gasped away the fire. Rhilander smiled weakly.

"You're soaked to the skin. Get on over to the barracks, get out of those clothes, and rub yourself down with a towel before you turn in. Somebody on guard'll see to your horse."

"Yes, sir."

Olson restored the bottle to the bottom drawer. He gripped the arms of his chair and tried to stand. He teetered perilously, grabbed one arm for support, straightened, and executed the feeblest excuse for a salute Rhilander had ever seen. So pathetic was it he would have burst out laughing, but his mood was too foul to let him. A bloodbath, Stoddard and every man under him, fifty seasoned fighters minus Olson, dead, probably scalped, their bodies hacked to pieces.

An entire company had been wiped away as if by the stroke of a pen. He thought about the captain's pretty, small-waisted, saucer-eyed bride with her eastern big city ways, her teas and tintype collection, her staunch and tireless defense of her husband's rights and welfare. Her morbid fear that he would be killed. He pictured her lying alone and lonesome in bed. No point waking her to tell her the good news. After reveille had blown would be time enough.

"Damn and double damn Dodge . . ."

"Sir?" Olson looked confused.

"Nothing," replied Rhilander. "Get out of here, go rub down, get to bed, skip falling out in the morning. And—"

"Sir?"

"Good job, soldier, good man."

5

Something woke Jubal. Before falling asleep he had been driving from inside the wagon, hoping to get them out from under the storm, but the horses, unable to make any real headway in the mire, had tired and rebelled against going farther. For the sixth meal in a row the family had cold food: dried beef, dried fruit, shriveled and tasteless peaches and apricots. One was supposed to bite into them and roll the piece around inside one's mouth to moisten it and draw forth its sweetness before swallowing it, but Jubal couldn't be bothered. Just get it down, drink some water, and get to sleep. He glanced through the horseshoe-shaped opening at the front. The horses stood stone still in their harnesses, rumps glistening, heads bowed, eyes fixed on the slough enduring, waiting patiently for the assault to lift. Jubal shuddered. Dampness had sneaked into his bones, displacing the marrow and substituting a chill, slushy fluid. It worked its way into his bloodstream and fouled and froze his blood and oozed through him. His heart felt as if it were shrinking with cold, and his nails showed a faint bluish tinge. Two days and nights and no sign of letup.

"And God said unto Noah . . . make thee an ark of gopher wood . . . A window shalt thou make to the ark . . . and, behold I, even I, do bring a flood of waters upon the earth, to destroy all flesh, wherein is the

breath of life, from under heaven; and every thing that
is in the earth shall die.

"And the flood was forty days upon the earth . . .
and the waters prevailed exceedingly upon the earth;
and all the high hills, that were under the whole heaven,
were covered . . . And every living substance was destroyed which was upon the face of the ground, both
man, and cattle, and the creeping things, and the fowl
of the heaven; and they were destroyed from the earth:
and Noah only remained alive, and they that were with
him in the ark."

His eyes became accustomed to the darkness. He could
hear Jeptha snoring softly, lying with his back to Lorna.
He spied the Dutch oven, the food supplies neatly stacked
in the right rear corner near the tailgate. His heart
wrenched.

"Hannah!"

Jeptha started as if poked by a stick; he sat bolt upright, kneading his eyes with his fists.

"Your mother's gone!" boomed Jubal.

"Oh my God."

"Pull on your boots, put on your slicker."

Jeptha turned to wake up Lorna.

"No, let her sleep," said Jubal. "We'll go. You take
the north side of the road. She can't have gotten far in
this."

Jubal fumbled with matches, managed to get the railroad lantern lit. He put on his oiled coat with the shoulder cape and large high collar and squam hat, the flap
secured under his chin. He wandered about calling her
name. Standing and listening, praying she would respond,
he could hear Jeptha calling on the other side. He had no
idea of the time. He guessed it to be about three hours
before sunup, as if the sun would rise in this. He could
not recall a downpour so determinedly, relentlessly heavy.

The terrain was rough in spots, the ground slippery, so
he had to be careful of his footing. Tall needlegrass and
bluestem predominated, but there were also shorter buffalo grass and blue grama. Soapweed abounded and clus-

tering prickly pear. And showy forbs: purple loco,
white-flowered beardtongue, lupines. Dear God, was she
out looking for wildflowers in this tempest? Her mind
must have unhinged completely. He searched and called,
telling himself over and over that she could not have
gotten far from the wagon. But the more he said it, the
less he believed it. He had a vague hope that she would
walk in a circle, as lost people often do, but he was
unable to anchor it.

He went back holding his breath, hoping fervently,
hanging over the tailgate looking inside, but she wasn't
there. Or Lorna. Jeptha appeared, his face ashen with
worry. He shook his head.

"Lorna's gone, too," said Jubal.

"Now she'll get lost!"

"No, she won't. Your mother may have headed back
down the way we came," said Jubal hopefully, but his
son's discouraged expression did not change.

"What do we do?" asked Jeptha.

"You head back down, I'll go on ahead. When you get
about a hundred and fifty yards, turn right and circle
back. I'll do the same to the south."

"But we already—"

"Just do it!" snapped Jubal.

Jeptha shrugged. They were preparing to resume the
search when a figure materialized out of the gloom. Two
figures. Lorna half carried her mother toward them. Father and son ran to help. Hannah was holding a fistful of
drooping, rain-sodden purple and pink lupines. They got
her into the wagon. She was soaked to the skin and
babbling incoherently. Jubal could catch snatches of sen-
tences, enough to get the meaning. She had been asleep.
She had dreamed of the baby; he had come to her as a
young boy, and he had taken her with him.

"Sun was out. Beautiful. Green meadows. Millions of
daisies. The bluest sky. His hair is just like Edward's. He
asked for you, Jubal. For his daddy. He's very happy
where he is. He told me. I didn't even have to ask."

Lorna covered her with a third blanket.

"She's shivering so she can't stop."

Jubal had loosened the bale on the lantern and gotten the top off.

"Find a tin cup and make tea over the wick," he said. "If we can get some down her, it may help."

She drank it all, but her shivering persisted. She began to cough. Lorna sat cradling her in her arms.

"Her feet were like ice when I took her shoes off. And feel her hands."

Jubal shook his head disconsolately and eyed Jeptha crouching opposite. He too looked ill.

"You all right?" Lorna asked.

"Mmmm. She already had a cold, you know."

"She'll catch pneumonia," said Lorna.

"Not if you keep her bundled up," snapped Jubal.

Lorna was feeling her forehead. "She has a temperature."

"Keep her warm as you can, she'll sweat it out."

"She needs a doctor."

"There's one at Fort Laramie," said Jubal. "Fletcher said."

"How far?" asked Jeptha.

"I don't know exactly, but it has to be over a hundred miles."

"There's nothing between here and the fort?"

"Not on the Overland Trail map," said his father.

"Can't we at least go on?" burst Lorna. "Must we sit here drowning, watching her die?"

"Don't talk so! She's not going to die." Jubal glared. "I'll see if I can start the horses, get them up on the high ground ahead; maybe it's not so muddy. Maybe they'll have more heart for pulling."

He picked his way forward to the driver's seat, jerked the whip from its holder, and climbed down, reins in hand.

Rhilander's attempt to gently break the bad news to Mrs. Stoddard failed. She fainted. When she came to, she came apart. He left her to Harvey Philips and went on to tell the other two widows about the massacre. That it had deteriorated into a massacre was not just a logical conclusion on his part anymore. An hour before reveille

CHEYENNE

he was awakened a second time by a messenger from
Dodge's temporary headquarters in Cheyenne. The man
informed him that Sergeant Olson's and his worst fears
had been realized.

It had stopped raining. Water dripped steadily from
the eaves and the parade ground was a swamp, but the
day dawned bright and clear.

He called on Private Mike Hannigan's wife, a laun-
dress at the fort who had been Mrs. Hannigan for a year.
Molly O'Flaherty–Hannigan was a fetching redhead with
permanently reddened hands and a defiant air about her.
Had she been a man, he thought, she probably would
have carried a chip on one shoulder, daring everyone she
met to knock it off. Tears glistened in her green eyes and
her lower lip quivered when he told her. He had come
upon her weeding flowers in a windowbox. She dropped
the weeds at her feet, standing silent, listening, letting his
words sink in like needles.

"All killed?"

He nodded. "They were badly outnumbered."

"Will the bodies be brought back?"

"They always are, when possible," said Rhilander.

"Will they be?"

"I think so."

"His has to be," said Molly firmly. "It can't be left out
there to rot. We're Catholics, you know. He must be
buried in consecrated ground with a priest officiating.
For the sake of his soul he must be."

"I understand."

"Are you a Catholic?" she asked.

"No."

"Then you don't understand. I'll have to go into town
and tell Father Boyle."

And that was that. His death had clearly staggered her,
but she'd recovered remarkably, in no more than half a
minute. His funeral required important preparations; her
religious conscientiousness took over for her emotions
and into the task she'd plunge. She had, as Mario Consolo
would have said, more grit than the bottom of the creek.
If she planned to cry, she'd be damned before she'd let him

see. Standing with her red fists locked to her hips, her lovely eyes brimming and softened by her unshed tears, she thrust forth her jaw and silently defied him to hurt her. Clearly, having said what he had to, she wanted him to leave. He was taking valuable time from a day to be devoted to arranging for her husband's soul's journey into the hereafter.

Consolo met him at the foot of the office steps as he was about to go in.

"The infantry and the cavalry had a baseball game scheduled for tomorrow afternoon. They want to know if you want to postpone it."

"It's up to them," said Rhilander.

"Oh no, they'll end up at each other's throats. Very intense rivalry; don't you remember the last game? They want you to decide."

"Tell them to put it off till next week."

"The infantry won't mind. They lost three quarters of their infield out there," Consolo added. "You all done telling the widows?"

"Yes. Thank God. I left Mrs. Stoddard with Harvey. He's much better at it than I am. She took it the hardest. Mrs. Van Winklemann was stunned, more than she showed, but fatalistic. She told me she expected it. Hannigan's wife was a brick. It's done, it's over, and now he has to have the proper send-off. Religion does come in handy at times like this."

"Spoken like a true atheist," said Consolo with a grin.

"Tell them to postpone the game. And when they do play it, there's to be no riot like the last game. They should only take their frustrations out on the hostiles as energetically as they do on each other. Tell them and come right back. I want you to mind the store for me, I'm going into town to have a little heart-to-heart talk with Major General Grenville Dodge."

"Lincoln—"

"Relax, I promise I'll control myself. I just want to get a few things straight. Bitter Creek is never going to happen to our people again. Never."

* * *

CHEYENNE

The reappearance of the sun revived the horses. They made eighteen miles before two that afternoon. The road dried quickly, but the deluge left it severely rutted, and Jubal was concerned lest one of the horses misstep and break an ankle.

Hannah's babbling kept on; Lorna took it to be delirium. She seemed to Jubal to be bearing the flag of pessimism. He waxed optimistic, hoping to pick up her spirits and erase the glum look from Jeptha's face. The boy even looked gloomy while reading, and he could not seem to concentrate. He kept looking back at his mother dozing in Lorna's arms, her lips moving silently now. She was sweating heavily. Again and again Lorna wiped her face and in seconds it would be gleaming anew. They came within sight of a creek which, from the map, Jubal took to be Lodgepole. The downpour had turned it yellow-brown and caused it to overflow. No sooner did Jubal sight it and draw Jeptha's attention to it than two riders appeared.

"White men," noted Jeptha. "I wonder if they've seen the train."

"They must have."

Waving as they came, they picked up speed as they approached. One was in his sixties, carrying a perfectly round paunch, although the rest of him above and below it, even his face and neck, were lean. He seemed to Jubal to be parts of two people. He was dressed like a parson minus the white collar. In place of it he wore a dark green silk ascot fastened in place by a pearl stickpin. His younger companion wore a tight-waisted black frock coat in defiance of the heat, close-fitting pants, expensive soft kid boots, a frilled white shirt with a high collar, and a flowing black tie anchored by a diamond cluster stickpin. A black stovepipe hat was perched on his head, and it gleamed like polished onyx in the sunlight.

"Pilgrims," he drawled, "welcome to Wyoming. My name is Rogers, that's with an *s*, Halliburton, and this is my friend and traveling companion, His Honor, Judge Arthur Shankland."

Jubal introduced Jeptha and himself. Both men's clothes

looked perfectly dry. When Jubal asked if they'd run into the storm, they told him that it had not reached more than a mile west of Cheyenne. Descending the eastern slopes of the Laramies, they had seen it at a distance moving toward them, and taken cover in a trapper's cabin until the sun reappeared.

"Did you run into a wagon train ahead?" Jeptha asked.

Halliburton and the judge exchanged glances. Jeptha sucked in his breath and held it expectantly with his teeth clenched.

"The wreckage of one," said Halliburton quietly. "Indians, a horde from the look of it. Grisly, really grisly."

"Killed every man, woman, and child," interposed the judge. "Looted and burned the wagons. Only thing left alive was an old cow wandering around loose, clanging her bell. Absolute carnage. Poor souls didn't stand a chance."

"One wagon was carrying a bunch of youngsters," said Halliburton. "They slaughtered them."

"How many children?" asked Jeptha bluntly.

"And what they did to the women," said the judge, "especially the young ones."

"How many children!" burst Jeptha.

The question repeated so insistently disconcerted Halliburton. "We—I—didn't count."

"Ten or eleven," said the judge.

"It was them," said Jeptha to his father.

"Your train?" Halliburton asked.

"We were held up back in Nebraska," explained Jubal. "Broke a rear wheel crossing a creek. Took us two days to ride to the nearest town and back with a replacement."

"Some luck to find a wheel that size out here," said the judge. "Luckier still you didn't catch up with them. No telling which ones did it, but there's a rumor going around that Red Cloud, chief of the Oglala Sioux, has joined forces with the Cheyenne."

Jeptha looked devastated. He hung his head, addressing the horses' rumps. "All massacred. Every one."

"Except Bossy." The judge looked to Halliburton for agreement. "I guess they didn't cut her up for meat because they had all they could carry of oxen. You should have seen the blood. They blew through that train like a Texas twister."

"You bound for Oregon?" Halliburton asked Jubal.

"The Willamette Valley."

"Good luck. Keep your eyes peeled for those redskins, though they're probably out of the area by now. You can lay over at Fort Laramie until the next train catches up with you. There's sure to be another behind. Treking all the way to the Willamette alone could be dangerous. Safety in numbers—"

The judge snorted. "Numbers didn't help those poor souls ahead. Yes sir, you boys and your busted wheel are luckier than you know."

Jeptha hung his head. He had plunged into a morass of misery. Jubal jerked a thumb over his shoulder.

"My wife is sick back inside. We heard there's a doctor at the fort. But it's so far. Would you happen to know if there's one closer? She's getting worse."

"Try in Cheyenne," said Halliburton. "It's less than twenty miles. Take the left fork about two miles up the line. People have been pouring into there lately like gnats swarming. You'll probably find a dozen doctors."

"Much obliged. She caught a bad cold in the rain."

"She caught pneumonia," said Jeptha.

The judge clucked and shook his head.

"Watch yourselves in Cheyenne," said Halliburton. "It's wide open, hell-raising around the clock. Everybody carries a gun. You might do better pulling up outside so one of you can go find a doctor and bring him to her."

They wished them luck and rode off.

"Salita Jane," murmured Jeptha. His eyes were still downcast. A tear dropped.

"I'm sorry, son." He groped for words of solace, but none came, none meaningful, comforting enough.

"We were going to be married, we planned everything—"

"I know. Wait, what are you doing?"

Jeptha had closed his book. He was getting down.

"I'm going to find them. I'll meet you outside Cheyenne. I won't be long. I just have to see."

"No."

"I have to, Jubal. I'll take the shovel. I have to bury her properly, bury them all."

"It'll tear the heart out of you. Don't!"

But there was no stopping him. Jubal watched him start out with the shovel over his shoulder.

"Wait, take one of the horses."

Jubal unhitched the leader's right-hand mate. He waved Jeptha away, the boy by now a helpless captive of his wretchedness.

"Outside Cheyenne. Look for us."

Dodge's striker had escorted Rhilander into the general's outer office–waiting room.

"I'll inform the general you're here, sir."

He clicked his heels, saluted sharply, and, rapping on the inner door, went inside, closing it after him.

Plumping into the overstuffed chair, unbuttoning his top button, and crossing his legs, Rhilander could hear muffled conversation inside. Then no sound. The striker came out. He handed him a sealed envelope.

"The general is in a meeting, sir," he explained. "He'll be able to see you shortly. He asked me to give you this, and is there anything I can get you, sir?"

"I'm fine, thanks, Sergeant."

Again the striker clicked and snapped off a salute capable of breaking a man's neck. He left. The muffled talking inside resumed, punctuated by occasional laughter. Rhilander checked his watch: 9:32. He turned the envelope over. His name was scrawled on the front.

Memo
From: Major General Grenville M. Dodge
To: Lieutenant Colonel Lincoln Rhilander

I have in hand the full report of yesterday's terrible tragedy at the Bitter Creek worksite. Against overwhelming odds your men fought gallantly. They died with honor, and their deaths, as the deaths of all those engaged in the continuing struggle to secure permanent peace in the territories, will not pass unnoticed by their fellow Americans. Each and every member of Company C was a bona fide hero, as I intend to inform the War Department. May you, their comrades, and their loved ones find some solace in the knowledge that they did not die in vain, that theirs was a sacrifice that will be acknowledged and long remembered by their countrymen.

Raucous laughter erupted within. Rhilander crumpled the memo into a tight ball and dropped it between his feet. His watch said 9:40. More laughter, more muffled talking. It sounded like three men, perhaps four. He switched from right leg over left to left over right and drummed the arms of his chair.

In a matter of hours, fifty men—the heart of Fort Russell's infantry—had been wiped out. Fifty men who never should have been assigned to the Bitter Creek site in the first place. Dodge knew that, knew it when he'd given the order, knew it when word of the massacre reached him, knew it when he dictated the memo. Why the memo? It wasn't s.o.p. Rhilander glanced down at the paper ball between his feet and wondered: were all those meticulously selected, flowery, lofty, meaningless words conceived and strung together to ease the general's conscience?

He waited. No one came in. The inner door remained closed. He continued to hear unintelligible talking and now and then bursts of laughter. Could whoever it was be swapping jokes? Ten past ten. He got up and began to pace. The outer door opened.

"Lincoln."

It was Major Hubert Walls, CO of Fort Fred Steele. Walls was tall, urbane, blessed with a classic Greek profile that melted women's hearts, and flowing mustachios that fetched his good looks into modern times. A ready laugh, a tough, fair, and altogether first-rate soldier. They greeted each other warmly.

"What are you doing here?" Walls asked, lowering his voice.

"What are you?"

"In town to check on a piece of property I bought.

Man has to plan for his future, you know. A year from next week I'll be the proud proprieter of a hotel. Oh, forgive me, I am sorry about that business out at Bitter Creek. Real tragedy."

Rhilander grunted and assumed a bleak look.

"It might not have been if the messenger had had the presence of mind to stop off at Steele and ask for help instead of riding all the way back to Russell," he said.

"We would have pitched in, but we didn't know."

"How could you?" said Rhilander.

"I *am* sorry. Say, did you know he's getting out?"

"Dodge? When?"

"Next week," responded Walls. "I guess he figures he can't go on straddling the fence indefinitely. Either he works for Uncle Sam or the U.P." He laughed lightly. "U.P. sure pays better. Lucky chap, his job's got it all over the hotel business. So what are you seeing him about?"

"I don't know that I will be. I've been sitting counting flies for three quarters of an hour already. He's in a meeting."

Walls cocked an ear toward the door. The voices could barely be heard.

"Does he know you're here?" he asked Rhilander.

"His orderly has been in. He said he'd be tied up awhile if I could wait. That was around nine-thirty." He shrugged.

"Looks like I'm out of luck. I should be getting back to the post. Again, I'm damned sorry about your bad news." He assumed a sheepish expression. "In a way I can't help but feel responsible."

"What do you mean?" Rhilander asked.

"He came to me right after a couple of his surveyors were killed, asking for a company to protect the workers out at the creek."

"Asking?"

"Politely ordering," said Walls. "I turned him down. From a top of 191 rank and file around this time last year before the order came down from Washington cutting strength by half, we're now down to 88 able-bodied. Two companies, Linc. He could have come to me on his knees, I wasn't about to hand over a whole company. We went at it pretty good. He could have flat-out insisted, but he didn't. I gambled he wouldn't. Everybody knows he's got one foot out the door and wouldn't want to be bothered squabbling with one of the help. What else are we? Of course I was holding an ace and he knew it. We lost six men up by Medicine Bow River two days after they cut our strength in half. Before Fort Russell was even built. I wasn't about to hand over half of what I had left. Not for the glory and profit of the goddamned railroad I wasn't."

"So he came to me." Rhilander shook his head.

"Believe me, I didn't send him."

"He didn't need sending, he knew where to head. And poor fool me, I practically set C Company in his lap. The son of a bitch didn't order, didn't demand, he sweet-talked me."

"He's good at it," said Walls. "Hey, don't get all worked up—"

"I'm not, not at him. At myself. I still don't understand how such a thing could happen. How so many Indians could get together and go on the warpath without his finding out and warning us? Where the hell were his scouts?"

"Down below chasing Arapaho, I guess," responded Walls. "I don't know, why don't you ask him?"

"I intend to."

"Ask, Linc, don't go accusing him." Walls looked toward the closed door. "I've got to get back. Nice seeing you."

"Good luck in the hotel business, Hubert."

"Not for a whole year. One more makes twenty, then good-bye boots and saddles. What about you?"

"Me? Retire?" Rhilander shrugged. "I haven't even thought about it. I've still got four years and no future plans. I haven't gotten around to that."

"It's never too early to think about it. God forbid the War Department cuts strength out here again. People back East, a flock of Congressmen, are clamoring for it. There's nothing as useless and as easily forgotten as a soldier after the shooting's stopped. Overnight he be-

A. R. Riefe

comes a waste of the taxpayers' money. People back East don't believe there's a war going on out here."

"I've got three new widows back at the fort who can tell them differently."

Walls shook his head grimly and offered his hand. Rhilander shook it.

"Good luck with him, Linc. See you."

Rhilander checked his watch. Twenty of eleven. One hour and eight minutes. The door eased open and a round, pink-faced artillery captain stepped out cradling a bottle of whiskey in his left arm. Dodge's aide appeared behind him.

"Colonel Rhilander? The general will see you now."

The inner office looked as if a whirlwind had passed through it. The desktop was in awesome disarray. Cartons lay about half filled with papers. Pictures had been removed from the walls. Smoke hung from the ceiling. Dodge sprawled in his chair, his shirt unbuttoned halfway to his navel. Commiseration welled in his eyes.

"Sit, sit, sorry to keep you waiting. Sorrier about what happened. Did you get my memo?"

"Yes, sir," said Rhilander.

"Oh, would you like a drink? Cigar?"

"No, thank you."

"What can I do for you? Name it." He swept the room with his hand. "As you can see, I'm leaving. Heading back to Omaha tomorrow morning. I've resigned. It doesn't take effect until next week, but I need the time to tie up all the loose ends, and believe me there's a thousand of them. So, what's on your mind? Oh, before you start, there's just one thing."

He roused himself from his chair and indicated the map on the wall behind him, the only decoration not yet taken down.

"Here, just east of Wamsutter. A number of Cheyenne Dog Soldiers have been seen in the area. They may or may not be associated with the bunch that attacked the worksite, but whether they are or not, there are thirty or forty of them and they should be driven out before they start something. Ounce of prevention, right?

90

Word is High-Backbone is leading them. Tom Everbach, the U.P. agent here in town—"

"Sir," interrupted Rhilander.

"Yes?"

"No."

"I beg your pardon." Dodge looked confused.

"Not again," Rhilander went on. "It's a little too soon for my boys. If Fort Steele can't handle it, give it to Fort Sanders."

Dodge hard-eyed him. "I'm giving it to Fort Russell," he said tightly.

"Keep it. This time we pass."

"I'm giving you a direct order, Colonel."

"I'm giving you a direct refusal, Mr. Dodge."

"*General* Dodge."

"Not anymore."

"Perhaps you weren't listening," said Dodge tightly, anger rising in his eyes. "My resignation doesn't take effect until next week."

"I heard you. But you did say you've resigned, so your intentions are clear. That's good enough for me."

"You're not listening. Protecting the railroad is our responsibility, whether you like it or not. I'm sorry about your men, it was unfortunate."

"It was unnecessary," muttered Rhilander.

"But the hostiles aren't going to sit on their hands, waiting for the period of mourning to end," continued Dodge.

"You son of a bitch."

"I'll give you five seconds to retract that."

Rhilander started to say something, changed his mind, spun on his heel, and walked out.

6

Cheyenne was unlike any town Jubal had ever seen. At first glance it looked as if the wind had thrown it together, a motley clutter of buildings, leantos, tents, and wagons on blocks that looked as if they were jockeying for position, interlaced with streets identified by temporary signs fastened to buildings, poles, even wires, many of the names already rendered illegible by the weather. The streets themselves were deeply rutted, quagmires baked by the sun and clogged with traffic. About the town hung an air of impermanency, a suggestion that everyone he could see was a transient. It was a surging, boiling mass of strangers, a many-headed monster threatening to absorb him like the sea swallows a drowning man.

A brass band blared from on a platform in front of the Big Tent Saloon. Miners, ranchers, drifters, trappers, clerks, gamblers, bullwackers, buffalo hunters, and railroad workers, war veterans all, flocked to listen to the military songs and stream into the tent to slake their thirst, gamble away their money, and find female companionship. The Big Tent was big indeed, a hundred feet long by forty feet wide, with a massive cathedral-like canvas top towering over the largest and most magnificent hardwood floor west of Chicago. To the left of the entrance stood a fifty-foot mahogany bar stocked with a bountiful array of liquor, food, cigars, cut glass goblets, ice pitchers, everything duplicated in a splendid French

CHEYENNE

mirror. Behind the bar above the mirror, hanging from the canvas wall, were numerous works of art. And just beyond the bar stood a collection of tables for gambling and drinking. Provocatively dressed hurdy-gurdy girls welcomed the patrons, herding them to the tables and to the rear to the dance floor. Occupying a platform on a scaffold ten feet above the floor was a band, minus the brass and drums playing outside.

The Big Tent was only one of forty saloon/dance hall/gambling casinos bulging with patrons. Men by the hundreds sought out the bawdy houses, from the cheap cribs offering the charms of one or two prostitutes to the imposing two-story building called the Double Decker, standing opposite the Presbyterian Church on the south side of Eighteenth Street, and acknowledged to be the biggest, most pretentious brothel in Wyoming, featuring the uninhibited skills of more than sixty females. The Double Decker's walls were the finest brick, the sills and lintels of its windows elaborately carved sandstone, its interior lavishly, royally furnished.

Traveling acts, everything from acrobats to touring zoos, performed in the variety saloon theaters. Nearly every building Jubal could see boasted a false front, some even attached to outsized tents.

Cheyenne was the sorest of eyesores, a monument to hasty and haphazard building, a junk heap of a town. People flocked to it, attracting droves of parasites bent on skinning them of their cash, valuables, and property in every conceivable way.

Jubal stood rooted, looking about. He had reined up a quarter of a mile from town. Jeptha had come back, having found the ashes of the train and completed his tragic mission. He said nothing about what he'd seen; he was too depressed to discuss it. Jubal was not curious. He could picture the massacre all too easily.

Hannah, meanwhile, had gotten much worse, coughing, spitting up blood, her lungs striving futilely to sustain her. Even in the sun she could not stop shivering. Her temperature had shot up. She complained of headaches and severe pains in her chest. Her breathing was shallow and she suffered from shortness of breath. Her color was high and tinged slightly blue. She would never make it to Fort Laramie. If she was to get any help, Jubal would have to find it in Cheyenne.

He stopped three people to ask directions to the nearest doctor, but none could help him. The fourth, a dark-haired, dignified older woman, came to his rescue.

"Dr. Gogarty. On Nineteenth near Eddy. Go to the end of the street, turn right and right again. The Gunshot Saloon is on the corner. There's a sign in the upstairs window. The entrance is one door up Nineteenth."

"God bless you, ma'am."

He pushed through the surging crowd, following her directions. He located the saloon and saw the sign in an upstairs window to the right. He thought about going back and fashioning a litter of some sort to bring Hannah into town, but decided he'd better check first and make sure the doctor was in and available. He ascended the stairs and knocked.

"Come in."

Aloysius Jeremiah Gogarty, M.D., was busy bandaging a gunshot wound. He did not look up when Jubal entered. He was short, pudgy, with a shock of steel-gray hair and yellow skin. He wore the emblem with the lyre, shamrocks, and clasped hands of the Ancient Order of Hibernia in America, hanging from a silver chain across his rumpled vest. He smelled faintly of stale liquor. His eyes looked as if they'd been taken from their sockets, bounced about, abused, bruised and reddened, and put back. He was nervous, fidgety, and obviously exhausted from practicing the healing arts fortified by too little food and too much drink. He coughed.

He finished with his patient, accepted payment, sent him out, and spoke to Jubal for the first time.

"Closing up for the day."

Jubal explained. Dr. Gogarty listened politely, hands joined behind his back, upper body bowed, eyes fixed on his well-scuffed shoes, forehead laced with deep black furrows.

CHEYENNE

"Your daughter have medical training?" He coughed into his fist.

"No sir," said Jubal.

"Well, it sounds like she's on the mark."

"Can you come out to the wagon?"

"Of course," said Gogarty. "I just have to lock up. Give me a second."

Jubal stood in the doorway watching him get ready to leave. He locked his cabinets, checked the contents of his satchel before snapping it shut, and motioned him to start down the stairs. He came toward the door, stopped two feet from it, snapped his fingers, and went back. He retrieved a pint bottle from a desk drawer, downed two stiff belts, corked it, jammed it in his jacket pocket, smiled self-consciously, and coughed.

"Let's go."

It was dark by the time they got to the wagon. Jubal was worn out from urging the horse to greater speed and worrying what they were speeding to. Hannah managed a smile of greeting. Jubal kissed her, lit the lantern for Dr. Gogarty, and left him to examine her in privacy. While they waited, he, Jeptha, and Lorna fed the horses.

"She's awfully weak," said Lorna. "The coughing takes away every bit of her strength."

"She's dying," said Jeptha.

"She's not!" snapped Jubal, so viciously it jerked Jeptha's head up and rounded his eyes. "How dare you say such a thing? What are you, a doctor all of a sudden, Mr. Brilliance? She's very sick, she's been sick before and gotten better. Haven't we all?"

Jeptha shook his head. "Not—"

"We have! That's enough!" He softened his tone. "What did you see ahead on the trail?"

"Somebody had already buried most of the bodies in a common grave. If the Indians don't dig them up, the coyotes will."

"You saw her body?"

Jeptha nodded. "All the Tuckers, even the baby. What

95

the Indians didn't take, they burnt or destroyed. What are we going to do if she dies?"

"She won't, damn you. Stop carrying on so!"

They heard creaking at the rear of the wagon as Gogarty climbed down. He peered around the corner.

"I'm terribly sorry," he said.

Lorna's pretty features hardened, contorting into suffering's mask. "She's dead!"

She threw herself against Jubal's chest, beating her fists weakly. She sobbed in his arms for a while, then recovered and set herself rigid, drew in a breath so hard it made her shudder, and started back.

"Lorna," he called.

The doctor blocked her with one arm. "There's nothing you can do, child. She didn't suffer. It's God's will." He crossed himself.

"Let me by," she said.

He lowered his arm. She started back. Gogarty's words had struck Jubal like a cannonball, staggering him where he stood. The agony that followed was torture, a creature with a scaly hide and sharp quills. It broke into his stomach and began thrashing about. Each point of its armor struck a different tender spot, sending pain radiating through him, rising into his trunk, descending to his loins and down his thighs, crimping and burning his veins.

He wanted to throw his head back and scream at the stars, at the God who had taken her from him. He wanted to die, to slip through the door into the realm of spirits and follow her, catch her by the hand and never let go. Wherever Death took them he'd be by her side. He could feel tears welling and swiped his eyes. He began to tremble, and the more he tried to control it, the worse it got until his teeth chattered absurdly.

Jeptha had followed his sister with Gogarty. Jubal joined them. The four of them stood peering inside the darkened wagon. Gogarty held the lantern high. In its glow Hannah lay eyes closed, arms folded across her chest, her expression contented, as if Death had politely invited her and she, obligingly, without fear or hesitancy, consented to accompany him.

Jubal had stopped shaking; he sighed and looked away. And the thing inside continued to ravage him. The separate stabbing pains became one; he felt like he was being burned alive. Jeptha clasped one hand, Lorna the other. A tremor passed through him, easing his agony, dulling it, dispelling his weariness. His son and daughter would be his support. They would be each other's. A link had been taken from them, but the ones remaining fastened together more strongly than ever.

Gogarty was watching them. He had lowered the lantern. He set it on the ground.

"About the burial," he said.

"Is there a cemetery?" Jubal asked.

"Sort of, the beginning of one." He pointed off. "South of town." He coughed into his fist. "Other side of the creek. I can make the arrangements."

"If it's not too much trouble—"

"I do it every other day. I'll send a wagon out with a coffin. Nothing fancy. Fancy's not available around here. The men who bring it can handle things. You *will* still be here—"

"Yes."

The three of them watched him wheel away in his fly, his satchel jouncing on the seat cushion, his horse prancing proudly, its glossy black mane riding the breeze. The sight of its energy tired Jubal. Exhaustion seemed to be assaulting him in successive waves, each time leaving his body less able to rebound. His heart felt as heavy as a tackle block. Its weight pushed him downward; his legs felt sinewless, his knees threatened to buckle. Above his waist he could feel only the block, no muscle, no pulsing blood, no vigor, nothing, hollow.

He looked upward; a million stars pulsed tirelessly against the shroud of night, lighting the way for the ascent of her soul. Hannah, Hannah, my love, my life.

"Tomorrow we'll have some kind of funeral," he murmured, "the best we can."

"This is horrible!" burst Lorna. "Heartless! To bury her in a place she's never even seen. So far from home. Among strangers. It's hideous!"

A. R. Riefe

Jeptha was gazing at his father. "And after we bury her, then what?"

Jubal had no heart for what he was about to say, but say it he did. "We go on."

"Without her? How can we? She was the one who held us together."

"We'll hold ourselves," said Jubal.

"It won't be the same. And sooner or later we're bound to run into the same thing the Tuckers did. I say we go back. Lorna?"

"What do you think, dear?" asked Jubal.

For a moment she did not answer. She stared off at no identifiable object, at the night. And shivered.

"I don't know, don't care. Excuse me, I have to find some place to sit and—"

She burst into tears and ran off.

"How can we go on without Mother?" Jeptha persisted.

"Will going back make it easier?" Jubal asked. "Will it soften the pain? How can it?"

"That's not what I mean. She was the one who would have made it right for us back there. She was home, Jubal, not the house or the land. I never wanted to come in the first place, but I did. I tried, even though I never did have your heart for it. Now I have no heart. I never want to see Oregon."

"We won't talk about it now," said his father. "We're not ourselves. This is no time to make decisions. We'll decide tomorrow."

"You want to go on, don't you?" said Jeptha.

"I don't know what I want."

"Lorna doesn't."

"Tomorrow, Jeptha, after the funeral. Do me a favor, fetch the Bible. It's in your mother's walnut chest. I want to read."

He read from Corinthians: "O death, where *is* thy sting? O grave, where *is* thy victory?" And from Revelations: "And God shall wipe away all tears from their eyes; and there shall be no death, neither sorrow, nor crying, neither shall there be any more pain: for the former things are passed away."

And Lorna heard him reading and came and sat beside Jeptha, holding onto his arm, listening. And in the words they found some comfort to ease their terrible grief.

───────◄7►───────

"You what!"

Lieutenant Mario Consolo's eyebrows jumped up his forehead and his dark eyes tested the confines of their sockets.

"I questioned his mother's marital status," said Rhilander.

"It's not funny, Lincoln. You apologized of course. Did he accept it?"

"I didn't apologize. How could I? I meant it."

"He'll—"

"Squash me, I know." Rhilander shook his head.

"What are you going to do? I mean, after you go back and apologize."

"I can't, Mario."

"You won't," snapped Consolo.

"He's resigned. He's out, technically if not physically."

It was an assertion that needed conviction in Rhilander's tone. He could feel none as he uttered it.

"He's not out until his resignation is acknowledged in writing, and that takes time," said Consolo. "You know the Army."

"You should have seen him. The monumental gall. He just has to have his way, no matter how outrageous his demands. Is each tie, each rail to be laid with blood on it? Fifty human sacrifices, that's what their deaths amount to. To the greater glory of the railroad, courtesy of Grenville Dodge. He has enough scouts to keep him up

100

on the Indians' movements. There never should have been a surprise attack, not by a force that large."

Changing the subject and putting the onus on Dodge did not impress Consolo. Rhilander suddenly didn't want to discuss the incident further. Consolo left, but not before he repeated his advice.

"Go back to town and apologize."

"I'll think about it."

He did. Pessimism flourished. He spent the rest of the day dutifully commanding: attending dress parade, disposing of paperwork, greeting the paymaster who came twice a year and arrived to cheering all the way from the entrance to the office by the men policing the parade ground. Late in the day, at the behest of Harvey Philips, he walked down to the stables by the creek to settle a dispute between the sergeant in charge and his superior, Lieutenant Crispin. Dudley Crispin III was new to Russell, to the Army. He was a graduate of West Point, which automatically invested him with a superior air. He was as green as a baby frog, unhappy, even somewhat disillusioned with this, his first assignment. He was uncomfortable in the presence of the whiskey-swilling, foulmouthed, raucous Sergeant Mason Bullard. The sergeant was fourteen years in the cavalry, broken more times than his memory could keep catalogued: for insubordination, drunkenness on duty, fighting and numerous other offenses. A much decorated veteran of the war, tolerated by a long string of superiors—including Major Philips and Colonel Rhilander—all willing to overlook his eccentricities and blistering disrespect for rank. They willingly paid the price for his experience. No man on any duty was more reliable and conscientious. But Lieutenant Crispin could not abide being yelled at and called Lieutenant Greenarse to his face, nor could he tolerate his orders being ridiculed or ignored. Noncoms, whatever their value, simply did not behave so toward their superiors.

Rhilander and Philips found them arguing heatedly, the sergeant standing crimson-faced, bull neck bowed, cursing eloquently, the lieutenant white with rage, making fists, filling the lungs in his scrawny chest through his prominent nose.

"How many times I got to tell ya, ya can't coddle a jug face," said Bullard. "They gotta know who's boss. They expect to be cussed 'cause it tells 'em ya care. It's music to their hairy ears."

"There'll be no more cursing, you foul-mouthed tramp! Look at your uniform, you're a disgrace to it. Do you ever bathe? Your bunk must be crawling with lice. You stink!"

"Why you puny, lily-livered, grass-ass son of a tea-sippin' bitch!"

"Sergeant!" bawled Rhilander.

Both froze, then straightened slowly, separating their nearly touching jaws. Color rose in Crispin's cheeks; Bullard looked his most menacing and growled resentment deep in his throat. He looked as if a furious hangover had him in its painful clutches. His shirttail was half out at the back, his uniform wrinkled and filthy, no hat, his hair askew, as wild as a maniac's, his boots mud-caked and broken down at both heels. He hadn't shaved in a week, hadn't washed his face; up close sleep could be seen clinging in minute yellow particles to his eyelids; his eyes looked on the verge of bursting their overloaded veins, to spatter him and anyone within range.

Crispin saluted. Bullard brought his hand halfway up to his head and down again in an excuse for a salute.

"What is it this time?" asked Rhilander wearily.

"What is it ever, sir?" grumbled Bullard. "Ever since he took over for Lieutenant Simons, he's fucked up the whole operation. Don't know what in hell he's doin' with a mule, don't know feedin', loadin', care or keepin'. Don't know nothin', don't wanta learn, won't listen, won't—"

"All right, all right."

Rhilander looked to the lieutenant, unable to conceal his sympathy. Crispin stiffened. His inhaling set his nostrils whistling.

"Colonel, sir, the cavalry manual, issue July 1, 1864, sets out specifically and definitely—"

"The manual, the manual!" bellowed Bullard. "He walks 'round with the goddamn thing open in his hand pickin' on this, that, and the other thing from mornin' till night that we don't do 'cordin' to the book."

"Sergeant—" said Rhilander.

"I say fuck the book! I say them that writ it never seen a goddamn mule, don't know muzzle from asshole. Shit almighty, I forgot more about the care—"

"Sergeant—"

"—and feedin' than ever was writ in all the books on mules, Army, Navy, any and all!"

"Shut up!"

"Yes, sir, just tryin' to explain."

Rhilander glared him to silence.

"Lieutenant, I admire your conscientiousness. The Army has rules, and it behooves us all to observe and respect them."

Crispin beamed. Bullard scowled.

"By the same token, a measure of leeway is not out of order. The sergeant has long experience with the mules. He does know how to get the best out of them."

Bullard glowed. Crispin looked hurt.

"It should be obvious to the two of you that running this stable falls somewhere between. Respect for regulations, respect for what seems to work, seems to be practical and useful that the book doesn't cover."

Both frowned.

"Frankly, I don't think the mules are the problem. It's you two. Neither of you seems interested in making concessions to the other. Why can't you give a little, try to see the other side of whatever it is you disagree on?"

"Disagree on everythin'," muttered Bullard.

"You, Sergeant, I want you to sit down and read the manual cover to cover."

"My eyes has got a little weak, sir. Printin' on a page jumps 'round and turns into specks."

"That's an order. You, Lieutenant, will put the book away after he's read it and work without it for three days. Work together, talk to each other like civilized humans, and discuss your differences calmly and rationally. Pull together as a team, not in different directions. Give it a try." He hardened his tone. "Make it work. If you don't, if you can't, I'll reassign you both."

"Oh Jesus," bawled Bullard. "You wouldn't—"

"You heard me. Now get back to work. You, Sergeant, start reading. This is your last fracas. No more, understand?"

"Yes, sir," said the lieutenant.

"Yeah," said the sergeant. "Yessir."

Philips was grinning to split his face. Rhilander shook his head and tried vainly to suppress a smile. The colonel's striker hailed them by the guardhouse.

"Visitors, sir, General Dodge and some others."

Rhilander's smile vanished.

"This may take some time, Harvey. Take over colors for me, would you?"

"Right," replied Philips.

His visitors were waiting on the verandah, six in all. Rhilander recognized all but one from before. Dodge was the only one sitting. He was in civilian clothes, a white crash linen suit and New York straw hat. Looking very much the civilian, thought Rhilander. He got up and greeted him.

"Can we go inside, Lincoln?"

"Of course, sir."

He brought the man Rhilander had not seen before in with them. He appeared to be about thirty-five, pale, muscular, with unusually deep set, heavily shadowed eyes, brooding, even mystical looking. He exuded intensity, his whole body appeared clenched.

"Lincoln, meet Lieutenant Colonel Rudolph Schwimmer. Rudy, Lieutenant Colonel Lincoln Rhilander."

Dodge cleared his throat. His eyes darted from one to the other. Comparing them? wondered Rhilander.

"General, I want to apologize for this morning. I—"

Dodge waved him to a stop. "Lincoln, I'm relieving you of your command. Rudy here will be taking over. It's rather abrupt, I know, so I'm giving you seven days to clear things up, personal and business. After that for a time I'm afraid you'll be in limbo until I can find a spot for you. You're welcome to stay on here until one opens, but of course you'll no longer be in command."

"You can't do this."

"It's done. As we speak the papers are being drawn up for my signature. I've already apprised the War Department. You'll remain in charge until midnight Tuesday, the seventh. Please find temporary accommodations for Rudy until you vacate your own. And while you're closing up shop, I'd appreciate it if you'd fill him in on what he'll need to know. Your staff, Major Philips, Lieutenant Consolo, and the others, will stay on, of course. This in no way affects any of them. I guess that's about it. Rudy, why don't you stay, give you two a chance to get to know each other. Get things off on the right foot."

With this Dodge waved good-bye, opened the door, walked out, and closed it behind him.

Left in the general's wake by his sudden departure, Lieutenant Colonel Rudolph Schwimmer reacted in embarrassment. Under other circumstances Rhilander would probably have felt sorry for the man; under these he was too stunned and too incensed to give even passing thought to his feelings.

"He's not getting away with this. This is *my* post. General Augur built it and gave me command, and by God, two star or no, I'm going to fight to keep it!"

Schwimmer shrugged. "It's between you two. I'm not in the middle, I don't want to be in the middle."

"I'm not blaming you!" flared Rhilander.

"I didn't ask for it. I was just passing through on my way from departmental headquarters to Fort Laramie. I stopped in to see him at General Truman's request to pay my respects and deliver a personal message. Next thing I knew he'd wired back to Omaha that he was reassigning me."

"Did he mention *why* he was replacing me?"

From the look on Schwimmer's face the reason Dodge had given him was anything but complimentary.

"Did he say I was insubordinate?"

"He said he needed a man in charge who could obey orders and not question them."

"A yes man."

"I'm nobody's yes man, Colonel."

"Did he tell you that we had an entire company butchered out by Bitter Creek the other day in a surprise attack? No warning, not a whisper. It shouldn't have happened, and with proper safeguards in place it wouldn't have. This morning he tried me a second time. Give me another bunch of lambs for the slaughter. I refused. I'm sure you're not interested in the details, but I was justified. His scouts didn't do their job the first time. I had no reason to think we'd fare any better the second. It was a suicide mission, Colonel; he made it so. What would you have done if you were me?"

"Orders are orders, Colonel."

"Thanks for the straight answer."

Corporal Salme stood at the wash-up trough in his long johns, sloshing his face with the tepid water, groping for the soap. Sergeant Olson, alongside him, handed him the shrunken yellow bar.

"You hear?" Salme asked as he lathered. "General Dodge kicked the colonel out for cussin' him to his face. Colonel Rye was sore about what happened over to Bitter Creek, him and the general had at it hot and heavy, word is. I hear Colonel Rye took a poke at him. Imagine hittin' a general? Blacked his eye."

"Wow," said Olson.

"Get Rye riled up, man's got a temper and a half. Now he's out."

"He already leave?"

"Soon," said Salme. "Gotta hang around a few days to break in his replacement."

"Shame. Rye's a good CO. Everybody liked him. Fair."

"Tough," said Salme. "My friggin' ankle's still red and sore from draggin' that goddamn ball and chain around the parade ground."

"What's the new CO like?" Olson asked.

"Who knows? Like most, I reckon—neat and tidy and a fuck-off boozer."

Major Harvey Philips sat on the front stoop of his bungalow smoking a cigar and nursing a hangover. Lieutenant Mario Consolo leered at his plight. He had just delivered the news. Philips's reaction was terse and left no doubt as to his opinion.

"It stinks. Dodge stinks. Who's Schwimmer?"

"I don't know. Linc doesn't either. From Omaha. Dodge pulled him out of his hat."

"It stinks. Where's Linc going?" queried Philips.

"Doesn't know yet. Fort Ruby between Salt Lake City and Carson City's open. Goddamn hellhole. Worst of the West. Can't keep a CO more than six months at a time. Highest desertion rate in the territories."

"Linc'll never accept it. He wouldn't give Dodge the satisfaction."

"What choice does he have?" asked Consolo.

Philips puffed, yawned, and jiggled his head, wincing in discomfort.

"He can turn in his leaf."

"He'll never," said Consolo. "Too proud."

"Six weeks at Ruby he'd turn into a falling-down drunk. They built a distillery close by. A rotgut called Old Commissary. Supposed to be pure. Pure poison. Is Linc sore?"

"Are you kidding? He's busting veins. He swears he's not going to take it without cracking a few balls, preferably Dodge's."

Philips puffed again. "It stinks. I wonder what he'll do, what can he do? I thought Dodge had quit."

"His resignation doesn't take effect for a few more days," continued Consolo. "Linc says he showed up wearing civvies. Son of a bitch just had to rub it in. Hey, where you going?"

"Over to talk to Linc. You come, maybe we can calm him down. Worst thing he can do is go off half powder and no cannonball."

* * *

The peace between Lieutenant Dudley Crispin and Sergeant Mason Bullard was of a temporary nature and in the minds of both, perilously fragile. But it was still in force well into its second day. Bullard's attention at the moment was focused entirely on a sick mule. Assisted by the lieutenant, he was preparing to administer a drench, using the stone bottle generally employed for the purpose.

"Let me do it, Sergeant," said the lieutenant.

"You sure you want to?"

"I want to do everything that has to be done around here, inasmuch as it looks like I'll be here for the foreseeable future. I've already gotten used to the smell, I might as well try my hand at the procedures. Talk me through it."

"Okay. Stand to the right there. Drench is always given on the right. I stand square in front of her. First thing, I ball out her cheek and while I'm doing it keep her head up; you pour into the cheek. A little at a time, and give her time to swallow, 'cause if any gets into her windpipe she'll cough and blow your hat off. You see, I hold her head up, but not too high. Too high and she'll cough for certain. All set? Go to it."

Crispin did his job dexterously and well. Bullard smiled approvingly.

"Balling her cheek makes a little pocket there so her tongue don't get in the way and she doesn't suck none up her nostrils, savvy?"

"Right."

"Good, fine, all done. All done, Edna dear, gonna make you well, little girl."

Edna sucked air for a bray. They petted her.

"You hear the latest?" Bullard asked.

"Removed from everything, stuck over here with the manure, I don't hear much."

"Colonel Rhilander's leavin'. Replacement's already here."

"I didn't hear a whisper," said Crispin.

"Happened yestiddy," continued Bullard. "Sudden like. There's them sayin' General Dodge booted him, others say he just up and quit on his own. But he'd never."

"Who's taking over?"

"Dunno."

Crispin narrowed his eyes. Bullard could see his wheels spinning, picking up speed.

"You figger on puttin' in for a transfer?" he asked.

Crispin started. He flushed.

"Can if you like," drawled Bullard. "Won't hurt my feelings none, only I wouldn't right away if I was you. I'd wait a week or so at least. Till the dust settles. Could be a lotta dust. I hear Rhilander's fixin' to fight to stay on. I dunno what he thinks he can do against somebody with General Dodge's clout, but knowin' Rhilander he'll try. He's a good CO. Whoever Dodge's got to take over has gotta go a long way to measure up to him."

"Bit of a hothead, wouldn't you say?"

"Shit, too, Dudley. Man's got balls, stands up for what he believes, for his men. I served under C.O.s that let the high brass shit all over 'em, an' smile an' ask if they'd like to dump a little more. Not the colonel. Man had some war record, too, which is how he got so high so fast. He went from shavetail to major in five months. He was under Hooker at Antietam. When ol' Joe got wounded an' was outta it, an' Mansfield, too: he got killed, George Meade took over. Rhilander, who by then was a cap'n, was George's right hand. They rallied what was left o' the First Corps near the North Woods, while the Twelfth was pushin' the rebs with evvythin' they had. Meade come out of it smellin' like a rose an' dumped some o' the perfume on Rhilander. Later on they did some job together at Gettysburg. Meade took over for Hooker just before the battle. First thing he did was swap Rhilander a silver leaf for the gol' one he got at Antietam. Him, Meade, got a brigadier's star in the reg'lar Army outta it for himself."

"I never realized Colonel Rhilander had such an exemplary career."

"Few do," said Bullard. "He sure don' blow his own horn like some. O' course Dodge is no slouch himself. With his record, I guess he feels safe kickin' the slats out from under anybody."

A. R. Riefe

"Dodge must have had good reason to replace him."

"Rhilander sure don't think so. The shit's gonna fly from here to Washington, watch and see. And, like I say, if I was you I'd keep my transfer application under my hat till it all blows over. No tellin' who's gonna be in charge around here for a while."

Rhilander and Schwimmer, the sudden, strange bedfellows in command at Fort Russell, both in full parade uniform, stood side by side reviewing the troops. The band led the march, flailing away at "The Battle Hymn of the Republic." Old Glory flapped proudly at the top of her pole, the petunias ringed by whitewashed stones at its base beaming pink and blue. The infantry minus C Company marched smartly by, with the cavalry following in perfect formation.

Rhilander and Schwimmer held their salutes as the parade passed, then slowly lowered them as it started into its circle around the ground.

"Who are those women on the other side watching?" Schwimmer asked.

"The laundresses."

"Laundresses?"

Schwimmer turned and eyed him skeptically. Rhilander remembered that this was his first post command, and numerous aspects of day-to-day life were unfamiliar to him.

"Prostitutes," continued Schwimmer, larding the word with a generous application of disdain.

"Laundresses," Rhilander repeated. "Not that some aren't a little loose and lax with the shades drawn, but they're here to do a job and they do it."

"Your idea?"

"Every post has them," explained Rhilander. "Most of them are married."

"To escape prostitution."

He seemed determined to pigeonhole them as whores. So he was a prude as well as a bootlicker.

"Married to enlisted men," Rhilander explained. "They do a job nobody else wants to and the majority are

110

ladies. They're paid five dollars a month for an officer's laundry and two dollars for an enlisted man's, and they're treated with respect."

Major Philips and Lieutenant Consolo, standing nearby listening, chanced a quick exchange of smirks. Rhilander continued.

"Aside from doing the laundry, they serve as midwives when a mother-to-be is in labor, and even nurse the sick. They turn out to watch dress just for something to do before work, and I guess because they like the sight of brass buttons."

"Who's responsible for them?" Schwimmer asked.

"They're responsible for themselves. We've no problems with them. Every post has laundresses," repeated Rhilander.

The parade had circled the parade ground, the band segueing into "The World Turned Upside Down." The music stopped, the order to halt given, and out of the ranks rode thirty troopers in two columns led by a first lieutenant. The men wore full field packs. A supply wagon appeared pulled by two mules and followed their dust. Rhilander turned to Philips.

"Harvey, what's that? Where's Hilliard going with those men?"

"On a mission," said Schwimmer. "My orders."

"What mission?" Rhilander persisted. "Where?"

"Over to a place called Wam—"

"Wamsutter." Boiling rage was beginning to darken Rhilander's face.

"General Dodge—" Schwimmer was beginning to look uneasy.

"Told you he got word that Cheyenne Dog Soldiers were seen in the area. He told me the same thing. I told him it wasn't a job for Fort Russell."

"He didn't request, Colonel, he gave me a direct order."

"Jesus Christ!" Rhilander burst.

"I saw no reason to question it. I could hardly begin my new assignment by disobeying his first order."

"Did he say anything about Bitter Creek?"

Schwimmer was glancing about somewhat self-consciously.

"Can we continue this discussion in the office?" he murmured, lowering his head.

"No need," said Rhilander. "Major Philips, all these officers, know what's going on. Harvey . . ."

Philips took two steps forward. "Sir?"

"Send a man to bring them back. Immediately. Tell Hilliard the mission's cancelled."

"Stay where you are, Major!" snapped Schwimmer. "Colonel Rhilander, *I* ordered them, *I* alone can rescind that order. I have no intention of doing so. I shouldn't have to remind you that I'm in command here."

They stood jaw to jaw. Rhilander slit-eyed him.

"You are indeed. Sorry, it slipped my mind. If you'll excuse me, Colonel."

He saluted. Evidently somewhat taken aback by Rhilander's failure to pursue the argument, Schwimmer was tardy returning the salute. By the time he did Rhilander had already turned and started away.

He had made his decision. The situation was untenable: the post couldn't function with two commanders, not these two. Somebody else would have to show the new boy the ropes.

8

Hannah's death nearly destroyed Jubal Hunnicutt. It
came so soon after the family's banishment from
the wagon train that he was hesitant to make a decision.
Suddenly he no longer cared what the family did, or even
whether he survived or died. Given the choice, he preferred the latter; life without Hannah would be no life for
him.

But thinking further he realized he had no right to
embrace such a drastic and simple solution to his problem; Jeptha and Lorna needed him thinking clearly and
courageously.

The aftershock of Hannah's passing that gripped all
three during and immediately after her funeral, such as it
was, did leave Jubal unable to make up his mind whether
to move on, go back to Pennsylvania, or call it a journey
and settle someplace in the area. Each choice had something to recommend it, each had its drawbacks. Jubal
finally decided.

Jeptha wanted to go back, but his father's suggestion
that they consider locating somewhere in southeastern
Wyoming was acceptable to him, even if his acceptance
was somewhat grudging. Lorna didn't care what they did.

They had driven back from the cemetery to where
Jubal had stopped the wagon the night before, the spot
where Hannah had died.

"I just can't see turning around and going back," he
said to Jeptha as they unhitched the horses. "There's

113

nothing there for us. The place is sold. We can hardly drive up and ask to buy it back. And I'm not all that interested in Oregon anymore, not without your mother."

"I'd be," said Jeptha quietly. "If Salita Jane were there when we got there."

"We won't know a soul there," said Lorna, contributing a full sentence to the discussion for the first time. "And if we do settle around here, we'll be close to Mother. I can come and put flowers on her grave. It got so she loved lupines, all the different colors, and the fleabanes and wild geraniums. She said mostly because they weren't yellow like most all the other wildflowers."

Having said this from where she sat just inside the bonnet at the front, she turned to straightening up the contents of the wagon.

Jeptha knelt and picked up a handful of dirt. It was loose and dry, despite the recent rain.

"Can you grow crops in this?" he asked.

"It's good, rich soil. You can grow most anything. There's rain in the summer, we know that."

"Amen."

Jubal looked off toward the town. "We wouldn't want to be too close to town. It's a terrible place."

"Terrible how?" Jeptha asked.

"Overcrowded, noisy, dirty, dangerous. Every man in the street seems to be wearing a gun. If we do stay, you and your sister should steer clear of there. No reason for either of you to go in."

"We're not children, Jubal, we can take care of ourselves."

"You're a greenhorn," said his father. "I don't mean to insult you, but you know you are. If for any reason we do have to go in, we'll go together, you and me."

"And leave her alone with the wagon?"

"Mmmm," murmured Jubal. "Good point. Right now, I'm going to leave the two of you to mind it and each other." He looked apprehensively toward the town again.

"Where are you going?"

"In to talk to Dr. Gogarty. He seems to know all about the area. He'd know if land's available, where and what sort, what it's suited to. With all the grass we've seen, I'm sure most folks hereabouts are cattle ranchers."

"We could be."

"I don't know the first thing about cattle, and you don't either. The smith sticks to his hammer, Jeptha. I'll be back soon as I can. Water the horses, let them graze, and help your sister straighten up inside."

Jubal started off on foot.

"Take one of the horses," Jeptha called.

"No, I can think better walking."

The decision to remain in the area had been made. Jubal chewed it in his thoughts, gleaning the possibilities it offered. Under the terms of the Homestead Act of 1862, a man could stake a claim to a piece of unoccupied land by living on it and cultivating it for five years, after which he could file for ownership. Dr. Gogarty would know where such land could be found. It was probably somewhere close by to the north. To the west the mountains rose, and who could say how far they reached across the territory. Cattle and sheep could graze the lower slopes, but fairly level land was preferable for crops.

And Cheyenne, for all its tawdriness, would provide a ready market for his crops. With the railroad coming through he could even ship produce east. The promise, the opportunity, began to take on a shine; with hard work the three of them could succeed. If only Hannah were there to share it.

Cheyenne swam mistily before his eyes.

The traffic was as hectic and boisterous as it had been the last time he'd been in town. He found the Gunshot Saloon, sidestepped a drunk being tumbled out the door, and climbed the stairs to Gogarty's office, only to be met by a sign on the door: "Back P.M." He sighed and went back down. A boy and girl were walking by, both about ten. She was in a polka-dot poke bonnet poking so far forward he could barely make out her features, and he was digging at the wooden sidewalk with his toe every other step, dulling the shine of his new high-button shoes. They stopped him.

A. R. Riefe

"If you're lookin' for the doc, friend, he's over to Lawyer Pinch's," said the boy pointing.

"We just seen him goin' in," said the girl.

The boy gave Jubal explicit and involved directions.

Aloysius Gogarty finished his drink and set the tumbler down with a loud clack, wordless invitation to his host to refill it. Attorney Cicero Sebastian Pinchot, a florid, flamboyant-looking individual who, even sitting, looked prepared to lunge—clenching and unclenching the ends of his chair arms, thrusting his massive head forward on his thick, vein-roped, red neck, pushing his words out like spat seeds in a gravelly voice—reached for the bottle without looking and poured the doctor another drink. The law office of Attorney Cicero Pinchot was small, dusty, smoky, and so cluttered it looked as if it had been upended and its furnishings and papers redistributed. It was the capital of the kingdom of disarray: gaping file cabinet drawers were overstuffed with folders jammed with papers, the overflow stacked on the floor creating an obstacle course from the door to the desk. The desk was missing one front leg, so a thick volume entitled *Illinois Statutes, 1840–1850* provided support. The semicircular window behind the desk admitted murky sunlight through its unwashed glass. Flies buzzed and alit on the windowsill, ambling amongst the books and dried bodies of other flies and the lonely corpse of a bumblebee.

Pinchot sat in his shirtsleeves without a tie, his collar open, in his hand a fan advertising Williams & Williams Funeral Parlor, 130 Twelfth Street, Denver, Colorado, stirring the sultry air in desultory fashion.

He was addressing Lieutenant Colonel Lincoln Rhilander.

"I'm not saying you don't have a gambler's chance, but he *is* in charge. He's got the right to hire and fire whoever, where- and whenever he chooses. You can interpret it as whim, as impulse, as anger, but it's not a violation of his authority. Hell, you're lucky he didn't bust you down to second lieutenant."

116

"He still may. The short of it is, from a legal stand-point I don't have a hope, much less a chance."

"I just told you I didn't say that. Aloysius, did I say that?"

"He didn't say that, Lincoln." Gogarty began to cough. A swig drowned it.

"You claim his stripping you of your command was unwarranted. And you blame him for the massacre."

"He blames himself. He's embarrassed. You should have seen his eyes when he blew up at me."

"In retaliation for your blowing up at him, refusing to obey his order, calling him a son of a bitch."

Rhilander shrugged and shifted his glance to the scat-tering of small black bodies on the windowsill. Pinchot rambled on.

"And you might think about something else. If that debacle out near Bitter Creek had never occurred, he'd still have every right to make a change."

"Yes."

"Buck up, he may be holding all the face cards, but you *can* challenge him. You can say he's treating you unfairly, he's prejudiced, he's picking on you for swear-ing at him. Did you apologize? Did you try?"

"I started to," said Rhilander.

"You didn't finish. Okay, why don't you? Go to him—"

"Crawl."

"Crawl," said Pinchot. "Tell him you're sorry. Give him a heartfelt spiel about, I don't know, what a blow the bad news was, the hardships of keeping the Indians in line, how occasionally you can't help letting your per-sonal feelings for your men—no, stay away from that."

"I refuse to lick his hand. Let's forget him. Within a few days somebody will be taking his place, taking over command of the Department of the Platte."

"Well, there you are. Go to *him*. Explain what hap-pened, that it was a fluke, you were insubordinate, you're sorry. In the meantime, ring in some of your old friends to testify to your character, your capabilities. General Meade, Joe Hooker—they'll stand up for you. Am I wrong or did you get a letter from General Grant praising your heroism at Antietam, lauding you to the skies? He's close as a brother to Edwin Stanton, the Secretary of War, he could talk to him."

"Dodge and Grant are old friends," said Rhilander.

"That needn't be a hindrance," said Pinchot. "It could work in your favor. If Grant were to speak up for you, Dodge'd listen to his old friend."

"I don't know—"

"Of course, as I say, it'd be even better if you could get a hearing with Dodge's successor. Who will it be?" Pinchot leaned forward.

"I have no idea," said Rhilander.

"Hopefully somebody who has no use for him, who'd jump at the opportunity to rescind his order. Would you say he's popular?"

"Very. His record's outstanding. Back East during the war and out here. And he's close personal friends not only with Grant, but Sherman and Sheridan. He's a good soldier and a good man."

"A saint," said Pinchot. "Okay, so you can't tear him down. As I see it, you have three options: one, go to Dodge with ashes in your mouth and beg his forgiveness—"

"Not a chance."

Rhilander sighed soundlessly. His chances of getting Russell back took the form of an unraveling rope in his mind. Pinchot went on.

"Two, petition whoever takes over for him for reinstatement."

"I don't know about that either."

"He'll probably pick his own successor," interposed Gogarty.

"Three, petition for a court of inquiry. I'm not up on the latest refinements in military law, but I do know even a private can request a hearing for redress of grievance, if you could call it that. We present your side of it and appeal for a reversal of the order. Now, he might not let it get to a hearing. He might not have the time or inclination to be bothered, or it might even be embarrassing to him. It's the sort of thing the newspapers like to grab onto."

"I don't know," said Rhilander wearily, suddenly bored by the sound of his own voice, repeating the words for the third time. What had appeared bleak when he walked in the door was now as black as his pocket. "Maybe formally petitioning whoever takes over for him would be worth a try."

"Now you're talking. He kicked you in the pride and it smarts, right?" Pinchot's tone sounded aggressively sympathetic. "But you did ask for it."

"I saw blood," said Rhilander. "He was so goddamn cavalier about it!"

"But now you've simmered down. Why not formally apologize and ask him to reconsider. The worst that can happen is he'll turn you down. Maybe he's cooled off, maybe returning to civilian life and taking on a cushy job will arouse a charitable streak. He doesn't sound like a vindictive bastard."

"There's something else that makes it even tougher. He's already replaced me."

"Oh." Pinchot pursed his lips thoughtfully as his face darkened. "You've already moved out?"

"I will shortly. Today. Find a place here in town." He looked from Pinchot to Gogarty and back to Pinchot. "I don't know if I can explain it, but believe me, this isn't just a matter of ego. When General Augur built Fort Russell and appointed me CO, he set me on top of the sky. And I set out to make it the best post in the territories. I worked like six men. We've got a great bunch, we're like a family with a camaraderie like—like the three musketeers, I guess you could say. The men respect the officers and vice versa, not like at some posts. I've got men on staff I wouldn't swap for anybody.

"I'm a bachelor, I guess you could say I'm married to the Army. Maybe I wouldn't feel like this if I were actually married. But Russell is mine, every brick, every board. To lose it like this, to have to start over someplace else, just thinking about it makes me sick. To move on knowing somebody else is in charge here, it's like some stranger moving in with the woman you love." He sighed. "What really gripes me is that the man he replaced me with doesn't even want the job. He's not interested."

"Who is he?" Gogarty asked.

Before Rhilander could finish telling them about Rudolph Schwimmer, the door opened. Jubal Hunnicutt stood holding his hat. The boy at the foot of the office stairs had given him directions to Lawyer Pinch's, ending with the jinx phrase, "You can't miss it." And of course before he found it, he had to ask directions of two other people.

"Mr. Hunnicutt!" boomed Gogarty.

He introduced Jubal to the others. Pinchot gestured him to the one remaining empty chair, removing a stack of papers from it so he could sit.

"I'm interrupting—"

"You're not," said Rhilander. "I was just about to go."

"Stick around," said the doctor. "I never see you lately. Let me buy you lunch at the Gunshot."

Rhilander smiled thinly.

Jubal told Gogarty why he had come looking for him.

"Cicero," said the doctor, "you know more about the land situation than I do. What would you advise?" He buried a cough in his fat fist.

"There's no land available anymore within a quarter mile of town," said Pinchot. "Or along the tracks east or west. The U.P. sent their land agent in about three months ago, he set up a tent, and began to sell 66 by 132 foot lots at $150 apiece. Some have already resold for a thousand. Before the cold weather sets in they'll be going for two thousand."

"I wouldn't want to be close to town anyway," said Jubal. "What about up beyond Lodgepole Creek?"

"There's land between there and Horse Creek, a little to the east toward the border. Between the mountains and Eli Leimkuhler's ranch. How big a piece are you looking for?"

"About a hundred and sixty acres," said Jubal. "I want to raise vegetables."

"I don't know if there's that much acreage, but you

could take a look. I don't know who owns the cattle ranch to the north beyond it, but if you do stake it out and settle there, you'll have to think about fencing: north and east. Keep the beefs from straying into your crops."

"That's a lot of fence," remarked Gogarty. "Two sides of a hundred sixty acres. How many feet on two sides of a square single acre?"

"About twenty-two thousand," said Rhilander.

Pinchot whistled low. "That's a forest and a half."

"Would you settle for less than a hundred sixty to start out?" asked the doctor. "Say half that?"

"I wouldn't," said Pinchot. "I say while you're taking, take all you can. Later on if you do decide to expand, it may not be there."

"I had thirty acres back in Pennsylvania," said Jubal. "I figure my son and I could work double that, and with hired help, three or four times as much."

The subject of conversation, providing temporary relief from dwelling on his own problem, inspired the colonel's interest.

"Maybe you could reach an agreement with your neighbors on the fence," he said. "Isn't any fence advantageous to the people on both sides?"

Pinchot chuckled without smiling. "Not really, Lincoln. Cattle ranchers are a peculiar lot. They all feel the whole outdoors belongs to their herds. They're perfectly willing to let their beefs wander just about anywhere. From a legal standpoint, Mr. Hunnicutt—Jubal, little of the land hereabouts is actually owned by cattlemen. They don't see any need to own it. They just let their cattle graze it. But a good part of that land is fenced, with gates to let the cattle in and out. Last year the ranchers organized what's called the Cattlemen's Territorial Courts, a rubber-stamp outfit, and the first thing they did was decree that it's no crime to fence public lands, but it *is* a crime to cut a fence.

"*Whether or not the property enclosed belongs to the man who appropriated and fenced it.*"

Jubal looked confused.

"I think he's talking about water," said Gogarty. He coughed.

Pinchot nodded. "Let's assume the land you settle has water, a runoff from Horse Creek or down from the mountains, running into irrigation ditches on your property. Let's assume that water is shared by one or more of your neighbors. Let's assume further that they're not ecstatic over you settling in their midst. So they set about diverting the water, cutting off the flow to your property and erect a fence to protect the diversion."

"You can't cut that fence," said Rhilander. "Can't trespass, so you can't redirect the water."

"That's right," said Pinchot. "Mind you, I'm not trying to discourage you, just warning you of what you could run up against. Of course, it'd be ten times as bad if you raised sheep. Cattle ranchers may not be overly fond of sodbusters, but they really despise sheepmen."

"But there's so much land," began Jubal.

"Even if there were ten times as much, he's talking about a feud that goes back to biblical times," said Gogarty. "Cattlemen claim sheep ruin the grass for cattle."

Jubal stood contemplating the situation for a moment.

The doctor shrugged. "Wherever you decide to settle, you're bound to run into some problems. At least up that far the Indians won't be much of a headache." He glanced at Rhilander. "Too busy picking on the railroad down here."

"What you shouldn't lose sight of is that it's public land to begin with," said Pinchot. "You're as entitled as the next man to settle it. Don't let anybody, red or white, discourage you."

"I say go get it," said Rhilander.

"Me too," said the doctor.

"I believe I will," said Jubal, beaming.

"That's the spirit!" boomed Pinchot.

"I know that area," said Rhilander. "If you can hold off until tomorrow morning, I'll go with you and show you around."

"I'd appreciate it."

"He's parked east of town," Gogarty said, then laughed

his way into coughing. "Stop off at the first Conestoga wagon you see."

Pinchot laughed. Jubal felt his spirit lift for the first time since Hannah's death.

"Let's drink on it. To Laramie County's newest settlers." Pinchot raised the bottle to the window and peered at it. "Oh my, John Barleycorn Gogarty has beaten us to it. Let's see if I can find a full one lurking about in all this tidiness." He located a full bottle and two additional glasses and poured.

"Say, how's about joining the three of us for lunch?" said Gogarty to Jubal.

"I'd like to, but my son and daughter are waiting back at the wagon." He turned to Pinchot. "My boy's eighteen; he wants to be a lawyer."

"Judas Priest!" burst Gogarty. "Don't encourage him, he'll end up despised by his fellow man, shunned, scorned, ridiculed, a blot on the family escutcheon."

"Shut up and drink," growled Pinchot.

Rhilander returned to the fort in a better state of mind. He hadn't changed his mind about leaving that day, but he did feel better about his chances of regaining his command. He even stopped off at General Dodge's office to attempt a second apology, only to be told that the general was on his way back to Omaha. He decided he would wait until the end of the week and follow. If an apology failed to change Dodge's mind, he'd approach his successor. If that failed it would be on to Washington. Hanging around Cheyenne while Schwimmer tightened his grip on his new command would be fruitless. Nobody was going to hand Russell back to him; he'd have to go out and take it.

Philips and Consolo met him in the orderly room. They drew him aside out of earshot of the two clerks.

"Schwimmer's in a great rush to make his reputation," said Philips. "After you left this morning, after his parade of welcome, he pulled a surprise inspection. He singled out A Company for slovenliness, lack of polish, and other capital offenses, sliced them up verbally, and sent them on a twenty-mile hike with full field packs and no water."

"How to win friends," muttered Consolo.

"Where is he now?"

"He's taken over your office," said the major. "What are you going to do, Linc?"

"What am I supposed to do, challenge him to a duel? Throw him out? It's his ball game."

"The enlisted men are getting up a petition," said Consolo. "They plan to get every man to sign it. They want him out and you back."

Philips nodded. "They're going to send it to headquarters in Omaha. And the officers are solidly behind you."

"Kill it," said Rhilander. Both started and stared. "No petitions, rank and file or officers. Tell whoever's circulating it I'm grateful for their support, but a petition could do more harm than good. To whoever signs it. When Schwimmer hears, he'll get a look at it and file the names in the back of his mind. You might remind one and all that this isn't a boy-pioneer summer camp. It's the Big Blue Club where the War Department's in charge, orders are orders, Schwimmer's in, and I'm out, courtesy of Major General U.P. Dodge."

"You mean you're not even going to try to get reinstated?" Philips frowned and Consolo looked mildly stunned.

"I'm going to try. I've just come from a long talk with Cicero Pinchot. My chances appear to be slim to none, but I'm trying. Only for the next few days, I'm going to have to hold my fire. Until Dodge picks his successor. In the meantime Schwimmer's in charge and I'd take it as a personal favor if you two see to it that he's treated with courtesy and respect."

Philips frowned. "No matter how big a horse's ass he makes of himself."

Consolo grunted. "How many enemies he makes."

"How he runs the place has nothing to do with my problem. No petitions, no pressures. If he gets the idea that I'm pressuring him, even indirectly, through anybody, it won't help me any. Understand? If he wants to hang himself, fine, only I'm not providing the rope. Now, if you boys'll excuse me. I'm going over to the office and have a word with the colonel."

Schwimmer had relieved Rhilander's striker of his duties. Apprised of this by the new man, Rhilander fleetingly wondered if this was the start of a succession of changes, if Philips and Consolo were also on their way out. He found his replacement behind his desk immersed in paperwork. Schwimmer looked up, smiled, put down his pen, and returned Rhilander's salute.

"Please, Colonel, when there's just the two of us, let's not be formal. Have a chair. Care for a drink?"

"No thanks," said Rhilander politely.

"I don't imbibe myself, never have, but that doesn't mean I'm intolerant of others' drinking."

"Colonel—"

"Rudy . . . Lincoln."

"I apologize for blowing up this morning," said Rhilander. "Of course you're in command, of course you were following his orders, sending men out."

"That's the job. Apology accepted. I apologize to you for neglecting to inform you." He clapped his hands and rubbed them. "What can I do for you?"

"I came to tell you I'm moving off post."

"So soon?" Schwimmer looked surprised.

"I know General Dodge asked me to stay on until next week to help you get settled, but you don't really need me. Major Philips and Lieutenant Consolo can fill you in on anything you want to know."

"Both good men."

Rhilander tilted his head and eyed him. "Will they be staying on?"

"Decisions, decisions, I suddenly seem to have my lap full."

Rhilander sensed that this was as good an answer as he'd get. "I'll collect my things. I'll be staying in town, at least for the next few days. There's just one other thing. I want to be straightforward about this, because I don't want you to think I'm plotting behind your back. I intend

to do everything I can—everything legal and aboveboard—
to get back my command."

"Your candor is commendable," Schwimmer said. "Have
you spoken to the general?"

"I missed him, he's on his way back to Omaha. Did he
happen to tell you who'll be replacing him?"

"No. I don't think he knows yet. I take it you plan to
approach whoever it is." Schwimmer suddenly seemed
interested.

"Yes."

Schwimmer smiled with no warmth. "I can't say good
luck."

"If necessary I'll go to Washington."

"You *are* determined."

"I am," Rhilander replied firmly.

"I can see why. This is an excellent post. I'm a lucky
man. My first command and one of the finest. Thanks to
you and your efforts, I'm sure. I want you to know, I
intend to keep it a first-rate showcase of military organi-
zation on the frontier. No laxity, consistent firm adher-
ence to regulations. Strict discipline tempered with
tolerance and understanding. As I said, I appreciate your
candor. I trust you'll appreciate mine when I say I plan to
work just as hard to hang onto this desk as you do to
reclaim it."

"Of course."

"I plan on being here a long time; I've already sent for
my wife and son. Mona's staying with her parents in
Bluffs, Nebraska, just outside Omaha. She should be
here in a few days with our boy. Louis is fourteen, the
image of his mother."

He got out a picture of the two of them. Pride swelled
his chest, flattening the wrinkles in his shirt.

"He has his heart set on becoming an engineer. He and
Gren—General Dodge have become quite good friends.
The general doesn't have children of his own. His brother's wife—they live in Bluffs—she, Elsie, and Mona went
through school together. Oh dear, I see I'm boring you."

As well as impressing him, telling him how close the
Dodges and the Schwimmers were. He stood up. He

seemed to Rhilander to be much broader and more muscular than he had looked when the general introduced them, as if his new assignment had infused him with a generous quantity of self-esteem.

He *looked* in charge, and impressively worthy as an opponent. Studying him, Rhilander resolved that whatever the outcome of his campaign, never again as long as he lived would he call a superior what he'd called General Dodge.

9

Lincoln Rhilander rode north with the Hunnicutts the next morning, crossing Lodgepole Creek to the valley stretching between it and Horse Creek above. Jubal waved the party to a halt, dismounted, and dug out a handful of soil. He examined it, then looked to his right. Cattle grazed freely west and north.

"That storm last week," Jubal said to Rhilander. "Does it always rain so hard?"

"It was a freak of nature. I've been here three years and never saw anything like that. The normal rainfall is generally well spread between May and the end of October. You can expect snow anytime between November and the middle of May."

"Are the winters severe?"

"Severe storms aren't common, but they can be bad when they do come. This past winter a blizzard raged for three days here in the southeast. The heaviest snows are apt to come in March, April, or May."

"I plant my potatoes in May."

"Not if the ground's frozen."

"After the last frost. How much average rainfall in a year?"

"I'd say about fifteen inches around here. As much as forty in the mountains in the northwest. That's solid forest."

"If I have a choice, I'd prefer to dry farm."

Rhilander furrowed his brow questioningly. "Dry?"

"He means depend upon natural rainfall," explained Jeptha. "Not irrigation."

"I suppose some farmers do rely on just the rain," said the colonel, "but most I've seen dig irrigation ditches. When the snows thaw in the spring, the water comes rushing down. By either method, people have been growing crops around here for ages. When the first white men got here more than a hundred years ago, they found the Crow growing corn, beans, and pumpkin along the Powder River. The men at the fort grow all kinds of vegetables. Cabbages the size of watermelons."

"I haven't seen a single fence," said Jeptha.

"You won't, this is cattle country. In Texas ranches are fenced, but not up here."

"Are there Indians?" asked Lorna, bracing herself for the colonel's answer.

He nodded. "All over. Shoshone to the west, Crow to the north, and Cheyenne and Arapaho around here. Blackfoot have come down from the north, and Ute up from the south. The Oglala and Brulé Sioux moved to eastern Wyoming from Dakota Territory about thirty-five years ago."

"Are they friendly?"

"The Shoshone. And the Crow, although the Crow'll steal anybody's horses."

"And the others are hostile." Lorna's eyes widened in alarm.

"The Cheyenne and Arapaho can be. And now, it seems, the Sioux are also on the warpath." He shielded his eyes from the sun's glare and looked southward. "Those three tribes are the reason why Fort Russell's here. Actually, a relatively small minority are hostile—young warriors. Their chiefs have no control over them."

"Then if we settle here, we'll be at risk every waking minute." She shook her head, but Lincoln was quick to note that neither of the men appeared worried.

"They could make trouble, but they'd rather pick on the railroad. The problem is that traffic on the Platte has been growing every year, and all the tribes are getting more and more restless, seeing what's happening to their country. Theirs because they were here first. Now the railroad's come—"

"We were told back in Sapling Grove there'd be Indians, dear," said Jubal. "There were in Kansas and Nebraska, and they're out in the Willamette Valley. I'm sure it's impossible to find an area out here where there are none. But the Army's here to protect folks."

"Not exactly here," said Lorna, pointing to the ground.

Rhilander grinned. Jubal looked from one to the other. He and Jeptha had ridden this far side by side, leaving the colonel and Lorna together behind them. He noticed, looking back now and then, that she rode very close to him, in his protection. And twice looking back he'd seen her staring admiringly at him. He *was* a handsome man, impressive in his uniform; young for a lieutenant colonel, perhaps not past thirty. And he seemed to enjoy her companionship as much as she did his. He seemed more relaxed this morning than yesterday, able to put his problem to one side while he was out guiding them about the area.

Jubal wondered why the general had fired him. Not that it was any of his business, but he was curious. From the little he'd heard about it in Pinchot's office yesterday, he gathered that Rhilander was not about to meekly forfeit his command. It was a bad break, he felt sorry for him. He hadn't told either Jeptha or Lorna about it, and might better hold off for a while before he did. Then again, she and the colonel were rapidly, determinedly getting to know each other; perhaps he'd tell her himself. There was nothing like the convenient ear and understanding of a sympathetic female.

He looked about them a second time.

"Can we go on?" he asked Rhilander.

"If you want. There's more public land north of Horse Creek, plenty."

"You mean go even farther from the fort?" Lorna asked. "From the railhead, from people? This piece looks fine to me."

"It is," said Jubal, "though it does run to the center like a shallow bowl. Heavy rainfall, a heavy runoff from the mountains could collect at the lowest point"—he indicated—"and rot the crop."

"So don't plant there."

"Dear, while we're up here, as long as we've come this far, why not look around? You walk into a store, you don't settle for the first dress you see, do you?"

Her expression said it wasn't the same thing. She looked to Rhilander for support. His expression said he'd rather not get involved in a family disagreement.

They continued north through partially staked cattle land, as evidenced by trampled and consumed grass, burnt out fires and now and then a sign: PROPERTY OF C.W. KNOX, NO TRESPASSING.

Rhilander fastened his gaze sidelong upon Lorna, riding slightly behind her, and kept it there. Unable to remove it. She was a vision, he thought. Perhaps because it had been so long—it seemed like eons—since he'd last seen a truly beautiful woman.

Knox's property ended at Bear Creek. They crossed the creek and ascended the opposite bank. Jubal shaded his eyes from the fire in the sky and whistled, impressed by what he saw. The land rolled gently all the way to the foothills of the Laramies, like a sea calming itself after a blow.

"Beautiful," he murmured. "Perfect."

"We don't know if it's staked or not," cautioned Jeptha.

"You can tell," said Rhilander. "There'd be at least the beginnings of clearing the sage brush. And some sort of sign."

They rode about for an hour. Jubal's enthusiasm grew like that of a small boy discovering one delight after another at the zoo. He selected a site for the house and, twenty yards from it, the barn, a silo, the corral.

"We can dig a well here. It's less than a hundred and fifty feet to the creek."

"How far are we from the fort?" Lorna asked Rhilander.

"Roughly a little over twenty miles."

"Twenty! Did you hear that, Daddy?"

"I heard. We can also draw water from the creek if we have to."

"The north branch is a long stone's throw up the way," said Rhilander. "You could draw from it for your acreage up above. You probably won't need to."

"We can clear this whole section of sagebrush and grass in a week." Jubal looked off toward the mountains. "Nobody owns that timber, do they?"

"It's yours for the taking. The best is at the higher elevations: Englemann spruce, fir. Just below it is lodgepole pine, and down lower, ponderosa pine and Douglas fir. The scrub in the foothills is worthless, mainly mountain mahogany, juniper, sagebrush. Whatever you decide on, how will you convert it to lumber?"

"Where's the nearest sawmill?" Jubal asked.

Rhilander removed his hat and scratched his head. "Nearest one is quite a ways." He pointed to the southwest. "At Davisranch. I'd say about twelve miles."

"Is there a road?" Jeptha asked.

"Of sorts. We could circle around and stop by there on the way back. There's a lot of building going on in the area. They're working eighteen hours a day. As soon as you file for the land, you should put in your order with the mill."

"We'll need planking for the barn, the silo, the floor of the house. We can use lodgepole pine logs for the house." Jubal looked from Lorna to Jeptha. "We can build it exactly like the old one back home."

"Home," murmured Lorna ruefully. "Where's the nearest town?" she asked Rhilander.

"At the moment, Little Horse Creek over toward the Nebraska border. I don't know as you could call it a town exactly. It's just a store and a stable, a few homes, maybe twenty-five people in all."

Jubal surveyed the majestic surroundings and breathed the fresh air deeply.

Rhilander smiled. "By the time you harvest your first crop the railroad will reach all the way back to New York. And the year after next it'll be complete, coast to coast."

"Hear that, children?" crowed Jubal.

"What do you plan to grow?" Lincoln asked.

"Just about everything, but potatoes will be three quarters of the crop, perhaps even more."

"I'll have my own vegetable garden by the house," said Lorna.

"Let's go back," said Jubal. "I have to file, I want this piece. This is where we start fresh. This is our Willamette Valley." Jeptha's face darkened slightly. Jubal noticed. "Our Pennsylvania patch in Wyoming. Feel that sun, you two, taste the air. Home at last!"

Jeptha tilted his head one way, then the other, suggesting at least a hint of skepticism. Lorna offered no reaction then, evidently thinking better of it. She kissed her father on the cheek, an obvious gesture of her approval. Rhilander watched her. She was so pretty, he thought, so much more of a woman than Stoddard's prissy wife and some of the others. He resolved to see her again, as often as he could before he left for Omaha—as often as would be decently acceptable, without being ostentatious, without rushing her.

She was beautiful.

Welcome to Wyoming, Lorna Hunnicutt!

10

Jubal filed for his land the next day. He put in his order with the manager of the sawmill for the lumber he would need and gave the man a deposit. He was told that the mill had a three-week backlog of orders. Everyone there seemed to be working feverishly.

They drove the Conestoga up to Bear Creek and across it into "New Pennsylvania," as Jeptha christened the property. The wagon was unloaded, the tents pitched, and father and son began to clear the area selected for the house and outbuildings. The bonnet and bows were removed from the Conestoga to prepare it to carry logs down from the mountainside about three miles away from the site of the house.

Early that evening Rhilander came in his dress blues to call on Lorna. In quest of privacy, they went for a walk along the creek. They had no difficulty communicating. He quickly decided that he had found a friend, one in whom he could freely confide. He told her about his run-in with Dodge. He did not try to either excuse or tone down his rashness or his swearing. Listening to himself describe the event, he sounded completely in the wrong, giving Dodge scant choice but to discipline him and as harshly as he had. But he was pleased and relieved when she sided with him, and cited Dodge's callous attitude.

"What a terrible waste of good men," she said, shaking her head. "So unnecessary."

"Exactly what I felt. And that's what made me so mad,

that and his supercilious way. Which I think was an act. I think it had stunned him and he felt as bad about it as I did."

"But he turned right around and demanded more men." She shook her head disapprovingly.

They sat on the bank of the creek. The water burbled softly by. A frog plopped into it. The sun hung suspended, fastened to the sky above the spruce and fir-timbered mountains, darkening their green to black. The air was still, as if with expectancy. The clouds were white feathers, freed from the tails of whooping cranes and eagles, brushing the pale, high sky. The whic-whic-ic of a quail sounded in the tall grass a few yards up the creek.

"What's that bird?" she asked.

"A male quail."

"How can you tell he's a male?"

"Whic-whic. The females are never that loud. He's probably out looking for a hen. More than one."

"Shame on him, the glutton," she laughed.

"Quails don't pair for life like some birds. The males usually keep a harem."

"You seem to approve."

"I don't," he said. "It's impractical. One woman at a time makes more sense to me."

"At a time."

"I mean one wife."

"At a time. Not like Brigham Young. You prefer to move from one to the next, to the next. How long does the relationship usually last?"

"You're twisting my words." He grinned and waggled a finger reprovingly.

She smirked and laughed again. "Just teasing." She sobered. "You're not—"

"Married? No. Not even a little. I've been too busy to meet any girls since I came here. Or at least, I was. That's something else about being kicked out. To go from sixteen hours a day down to nothing but waiting . . . This is turning into a very long week."

"When are you going to Omaha?"

"Monday."

"For how long? Of course, that depends upon what luck you have."

He freed a blade of grass and began chewing. "I should know one way or the other within a couple hours."

"You said Colonel Schwimmer's wife and son are on their way here?"

"He didn't lose any time. He's my big problem. He's already in place and going at it with his sleeves rolled up."

"Do the men like him?" she asked.

"I'm afraid that's not one of the requirements of the job."

"But do they?" she persisted.

"His first impression didn't exactly hearten the rank and file. He sees himself as a strict disciplinarian."

"Were you strict?" she asked.

He smiled. "Could you make that 'are you'?" He sighed and gazed off into the distance, then shook his head. "I can't accuse him because I resent him, but he sure seems to want to carve a reputation for himself in a hurry."

"Cross your fingers, maybe he won't get the chance. Maybe after next Monday he won't be around."

He grinned. "Bless you, Miss Hunnicutt. That's what I need, somebody cheering for my side."

She set her hand over his, and they sat in silence.

Four hundred ninety-three miles of shining rail stretched from Cheyenne to Omaha; with thirty stops the trip took nearly eighteen hours. Whizzing along at a steady forty miles per hour, it was like traveling through time. No one minded the boring, yellow, flatness of Nebraska, the rattling, the racket, the marble seats, the smells, the soot. It was an exhilarating experience—Cheyenne to Jupiter by way of Mars, Venus, and Mercury.

Lorna, Jeptha, and Jubal saw Lincoln off at seven in the morning. How Lorna could look so pretty at that hour amazed him; he did appreciate their showing up. Cicero Pinchot did also. They all wished him well, and Lorna handed him a four-leaf clover. He had wrapped it carefully in his handkerchief. He got it out now and unfolded it. He'd never thought of himself as superstitious, but in his present plight he was willing to accept luck from any source. Lorna was his luck, he decided; she believed in him, she was rooting and praying for him.

The train had just chugged and whistled its way out of North Platte, roughly halfway to Omaha. He glanced at his watch: 5:55. The sun was lowering over the Sand Hills behind the train. If they stuck to the schedule they'd arrive in Omaha around 3 A.M. He could wangle a visitor's bed at headquarters, sleep until seven or so, get up, freshen up, drink two cups of black coffee to clear his head, then go looking for General Augur. The last Rhilander knew he'd been on duty there—if one could call shuffling papers and waiting for the last days of his thirty-year hitch to move behind him duty.

General Christopher C. Augur had been as much a father as his superior to him since they'd both arrived in the West. "My boy, I'm appointing you CO of a brand new installation. Fort D.A. Russell, Wyoming, on Crow Creek. I planned and supervised the construction. You'll be in full charge—infantry *and* cavalry, and plenty of redskins to keep you sharp and ready. Cheyenne, Arapaho, Sioux, Ute, all the rascal tribes. A fine post, you'll like it, you deserve it, it's yours."

"Mine."

Across the way an elderly lady in a heavy brocade dress and lace collar so high it looked as if her head was sitting in a crocheted bowl, threw him a questioning look. He smiled, telling her he wasn't cracking up.

For all its speed and convenience, the train was a distant second best to stepping out the door of his hotel room and into the room opposite to confront Dodge's successor and thrash things out. The suspense had to end. It would be much better than carrying it like a horse anchor in the pit of his stomach for five hundred miles. Tomorrow was Tuesday; Dodge would be at his $10,000 a year job—nearly double the peacetime pay of a major general.

Who would he pick to replace him? And would General Augur know the man well enough to put in a good word for him? Holding the four-leaf clover in his handkerchief, he willed hope into it and wondered: did four-leaf clovers yield their luck to people who fashion their own coffins with their tongues? If he'd pulled dumber stunts in his life, he couldn't recall what or when!

He groaned in his gut. A thousand mile round trip might set a record for a waste of travel. Still, if he got nothing else out of it, he'd at least have a chance to shake hands with General Augur, probably for the last time. In a few weeks he'd be retired and back home in New York in civilian Sunday best for the first time since 1837, an ox out of his yoke, devoting much of his considerable free time to poker, smoking cigars, and fishing off Montauk.

The conductor came through announcing Lexington. He thought of getting off for a quick bite, but he wasn't hungry. He dozed and thought of Lorna, picturing her standing on the platform waving, the sun lending her hair the look of finely spun gold. Where had she been all his life? More to the point, where had he been?

Worry struck. What if he arrived in Omaha to be told he'd been reassigned?

"Make arrangements with one of your former staff at the fort to forward your things to Fort Assiniboine, Montana." A shot from a Sharps distance to the Arctic Circle. And just as cold seven months of the year. Or Fort Huachuca, Arizona, where on a cool day the temperature dropped under a 100°. Or Fort Ruby, the country club, protecting the Overland Mail route from Salt Lake City to Carson City, Nevada, and boasting all the luxuries and comforts of a Turkish prison.

He fell asleep and dreamt of Lorna and slept through Lexington, Kearney, Hastings, and all the stops that followed, awakened by the conductor bawling "Omaha, Omaha, last stop Omaha."

General Christopher C. Augur had been assigned an office too small for his rank, not to mention his size. He stood six feet four with his boots off, aging sinew and

CHEYENNE

sagging flab surrounding a corporation of massive proportions. His stomach looked like a medicine ball shoved between him and his middle desk drawer. A cavalry man, he had not sat a horse for nearly four years—to the relief of the horse, Rhilander was sure. A stogie was jammed in the corner of the general's mouth; whatever the brand, it smelled sadistically foul. Rhilander got a small whiff of it, which was enough to roil the juices in his coffee-drenched but otherwise empty stomach. Augur did not drink to excess, but he suffered grievously from insomnia, and his bulbous eyes were terribly bloodshot. His spirits, however, were good. He smiled, chuckled easily, and was quite pleased at his protege's unexpected appearance. Rhilander told him why he'd come. His next-to-last meeting with Dodge in Cheyenne and its abrupt ending intrigued Augur.

"You actually called him a son of a bitch?"

"Yes," admitted Lincoln.

"To his face?"

"Yes."

"That was stupid," Augur snorted.

"Yes."

"From what you say, you had good reason to be upset, but that's hardly excuse to question his mother's marital status. And it seems to me, if I understand you rightly, when he first asked you for men and you agreed to supply them, you regretted it. But you didn't have the gumption to refuse him, and that made you as mad at yourself as you were at him."

"Yes."

"Please stop saying yes."

"I'm only agreeing," said Rhilander.

Augur sucked his stogie, ringed the ceiling with smoke, and aimlessly patted his paunch with his free hand. The anchor of suspense in Rhilander's belly had given way to a mass of cold jelly. Why the devil had he bothered to come? Why make the trip? Why not swallow his punishment, dally in Cheyenne until he was reassigned, then pack up and leave?

"Fine business," rasped Augur. "Lovely."

139

The little office seemed to shrink around them. A lone fly buzzed above their heads in erratic circles, as if looking for a way out. Rhilander cleared his throat. Augur's red eyes flickered and settled on him.

"Sir, do you know who General Dodge picked to take his place?"

"You're looking at him."

He suddenly felt confident, optimistic, and he had to consciously strive to keep from displaying his relief in a smile.

"You—"

Augur nodded. "Commander pro tem, Department of the Platte. The last bone the Army can toss in this old warhorse's lap. And you want me to restore your command."

Augur puffed and eyed the closed door behind his visitor. What does that mean, thought Rhilander, why can't he look straight at me? Is it that what he's about to say won't let him? That even before it comes out it's troubling his conscience? Augur cleared his throat.

"Fill me in. Who did Grenville pick to take your place?"

"Lieutenant Colonel Rudolph Schwimmer."

"Ye gods!" The stogie dropped from the general's mouth. He caught it deftly.

"Sir?"

"Nothing, nothing."

"Colonel Schwimmer was on his way to Fort Laramie. He stopped off in Cheyenne to call on the general."

"And Grenville drafted him. Plucked him out of the air." Augur shook his head slightly.

"Why did you say 'ye gods'?"

"Did I? I guess I did. Don't misunderstand, I'm not knocking Schwimmer. He's a good man, but giving him command of a post surrounded by hostiles? I don't believe I've ever heard of a worse mismatch. Do you know what he did back here? Chief finance officer. He was an accountant in civilian life, volunteered, got into Army finance, and worked his way up. He doesn't know one end of a Springfield from the other. Oh, he's not stupid, and he's not lazy. A bit of an egomaniac and stubborner than a deaf burro, but a good officer."

"Finance officer."

"Amazing," said Augur. "If you gave me six days, I wouldn't be able to think of a more unlikely choice. But he was in the right place at the wrong time for you. Now he's in and you're out."

"So that's it."

"Take it easy, don't go jumping down into your boots, and let's not see any of that famous temper of yours." He leered. "Don't go calling *me* a son of a bitch."

Augur eyed him steadily. His stogie continued to cork the corner of his mouth as if permanently lodged there. The ash dropped off, revealing the stogie had gone out. He began to chew.

"How long you planning to stay in Omaha?"

"I just came for this," said Rhilander. "If something can't be worked out, if I can't get reinstated . . ." He shrugged.

"Ye gods, don't give up so easily. Look, why don't you go over to the officers' mess and get yourself a decent breakfast. Make the rounds, say hello to some of your old friends. Grenville's gone, you won't bump into him. Come back this afternoon, say two o'clock. Give me time to chew on this thing."

"If there's no hope, I don't want to waste your time."

"Son, I've got twenty-four days before I hang things up. I've got nothing but time. Besides, we go back a long way. In a true friendship mutual indebtedness goes on and on. It's one of the things that keeps two people friends, so don't expect me to turn you down cold and slam the door. I'll see what I can do. Two o'clock."

"Thank you, General."

He couldn't enjoy breakfast; lunch was the same: the butterflies of anticipation and worry appropriated his stomach for their maneuvers. Between meals he met and talked with old friends. None seemed aware that he had been kicked out, and were surprised to see him away from Russell. He didn't explain his reasons for coming, which kept most of the conversations at a level of hearty banality: How's Russell? What are you doing here? How about a drink tonight? How's Harvey? How's Mario? You still single? How are the Sioux treating you?

He was grateful to Dodge for not heralding his dismissal far and wide.

After lunch, two o'clock seemed to move further and further away into the afternoon. It seemed like years before he returned to Augur's office. Even before accepting the general's invitation to sit, he tried to read his expression; was it to be good news or bad? Nothing in his face or eyes offered any clue. Then, recognizing Rhilander's unease, Augur broke into an affable smile.

"You have lunch? I skip it." He patted his belly. "I've got to lose a few pounds. Can't go home looking like a whale. I have a good breakfast and supper, no lunch, no sweets, no bread, except an occasional heel off a loaf of rye. You know how I love my *knuscht*." He cleared his throat. "I've given your problem a good deal of thought. I've tried to examine it from both sides: yours and Schwimmer's. I think I've come up with a solution. You may not like it—"

Rhilander's heart sank and thudded to rest.

"But if you think about it, it's not all that bad. More important, it's the best I can do. I'll explain it, and please don't interrupt."

He cleared his throat again and turned in his swivel chair, then fastened his attention to the wall at Rhilander's left. He tented his fingers over his paunch.

"He's in command, you're out. Oh, before I get started, I got this in the mail this morning." He held up a sheet of paper folded twice horizontally. "Brace yourself. Lieutenant Colonel Schwimmer is now a full colonel."

"Oh my God."

"Ssssh. Grenville's last order before he stepped off the wagon. Not only a rise in rank for Schwimmer, but I see it as a reminder to me that he's replaced you. Okay, he's in command, but from now on, only over the post *at the post*. If you're willing to return, if you're willing to ignore your pride and accept him as your commanding officer—and I mean accept, without snide remarks or attempts to undermine his authority—you can go back as field commander."

"I don't under—"

Augur's hand came up, cutting him off. "*In full and absolute charge in the field.* He can't second-guess you, can't countermand your orders, he'll have no power over you and your authority *in the field.* Or what you decide to take into the field."

"But—"

"Quiet. He's never been in charge in battle. No field training, no experience. He belongs behind a desk, and he's comfortable there. In the field he'd be a washout, probably crack under the strain or issue idiotic orders, sacrifice men unnecessarily. The point is, Lincoln, he *knows* he's no field officer."

"He's still not going to like sharing the command," said Rhilander.

"Oh, it may bruise his ego, but in his heart he knows his limitations. And your strength. He's not stupid. He's honest, practical—"

"Practical? Ha!"

"You two cooperating could do a lot for each other that neither of you could accomplish by yourselves. For one thing, he'll be relieving you of all the paperwork, except for skirmish reports, all the reports in triplicate, official correspondence. You despise paperwork, he dotes on it. He was born holding a pen.

"On the post he'll give the orders. In the field you will. If he should decide to come along, he'll be under your command, despite outranking you. That's no first in this man's army. Son, I know it sounds awkward, but I think it can work if you both try." He paused, cleared his throat, injected something like menace into his tone, and went on. "That's the best I can do. If you don't like it, you'll go back to Russell and sit until another spot opens up."

"Fort Ruby," said Rhilander.

"Very likely. They change COs out there every six months. Lincoln, don't decide in the next ten seconds. Think about it, weigh the pros and cons, make two lists if you like. But whatever you do, don't lose sight of one thing: right now as we sit here jawing, he's in charge and you are out."

"What makes you think he'd want to share command?" Rhilander asked.

"In the short time you worked with him—"

"One day."

"Was he hard to get along with?" Augur asked. "Or was it that the situation was awkward, and that's the real reason you got out?"

"I guess."

"Yes or no!" snapped Augur. He swiveled back a quarter turn and slit-eyed him.

"Yes."

There was a long pause. Augur tapped the tips of his tented fingers. Rhilander hung his head, stared at the floor, and scratched the back of his neck with both hands. Then he straightened.

"All right, let's say I go for it."

"Either you do or you don't!"

"Okay, sure. And, General, I am grateful. I may not sound it but—"

"Oh, shut up."

"How do I get him to go along with it? How do I even approach him? It's pretty touchy."

"I'll write him," said Augur. "I'll be as discreet as I can be. It'll all be in the wording. Another thing, don't go back right away, not until he's had a chance to digest the letter and respond. When we hear from him—"

"He could turn it down." Rhilander sucked in a breath and shook his head.

"He could, but you wouldn't expect me to can him for that."

"I didn't say that—"

"Only kidding," rasped Augur. "Boy, you should see yourself. Where's the funeral? Seriously, let's see if I can talk him into it. If he's willing to try it, I'm sure he'll make an honest effort. And you see that you do the same. On the other hand, if he doesn't go for it—"

"Hello, Fort Ruby."

"Don't jump to conclusions, Colonel."

"Lieutenant Colonel. He's the colonel," said Rhilander.

Augur eased open the bottom drawer and got out an unopened bottle of bonded bourbon.

"Take this, go tie one on, sleep it off, and get up tomorrow with your spirits a notch higher. Is that asking too much after what I've just done for you?"

"No, sir."

Augur burst out laughing. "Get out of here!"

◄11►

Building the house was tedious work. The trees had to be felled, trimmed, sawed by hand into logs, and carried by wagon to the site. It was hot and hard work, but by Tuesday—Lincoln's first day at headquarters—it was well under way. Lorna was in a nervous twitter wondering how it was going for him. Her fingers ached from crossing them every time she thought about it. Her concern took somewhat of a melodramatic turn that amused Jubal and Jeptha. They sat around the cook fire discussing the colonel and his dilemma.

"I don't understand why he's so set on getting Fort Russell back," said Jubal airily. "It seems to me one post is the same as another. If he doesn't get it, they'll send him to Arizona or California—"

"Arizona!" burst Lorna. "California!"

Jubal winked at Jeptha sitting on the other side of the fire. Lorna saw him.

"Will you two stop teasing me!"

Jeptha looked hurt. "I haven't said a word."

"Why must you always gang up on me?"

"We're not," said Jubal. "Settle your feathers, little girl. He's smart, he can handle things. I'm sure he'll be back in a few days with good news."

"How do you know that?"

"I don't, I—you like him, don't you?" Jubal asked.

"Don't change the subject. How can you be sure he'll come back with good news? Can you see into the future

146

all of a sudden? The surest way to jinx somebody is to say flat out that he or she has won. He stands about one chance in a hundred of getting his fort back. And if he doesn't, he'll have to leave. Maybe not for Arizona or California, but somewhere too far, so we won't be able to see each other. I'll never see him again!"

Tears glistened, she swiped at her nose and turned her head. Jubal got to his feet and dusted off the seat of his trousers.

"Here, here, don't get upset."

"I love him!" She paused and looked from one to the other. "Does that shock you?"

"Not really," said Jeptha. "The way you've been carrying on the last few days we'd be shocked if you told us you didn't."

"You're so smart, Jeptha Hunnicutt, why don't you stick your big nose back in your stupid book?"

"Now, stop before you start, you two."

Jubal moved to her and took her hands affectionately. "Honey, I couldn't be happier for you, I mean it. He's a fine fellow, but isn't it a little sudden?"

"So? Sometimes it happens suddenly."

"Does he love you?" Jeptha asked pointedly. "Did he tell you he does?"

"In . . . so many words, yes."

"What words?" persisted Jeptha.

"Never mind."

"That's enough, Jeptha." Jubal thought a moment, his eyes on the dwindling fire, his hands jammed in his back pockets. "If he doesn't get his job back, if the Army does move him on, what then? Will he ask you to marry him and go with him?"

"I don't—I guess. Yes."

"So when he proposes, you'll say yes," said Jubal.

"I . . ."

"You're not sure?" he asked.

"I'm sure. Yes, I'll accept."

"It sure is a little sudden, though. A lot."

"That doesn't mean anything," she blurted, her tone becoming increasingly defensive. "Time has nothing to do with it. People can be together for ten years or ten hours. You either fall in love or you don't."

"And you two are in love."

"*She* is," said Jeptha. "That's half of two."

She seethed. "So is he!"

"Well, I think that's just fine," said Jubal. "I mean it. If he's the man who'll make you happy, then he's for you. He's going through a trying time, and having you to talk to is the best thing that could happen to him, short of getting his job back."

"I don't see how you can compare the two."

"You know what I mean," said Jubal. "I'm sure he does appreciate you mightily."

"It's more than appreciation!"

"He loves you. That's nice. I mean, it's beautiful. Did he say when he expects to be back?"

"When everything's settled," said Lorna. "Maybe Thursday or Friday. The train takes less than a day from here to Omaha."

She began to gather and scrape the dishes to take down to the creek to wash. They stood watching her make her way down the slope.

"What do you think, Jubal?" Jeptha asked.

An owl hooted in the distance, a wistful, lonesome call; the breeze moaned as it twisted down from the heights, beating against the tall grass, marking the path of its wandering, and hurrying after Lorna down to the creek.

"I don't know what to think. I just wish he could settle his problem one way or the other. I hope he does love her as she says, and not that he's interested in her just because she's sympathetic."

"She's sensible. She can tell the difference," said Jeptha.

"Only if she chooses to. Oh, she's in love, all right. It sticks out like a plow beam. I just hope she doesn't end up getting hurt and deserted."

"He wouldn't leave her."

"Who knows what he'll do?" said Jubal. "I really don't know him. None of us do, not even her. It's too soon."

*   *   *

CHEYENNE

On her knees at the water's edge, Lorna scrubbed the tinware with sand, rinsed it, and thought about Lincoln. Even before he left he was in her thoughts when they were apart. She wondered about the things that set an army wife apart from other wives. Above all else one had to share a husband's fondness for the service, and his willingness to be shunted from post to post. Danger was always lurking close by, and the wives were subject to a caste system: an officer's wife wasn't supposed to mingle with enlisted men's wives, which seemed ridiculous. Who honestly cared if a good friend's husband was a private or a general? But that was the system in place; it affected the couple's social life, where they lived, what they could do, and with whom. Rank was the measuring rod. Yet restricted to the post as most army wives were, obliged to create their own social life, keeping the caste system in force could be terribly awkward. Only one or two class-conscious officers' wives could make life miserable for the majority, and of course the commanding officer's wife was thrust into the role of mother superior.

Some of the more obvious possibilities for conflict seemed downright heartless: a corporal's little girl couldn't play with a captain's little girl, even though they might hit it off beautifully. A lieutenant's wife and a private's couldn't stitch a quilt side by side. Segregation reigned, and in such a relatively small community it had to be a strain for some if not most.

And being an army wife meant living, eating, and sleeping by the bugle calls.

She'd also heard the Army discouraged men from marrying, simply because life at even the best posts was boring and restrictive, ill-suited to women. Some wives simply couldn't stand the tension and ended up divorcing their husbands or running away.

Hardest of all would be standing helplessly by as he led his men into battle, possibly a massacre like Bitter Creek. There was nothing to do but pace and wait for their return. If the officers and enlisted men's wives had one thing in common, it was when the bugles sounded officers' call and company commanders assembled for orders,

A. R. Riefe

every wife—regardless of her husband's rank—watched the men leave and turned to waiting in silent dread.

Still, she mustn't think black of it all. When she and Lincoln were married it would not be the Army she'd be marrying. Eventually he would retire.

Would he propose? She felt intuitively that he would, whatever news he brought back. She had never even heard of General Grenville Dodge before meeting Lincoln, but she disliked him intensely for what he'd done.

"Poor dear Lincoln . . ."

He did need her and he realized it. She could read it in his eyes, could see the longing. He had a wistfulness about him that only a woman could dispel, along with a sort of self-imposed air of isolation. Of course, he *was* post commander; in his position he had to maintain aloofness, though he was clearly not incapable of friendship.

"Poor dear."

She missed him tremendously, and it was impossible to hide it from her father and brother. She closed her eyes, turned loose her imagination, and there he was, smiling, so handsome in his dress blues with his saber by his side. And on horseback, with his shoulders squared and his back ramrod straight, he looked like a prince leading his troops into battle. She looked off to the east. What was he doing at this very moment? Was he thinking about her or did he have too much else on his mind? Did he lie in bed at night thinking about her as she did about him?

She suddenly ached to feel his arms around her. He had not yet held her; he wasn't so forward as to presume he was entitled to. She wished he would embrace her, kiss her, express the love they shared with more than their eyes.

"Patience."

It was nearing midnight. He lay in bed thinking about her, and wished she could be there to discuss Augur's idea. She could be objective when he himself couldn't begin to be. He could too easily tell himself he didn't like Schwimmer, but that would be petty. He had no real reason to think ill of him. It wasn't easy for the man; he

150

certainly hadn't been much help, walking away with his hurting pride and simmering dander.

How would he react to Augur's proposal? If he bought it, it would be worth the best effort both of them could give it. Would it work? Could it? He'd never heard of such an arrangement: shared command. Still, when Augur looked him in the eye and told him straight out he believed it could work, that in effect only the two of them could make it fail, he could see he was being honest. But he did wish she was there so they could discuss it.

He wished she was there to hold in his arms. Whoever invented the phrase "head over heels" knew whereof he spoke. He'd fallen so hard it had bruised his heart. She was almost twenty, he was thirty-three, but his own mother and father had been separated by twenty-two years and he'd never seen a happier marriage. He'd never been in love before, not like this. Better late than not at all. How long would he have to stay in Omaha, how long would Schwimmer make him? Augur had contacted him and proposed his idea. Give him a day, two at most, to consider it. If he rejected it, what then? Augur would be sympathetic, but there'd be nothing further he could do; he'd as good as told him that. He'd have to ask his permission to go over his head to Washington, to Secretary of War Stanton, some authority who'd listen.

He prayed it wouldn't come to that, that Schwimmer would be reasonable. But why should he be? He was in command, so why should he take on a partner? Augur seemed to think he would for the reasons he'd set forth, but would Schwimmer see it that way? It took a big man indeed to publicly concede his shortcomings. He'd be voluntarily assuming a label for all the officers and men to read: "Suitable for desk job, useless in action."

His thoughts grated to a stop as the outer door creaked open and closed, and heavy feet stumbled across the floor. A second door opened and closed. A man's stage of intoxication can always be determined by his walk.

The moon angled a beam through the single window,

washing the floor. A spider scurried into the light, then vanished under the bed.

He did hope Schwimmer wouldn't force him to go on to Washington. If he had to, it would be at least two weeks before he saw her again. Two days' separation was too long. His conscience stirred. His career was in temporary shambles; would it be fair to her to propose at such a time? Fair to drag her off to Ruby or Assiniboine away from her father and brother? Fair to break up the family so soon after Mrs. Hunnicutt's death? None of them had had time to recover fully from it.

He smiled wryly, life had been so uncomplicated just a week ago. Before Bitter Creek, he'd been in a rut, yoked to routine with only sporadic action to relieve the monotony. How dull life had been could be measured by the arrival of the paymaster. One would imagine President Johnson had shown up for all the excitement it sparked. Things were so simple then and so discouragingly involved now.

"Your move, Rudy."

He fell asleep and dreamt about her.

"He's agreed," said General Augur, waving the telegram, and flicking on the Augur glow of friendliness.

Relief was all Rhilander could feel. He emptied his lungs slowly. "Bless him."

The general pursed his lips, crinkled his brow into deep, black furrows, and squinched his red-laced eyes. "I wonder—"

"What?" asked Rhilander.

"If we've overlooked something, that he's yellow. That would certainly make him decide in your favor."

"We'll never know what kind of courage he has if he sticks to his desk."

"Make it work, Lincoln, I mean it."

"It'll take us both."

"It's mainly up to you," said Augur. "I'm not saying you'll have to toss roses at him and kiss the hem of his toga, but once in a while—"

"I'll have to bend."

"You will. Let me give you a little advice. When you board your train back to Cheyenne, leave that notorious temper of yours here. It wrecked you with Dodge. You've been lucky beyond belief to come out of it this good, so don't let it ruin things with Schwimmer."

He stood up and offered a hand the size of a baseball glove and a grip like a Cyclone wringer. Rhilander shook hands gratefully.

"I owe you," he murmured.

"Get out of here. Goodbye, good luck, and if you run into Moch-Peah-lu-tah and his Oglala-Tetons, tell him I said to keep a short rope and a strong one on Crazy Horse."

Rhilander understood the white man's name for Red Cloud and the mutual admiration the general and the chief shared for each other.

"Three more weeks and you're gone," he said.

"Twenty days."

"I'll miss you, General. You've done so much for me, and now this."

"I'll miss you, Lincoln."

Rhilander felt a surge of fondness and admiration for this aging giant, a gray warrior in the twilight, preparing to pack up his memories and go home.

He too would be heading home with the best, perhaps the only feasible resolution to his problem tucked in his self-esteem.

─────────●◄*12*►●─────────

Lorna brought Jubal and Jeptha a dipper of water from a quantity taken two days before from the creek, boiled, and cooled. Construction of the house proceeded slowly. The doors, window frames, floors, and other parts had to wait for delivery of the lumber from the Davisranch sawmill. Until the house was completed they would continue to live in their tents.

"I'm using muscles I haven't used since back in Pennsylvania," said Jubal. "What are you looking so down about, honey?"

"Nothing."

"Colonel Ryebread," Jeptha snickered.

She scowled and was preparing to upbraid him when the sound of a horse approaching from the other side of the creek drew their attention. Rhilander waved his hat and shouted. He came splashing across. He jumped down, grabbed Lorna, and swung her about; then, realizing that his impulsiveness was out of order, he backed away from her.

"It's good news! Good news!" she burst.

Jubal and Jeptha crowded around. Rhilander sketched the details for them. When he explained the arrangement, Lorna's face darkened. When he was done, they walked off down by the creek. They sat under the largest of four cottonwoods, a spot they had come to favor. A plump brown-capped, chestnut-backed chickadee cheecheed and zay-zayed wheezily from an upper branch, and

154

the sun set the pale green, sharply pointed catkins studding the branches shining.

"I came straight here from the station," he said.

She had yet to express an opinion about what he had told them. He wished she would. She seemed to need prodding.

"It's the best General Augur could do for me," he said. "I know it must sound unconventional—"

She shook her head, a simple gesture of complete dismissal of the idea. "It'll never work."

"We won't know unless we try. Schwimmer's agreed. It'll really be two separate and distinct posts; his at home, mine in the field. I mind my business at the fort, he minds his in regard to all military action."

"You amaze me," she said.

"You think I'm being naive. If I am, so is the general."

"I didn't say that."

"That's what you're thinking," he said.

"How do you know what I'm thinking?"

"Lorna, Augur could have refused to do anything for me. After all, I've already been replaced. All in all, I have to consider myself very lucky."

"*Have* to?"

"You know what I mean."

"I'm sorry, Lincoln, you're not back here twenty minutes and I'm already throwing cold water. Not a very friendly reception. It's just that, well, it's all so terribly unfair. It's all spitefulness on Dodge's part, nothing else." She seized his hands, squeezed them, and smiled radiantly. "But at least you're getting back your command."

"Half of it."

"If anyone can make it work, you can. I just hope Schwimmer doesn't take advantage of you."

"How can he?"

She sighed, affirmation that she did think he was being naive, he thought. But then she was on his side, and any reservations she had were only because she was loyal. Because she loved him.

Did she?

"Yes," he said aloud.

She looked puzzled.

"Nothing," he said. He stared so long and resolutely that pink came to her cheeks. "I've missed you so—"

"I've missed you worse. People say keep busy and the time passes and you won't miss someone so much. It's nonsense. I've been working clearing grass and sage brush, and every hour has been harder than the one before."

He drew her to him. "We must never be separated so long again. It's been a week."

"Five days, eight hours," she said, and set her hand to his cheek. His heart filled his chest with warmth.

"How many minutes?" he asked and checked his watch.

"Seventeen. I love you."

"I love you, Lincoln."

She kissed his cheek. He embraced her and kissed her soulfully, all his feeling, his love and hunger for her held in check in his absence pouring into the kiss. She held his mouth to hers tenaciously. When their lips finally parted he got to his feet and pulled her up.

"Come, let's tell your father and Jeptha."

"That we're in love? They already know." She laughed lightly. "As if I could hide it."

Again he kissed her, then held her at arms' length and searched her eyes. In an instant all his troubles seemed unimportant, trivial, obscured by the glow of their love.

"Do they know we're going to be married?" he asked.

"Oh, Lincoln—"

"What?"

"I feel like the ground is dropping from under my feet. To think I had to come all this way to fall in love." She touched a finger to his lips, holding it briefly. "Oh, how I hope this thing with Schwimmer works for you. If there's anything I can do. I know! Mrs. Schwimmer should be here by now."

"I guess," he said.

"Why don't I make friends with her, talk to her, get her in our corner?"

"Pit her against him?"

"No, no, just make sure she understands how it can work and that it's best for you both," she said.

"I don't think that's a good idea."

"Why not?"

"Lorna, it's our pickle, his and mine. We're the ones who have to deal with it."

"How do you know he can?"

"How does he know I can? We'll just have to work at it. But you haven't answered my question."

"You didn't ask it."

"Here goes. Will you marry me, Miss Hunnicutt?"

"I guess." He reacted. She laughed, then her expression became deadly serious. "Yes, I'll marry you, Colonel."

They kissed, he swung her about joyfully. "Thank you, Miss Hunnicutt. Only one thing."

"What?"

"I should ask your father's permission."

"Isn't it a little late?"

"It *is* proper," he said.

"Do it."

"You don't think . . . I mean, there's no possibility he might turn me down."

"You won't know till you ask," she said.

"You're a big help."

Hand in hand they walked back to the work area. They came within twenty yards of Jubal; he was carrying one end of a log, Jeptha the other, when Jubal's end slipped from his grasp and landed on his foot. He roared and hopped about on the other foot. His face turned crimson and he began to swear.

"Maybe another time," said Rhilander quietly.

Lorna burst out laughing. Jubal saw.

"What in blue hell is so funny, missy!"

Rhilander walked past him with his eyes averted and set about helping Jeptha with the log, deciding to let the two of them have it out.

It would have to wait.

⏴13⏵

Mona Schwimmer was a buxom redhead who had a nervous habit of lowering her head and peering at people with the tops of her eyes. Her hair was magnificent, a natural dark red, but her face was not pretty. It was not homely, either, but simply unmemorable. Rudy stood his tallest and chestiest, and beamed his proudest introducing them.

"Welcome to Fort Russell," said Rhilander. "How was your trip over?"

"Steaming hot, but more comfortable than a stagecoach, and not nearly as dusty. I despise stagecoaches, don't you?"

"Despise is the word."

This pleased her, and she tried a smile. Genuine if self-conscious, he mused. He wondered how Lorna would get along with her. She was at least twelve years older, and would probably try to mother her when she found out Lorna had lost her mother. Mona would never get away with it, and they could never be sisters, but friendship was possible. He wondered if Mona Schwimmer would turn out like Colonel Butterick's wife over at Fort Bridger; Mable Butterick reputedly tyrannized the other wives and the children, exercising a firmer hand than did her husband in command of the troops. Their husbands' rank did go to some wives' heads, although Mable was such an extreme case she had gained a reputation as a caricature of the type: appointing herself judge and jury over all civilian squabbles at the post, even the domestic ones; lecturing the other wives on bringing up their children; manipulating as many lives as she could at any one time. Mona Schwimmer couldn't possibly be another Mable Butterick. Mike Hannigan's widow, Molly, for one, would give her back as good as she gave.

He was being unfair: why assume she'd be a problem for Lorna, him, anyone? She was probably friendly, fair, and not at all high-handed.

"Where's Louis, my dear?" Rudy asked. "I want him to meet the colonel."

"Out looking for bugs." She beamed. "You know Louis, Rudy. Natural history fascinates him, Colonel."

"Please call me Lincoln, Mona."

She tittered, pleased. "Animals, snakes, birds, bugs, plants, everything. His appetite for knowledge is voracious. He's terribly bright."

"Lincoln, we're going to have to find you quarters," said Rudy. "It shouldn't be difficult. You can always rank out the low man on the totem pole."

"It might be best if I stay in town."

"And go back and forth? That seems like a lot of trouble to put yourself to."

Maybe, reflected Rhilander, but it also may be worth it; the more time he spent away when he really wasn't needed, the better for the arrangement. Then again, he was supposed to be meeting Rudy halfway—in everything. Keeping clear of the fort when he wasn't absolutely required to be there didn't exactly qualify as cooperation.

"Perhaps you're right. I'll work something out."

Harvey Philips's wife had deserted him the year before, he recalled. Perhaps he could put up with a roommate until Lorna officially became Mrs. Rhilander.

Mona excused herself, leaving colonel and lieutenant colonel with their first opportunity to discuss the arrangement. Rhilander got off on a friendly foot.

"Congratulations, *Colonel*."

"Thank you. Lincoln, I want you to know right off that I intend to do my best to pull together in this thing."

"I will. I give you my word."

They shook hands. Rudy beamed, then sobered.

"When you do go out to engage the hostiles, if you don't mind I'd like to talk it over with you. I'd like to learn about your strategy and tactics."

"Of course."

"I promise I won't find fault, even question. And would you mind if I went along sometime? Strictly as an observer, of course. There's no substitute for experiencing action firsthand, right?"

"You're welcome whenever you like," said Rhilander, thinking as the words came out that he was probably sticking his neck out. Augur had repeatedly emphasized the importance of keeping their areas of authority separate. To deliberately ignore the lines could be asking for trouble.

"Of course, if you have any ideas on running things, on my policies here, I'll be happy to listen," added Rudy.

They talked for another twenty minutes, mostly about the day-to-day running of the post, Rudy's continuing predilection for what the older noncoms called "chicken-shit discipline." If that was to be his style of command, so be it. Presently Rhilander excused himself, they shook hands a second time to confirm the arrangement, and he went looking for Philips. He found him at the sutler's paying his bill. Rhilander steered him out of the sutler's earshot and told him what had happened in Omaha.

"Sounds screwy as hell to me," rasped Philips. "How did Chris Augur ever make general with flea-brained ideas like that?"

"Don't knock him, Harvey. He wanted to salvage something for me. Maybe I can't have all the apple, but this way I at least get a share."

"Do you know what that horse's ass had D Company doing yesterday? He didn't like the way they drilled the day before so he sent two men out each with a fifty-pound sack of corn. They strewed it all over the parade ground, and D Company, every man and the officers, spent all day and half of last night picking it up. Every kernel. That's his idea of discipline. Like it?"

Philips's breath smelled foul. He was a little drunk. The sutler, a big, greasy, and perpetually scowling Frenchman, stared from one of them to the other from behind the counter. His chin was stained with tobacco juice and one eye was partially closed and swollen. Proof, reflected Rhilander, that he was one storekeeper who evidently didn't think the customer was always right.

"I forgot to mention, while I was away he was promoted to full colonel."

"I know, he announced it. The son of a bitch . . ." Philips glowered.

"Relax."

"Thank your friend Dodge."

"To answer your question, whatever he does in the name of discipline, in anything else here on the grounds, I can't criticize. That's the deal, Harvey. I've salvaged something and I don't intend to jeopardize it. I made a mistake, a doozie. I'm not going to make another."

Philips shrugged. "Whatever you say."

He started for the door. Rhilander stopped him.

"Harvey, don't. We're friends, I value your opinion."

"Maybe, but this time you don't want it. What you want is for me to encourage this farce, what you call the arrangement. You're looking for ways to rationalize it, some you haven't thought of yourself yet. I haven't got any, go ask him."

"Thanks."

"You're welcome."

Again he started off. Rhilander bristled.

"I didn't come looking for you to discuss it. Believe it or not, I was wondering if I could move in with you. Temporarily."

"If you want."

"On second thought, forget it."

Philips waved over his shoulder and went out.

Rhilander made plans to move his things into a large room attached to the sutlery. He didn't resent what he could only construe as Harvey Philips's reaction over his failure to regain sole command of Russell. He could see that Harvey had it in for Schwimmer. Ironically enough, it was because of his loyalty to Rhilander. Harvey didn't resent the arrangement as much as he was disappointed with it. Rhilander had known him long enough to know that he took disappointment with about as much tolerance as a spoiled nine-year-old. Mario Consolo, on the other hand, took Schwimmer's arrival and its consequences in stride. He could live with it if the other junior officers could. Every man, if he was at all realistic, had to expect a change in command once in a while. Nothing was forever, especially in the Army.

Lorna sensed that Lincoln was thinking over the situation at dinner, so she tried to keep the conversation on lighter matters.

"What's Mrs. Schwimmer like?"

"She doesn't like stagecoaches and she has lovely natural red hair."

"My, but we're observant. Is she nice?"

"She seems so," he said.

"Pretty?"

"Plain."

He inched his hand across the table between the single daisy in its slender vase and her coffee. The restaurant was crowded and noisy, the three waiters trudging about looking desperately harried, catching orders and demands from all sides. He covered her hand. She turned hers to clasp it.

"Are you done?" he asked. "More coffee?"

"No. Can we get out of here?"

"I'll get the check. Shall I take you back to the house?" he asked.

"My tent, you mean. Later. I want to see where you live."

"It's not much to see, one room, not even a closet. Besides, I'll be moving back to the fort tomorrow morning."

She was gazing at him. "Before you move out I want to see your room," she said evenly.

He understood.

*   *   *

CHEYENNE

They hadn't planned it. He got the feeling as he mounted the backstairs behind her that it was more that she hoped for it, seeing it as an opportunity to prove her love that she could not let slip by. There would be no privacy in his new quarters at the sutlery. This would be their first and perhaps last chance, at least for the time being, to be alone.

They sat on the edge of the narrow bed in the small, bleak, sparsely furnished room, arms around each other. The mattress sagged so the position was uncomfortable. Still embracing, kissing passionately, he eased her down. He could feel her begin to tense.

So it was her first time. He wondered if they should go through with it, but decided it wasn't his decision to make. Her kisses were becoming more ardent, her cheeks were flushed, her voice husky; she was aroused. If she wanted to stop she could not, and neither could he.

Gently, his conscience warned him. Give yourself to her, don't take her, don't!

They lay under the sheets. Her flesh fairly burned under his touch. She groaned.

"What?" he asked.

"I can't stop shaking, I feel like such a fool—"

"No, no, I feel like an oaf. I'm so clumsy."

"You're not. Hold me."

He held her; gradually she mastered her nervousness, at least to the extent that she stopped trembling.

Oh Lord, she thought, he knows it's the first time for me. How can he not? What must he think? No matter how much it hurts, I can't cry out.

I can't hurt her, he thought. What am I doing even touching her? But it was past the point of stopping. In spite of her unconcealable nervousness, she wanted him. He slid his hand between her thighs, setting them quivering.

"I'm sorry," she murmured. "I'm being such a baby . . ."

Gently, tenderly, he eased his fingers between her lips, finding her clitoris, stroking it. She drew in a long breath. He could feel her tense, more, more, then slowly relax. She brought her hand down and moved his probing fingers higher, then began working herself against them, coupling their movements. She moaned softly and moved faster. He held his fingers rigid, letting her work against them. She pressed her hips upward, panting, sinking her teeth into her lower lip, and tossing her head side to side. Her eyes took on a glazed look. He was stiff, but he hesitated to mount her, worrying that pressing his head against her lips would frighten her. Again she grabbed his fingers, manipulating them, pushing them higher and deeper.

"Ahhhh, darling . . ."

He withdrew his fingers and lifted himself over her. Her hand gripped his member and guided it to her lips.

"In me, in me," she rasped.

"Easy . . ."

Slowly he thrust it forward, parting her moistened lips. He was only partially in when she suddenly bucked and cried out. She froze, then bucked again, driving against him so violently he was astonished. She bit her lip hard against the pain, shuttering her eyes, moaning, panting, writhing uncontrollably.

"Ahhhhhhhhhh . . ."

He came with her, flooding her. Their mouths met passionately, his tongue gliding over hers as he continued to pump. The moon slid behind a blue-bruised cloud, and stars peered down as they separated and lay back.

He kissed her lightly on the forehead.

"Are you all right?" he asked.

She smiled dreamily. "Is it always so glorious?" she murmured.

"It can be."

"Can we go on?"

"Soon, my darling."

"Very soon, my husband."

It was nearing midnight by the time he got back to the fort. Every window was dark except one. Schwimmer was evidently still at his desk in the office. Wick work, as Christopher Augur used to call it. There were things about the colonel he could criticize, reflected Rhilander, but he'd never known anyone who worked longer hours.

CHEYENNE

The room he'd appropriated next to the sutler's was twice the size of his rented room in town. Rather than return to town after taking Lorna home, he decided to try out his new quarters. He kicked off his boots, stripped off his shirt, and began to wash up. He studied himself in the glass.

"You're in love, Rhilander. You of all people. What happened?"

She happened. He felt content. Even the fragile arrangement he had with Rudy and the challenges it threatened didn't worry him. They would work things out.

God, but she was a marvel! He had to have hurt her, but there had not been a whisper of complaint. Nothing but love, tenderness, complete capitulation to the demands of their hearts. When could they be married? They hadn't gotten around to discussing dates yet. First let them finishing building their house before he whisked her away. It could not be very nice for Jubal and Jeptha, but he had proposed and she'd accepted.

He still hadn't formally asked Jubal's permission to marry her. She'd said it wasn't necessary, but he wanted to. He liked his future father-in-law and valued his friendship and respect. Besides, he wanted to do things properly—join the family, not invade it.

Harvey Philips would stand up for him; their tiff wasn't serious, he would apologize. Harvey would welcome the good news as would Mario.

A knock sounded. He turned from the glass. The door opened revealing Mona Schwimmer. She wore a crepe robe of pale rose embroidered up the front of the skirt and a frilly white cotton blouse. Her beautiful hair was pinned up. She closed and bolted the door behind her before he could say a word. She was agitated, she looked troubled.

"Colonel—"

"Mrs. Schwimmer, what—"

"I need your help."

"You shouldn't be in here like this."

"Nobody saw me. I have to talk, please."

"Mrs. Schwimmer—"

"Mona. Lincoln. Don't make me leave, I beg you. You must help me!"

"Shhh . . . Calm down, what's the matter?"

She was pacing; she had her hanky out and was tugging at it, and sweeping her fists up and down in front of her. He hadn't noticed when Rudy introduced them earlier, but it was obvious now that she was neurotic. Her cheeks were flushed; every few words her voice cracked, she couldn't stand still, couldn't keep her arms still. She was out of breath, as if someone had been chasing her and she'd come barging in to hide from them. She was pathetic.

"Sit down," he said. "Relax."

"I can't, I mustn't. You probably think it horrible of me, bursting in on you like this so late, but I don't know who to turn to. I don't know anyone else here."

She stopped, her hand going to the side of her head. She had stopped pacing, she swayed slightly. He moved to her to catch her if she passed out. But she shook it off and went on.

"You don't know what it's like." She laughed brittlely. "How could you? How could anybody?"

"What are you talking about?"

Her reaction said he was being dense. "Him, what else? Rudy." She resumed pacing. "It's going to be just like back in Omaha, working till all hours. Coming home at three and four in the morning. All he does is work!" She stopped. "He doesn't know I'm alive! Or Louis!"

"Sssssh—"

"Even when he's around, he hardly says a word. Work! Work! It's a sickness with him. Every *i* dotted, *t* crossed, every column added up four times. Four times! Oh, but he's proud of what he calls his wizardry with figures. They're sacred to him, he worships them. Ignores me. I don't exist. I'm a woman, Lincoln, I have needs, desires. I'm a human being! Turn your back."

"But—"

"Turn around!"

He turned. He could see her in the mirror. She hastily undid her blouse, jerking the two sides apart. Underneath she was naked. Her breasts were huge, gleaming

166

like ivory, the nipples pink, firm, erect. She was perspiring; she began to pant sensuously. Before his initial shock passed and he could find his voice, she ran to him, throwing her arms around him, rubbing her breasts against his chest.

"Beautiful, aren't they? Feel them."

Her hand grasping his was like a vise. She ran his hand over her breasts.

"Mona, for Christ's sake!"

"Take me, take me, I beg you! Give me your cock!"

She dropped to her knees and began tearing at his fly. He pulled free, backing against the washstand and upsetting the basin. It shattered on the floor, sending water streaming in every direction.

There was a loud knock. Both went rigid.

"Lincoln? Are you awake? I saw the light. It's me, Rudy—"

"Oh my God," murmured Rhilander.

Before he could move she had shot to her feet and was clawing at her hair, ripping the pins from it. It tumbled down in disarray. She tore at her blouse savagely, ripping it from her shoulder. She flew to the door.

"No!" burst Rhilander.

She threw the bolt, wrenching the door wide. There stood Rudy, eyes gaping, mouth wide.

"Mona—"

She hurled herself into his arms sobbing loudly, caterwauling.

"He tried to rape me. Rudy, save me!"

"I never touched her," rasped Rhilander heatedly.

Rudy had fixed his gaze on him and still held it.

"He raped me! He did, I swear!"

Rudy eased her from him, still holding eye contact. When he spoke his tone was restrained, perfectly calm.

"Fix your clothes and go home, dear."

"Rudy! Darling!"

"Go on, I'll be along."

"He raped me!"

"Go home, woman!"

A. R. Riefe

She fled. Schwimmer came in and closed the door. He looked heavily weighted with weariness.

"I never went near her," Rhilander went on.

Rudy's upraised hand stopped him. In an instant it was all clear to Rhilander, the reason for the man's passive reaction, his dismissal of her, all but shouting her out the door. Rhilander nodded.

"This isn't the first time this has happened," he said quietly.

Rudy had broken his gaze from Rhilander's; he fastened his gaze on the floor.

"Not the second. Not even—what a fool I am. I thought bringing her out here from Omaha would be a healthy change for her, and Louis. I thought—wishful, stupid thinking. She'll never change. She's a . . . a nymphomaniac."

"Is she? Or is she normal?"

Schwimmer didn't immediately respond to this. He lifted his eyes and averted them, pretending interest in the window.

"May I sit down?"

"Sure."

"You're right, of course. Normal. But intensely, unbelievably frustrated, thanks to me. I'm the world's worst husband. I'm amazed she didn't leave me years ago. Terrible husband and father."

He looked back at Rhilander. And in that instant Rhilander felt a great surge of pity.

"I used to try. Oh, I've long since given up." He continued to look at Rhilander, appealing for understanding. "I'm a washout at both. Some people just aren't any good at marriage. Even worse raising a family. I work. It's all I know how to do, all I love, God help me." He smiled wistfully. "At least I can be honest about it, eh?"

"Rudy—"

"Some time back, the day after Louis's ninth birthday, actually, I took the afternoon off. Can you imagine me taking a whole afternoon off? We went fishing. Ghastly mistake. We weren't out in the boat twenty minutes before I began to get fidgety. Sitting there doing nothing

168

was suddenly driving me crazy. He sensed it. And this is the worst part: it made him feel bad, Lincoln, that he was making me uncomfortable. The poor lad. Here *I* was making a total disaster of the afternoon and *he* wanted to take the blame. Imagine how that made me feel."

"You don't have to talk about it."

"I want to. It's a chance to remove a few of the pins from my conscience. The trouble is, the months go by, the years, and then you suddenly catch yourself. You realize what you're doing to your wife, you fall all over her with apologies and swear it'll be different. Only she's heard it all before, she knows you don't know how to change. Any attempts you make fall flat. It's not spontaneous, you see. Love, affection, attention can't be scheduled, they have to be spontaneous. Listen to me, I'm an authority on all kinds of marital neglect. Past master.

"Some people just shouldn't get married. Only a husband can't tell his wife that, of course. As if Mona didn't know. But it's true, for people like me marriage is very unwise. Unwise? My God, it's criminal! That's enough, keeping you up to listen to my troubles isn't very sporting of me."

He got up from the edge of the bed and went to the window, looking out at the darkness.

"I'm sure you wonder what I'm doing here so late." He turned and smiled sadly. "I can assure you, I didn't come to unburden my soul."

"You saw her come in," said Rhilander.

"No. I was surprised to find her here, though I don't know why. This came by messenger about eight o'clock." He dug in the breast pocket of his shirt and brought out a folded telegram.

It was from departmental headquarters, signed by Christopher Augur. It was unusually long, but specific, the facts clearly laid out. A scouting report had come in to Fort Fetterman, the intelligence that Crazy Horse was collecting the youthful hotheads and renegade elements of the Sioux and allying with the Cheyenne and smaller groups of Arapaho and Gros Ventre to launch a holy war against the white intruders in their territories. Large num-

bers of Indians had been seen near the southeast fork of
the Tongue River more than two hundred miles to the
north, just below the Montana border. Trails fifty feet
wide made up of powder six inches deep confirmed the
gathering of the malcontents. Crazy Horse, the blue-
eyed, pale-skinned *potanka* with the light brown hair had
already established himself as a genius at tactical cavalry
warfare. He was friendly with Red Cloud, with Gall,
Rain-in-the-Face, Hump, Fat Bull, and other ruling red
rascals, and the only one among them capable and respected enough by all to weld them into a fighting force.

Rhilander recalled all this as he read the telegram. He
also knew that Crazy Horse was a brilliant strategist in
not just battle, but in the hound-and-prey maneuvering
all over the landscape that preceded the fight. Augur
emphasized that he must be taken out of the game before
he caused serious trouble. A single successful large-scale
raid would rally a horde of additional hostiles to his
lance. If he could be neutralized—better yet, eliminated—
his army would dissolve overnight, for not one of his
young cronies could fill his moccasins.

Rhilander was hereby ordered to take command of an
expeditionary force, move north to where Crazy Horse
had been last seen, track him down, and speak with him.
If the chief eluded him or declined to parlay, the colonel
knew what his next step must be. Every installation in
Wyoming had been alerted as far west as Fort Bridger,
as far north as Camp Brown; every post commander
ordered to contribute men and materiel to the effort.
Lieutenant Colonel Lincoln Rhilander would assemble
his force at Fort Fetterman seven days hence. There was
little time to dally.

Rhilander crumpled the telegram. "We'll ride out in
the morning," he said.

"I'm coming."

"Rudy—"

"We agreed, Lincoln. You did. I can go along on any
mission as long as I concede overall authority to you. In
the field, in preparation, on the way. I do. No argument,

I promise you." He moved closer. His eyes glistened. "I just want to see some action."

"We can't both go."

"Why not?" asked Schwimmer. "Harvey Philips can mind the store. How long will it take, do you think?"

"It could drag out until winter. Crazy Horse'd love that. He'll likely do his damnedest to make it happen. Rudy, you do have every right to come along, but not this once, please. You're needed here. What if the Sioux and Cheyenne down here, those that don't throw in with Crazy Horse, take advantage of our pulling out in strength and start harassing the railroad in earnest? I'm talking about a Bitter Creek every other day. I'm going to have to take at least half of our people. Three of the four howitzers, as much ammunition as we can carry."

"That's your department, whatever you say. Only I want to go. I have to."

"Have to?" Rhilander studied him.

"I've never seen any action. Never had the chance. Now I do. I want to, and come home and tell Louis about it." He paused and looked away. "I want him to know that his father is a soldier."

"He knows," said Rhilander.

"Be serious. I'm a number juggler in uniform, with no idea how I'll react under fire. I could turn out the worst sort of yellow belly. No, I won't be a coward. But if I don't try, I'll never know how brave I can be. Nor will Louis. Please. I don't expect to come back with the Medal of Honor. I just want a taste of action. It's terrifically important to me, Lincoln."

Rhilander didn't like the idea; the situation, if and when they encountered Crazy Horse, threatened to be bloody and difficult. He didn't need a company clerk by his side, at risk, getting in the way, meddling, muddling. He didn't want to have to worry about somebody else's skin along with his own. And yet Rudy was right, he had a right to go; it was in the contract.

Still, what would General Augur think? Both commanders running off to engage the hostiles would upset him. Not that Harvey couldn't handle things in their absence, but Augur had been very clear about the division of responsibility, harping and harping on it. And here, in the first to-do to come along, they would be ignoring his instructions. And what made it worse, this was a campaign, not a skirmish at the railhead; it could drag out till spring.

"What about your wife?" Rhilander asked.

"What about her?"

"She just got here and you want to leave."

"I hope you don't think I'd be deserting her. I wouldn't. She'll like the idea. I'm not around when I'm around, so what difference is it if I'm three hundred miles away? Besides, I'm sure she shares Louis's reservations about me, about my manhood, if you will. I'm sure she'll be as proud as he when I come back."

If, reflected Rhilander, at the same time suspecting that if he were in Rudy's place, he'd grab the same opportunity. Knowing he had no experience under fire, Mona would probably worry herself to distraction, but when they did come back, mother and son would be welcoming a new Rudy, one both could appreciate and respect a good deal more.

"It's late," said Rhilander. "I should turn in."

"Let me help pick up the pieces of the wash basin."

"Don't bother, they can wait until morning. Can we get together in your office right after guard mount? We have to figure out who goes, who stays, all the little details."

"I can go back to the office now and work on the logistics," said Schwimmer.

"No. Just go home and to bed."

"What? Oh sure, sure, I see what you mean."

Rhilander stood in the doorway watching him walk away. The instant Rudy vanished into the darkness, he sighed. Poor fellow, he'd picked himself a formidable adversary for his baptism of fire in Crazy Horse. How would he react when he faced him? How would any of them, himself included?

He yawned and closed the door.

"What a day, what a night, what a life."

14

"**H**ow long will you be gone?" Lorna asked, unable to disguise the anxiety in her voice.

"Perhaps a month," he replied.

"Dear God!"

They sat under the cottonwood by the creek. He estimated he had less than ten minutes to devote to her before he headed back to the fort. He had waited until now to tell her, preferring to do so in privacy. They could hear Jubal and Jeptha working on the house up above. A thrush sang above their heads. Purple lupines nodded and basked in the sunlight. No sooner had he gotten there than Rhilander had taken Jubal aside and without preliminary discussion asked him for Lorna's hand. Jubal had not hesitated, either. He practically bellowed his blessing, he and Jeptha both pumping Rhilander's hand. And despite the fact that it was not yet mid-morning, Jubal insisted they toast the happy couple with a generous dollop of sourmash whiskey from a jug a friend with the ill-fated wagon train had given him back in Kansas.

Sourmash telegraph battery acid, he could still taste it. Perhaps in a day or so the sting would go out of the roof of his mouth.

"Perhaps we won't be gone even that long," he said.

"Perhaps even longer. I know, it's your duty."

"It could be worse, sweetheart."

Her concern was beginning to make him feel uncomfortable. What a hell of a time to have to go away, he mused.

"It's certainly going to be dangerous. But I know it's your duty."

"There's an echo around here," he said.

She was unable to keep from grinning. She leaned over, kissed him on the cheek, and smoothed back his hair.

"Be careful."

He nodded. "I've never had a more important reason to be."

"Keep that in mind." She got up and straightened her apron, then took it off and folded it. "I'll go back with you."

"Would you?"

"Try to stop me. I'll see you away with all due ceremony, Colonel, and before you leave you can introduce me to Colonel Schwimmer's wife."

"Oh."

"What's the matter?"

"Nothing. Sure I'll introduce you," he said.

Thoughts careened and clashed so he was surprised he couldn't hear as well as experience them. He hadn't seen Mona today; she hadn't come near the office when he and Rudy met earlier to plan the logistics of the search for Crazy Horse. How, he wondered, did Mona feel about her rejection after a night's sleep? About her rejecter? Was she licking her wounds? Had she put him out of mind? Was she suffering unbearably and hating, despising him for it? How capable was she at making and holding a grudge? If she did despise him as much as he pessimistically thought she must, would she take it out on Lorna in his absence?

She'd have to be malevolently petty to do such a thing, but it was possible. Anything was with somebody that unstable. Worse, she could lie to Lorna, paint all sorts of lurid pictures of him as the vicious rapist she had successfully fought off. Lorna wouldn't believe it, but others who heard it might.

If only he knew Mona. But he had no yardstick for

measuring the intensity of her frustration with Rudy. What brought it to the surface, if she delighted in hurting others . . . Rudy hadn't said a word about the previous night when they'd met that morning, nothing about his conversation with Mona when he finally got home. If they'd had a conversation.

They started back, crossing the creek and following the narrow, dusty road toward the fort four miles north of Cheyenne. And Mona, he thought wearily. He glanced sidelong at Lorna. She seemed preoccupied, as well she might be, considering the circumstances. He tried to cheer her.

"We can set a date for the wedding as soon as I get back," he said. "Okay?"

"Yes. Fine. I hope with that to shoot for, you'll get back as fast as you can."

"As fast as Crazy Horse ordains."

It wasn't intended as a joke, just something to lighten the weight of the moment. It failed. They rode on in silence. Ahead the tall grasses danced and shimmered in the sunlight, crowding both sides of the road down to Little Horse Creek. Midway between Little Horse and Lodgepole creeks marked the halfway point to Fort Russell.

"What is it?" she asked.

He could feel his throat drying slightly. He hated to bring it up, but it was speak now or forever hold, he thought ruefully.

"I met Mona Schwimmer."

"I know, you said."

"I mean since Rudy introduced us. I—she—"

"Darling, what are you trying to say?"

She reined up, eyeing him questioningly. He recounted Mona's visit, Rudy's coming to the door, and, after sending her home, explaining her problem. He didn't have the heart to quote the poor man's soul-baring speech word for word, but gave her the gist of it, expressing his sympathy. He found himself groping for words. She interrupted.

"The poor woman. Poor Rudy. When she started screaming rape, you must have gone into shock."

"For a minute I thought my heart had stopped dead on me," he went on. "It was all a terrible mess, only I figure you should know. I mean God knows what she'll say when I introduce you, and after I leave. Best be prepared for the worst. She's terribly lonely, poor woman. She needs somebody she can talk to, confide in desperately."

"Don't they have a son?"

"He's a loner, from what I gather. Rudy's very self-conscious about them. Blames himself, of course, only doesn't do anything about it. It's a problem and a half."

"You take care of him, I'll take care of her," said Lorna.

"And Louis'll take care of himself. He'd prefer it that way."

They crossed Lodgepole Creek, and ten minutes later, Fort Russell broke the horizon.

15

The column would be moving out shortly. The regimental band had already assembled at the northern point of the diamond-shaped parade ground, the tubas and other brass instruments dazzling under the bright sun, flags unfurled, drummers practicing their rattles and rolls. Along the northeastern side of the diamond, wives, children, and off-duty men formed a long, straggling line to watch the departure. Horses were being brought up from the stables in a steady stream. Two—not three—of the four howitzers were being readied to accompany the column. An air of excitement and apprehension pervaded the scene. Apprehension in Rhilander's mind, nursing the knowledge that post strength would be reduced by half when the last strains of "The Girl I Left Behind Me" faded and the dust raised by the departure resettled on the parade ground.

Mona Schwimmer had made a remarkable recovery from the night before. She looked as if she'd slept ten hours; she was composed and generously friendly toward Lorna when Rhilander introduced them. Louis stood by, holding a mason jar with a whiptail lizard coiled in it. The boy looked like his mother: her hair, her curious on-again off-again smile, deep-set staring eyes, and all but nonexistent upper lip. Louis was fourteen; he acted about nine in gushing about his captive to Lorna.

"Are you free the rest of the morning?" Mona asked her pointedly. "Can we have tea and chat?"

About what? wondered Rhilander. But he had warned Lorna, she could handle Mona.

"I'd love tea," she replied.

Mona beamed. "I want you to tell me all about Cheyenne."

"I'm afraid I've yet to even see it."

Rudy interrupted hesitantly to kiss her good-bye. He shook Louis's hand and instructed him to take care of his mother in a self-conscious manner. Rhilander walked Lorna out of the Schwimmers' earshot, held her, and kissed her. When they broke, her eyes were glistening.

"None of that," he murmured.

"I'm not crying."

"If we send anyone back—it might be necessary—I promise I'll send a message."

"I hope it's not as long as you think," she said, searching his eyes.

"I didn't say it was going to be long."

"But you think it will, I can tell. What if winter comes and you still haven't found Crazy Horse?"

"We will," he said.

"You'll end up fighting him, won't you? It can't be avoided."

"It can be postponed. You must look at the brighter possibilities: he could run away to Canada, he could quarrel with his Cheyenne friends. He and Bat don't like each other. Bat doesn't like anybody, even his own."

"Bat?" she asked.

"We pale-eyes call him Roman Nose."

The band finished tuning up and broke into "The Girl I Left Behind." He grasped her hands.

"Say good-bye to your father and Jeptha for me. And don't worry."

"Of course I'll worry. I've already decided on that."

He grinned. "I love you. Take care."

They kissed again and separated. She waved discouragedly and headed across the parade ground, towed by Mona. Louis walked backward with them, watching the column assemble. The cavalry would lead the way, followed by the infantry, with the wheeled vehicles bringing up the rear. The troopers marched with weapons slung, horses curried, wagons clean and tight, gear saddle-soaped to a gleaming black. Every man carried his own gear and blanket, canteen, rations for seven days, to be replenished at Fort Fetterman before embarking on the search for the hostiles. Each man carried a Spencer repeating rifle with 140 rounds of ammunition and a Colt's Army revolver with 50 rounds. Four pack mules carried the company's medical supplies and 4,000 additional rounds of ammunition for the rifles.

The column streamed out, heads high, guidons flapping, sunlight bouncing off the saber scabbards. Ten minutes later, out of sight of the post, they settled down to chewing at the two hundred miles separating them from Fetterman. A snaking line of men, horses, and wagons moved in columns of four when the terrain permitted, but it would dissolve into a vulnerable single file across rougher country. No band played now; the only sounds were those of men on the march. Cups and skillets hanging from packs set up a cacaphonous rattling clashing with the thud of heavy boots, the creak of saddles and harness, the grinding of wagon wheels, the occasional gusty snorting of the horses.

Rudy, riding about six lengths ahead of Rhilander, reined up sharply to let him catch up. They rode side by side to the left out of the line of march.

"Lorna and Mona seemed to hit it off," said Rudy.

"Very well," said Rhilander.

"I hope they can be friends. Mona needs somebody. I worry so about her."

"What did she say when you told her you were going along?"

Before he could respond, Rhilander noticed that men were hoisting their canteens and drinking as if there were a well every mile all the way to the Platte River. The streams and creeks they would be fording enroute were for the most part muddy trickles whose water had to be strained through cheesecloth and boiled before being consumed.

"Mario!" called Rhilander.

A. R. Riefe

Lieutenant Consolo came galloping up. "Sir?"

"Pass the word up and down the line. Every man, including officers, two swallows from their canteens. Any man caught sneaking a third one before the first halt will be severely disciplined."

Seconds later the grumbling up and down the line affirmed that the order was being obeyed. Rhilander had returned to the conversation. He repeated his question.

"She was all for it," replied Rudy.

"She liked the idea?"

"It'll be good for us to be apart for a while. You'll see, Lincoln, you and your lady. By the way, she's lovely. It's easy to see why you're smitten. You think we'll be long catching up to Crazy Horse?"

"Only as long as he wants us to be."

"I don't understand."

"We haven't been on the road an hour yet, but I guarantee he already knows we're on the way. He'll know where we assemble and when. What our strength is. Our firepower. When we pull out and where we are from then on practically every step of the way."

"Good God. If he knows all that, what's to prevent him from ambushing us?"

"Nothing I know of. There's only one thing in our favor, one thing that begins to approach evening things up. When we leave Fetterman, our scouts will precede us by a day's march. We'll get back a steady stream of reports. And if the reports of his numbers are anywhere near accurate, he'll be leaving a wide trail. He probably has women and children with him. He won't try to ambush us with them nearby. What he may do is try to lead us into a trap of some sort. What we have to do is track him down and meet with him before he decides to attack."

"What can you possibly say to him to change his mind?"

"Not much, I'm afraid. Look—"

Directly overhead a lone buzzard carved the blue sky in circles a quarter mile in diameter. The sudden appearance of such an ominous omen was not lost on Rudy. His expression said more than any words he might utter.

* * *

180

CHEYENNE

Louis followed the column's dust for a couple hundred yards, leaving his mother and Lorna standing in shadow at the edge of the now deserted parade ground. Mona's eyes were downcast when she wasn't looking off apprehensively after Louis, making sure he didn't wander too far from the post.

"I let Rudy go as easily as if I'd asked him to go to the store for me," she said grimly.

"He wanted to," said Lorna.

"He has no experience fighting, he's not trained for it. As long as I've known him I don't think he's fired a gun more than six times." Mona had been aimlessly toeing the dusty ground. She looked up, her eyes steeped with worry. "It's going to be terribly dangerous, isn't it?"

"It may not be dangerous at all, not if they don't catch up with them," rejoined Lorna.

"But they're bound to." Mona stared. Her eyes seemed to grow larger with every passing moment. "It doesn't worry you, does it?"

"Of course it does."

"You don't show it." Mona laughed thinly and waved to Louis to come back. "I wear my feelings on my sleeves. But I'm so afraid for him. I'm already worried sick. He never should have gone. I love him."

It seemed out of context, a strange thing to say, thought Lorna; it came out sounding as if she thought Lorna questioned her love and loyalty. Probably because of what had happened in Lincoln's quarters. Pity roused itself in Lorna's heart; the woman was suffering so, a keg of dynamite threatening to blow. This separation from her husband for heaven only knows how long could backfire. Instead of giving them a rest from each other, the suspense, the waiting, the strain could cause her to crack. She already had too many demons assaulting her without adding worry over him in battle.

Why, Lorna wondered, had she let Rudy go, even encouraged him? The answer was that he wanted to so desperately. Even had she wanted to, there was no way to prevent his going. He saw it as a God-sent opportunity to redeem himself in the eyes of his wife and son, and in his own. Was that his hope? From the little she'd seen of him, and what she'd heard from Lincoln, Rudy's chances of coming back a hero or even just a changed man were discouragingly slim.

Nevertheless, she could understand why he felt he had to go. Louis came up to them. His normally pale face was flushed with excitement.

"Oh, Mother, I wish I could go with them!"

"I'm glad you can't," said Mona, setting her arm around his shoulders and smiling out of the warmth of her heart for the first time that morning. "Mother needs you here. You're the man of the family while Daddy's gone." She smoothed the hair from his forehead and gazed off into the distance.

Jubal had gone off to Davisranch to pick up some lumber in the small wagon he had bought in Cheyenne the previous week. Left by himself to work on the house, Jeptha quickly became bored, and when Lorna didn't return from the fort, he decided to give in to his growing curiosity and ignore his father's warning. He took one of the five horses left behind and headed for Cheyenne. If Jubal got back before he did, he'd tell him he'd gone in to buy oats and bran for the horses. At that, he didn't feel any need to justify his visit. It was his father's decision to call him a man.

"I believe I'll have myself a drink of liquor in town," he said to the horse, patting its neck and heeling its barrel to pick up the pace.

Entering town leading his sweating horse, Jeptha surveyed his surroundings in wide-eyed disbelief. The ceaseless activity, the noise, the crush of so many unsavory men and women, the color, the electricity, mesmerized him. It was like being tossed into the most dangerous area in a jungle, surrounded by wild beasts and snakes, poisonous plants, menacing vines, thorn-studded shrubs, quicksand pits, and a host of other threats.

He hurried his step to the refuge of the nearest saloon, which happened to be the Capitol, one devoted more to gambling than drinking, which the owner considered only a sideline to bilking the unwary and naive faster and more thoroughly with poker, faro, dice, and roulette. The place was mobbed. Jeptha stood waiting his chance for sixteen inches of space at the bar, his right hand in his pocket clutching his money. While he waited he looked about. He had never seen so many pretty women together in one place in his life. Perhaps pretty wasn't the word, but they were clearly striving to make themselves look pretty with mascara, lipstick and powder, hair dye and bleach, and fetching costumes that left almost nothing to the imagination. They glided about, the ostrich feathers planted in their hair bobbing lightly, pausing to lean far enough over tables to show most of their charms, accepting drinks from customers, laughing gaily, clutching inviting arms, and now and then stuffing paper bills down their cleavages.

Jeptha had never seen such goings-on; he could feel his cheeks redden and sweat beads warm his upper lip. He finally made it up to the bar, feeling for and finding the rail with one foot and separating a half dollar from the change buried with the few bills he was carrying deep in his pocket.

"What'll it be?" growled the bartender, eyeing him so sternly Jeptha felt he'd been caught with his fingers in the man's billfold.

"Ah . . ."

"Speak up, ain't got all day."

"Hey, Jack, two more gins down here!" called a man four down on Jeptha's left.

"Comin' right up. Speak up, boy."

"Whisk—scot—bourbon. Bourbon."

"You sure? You don't sound like you are."

"Bourbon."

A tumbler was set sloshing in front of him.

"One dollar," said the bartender.

"A dollar? For one drink?"

"Welcome to Cheyenne, pilgrim."

Jeptha recovered, paid, and picked up his glass. The man to his right bolted his drink. The man to his left did likewise. A man drinks a man's drink in manly fashion, reflected Jeptha. He stiffened, drew in a cavernous breath, and bolted his bourbon. And exploded in a fit of coughing so severe it all but split his throat. The man to his left clapped him on the back repeatedly, the man to his right shoved a glass of water at him. Jeptha downed it in one gulp. By now he was the target of everybody's laughter. His cheeks flushed with embarrassment, and his eyes watered so he could scarcely see. His mouth and throat burned so furiously and insidiously he had to pant like a blown mustang.

"Drink it slow, boy," said the man to his left.

"Now you knows why they calls it firewater," said the man to his right, his round face pink from laughing.

Before Jeptha could move to stop him, the bartender refilled his glass.

"One dollar."

Intimidated by his scowl, Jeptha couldn't even murmur protest as he fished for another dollar and laid it on the mahogany. Then he picked up his drink and retreated, slinking out of the pack toward the rear of the establishment. He found his way to a circle surrounding a whirling roulette wheel. Watching the ball dance and click, he tightened the bolts of his resolve and began slowly sipping his drink. Even in tiny amounts it tasted like scalding, rotten cider, but he made up his mind to swallow every drop if the last one killed him! He eyed the deep amber, brackish-looking liquid and past it at the bouncing white ball and felt eyes on him. Slowly he lifted his own to meet them. On the other side of the wheel, dressed in a black silk and sequin gown so tight it looked stuck to her willowy, well-endowed form, stood an almond-eyed beauty with the rosiest, fullest, most sensuously inviting lips he had ever seen. They were the focal point of her beautiful face. They were so striking her other features seemed to pale and blur. They beckoned, invited, promised wild, sinful, scandalously tempting acts and experiences that set his imagination whirling. And as he gazed, her full lips rose at the corners in a smile, revealing shining, perfect teeth. A laugh like a small silver bell floated from her mouth, and she turned to say

something to a tall, dour, expensively dressed man standing beside her. He smiled.

They're talking about me, thought Jeptha self-consciously. It didn't bother him. What did was that his
heart had shattered. Suddenly he was consciously striving
to keep from trembling, aware that the surging of the
drink in his glass would betray the effect her presence
was having on him. As if his face hadn't already given
him away!

There was only one thing for it. He eyed his tumbler
again, he'd sipped very little, lowering the level less than
a quarter inch. Again he took a deep breath and hurled it
down. He suffered, he died, but did not cough, gasp, or
react in any way. But even as he resumed breathing,
sucking air in to cool his blazing throat, the bourbon
struck bottom. Nausea spread and rose swiftly from the
pit of his stomach; dizziness fuddled his brain. The spinning ivory ball split into two balls, and each of these into
two: four balls whirling, circling four wheels, four of
everyone on the opposite side of the table, including her.
His stomach flipped and became a bucket, upended and
pouring out nausea, his brain spun wildly, blackness rose
like a tidal pool before his eyes. He plunged. The last
sight that registered was the revolving ceiling. The last
sound he heard was the mumble of voices giving way to a
chorus of raucous, derisive laughter.

When he came to it was to the chilling discovery that
his head was split cleanly in two. His brain had been
bisected as well. Furious and unabating pain arced between the halves. He was unable to focus in the dim
light, and dared not fill his lungs for fear of aggravating
the pain. He had to settle for timorous gasps, getting just
enough air to keep from slipping back into unconsciousness.

Gradually he found himself able to breathe deeper; it
dulled the pain, it drew together the halves of his skull,
restoring his brain. The ache that lingered now began
seeping upward to and out of his eyes, swelling them in
their sockets. He foolishly tried to rise on one elbow. A
gentle hand pushed him back down. He groaned and
covered his eyes with the heels of his hands. A hand

slipped under his head, raising it slightly, then a little more. He sipped the cool water. It revived and refreshed him. He tried to gulp it, but she took away the glass.

"Later."

The room was small, crushed by a low ceiling. In one corner stood a chinoiserie screen with silken underclothing draped over it. He could smell incense, a vague, pleasing, exotic odor insinuating itself on his nostrils. Both window shades were drawn to within six inches of the sills. He could see darkness outside.

He jerked upright, swinging his legs over the side of the bed, bracing himself with stiff arms to keep from toppling. The dizziness spent itself, leaving only his headache. It throbbed so he could almost hear ringing.

"What time is it?"

"Does it matter?"

He looked up and saw her for the first time. She wore a kimono splashed with enormous bright flowers on a black background. The sash was tightly secured around her waist; her breasts stood high, the material taut against them. She smiled.

"You are not much of a drinker, are you, *mon cher?* Why did you do it, bolt it down like it was lemon squash?"

"How did I get here?"

"Does that matter? It is my room." She laughed. "Don't look so, you are safe, I would not dream of taking advantage of you." She winked. "At least not in your present condition. And how is your present condition? Will you live?"

"I'm fine, thank you, all recovered. Thanks to you."

"A gentleman in distress, what else would a lady do? What is your name?"

"Jeptha Hunnicutt."

"Jeptha. Biblical. Wasn't he a great warrior? Are you?"

"I hardly know one end of a gun from the other. But I see you know your Bible, miss . . ."

"Delise Giradoux. My friends call me Emerald. Because I'm so fond of them." She laughed. "Alas, I'm afraid I am not in the Bible."

"You're French."

CHEYENNE

"My father. My mother was a Teton Sioux, but they were legally married. Both are dead. So, what brings you to Cheyenne, Mr. Jeptha Hunnicutt?"

He explained, leaving out Hannah's unfortunate death; he wanted the lady's respect rather than sympathy. He wanted her to see him as the man he felt he was in her presence—in her bed. She began buttoning his shirt for him, and this simple act had a nearly devastating effect on him. As she leaned close to him he could smell her perfume; it vied with the fragrance of the incense. A slender wisp of smoke rose lazily from the little Aladdin's lamp-shaped burner on the table. Her nearness, her fingers closing his shirtfront set his heart thudding. He wanted to throw his arms around her, but of course would never dare to. Her cheek was very close to his, those marvelous, awesomely beautiful lips gleaming in the faint saffron light of the single lamp on the night stand. She looked up from her task to smile at him. He had to get back, he thought. Jubal would be furious with him, and Lorna would be worried. But first he had to tear himself away. He suddenly wanted to stay forever.

"What am I doing?" she asked.

He swallowed, but he could not make his voice work. She began to unbutton the buttons she had already fastened. She undid them all and lifted back the halves of his shirtfront, baring his chest. She ran her hands slowly down it, then slipped his shirt over his shoulders and down his arms. The flat of her hand glided back and forth over his chest. He sat stiffly upright, scarcely daring to breathe. She lowered her head and kissed his chest lightly; he nearly cried out. He slipped a hand behind her lowered head to keep her lips against his flesh.

She raised her head and smiled. Then she sobered, and leaned forward slowly to kiss him. He plummeted into her mouth, overwhelmed and overcome by her kisses.

Holding his mouth to hers, she laid him prone, unbuckling his belt and drawing off his trousers, exposing him. He stared upward at the low ceiling, catching his breath fitfully; he could feel himself hardening. Her lips parted from his, moving down his neck and chest to his stomach and below. He closed his eyes. Then her mouth left him.

"Look, Jeptha Hunnicutt," she murmured. "See what I have for you."

He opened his eyes to find her standing by the bed smiling down at him. She undid her sash, the folds of the kimono separating. She lowered it over her gleaming white shoulders and dropped it soundlessly to the floor. Before he could speak, she dropped down beside him as lithely as a panther, setting her side firmly against his.

"Oh Lord . . ."

She tittered and took him in her arms, pressing her breasts against his heaving chest. Her smooth hands cradled his face, and she pulled him closer to kiss him again.

◄16►

The four barracks and seven officers' quarters of Fort Fetterman, situated just below the River Platte were isolated from the remainder of the post by an eight-foot-high plank fence. The fence was old, rotting, barely able to stand erect, and so dry that if one dark night it were to be set fire to by attacking hostiles in minutes it would have surrounded the living quarters with a wall of flame. The fort's complement had been almost tripled by the arrival of Colonel Rhilander and his detachment from Fort D.A. Russell and men from the other forts in southeast Wyoming. The force assembled under Rhilander's command totaled more than six hundred officers and men. The dozen or so Indian scouts, mainly peaceful Shoshone and Crow, had returned from the field to report that Crazy Horse and his Cheyenne allies were encamped near the south fork of the Cheyenne River, two days ride to the northeast.

Crazy Horse had been there for nearly two weeks, Rhilander learned, and there seemed little reason to expect him to move for a while.

"How long 'a while' is, who knows?" he remarked to Colonel Schwimmer and Mario Consolo as the three stood by the north gate of the fort corral and looked toward the thick stand of trees blocking view of the river beyond.

"You thinking of going up there and parlaying with him?" asked Mario.

A. R. Riefe

"If that's possible." Rhilander knelt and drew on the ground with a stick. "Let's say he's camped about here. What we could do is surround the area in force just to give him a good look at what we'll be preparing to throw at him. With our artillery, the two howitzers we brought with us and the two each from Fort Payne and Fort Reno prominently displayed."

"If he does agree to talk," said Rudy, "what will you say to him?"

"What we have to show him will be threat enough," said Rhilander. "I'd best be friendly and diplomatic. Our objective, obviously, is to get him to disband."

"Failing that, you can at least find out what he wants," ventured Consolo.

"Mario, what he wants is for the whites, soldiers, and settlers alike to pack up and leave Wyoming." Rhilander chuckled thinly. "Somehow I can't picture myself agreeing to that. Still, we should talk before he pulls out."

"What do the scouts say about that?" asked Rudy.

"They'd only be guessing, unless they can crawl inside Crazy Horse's head. Mario—"

"Sir?"

"Inform all officers that we'll be meeting at sixteen hundred hours in that empty building down by the magazine. When you've done that, get with Captain Murphy, the supply officer, and the two of you get up a list of what we have on hand: weapons, ammunition, food, blankets. A rough estimate will do. Tell Lieutenant Crispin and Sergeant Bullard they'll be in overall charge of horses and mules. Every animal is to be checked for fitness and condition. Lame shanks and the sickly we don't need. That's all."

Consolo saluted, Rhilander flipped acknowledgment.

Tashunka Witko, whom his enemies called Crazy Horse, was unaware that some West Point military instructors were already calling him the greatest Indian cavalry tactician who ever lived. This praise would not have impressed him, for he held an implacable hatred toward all whites, and their words—whether complimentary or unflattering—held no meaning for him. He was not yet twenty-seven years old, but already an Oglala *potanka*, warrior chief. He sat in the open in front of his tepee, surrounded by the stink of rotten meat and body odor, with his father Worm, the seven-foot-tall warrior Touch-the-Clouds, and Dull Knife, a Cheyenne chief, who had joined his warriors with the Sioux.

The four of them were painted for war, Crazy Horse displaying lightning-flash marks and spots denoting hail. The body of a freshly killed hawk lay by his side. He would carry it into battle to draw its quickness, courage, and strength from it. He also had a bright red trade blanket that he would use as a cape.

Had he not been painted for war, had he worn white man's clothing instead of buckskins and moccasins, he might easily have been taken for one of his blood enemies. His hair was not Indian black but light brown, his skin pale, his eyes not dark brown but blue.

The conversation focused on one point: the six hundred newly arrived soldiers assembled at Fort Fetterman, their howitzers, Spencer repeating rifles, the imminent threat they posed, and what should be done to neutralize them. Numerous suggestions had been thrown into the pot of discussion, but all of them were discarded. The last word was Crazy Horse's. He stuck his knife in the ground.

"When its shadow is as long as it is high, we go," he said.

"To attack Fort Fetterman?" Worm asked in undisguised surprise.

The fear in his father's tone irritated Crazy Horse.

"To attack the box where the soldiers sleep," he responded, smiling icily.

Cryptic as it was, this answer was all the explanation his listeners would get. He rose, picking up his red robe and tying two of the ends around his neck. Then, using rawhide thongs, he fastened the dead hawk to his side. This done, he surveyed the camp. All eyes were on him expectantly, all his men painted for war, standing motionless, holding their breaths, waiting for his order.

A. R. Riefe

"Commah-dawa. Commah-ah-acha-ah, nema pah!"

The roar that went up frightened the gaunt-ribbed dogs lying by the cook fires and startled the squaws and children. But when understanding dawned on them they smiled, and the boys joined their fathers and older brothers in the cheering and whooping.

It was past midnight. Rhilander had slept and awakened, and now lay unable to fall back to sleep. He thought about Lorna, missing her desperately, wondering if she missed him. Love was as consuming as the poets contended it was; it flowed through his veins and filled his heart. He also wondered about Mona Schwimmer, and whether Lorna and she had gotten to know each other. What a strange and strained relationship Rudy and Mona had. Like teetering on a tightrope, each holding back from the other, guarding their secrets, unable to communicate.

He propped himself up and looked over at Rudy snoring softly. Whether they met with Crazy Horse or not, there was bound to be a battle. He'd have his hands full keeping an eye on things, so it would be impossible to watch Rudy. He'd be on his own.

Poor man, he thought, with his conscience harder on him, more demanding of him than his wife and son ever could be. He had noticed that neither had said good-bye to him with any reference to what he would be going up against. Mona had not cautioned him to be careful, Louis hadn't asked him to bring back an Indian knife or some other souvenir of battle as most boys would have.

Sleep continued to elude him. He couldn't rein his thoughts. He got up, found a stale and somewhat frazzled cigar at the bottom of his bag, and lit it. Sitting at the foot of the bed, he could look out the window at the black night: no stars, no moon. Beyond the fence the flagpole rose, piercing the gloom, the wind snapping its rope. Mario had given him the report on supplies he'd worked up with Captain Murphy; Crispin and Bullard had yet to finish their inspection of the horses and mules.

They'd have to before tomorrow night. At six the following morning they'd be pulling out.

It was all so different now, he thought, going up against the hostiles, knowing she was back there waiting, worrying. Before, when he'd had no one, it seemed far easier. If he were killed he'd be leaving no one behind to mourn and suffer. It did seem an unfair burden to put upon her, a penalty she had to pay for loving him. It was different in other ways. In a sense their love for each other divided him; part of him was still back there.

For the first time since enlisting he had begun to think about getting out. Before Lorna he had no reason to even weigh such a decision; now . . . The Army was a miserable life for a woman, for the Molly O'Flaherty-Hannigans, the Mona Schwimmers. Whatever a man's rank, the life he forced upon his wife and children was not the life women would choose for themselves—which accounted for the number of divorces and desertions. Harvey Philips's wife hadn't left him so much as she had the Army. She couldn't stand the regimentation, the living conditions, the caste system that made it mandatory to snub the wives of the noncoms and enlisted men, the absence of feminine frills that so delight a woman.

It was no life for Lorna. She'd try to fit it, but his conscience wouldn't let him encourage her. She was too free spirited to conform.

He drew on the cigar, only to discover it had gone out. He dropped the stub in the fire bucket. Outside low in the sky he spied a shooting star. No, shooting stars aren't orange. Another, another. Rifles cracked. The two guards on duty at the palisades gate were easing it open to see what was going on. He threw up the window.

"Close that gate! That's an order! Move!"

They hurried to comply. He opened the door and shouted the building awake. Other doors opened almost immediately. Rudy was awake, rubbing his eyes.

"Get your clothes on quick!" burst Rhilander. "You wanted action, it's here."

Fire arrows stitched the sky over the fence. One, then another thudded against the building. Men were running

A. R. Riefe

back and forth with sloshing water buckets, yelling, confused, frightened. Rhilander and Rudy fumbled on their
clothes, drew on their boots, and ran out. A sergeant
came rushing up saluting.

"Indians, sirs, attacking quarters as a diversion, sirs, to
raid the corral!"

"Bastards," muttered Rhilander.

The bugler was sounding assembly. Half-dressed men
came running into formation. Colonel Whiteside, a gruff,
white-haired, burly bear, began yelling them to action.
The gate was pulled open. Outside, a horde of warriors
armed with bows, lances, a few ancient Henrys, and a
few modern Spencers spread the width of the grove of
trees just beyond the corral. A scattered few were climbing into it; others were working at the gate. Rifle fire
killed each group of three or four attempting to break the
chain locking the gate to the post. Inside the horses
milled about wide-eyed with terror, neighing nervously.

The attackers, having showed their considerable strength,
now retreated to the cover of the trees, leaving the next
suicide squad to work on the gate. Meanwhile, the few
savages who had gotten over the fence and among the
horses were using them as cover while they smashed and
removed boards, opening an exit. The fear-stricken horses
surged forward, stampeding through it, the crush of their
bodies knocking over the entire north side of the corral.

The soldiers did not stand and ogle, even though they'd
been surprised. For the moment the horses were lost.
Any attempt to check their flight before they vanished
into the trees would only endanger them. Colonel Whiteside
concentrated on the grove and the attackers now concealed behind trees or crouching in the underbrush. The
hail of fire arrows continued. The bucket brigade drowned
every blaze before it could take hold, except those ignit-
ing the barracks nearest the corral, closest to the marks-
men. It went up like a haystack, the last few occupants
fleeing just in time.

The howitzers were brought up. The first salvo, three
of the six pieces discharging case shots, stirred havoc
among the attackers. Trees toppled, and Indians fled

194

screaming and splashing across the river to their waiting ponies. Swinging sabers and firing as they moved forward, the troopers pursued on foot. Rhilander and Rudy ran with Mario Consolo.

"Get the horses there!" shouted Rhilander.

Many had gotten as far as the trees and now stood frozen out of fear of the carnage surrounding them. A twelve-pound ball toppled a large cottonwood, striking one horse flush in the haunch, buckling its legs, and killing it.

But now, thanks mainly to the impact of the howitzers, the tide had swung in favor of the troopers. As they streamed through the trees in pursuit, scores of horses were caught and mounted, many double. The few men unable to mount moved ahead on foot, splashing through the shallow water. And the night air rang with the screams of the Indians punctuated by shots and the sporadic thunder of the howitzers.

Rhilander studied Rudy askance as they rode side by side, trying to figure what was passing through his mind. He appeared to be enjoying himself, eager to catch and engage the hostiles. But he had yet to be shot at or even directly threatened. The true test was still to come.

They rumbled north toward Box Creek, the fleeing Indians pounding a path a hundred yards wide over blue grama and blue grass, needle and wheat.

Consolo came riding up alongside Rhilander.

"I guess this means you're not going to get to talk to Crazy Horse after all," he said, grinning. "It looks like he's not in the mood."

"Me either," muttered Rhilander.

The glare of the rising sun turned the sky white even before the sun could be seen. Crazy Horse had not slept, nor had Dull Knife or Touch-the-Clouds, yet none of them showed the slightest fatigue; they were alert and ready for the next phase of the encounter. Crazy Horse had ordered a halt on the north side of Box Creek behind a natural fortress of low hills flanked to the east by a shallow gorge. There were few trees, but sagebrush abounded, thick masses of it ascending the hills and girdling the level spot in the center where the Sioux warrior of warriors had spread his red trade blanket. He, Dull Knife, and Touch-the-Clouds sat cross-legged on three sides, leaving one side open for summoned subchiefs to approach.

Crazy Horse was annoyed and disappointed. He had been grumbling to himself ever since they had stopped to take temporary refuge and work out a strategy for dealing with their pursuers. The sleeping fort had reacted to the allies' attack quickly. The corral had been emptied of horses, but the howitzers and repeating rifles had driven the braves back before the soldiers' mounts could be taken away.

"About half of them found horses," said Dull Knife. "Many double mounted. They are slow, but they are coming."

His words came slowly from low in his throat; he was at least ten years older than Crazy Horse, more experienced in battle, a longtime leader of his people. Still, he did not seem to resent the younger man's superior position. If he was secretly envious, he did not show it. He never raised his voice in anger or argument, and for that reason everyone listened when he spoke; whatever he said in serious discussion was said only after profound thought and consideration.

He had led his people in many battles, not always successfully, but never without courage and intelligence. He was of medium height and build, unprepossessing in appearance, but his deep, commanding voice set him apart from his warriors. One other thing served to confirm his status, the single withered scalp hanging from his belt sliced from the head of a cavalry lieutenant colonel, the luckless officer's silver stars sewn on the inside. And it was Dull Knife's engraved steatite buffalo bowl peace pipe that Crazy Horse had smoked when the two agreed to join forces against the white intruder.

Touch-the-Clouds was all height, sinew, hatred for the whites exceeding even that of his two companions, and an eye with a rifle that amazed all who had seen him shoot. His weapon was a battered, tack-studded, breech-loading Christian Sharps, a buffalo gun boasting a phenomenal range. "Shoots today, kills tomorrow." His prize war trophy, however, frustrated him; rarely could he fire it, simply because the .50 caliber ammunition was so hard to come by.

Crazy Horse liked both his companions of the red blanket. More important, he trusted them. Having a common enemy was perhaps the surest guarantee of loyalty. Loyalty he demanded, unquestioned and steadfast, and he got it.

But at the moment his temper appeared on the verge of giving way. Dull Knife could see it.

"They are about two hand-swings of the sun behind us," he said. He pointed to the northeast. "There is a hill just beyond the water that winds like a snake. A hill with many boulders and ravines, good hiding places, perfect for ambush."

Crazy Horse ignored his words. "I want ten of your dog soldiers."

He drew with his finger on the blanket. "The soldiers will come up here and cross the creek."

He pointed to his left. "We will be moving toward that cloud there."

He pointed in the opposite direction. "Your men will show themselves there."

"Decoys," interposed Touch-the-Clouds.

Crazy Horse nodded. "Pretending to be wounded stragglers. The soldiers will catch up with them."

"And shoot them," said Dull Knife resignedly, looking down at the blanket.

"Then continue in the direction they are heading, thinking we are up ahead," Crazy Horse went on.

"Why not stay here?" asked Touch-the-Clouds. He gestured their surroundings. "There is good cover here, a good place to defend—"

Crazy Horse scowled contemptuously. "Defend? Attack is what we must do, and cut them down before they can fire their cannon." His face softened as he looked toward Dull Knife. "Your hill up ahead will be our ambush for them, and before the sun is overhead I promise you another officer's scalp for your belt."

Rhilander was having second thoughts over his snap decision not to bring at least one howitzer with them. But double-riding had slowed the pursuit as expected, and hauling howitzers would have reduced the pace to a walk. The horses were tiring fast as they splashed across Box Creek. The weary troopers assembled on the opposite bank around Rhilander and the other officers. Colonel Whiteside was not among them, having remained to protect his post with a skeleton force.

"They been leaving us a trail as wide as Wyoming," said Mario Consolo.

Rhilander's attention was on the ground. "Only up to here. From the look of it, they got this far and scattered." He smiled grimly. "Or so he'd have us think."

"Colonel, sir." A baby-faced lieutenant of dragoons had come bustling up, sweeping nimbly down from his saddle. He pointed northwest. "It's them, sir!"

As one man, the body of troopers came alive.

"Hold it!" boomed Rhilander. "Lieutenant Crispin, Sergeant Bullard, go have a look. Come right back, make it fast, take care."

Their horses sprinted away and back they came before the second hand on Rhilander's watch could complete its circle.

"Stragglers, Colonel," said Crispin.

They caught up with the ten Cheyenne easily. They were spread out, each one separated by a distance that prevented their talking to one another in normal voices. They staggered, exhausted, and dragging themselves. They were quickly rounded up. Only three turned out to be actually bleeding, and from what Rhilander could see their wounds were minor.

"Decoys," he said. "You, I'm talking to you. Where's Crazy Horse?" He mimed a headdress and pointed in a number of directions.

The brave looked barely sixteen, skinny as a pole, and unarmed. He'd lost one of his moccasins. He was filthy, his legs caked with dust halfway up to his knees. He sneered and spat. Sergeant Bullard moved forward and cuffed him, knocking him over.

"As you were, Bullard!" snapped Rhilander.

"Where is your chief?" asked Rudy, obviously feeling the need to take an active part.

"Never mind," said Rhilander. "Wherever any of them point, they'll be just throwing us off the track. Mario."

"Sir?"

"Assign four men to take them back to Fetterman."

"Take them back?" Consolo asked.

"You heard me. Rope them together. If they don't get them there alive, they'll answer to me in spades. Get on it." Rhilander rose in his saddle. "Listen up, everybody. We'll keep going." A loud groaning swept through the ranks. "We'll split up. Major Daltry—"

"Sir?"

"You'll move northwest on a line with the southeast bend of the Powder River. Check your map and head straight for it. The rest of us'll head northeast. As we progress, obviously the distance between us will widen. Station outriders to maintain contact when we get out of sight of each other. We'll keep going till we see signs of them. Or until we reach Montana."

"The horses'll never make it," grumbled a man behind Rhilander.

"Who said that?" he snapped, swiveling about.

All eyes were on the culprit, who stared sheepishly at the ground. Rhilander glared.

"Dismount, trooper."

"Sir?"

"Get off your horse. Give the reins to a walker. Let's hope your boots are a decent fit."

Two scouts came galloping down out of the hills.

"No sign of 'em, sir," said the older one, a grizzled, red-faced, shabbily dressed man, and one of only two white scouts with the company. "Ground's hardpan, no grass, no sign of a track."

"Let's move out. You first, Major."

Rhilander frowned. They'd be riding into an ambush.

A. R. Riefe

He glanced back the way they had come. *He* was splitting his strength; was Crazy Horse? He sighed. It always came down to a guessing game.

"What are you thinking about?" asked Rudy.

Rhilander managed a wry smile.

Jubal was furious. He stood with his fists grinding his hips, scowling fiercely as Jeptha dismounted and came toward him. Lorna joined them.

"Where have you been? You weren't here when I got back from Davisranch and that was four hours ago."

"Daddy, please—" said Lorna.

"Stay out of this, little girl. I'm talking to you, boy."

"Man, remember?"

"*Man,* is it? When are you going to start acting like a man? And not like a snot-nosed schoolboy?"

"Daddy!" burst Lorna.

He waved her away and grabbed Jeptha as he passed, seizing his shirtfront and swinging him around.

"I'm talking to you!"

Jeptha pulled free. "You keep your hands to yourself, Jubal," he said tightly.

Jubal slapped him, sending him staggering to one side. Jeptha started for him. Lorna pushed between them.

"Stop it, both of you! Jep, where *have* you been? We've been worried sick."

"In Cheyenne," snarled Jubal. "Where do you think? Carousing, drinking, can't you smell? Carrying on, squandering money in some filthy hole—"

"Yes, I went to Cheyenne."

Jubal bristled. "I told you never to go near there. How dare you disob—"

"I go where I damned please!"

"Listen to him, cursing."

"I'm not a child, I don't have to answer to either of you. Get that through your head, *Father.* I'm a man!"

"Oh yes, keep saying it and maybe you'll believe it. Nobody else does. There's shame on your face and guilt in your eyes. From drinking, sinning, God knows what else. God help you!"

"Leave me alone, damn it!"

"Now he curses me to boot. Oh, I'll leave you alone. My pleasure. I'll not speak to you again. Get out of my sight and stay out!"

"Gladly!" burst Jeptha.

"Will you stop it? You sound like two bickering little boys."

But Jeptha had walked off in one direction and Jubal was walking off in the other.

The opposing sides came together on a battleground that turned out to be a boulder- and ledge-covered hillside overlooking the drying terminus of Cow Creek, twelve miles from the Box Creek hillsite. Rhilander's two columns had maintained contact with strategically positioned outriders. Crazy Horse's forces were firmly entrenched in the hillside. But the troopers had ventured too close. The Indians had opened fire. The bluecoats retreated, reassembled, and returned fire. Now all hell was jumping from the pit. Rifles cracked, smoke puffs ascended the bright sky, bows twanged ominously, arrows whirred, lances rattled to rest or found their way into dusty blue tunics. Lieutenant Crispin, standing near the center of the action, slashing with his saber, his face chalky with fear, took a lance thrown from so close and with so much force it passed through his chest and out his back six inches. Before he hit the ground Sergeant Bullard was on his assailant with his saber, cursing and hacking him, lopping one arm cleanly from his shoulder, then running him through. Vengeance his, he swung about holding his dripping saber high in triumph, waving it, grinning, roaring, catching an arrow in the left eye, plowing four inches into his brain and freezing pure astonishment on his face at being so suddenly and rudely deprived of his immortality. As he fell he snapped the shaft in two, the broken end striking a rock and driving even deeper into his brain.

A burly dragoon, a corporal fully six-and-a-half feet tall, swung a saber in each hand, cutting a bloody swath through a dozen savages swinging war clubs just as wildly.

But the giant in blue appeared to be charmed. His long reach and the fury of his swinging kept every club at bay. None of them touched any part of him while he downed his attackers one after another.

Until he came up against a warrior six inches taller than he, wielding a nine-foot lance like a war club. Touch-the-Clouds accepted the corporal's challenge to duel, knocking away one of his sabers, sending it rattling down a ravine. In an instant the scene took on classical dimension. It was like two mythical giants fighting to the death over an innocent maiden chained to a nearby rock. The footing was uncertain; at any moment either could misstep, fall, and leave himself open to the other's death blow.

Rhilander and others on both sides stood watching them. Hand-to-hand struggles halted as everyone became absorbed in the contest. Both men were agile for their height, strong and seasoned fighters. Touch-the-Cloud's lance was tipped with steel, but he made no attempt to stab the corporal with it, contenting himself with parrying his every thrust—hoping, it seemed, to exhaust him. On and on they dueled, Touch-the-Clouds stony-faced, the corporal leering. Gradually it became not so much a duel of weapons but a deadly endurance contest. Which one's arms would give out first? Which weapon would fall?

They fought at a furious pace for nearly ten minutes before the corporal's arm began to slow, the point of his saber dip, the muscles of his jaw tightening perceptibly with the growing strain. And Touch-the-Cloud's parrying grew steadily weaker and more sluggish. Both were sweating profusely under the fierce sun. Rhilander and everyone else looking on could see the corporal had only six or eight more thrusts left in his arm. But as if to answer the colonel's concern, he promptly flipped his weapon to his other hand. In his left the saber was not nearly as effective, but good enough to enable him to keep on fighting.

If there was an edge in the contest it went to Touch-the-Clouds; Rhilander figured his lance must weigh less than half as much as the saber, and two handing it was not as strenuous as the corporal's thrusting. Touch-the-Clouds began to close in, forcing his opponent to retreat, feeling with one foot behind him for level ground.

Finding it, setting both feet, he roared to the attack, driving his blade forward with both hands like a medieval two-handed sword. Touch-the-Clouds skipped nimbly back to avoid the thrust, bringing his lance down hard against the blade.

The lance snapped in two, but the corporal's next thrust caught the warrior just under the heart; blood gushed from it, draping his upper body in crimson as Touch-the-Clouds sank to his knees and fell over dead.

For a long moment everyone stood motionless. Then, as if obeying a signal, the battle resumed on every side.

The troopers held a decided edge in firepower and used it to advantage. At their officers' direction they dispersed, many retreating down the slope to the creek and spreading out beyond range of the savages' arrows. They began picking them off at a distance with stunning accuracy.

The battle raged for another half hour until a shout went up from above. Immediately the Indians began fleeing up the slope and over the top. In seconds every one had vanished, leaving their dead and wounded and their enemies too exhausted to give chase. Rhilander plopped down onto a rock, his smoking revolver feeling as if it weighed thirty pounds. He had taken an arrow through his jacket sleeve, but luckily it had only passed through the fabric. He had lowered his head and was breathing deeply when he stiffened abruptly. Consolo stood looking down at him.

"You okay?" he asked.

"I'm fine," responded Rhilander. "You . . ." He stopped short. "Where Rudy?"

"I haven't seen him."

Rhilander was on his feet looking about, shading his eyes from the glare. "My God!"

"I'll go find him," said Consolo.

"He's dead, he must be," said Rhilander. "Damn it, I knew I should have stayed with him."

Consolo went off to look.

Trooper casualties turned out to be surprisingly light. Only thirteen had been killed and about thirty seriously wounded, but most were able to travel back to Fetterman. The Indian dead count totaled well over a hundred. The hillside resembled a burial ground, its contents pushed up out of the graves by some subterranean force. Every rock Rhilander could see around him glistened with blood; discarded and lost bows and lances littered the area. A dying brave keening loudly, begging the attention of the Great Spirit, raised one arm feebly then collapsed, as if to signify the end to the confrontation.

Consolo came back to where Rhilander sat resting. "You'd better come, Lincoln."

"I knew it!"

"He's not dead, not even wounded as far as I can make out."

Rudy was hunched between the walls of a shallow ravine, his knees drawn up to his chin, forearms clasped tightly around them. He was shuddering violently, moaning, his eyes wide and wild. Sputum dripped from one corner of his mouth and his face gleamed with sweat. As Rhilander stared down at him he began to twitch convulsively. Rhilander knelt and lay a hand on his shoulder.

"Rudy—"

Rudy jerked his head and looked straight at him, through him without seeing.

"It's okay, it's all over."

Rudy's jaw dropped, he gasped and began screaming, shrieking like a woman in agony. Rhilander jumped down and gripped his shoulders, shaking him until he finally quieted down. But he only resumed his twitching and moaning. This, thought Rhilander, was fear so powerful, so all-consuming it stopped the brain and set the nervous system thrashing about uncontrollably in the confines of the body.

But it was Rudy's eyes that frightened Rhilander, evoking more than pity; fear for his sanity, concern that the shock he had undergone and that still gripped him was so severe he would never recover from it.

He continued to shudder and twitch, but his moaning

gave way to quiet sobbing, then whimpering. Strangely, no tears came. His eyes remained enormous and wildly gaping, with no hint of recognition in them. And they looked dead.

"Poor bastard," murmured Consolo.

He looked mutely toward Rhilander. The colonel paid no attention, avoiding his eyes; he was still trying to get Rudy under control. It didn't appear possible. He finally gave up. They stood looking down at him still sitting huddled between the walls at the mercy of his monster, staring, shuddering, whimpering.

"We'll have to clean up here," said Rhilander. "Let the men rest. We'll go back to Fetterman. Short horses as we are, there's no sense going on. We'll catch up with Crazy Horse another day." He nodded toward Rudy. "Give him an hour to calm down, then collect a couple of men and the three of you take him back."

"To Fetterman."

"Home. Russell. He's had the baptism he wanted. He'll never ride out again, not as long as I'm in charge. This is my fault, you know."

"Bullshit, how could you know it'd do this to him?"

"I thought about it. I did. The point is he shouldn't have come," said Rhilander. "I should have made him stay at Russell. I could have."

Consolo shook his head, disagreeing. "You're wrong. If he didn't come this time, he'd come the next. This would have happened sooner or later."

"Take him back to his wife and his boy. Poor man."

"He couldn't run," said Consolo. "Look at him, he can't even stand."

As the lieutenant said it, Rhilander thought he saw disdain in his expression. When he responded, he was careful to make it sound like an order.

"Pity him, don't condemn him."

"There but for the grace of God, I know," said Consolo.

"I mean it. It's not his fault God didn't give him a stomach. I've never known anybody who wanted one more."

"God doesn't give guts, Lincoln, you build your own."

"He tried. You be patient with him. When he comes out of it he'll be so embarrassed he'll despise himself. Help him. And no talking behind his back. He's shouldered himself the heaviest cross a soldier can bear. The last thing he needs is criticism and ridicule. I don't have to draw pictures. And one thing more."

"Yes?"

"Strip him of his pistol," said Rhilander. "Now, before he comes around."

"Won't that be like telling him we don't trust him not to kill himself?"

"It will, he's not stupid. But better that than he do it."

"If you say so—"

"That's an order, Lieutenant." He softened his face and his tone. "A favor to me if you like. I've enough on my conscience already, thank you."

17

For four days father and son refused to speak to one another, even though they worked side by side. The house was so near completion that Jubal began working on the barn. Lorna tactfully resisted the temptation to bring them together by the scruffs of their necks and cajole or browbeat them into agreeing to a truce. Given a couple more days, she reasoned, the bruises from the harsh words would fade, the wounded pride would mend, and reconciliation would take place.

She left them in the morning to see Mona at Fort Russell. She found her with Louis; they seemed in good spirits, as if they'd made a pact not to worry about Rudy. In Lorna's mind she was sure Lincoln would be looking out for him, no matter how busy he got.

Two days earlier she had gone to the fort and was with Mona when they ran into Harvey Philips. They'd had a long talk about the mission, and the major had assured them it would be nothing like Bull Run. He didn't try to fit either of them with rose-colored glasses, he simply set out the situation and examined the most logical possibilities and consequences in such a campaign. He praised Lincoln's experience, abilities, courage, and leadership, adding that Colonel Schwimmer and the others were fortunate to be able to serve under him.

Lorna felt better about things afterward. She took a vow of optimism when she returned home that afternoon.

She and Mona walked toward the creek, Louis trailing

behind, talking to himself as usual, stopping to examine insects and plants. Why he would want to tag along, Lorna couldn't understand. There was much about him that mystified her, leaving her wondering why he was so different from boys his age. But there he was, a few yards behind them, carrying on like an eight-year-old.

"It's not that I'm optimistic," said Mona. "It's more like I'm worried out. You can only worry so much before you begin to feel foolish. It always happens to me, although I've never had to contend with Rudy's going off to battle Indians."

"They still may not."

"But he wants to, and if not this time, it'll be the time after. Men amaze me. Climbing mountains, beating their way through jungles, running at cannons. Actually it's not the need to prove themselves *to* themselves, you know, it's an absolute compulsion. If they don't, what's left but that they lay down and die? I have three brothers, all the same. My brother Andrew, he's the oldest, decided he just had to fight a bull. Can you imagine? Can you imagine you or me, any woman, just having to fight a bull? So desperately that your life stops right there until you do?"

"And did he?" Lorna asked.

"He did. He was gored and he'll never walk again, but he fought his bull."

"That's amazing."

"I don't think so, I think it's common as clams. My husband's out fighting his bull right now. Let's go back and have tea, shall we? I'm in the mood for it. Louis, dear heart, we're going back now. For tea."

"Oh good."

Lorna had never been in the little house before. It was as barren inside as out, the walls bare boards, an oval rag rug on the floor, not a swipe of paint anywhere, not even pictures on the walls, with the exception of Rudy's and Mona's wedding picture. The place felt more like a temporary stopover than a home. Lorna imagined all the officers' quarters looked pretty much the same, with each wife gussying things up as best she could in direct relation to her husband's rank and salary. She had no idea what Lincoln was paid, but even if he'd been a general and in a position to buy the finest furnishings, there was no way she could see to transform these dismal surroundings into a cheerful, comfortable home.

Outside, horses were pulling up. Louis ran to the window, nearly spilling his tea.

"It's Daddy! Mother, it's Daddy!"

"It can't be," said Mona. But, Lorna noted, her expression was hopeful.

With the colonel was Mario Consolo and two privates. All four looked as if they'd been riding for days, dust-caked and weary, their horses on the brink of collapse. Rudy dismounted, said something to the others, returned their salutes, and off they rode. Mona and Louis ran out to welcome him; Lorna stood in the doorway, looking off toward the rapidly vanishing lieutenant and his companions, wishing Consolo had stayed long enough to answer a few questions. But Rudy would know what had happened, how Lincoln was. She turned her back to give husband and wife privacy as they kissed.

"Oh, Rudy, darling."

"Now now, my dear, let's have no gushing. This is cause for celebration, right? Louis, my boy, have you been taking good care of your mother?"

"Yes, Daddy. Did you fight the Indians? Did you kill some? Was it terrifically dangerous?"

Rudy laughed and seemingly for the first time noticed Lorna inside the house. "Miss Hunnicutt, good news. We did engage the red rascals, a few casualties, very few. Lincoln is just fine, not a scratch."

"Thank God. Where is he now?"

"Back at Fort Fetterman, I believe."

"Will he be coming back here soon?"

"I don't know what the plan is." He smiled affably and winked. "Not my department, remember?"

"Are you wounded?" Mona asked him.

"No no," said Rudy hastily.

"Why did you come back?"

"Had to. Got my taste of action. That's all I wanted.

A. R. Riefe

Besides, I've too much work back here to stay out in the field."

"You're sure you're all right?" Mona persisted.

"Don't I look it? I've never felt better. Just tired."

"What happened to your gun?"

"Lost in the fray, I'm afraid." He laughed lightly. "Somebody got a souvenir."

Louis was carrying the last of his father's gear into the bedroom. The boy was fairly exploding, he was so proud. Rudy seemed in a lighthearted mood, Lorna reflected, almost jocular. No doubt enormously relieved to get back without a scratch. She certainly would be!

"Did you bring me back a souvenir?" Louis asked.

"A scalp, perhaps?" Again Rudy laughed. "Too busy to think about souvenirs, my boy."

"Daddy's brought back the nicest souvenir he could, Louis," said Mona, brushing the boy's hair back from his forehead. "Himself unharmed, thank the Lord. Promise me never again, Rudy, please."

"I promise."

"Tell us everything that happened!" shrilled Louis.

"Patience, I will. Right now I'm going in to lie down before I collapse and you have to carry me in." He started toward the room.

"I'll be going," said Lorna. "Welcome home, Colonel," she called after him.

Mona signaled her to wait and went in after him. But in less than five seconds he was already lying facedown on the bed in a deep sleep. She pulled his boots off, covered him with a light blanket, kissed his cheek, and went out, closing the door softly. Lorna was standing outside the house with Louis. Mona joined them.

"He's already asleep," she said. "Don't go, you haven't finished your tea."

"I'm saturated I've drunk so much," said Lorna. She squeezed Mona's hands affectionately. "I'm so happy it all turned out fine."

"It did after all, didn't it? And I'm happy for you."

"Lincoln's not home free yet. Lord knows when he will be. I think I'll go pump Mario Consolo."

"Better hurry, before *he* falls asleep," said Mona laughingly.

She was ecstatic. And Lorna was happy for her; if only Lincoln would come back. She looked out the window wishfully. No sign of anyone.

"Can I go in and talk to Daddy, Mother?" Louis asked. "Please, please—"

"Not now, dear heart. We must let him catch his breath and nap a little. In a while."

"Oh rats!"

His mother eyed him. "Louis—"

It was as far as she got. The gun discharging inside the closed room sounded like a cannon fired down a well. It shook the entire house. Mona gasped. Louis screamed and covered his ears. Lorna blanched and stiffened, then rushed to the bedroom door, pushing it open a crack, then wide. Smoke came billowing out. The stink of cordite struck and stung her nostrils.

Rudy lay on his back on the bed, his arms outstretched. The smoking pistol was still in his right hand. The bullet had passed through his head, driving against the wall beside the bed, denting it slightly before dropping to the floor.

18

Crazy Horse, Dull Knife, and their followers fled north to the Powder River country and there dispersed, but only to temporarily thwart any organized pursuit. Rhilander and his men returned to Fort Fetterman. Scouts came drifting back with reports that Crazy Horse himself with a handful of followers had been seen camped near Nine Mile Creek, south of Meadow Creek, north of Dugout Creek, and even as far up the line as Wild Horse. Rhilander could only conclude that he was on the move, which served to reaffirm his decision to let him run for now. Given time, Crazy Horse would come to him. Not to parlay, to be sure, but to fight. His prediction was grounded in simple logic. The Sioux and Cheyenne and whatever other tribes they might gather to their war lance would not rest until the white man was driven from their lands.

The expeditionary force was dissolved. Rhilander and his men returned to Fort Russell four days after Rudy, Mario, and their escort had come back. Consolo and Harvey Philips met with Rhilander in the office, now his office once again, and told him of Rudy's suicide. Rhilander sat listening in shocked disbelief.

"Didn't I tell you to disarm him?"

"We did," said Consolo.

"He evidently had another pistol in his bedroom," said Philips. "Protection for his wife and son, obviously. I wasn't there, but we both talked to Miss Hunnicutt after.

Couldn't talk to Mrs. Schwimmer or the boy. They were both in shock."

"What did Lorna tell you?" Rhilander asked. "I mean, did he give any inkling—"

"That's just it," said Consolo. He stood looking out the window, his back to the others, his words muted. He too was devastated by the tragedy, in spite of his not being at all close to Rudy. "On the way back, by the time we got to the Laramie Mountains and started around them, he'd snapped out of it. He was perfectly calm and coherent. Mortally ashamed of himself, of course, but his spirits were up. I remember thinking it was almost like he was immensely relieved that it was over and that he'd come out of it alive. *How* didn't seem to matter."

"But you just said he was ashamed."

"Only at first. Within a couple hours—"

"Didn't it occur to you that he was putting on a show for you?" Rhilander asked.

"Sure it did, but it wouldn't have helped to tell him that. He talked and talked, he hardly stopped."

"Didn't he resent your taking his gun away?"

"Didn't say a word about it," said Consolo. "Just handed it over."

"He had no need to say anything, Linc," interposed Philips. "He knew he had the gun back here. I'll bet the second he snapped out of his fear he made up his mind to kill himself."

Consolo turned from the window and nodded. "And the way he was acting was just to keep us from suspecting."

Rhilander listened with one ear. He'd have to forward a written report to departmental headquarters describing the operation. And a separate report on Rudy. Better he submit it before it was asked for. What could he say? How would he describe his conduct, the sheer terror that sent him scurrying into hiding to sit jibbering and quaking?

He'd have to try and explain why Rudy had come back and killed himself, why no one anticipated it and taken steps to prevent it. C. C. Augur's successor as commander, whoever he was, would probably want to know why Rudy had gone along in the first place, why Rhilander hadn't ordered him to stay home. It was within his authority. And had he done so, Rudy would have had no option but to obey or go on report.

"Do either of you know where Lorna—Miss Hunnicutt, is now?" Rhilander suddenly asked.

"Probably in town," said Consolo. "Mrs. Schwimmer and the boy are taking the body back to some little burg near Omaha."

"Which train? What time?"

Consolo shrugged. From his expression Rhilander could see that Philips didn't know, either. The colonel got up.

"I'll be back in an hour. Take care of things for me. Jesus Christ, I hate this."

"Don't we all," said Consolo. "I didn't like the man, and it may sound stupid, but if he had to die, why couldn't it have been in battle?"

"You know something?" ventured Philips. "I don't think he wanted to kill himself."

Rhilander stared. "What are you talking about?"

"I think what he wanted to kill was his shame. He couldn't shed it, couldn't live with it, so why go on?"

"I think—" began Consolo.

"Who gives a bloody damn what either of you think!" snapped Rhilander. "The poor bastard's dead. Leave him in peace for christsakes, find something else to philosophize about."

Lorna, Mona, and Louis watched the coffin being loaded aboard the baggage car. The station platform was crowded. The laughing and shouting was loud and irritating. If Cheyenne knew about the tragedy, it quite obviously didn't care. Of course, thought Lorna, the town couldn't know and couldn't sympathize with the dead man's loved ones beyond glancing their way out of curiosity, noting their red eyes and sad faces. The whistle sounded two long blasts.

"Boarrrrd, all aboard!" shouted the trainman.

Lorna held Mona by the forearms and kissed her cheek. "Write me, please."

"I will."

"Promise."

"I promise."

Lorna put her arm around Louis. "I'll miss you both."

"I wish you could come with us, Miss Hunnicutt. Mother will miss *you* dreadfully, won't you, Mother?"

"Mmmm . . ."

Mona had emerged from her shock into a fog of sorts. She seemed to be mentally drifting. She was slow to respond, reluctant to talk at all. Louis was coming out of it much faster. He really hadn't known his father in the way most boys his age knew theirs, which seemed to be working in his favor. The pain of loss was there, but it wasn't as severe as his mother's and wouldn't last as long. He seemed more concerned with her suffering. Admirable, thought Lorna; it was also forcing maturity down his throat. Perhaps, she reflected, now that the mantle of man of the family had been placed on his shoulders, he'd be able to fill the role.

Mona was cried out. She looked past Lorna when she said her good-byes and thanked her for all she'd done for them both. Lorna watched them board, Louis's slender hands gripping the grab bars to pull himself up the steps, and decided this tragedy was an octopus, reaching forth with its tentacles into so many areas separate and apart from the suicide itself: into Louis's future; what was it to be without a father? Into Mona's bed without a husband. Into her conscience, where self-criticism for Rudy's action would linger and fester. Already regret over her failure to support their marriage was evident in the guilt in her eyes and voice.

Pausing on the vestibule plate, Mona turned and waved and tried desperately to smile, but could not. Lorna did and blew a kiss. They disappeared into the car.

The whistle sounded its double blast again. The last passenger hurried aboard, the last door slammed, steam whooshed from behind the wheels, and the train lumbered away, carrying grieving mother and son out of Lorna's world.

She stood watching the caboose vanish around a bend.

A. R. Riefe

She turned to go back to her waiting buggy parked at the front of the station. She stopped short.

Jeptha!

With a woman on his arm, a beauty, slender, expensively dressed, exotic and sophisticated. Far too worldly for a mere boy with barely one foot into manhood. They were talking and laughing. Lorna ducked behind the corner of the building, peering out. They seemed to be heading toward the center of town. Her arm slipped through Jeptha's and he patted her hand. He kissed her cheek, holding his lips against it. Not a friend-to-friend kiss, not the way he slowly brought his lips away and whispered something in her ear that caused her to laugh and shake her finger reprovingly.

"Jep Hunnicutt," murmured Lorna. "What in the world?"

19

She shuddered in his embrace and gasped lightly. What? he asked with his eyes.

"Nothing, it's like a current passed through me. It's you, that's the effect you have. Hold me tighter, Lincoln, it's been so long."

"Thirteen days, thirteen years."

They kissed. Sunlight splashed the wall at the foot of the bed. In the street below a gun went off; people were laughing, shouting. The crowd surged like a dam giving way under pressure. Another gun fired. Lorna and Lincoln heard nothing. Two hours earlier she had taken a room at the Meadowlark Hotel in the center of town. Lincoln had stationed himself in the lobby so that he could overhear the desk clerk telling her the room number and had come up the backstairs minutes after. Both confessed to feeling like sneak thieves, skulking about in a strange hotel, but it was the only way they could meet in privacy. He didn't want her coming to his quarters at the fort.

They had already made love, all but flinging themselves at each other in their eagerness. It seemed like a lifetime since last she'd felt him inside her. When he entered her, even though she tried to restrain herself, she could not. She justified her failure by telling herself that command of one's emotions was the last thing one should think about in the act; to think at all was unnatural.

Curiously, when it was over and they separated, inhibi-

217

A. R. Riefe

tion and modesty came winging into her conscience. Even before they sat up, kissed, and sat gazing adoringly at each other, her first thought was to pull the sheet over her bare breasts.

"Thirteen years," she murmured. "Lost, gone forever. Make love to me again, my darling. And again. We must never leave this room."

He laughed. "Please—"

She kissed him soulfully. "My husband."

"My beloved wife. And when can we get married? You promised when I came back."

"Next week," she replied.

"Why not tomorrow?" he countered.

"Patience, I have to make preparations. My wedding gown, the church, the minister. Next Saturday."

"That's nearly two weeks. *This* Saturday. I can get the church and minister—"

"Next."

She felt immensely content and sinfully happy. Then a thought came. She frowned and shook her head.

"What?"

She told him about seeing Jeptha earlier that day with the woman.

"Did he see you?" he asked.

"No, thank the Lord."

"Are you going to tell him you saw him?"

"No!" she burst.

"Why not, don't you think you should?"

"What if Daddy finds out from somebody else? I'd be the first one Jep would come storming to. Besides, it's none of my business."

Lincoln had lowered his head and begun picking aimlessly at the corner of the pillowcase. He avoided her eyes, which seemed to be asking for approval. He could not give it.

"He's your brother, darling. Sometimes you have to take risks in close relationships."

"I don't know about this."

"Who was the girl?"

"Woman," corrected Lorna. "I never saw her before."

218

CHEYENNE

She described her. She had not even finished doing so when he recognized her.

"Delise Giradoux. They call her Emerald."

"You know her?" Lorna was shocked.

"I don't *know* her, definitely not in the sense you imply."

"I'm not implying anything."

"Okay, okay." He went on. "She's a half-breed, woman of the world, an institution in the area."

She laughed. "You make her sound like a building. . She's beautiful."

It was acknowledgment of an obvious fact, not a compliment.

He nodded. "She's also dangerous. And notorious."

"Who *is* she? *What* is she, a prostitute?"

"Not exactly . . ."

"What does that mean? She either is or isn't."

"I wouldn't call her a prostitute, not the hog ranch variety at any rate."

"Some other variety . . ."

She was seizing on the subject like a starving dog snatches a bone. And getting more and more upset, the big sister girding for battle against the enemy that dare take advantage of little brother.

"She sleeps around," he went on, "but for a purpose, not a paper dollar. She's out to hook a rich man and take him for everything. I hear she's made a career out of loving, taking, and leaving. She went with a friend of mine for a while. A short while. A major's hundred and fifty a month pay is hen feed to her sort."

She bristled. "What in the world does she want with Jep?"

"A good time."

"Bitch!"

"Now, darling, pull in your fingernails. She won't hurt him." He smirked. "She *will* educate him. Oh my—"

"He doesn't need educating from her sort!"

"He's nineteen. Shouldn't he be the judge of what he 'needs'? It sounds like whether you like it or not, he wants to be educated. Oh my—"

" 'Oh my' what!"

"I'd love to be a fly on the windowsill when Jubal hears." He raised his eyes and whistled softly. She exploded.

"It's not funny!"

"I'm sorry, of course it's not. But honestly, there's no reason to worry. The worst he'll come out of it is sadder but wiser. In the meantime let him sow his oats. Look at it as a learning experience."

She turned from him and talked to the window. Her fury was building, her tone heavy with loathing when she spoke.

"She's twice his age," she said icily.

"She's about thirty."

"She *looks* twice his age."

"Kiss me," he said.

"No."

"No?"

"I'm too upset. He's such a hopeless innocent. Why can't he pull his nose out of a book long enough to see life as it really is and grow up? She'll break his heart. All she's doing is amusing herself, using him."

"He's certainly using her," he said.

"Don't be vulgar."

"Come on, loss of virginity isn't a capital crime. You want him to grow up, it's in the works."

She sighed. "I suppose," she said softly.

He turned her back so their eyes met. "It's his life, Lorna. He's got to do things his way even if he does them wrong. And he will with or without you or Jubal's approval or blessing."

"Talk to him, Lincoln, he'll listen to you."

"And what would I say, stay away from her? No, darling, I'll stick my nose in only if there's trouble."

"What trouble?"

"I don't know," he hedged uncertainly, feeling that he could kick himself for letting loose the word.

"What?"

"Nothing."

"What trouble!"

"Nothing, anything, how am I supposed to know?" He shook his head. "It's only that a woman like Delise Giradoux is no stranger to trouble. Hubert told me that at least two duels have been fought over her."

"What if one of her jealous old flames shoots him?" Her eyes were wide.

"That's nonsense. You don't really think he's going to get into a duel."

"He hardly knows one end of a gun from the other. Oh Lincoln, what are we to do?"

He was rapidly getting fed up with the whole thing. It simply didn't warrant such deep concern.

"Talk to him if you think it'll do any good," he said.

She brightened. "Maybe I'll talk to her. If she has a grain of decency, she'll let go of him." She darkened. "I can't, he'd never speak to me again."

"I'll talk to him," he said wearily. "Only at the right time, when we're talking about something else and I can slip into it comfortably. I wouldn't want to get off wrong with my future brother-in-law."

That seemed to satisfy her, if only for the time being. They kissed and lay back down, the sheet slipping from her breasts.

It felt glorious with him inside her. Sublime! His every gentle stroke increased the flush of excitement, and as he aroused her she felt more a woman, more in command of her sexuality.

He turned to her breasts, warming them with his touch. He kissed her nipples, her earlobes, her mouth, the palms of her hands, her inner thighs, and stroked her, stoking the fires. The flow she felt seemed to spring from her body and tint the walls and ceiling in a roseate hue.

And while he explored he whispered his love.

20

Jeptha Hunnicutt was in love. He had felt it with Salita Jane Tucker—the inability to touch the ground with his feet and the quickening of his heart at sight of her. But with Emerald it was different. He was. He felt years older than when the wagons were nearing Wyoming and the Indians massacred the Tuckers and the others. Now he was a man in love with a woman. Emerald thought of him as a man; he could see it in her smoldering almond eyes.

He considered buying a gun; every man in Cheyenne carried one, except Dr. Gogarty. Jubal didn't and probably wouldn't approve, nor would Lorna, but he didn't need their approval. Jubal was coming around; his father wasn't pleased with his son's newly found independent attitude, but he was beginning to accept it. He had little choice but to and, reflected Jeptha, maybe he even respected him for it. Although he'd never say so. Yes indeed, maybe he should start wearing a gun. He must ask Delise, she'd advise him.

He bounded up the stairs to her room. It was Sunday, a lovely day; they were going on a picnic down to a place she knew near Borie, just above the Colorado border. Her room was in the rear of the building and overlooked a small corral attached to the stable next door. As he neared the door he could hear arguing inside. A man. He raised his fist to knock but did not. He eavesdropped.

"You're going to learn to do as I tell you!"

He tried the door. It was bolted. He pounded on it. The man opened it. Black mustachios swept across his lip. He was in his gartered shirtsleeves, his flowered vest unbuttoned. His face was red from shouting. The sickly scent of cheap lilac came wafting out. Emerald came up and opened the door wider. She was still in her kimono, her hair not yet fixed, without makeup. One eye looked red and swollen.

"Jeptha . . ."

She looked surprised to see him as if, he thought, she'd forgotten they had a date. Her hand started for her eye self-consciously, then stopped. She glanced at the man filling the door.

"Come in," she said. "This is Mr. Freeling, an old friend. Oscar, this is Jeptha Hunnicutt."

O.K. Freeling, owner-manager of the Two Mile Ranch, greeted him effusively, seizing and pumping his hand.

"Pleased to meet you, son. You're the Hunnicutts who settled that land up above Bear Creek, right?"

"Yes."

He didn't like Oscar Freeling, didn't like his patronizing tone and look; he was laughing at him. The next thing he'd turn to her and accuse her of robbing the cradle. Jeptha set his jaw; how he'd love to smash the smirk from his face!

"Welcome to Wyoming. What are you and your dad going to do up there, cattle? Great cattle country."

"Your eye," said Jeptha to Emerald. "He hit you."

Again her hand started toward her eye. "It's nothing, a little misunderstanding."

"You like to hit women, do you? Does it make you feel big, superior?"

Freeling's smirk vanished. "Get off it, sonny, it's none of your business."

"I'm making it."

"Don't, Jeptha," said Emerald, eyeing him anxiously. "Please don't start anything."

"It appears it's already started." He scowled at Freeling. "Why don't you hit me? Come on."

Freeling chuckled brittlely. "Take it easy, sonny. I don't pick fights with striplings."

Jeptha smashed him in the jaw. Emerald screamed. Freeling staggered and retreated, his shocked expression quickly giving way to anger.

"You little snot . . ."

They were suddenly swinging toe to toe. Freeling was not as big, not nearly as fit or as fast, but he had no qualms about fighting dirty. He closed, feinted to distract Jeptha, and brought up his knee sharply. Jeptha's groin exploded in pain and down he went, groaning. Emerald screamed again and dropped down beside him. Freeling snickered, slammed on his hat, and went out.

"Are you all right?"

"The dirty scum . . ."

He sat up, his hands locked to his crotch. He was in agony, sweating and shaking.

"You're white."

She helped him to his feet and over to the bed. He sank wearily down.

"Let me get you a glass of water."

"No, I'm okay, it'll pass. It's already going away. Why did he hit you?"

"It's nothing."

"None of my business."

She had taken up her hand mirror and was examining her eye. "He's an animal. I try to keep out of his way, but it's impossible. *Sacre mere,* I won't be able to show myself on the street for a week this time."

"It's happened before? Who is he, what is he? How do you know him?"

"He owns the Two Mile Ranch."

"I've heard of it. Good God!"

He noticed her wrists; they were red and raw from twisting, and by now her eye had puffed up so it was beginning to close. Above her left breast a bruise was beginning to appear.

"He didn't just hit you, he beat you up! I'll kill him!"

"Jeptha, don't, I'm all right. He's done worse than this. Forget him. Are you feeling any better?"

"Never mind me!"

"Jeptha, don't. You lie down and rest. I'll get ready."

"I don't want to go," he rasped.

"Oh don't be like that, *mon cher, mon chevalier*. We'll go, we'll have fun."

"It's almost seven o'clock, where is he!" snapped Jubal irritably.

Lorna had finished cleaning up the supper dishes. She sat at the kitchen table darning socks while he paced and groused and stared flinty-eyed out the window. He was probably more worried than angry.

"He did tell you he was going out," she said. "Didn't he say when he might be back?"

"No, or where he was going or why. Headed straight for town, I'm sure. Where else would he go?"

She put down her work. It was time he knew, she thought. "Daddy, he has a girlfriend."

"He what?"

"I found out inadvertently. I'm sure he's with her."

Jubal stood with his hands on the back of a chair. "Who is she?"

Lorna told him what she knew, taking care not to betray her resentment against Delise Giradoux.

"You found out 'inadvertently'? What does that mean?"

She told him about seeing them at the railroad station in the crowd, and later learning from Lincoln who she was.

"He does have a right to see somebody, Daddy. He's been terribly lonesome since Salita Jane was killed. He loved her."

"Puppy love."

"It wasn't. She wasn't a child and neither is Jep. That's the whole thing, he's not a schoolboy anymore. Men his age are married with children. All he wants is for you to acknowledge that he's a grown-up."

Jubal sighed. "You're right, dear. I've been carrying on like he was six. He really hasn't done anything, except run off to town against my orders."

"That's my point, he's too old to order. Ask, don't

A. R. Riefe

order. Treat him like you treat me." She came up behind him, put her arms around him, and kissed his cheek.

"I love you, Daddy, and so does Jep. Just back away a little, give him breathing room. He'll be fine. And you two will be closer than ever."

This prompted a twinge of guilt. Who could really say if he'd be fine, now that he was a fly in the spider's clutches? Tomorrow was Monday. She'd go out to the fort first thing to ask Lincoln to come to dinner and talk to Jeptha. If there was anybody he'd listen to on such a touchy subject, it would be Lincoln.

Harvey Philips sat with Lena Dawkings at a corner table. She was sober and Philips was feeling quite relaxed, although not yet drunk. It was, however, his intention. Now that the colonel was back, it was no longer necessary for him to stick close to the fort and command. He'd sneaked away by himself, not telling Rhilander or Mario Consolo where he was going. It was nobody's business where he spent his off-duty hours, especially since he no longer had a wife.

At the next table sat O. K. Freeling in one of his nineteen brocade vests, chomping on a cigar. With him was an almond-eyed beauty who affected a French accent and laced her speech with French phrases. One of her almond eyes was so puffed up it was almost closed. Between studious examinations of the rye in his glass and sippings of it, Philips listened to their conversation. Freeling had recognized the major when O. K. and his companion sat down, greeting him too loudly and too obviously for Philips's taste, though when Freeling magnanimously stood him to the drink in his hand, the man's boorishness didn't bother him quite so much. A couple of junior officers and a few enlisted men were also present. Indeed, uniforms made up the majority of patrons. The roulette wheels rested, no poker games were in progress.

"Lena, my lovely," murmured Philips slightly slurringly. "Have you ever thought about the meaning of life?"

"You're drunk, Harvey."

226

"Not yet. I'm serious, what meaning does anybody's life have? King or commoner, war hero, tramp, anybody?"

"I don't know, I never got past the fourth grade."

"My dear, you don't need an education to form an opinion on a philosophical point. I think life has no meaning. None. Zero. I think it's entirely illusion."

The blank expression draping Lena's face deepened. "What's illusion?"

"A deception, a mockery. And the same goes for death."

"You're drunk, Harvey."

"He proposed," said Delise and laughed.

"He didn't—"

Freeling shook his head. Philips, his back to their table, listened. Lena drank. Emerald went on.

"After you left I took him on a picnic. We sat under a tree nibbling sandwiches, drinking wine, the birds were singing, it was balmy, beautiful. *Quel beau temps!* It put him in an amorous mood, *mon petit chevalier.*"

"And what was your answer?" Freeling asked.

"Oh, I accepted, *sûrement.*" She laughed. "How could I refuse him, he swept me off my feet! And this afternoon were your ears burning, *mon cher?*"

"Why should they?"

"When he wasn't pouring his heart out we talked about you. I told him what a brute you were. He was so *sympathique*. He's so precious."

"He's a little boy, you should be ashamed. You shouldn't have told him you'll marry him."

"How could I resist such a flattering proposal?"

"He—" Freeling's jaw dropped. "My God." Emerald was sitting with her back to the door, Freeling with his to the wall with a good view of anyone coming in. "Speak of the little devil!"

Jeptha had come in. He stood just inside the door. He was wearing a six-gun that looked almost ludicrously out of place on his hip. Major Philips looked his way, but didn't recognize him, since he'd never seen him before. Jeptha stood about two feet inside the door. He looked about and spied Freeling with Emerald. He was surprised

A. R. Riefe

to see her, but not enough to cause him to waver from his purpose in coming.

"You slime!" he burst and went for his gun.

Chairs scraped the floor. Women screamed, Freeling ducked, Delise shrieked.

"No!"

One of Freeling's two bouncers had been leaning on the end of the bar when Jeptha came in. He had walked in front of the man, ignoring him, turning to his right to survey the room, spotting Freeling. He got his gun only partway out of its holster before the bouncer grabbed him from behind, pinning his arms and snatching away the gun. Jeptha cursed, broke free, and lunged at him, but the bouncer brought up the gun, setting the muzzle against his chest. Freeling was on his feet, watching in amusement.

"Jeptha!" shrilled Emerald.

"Shut up," snapped Freeling. "Get him out of here, Bert!"

"Yes sir, Mr. Freeling."

Jeptha went out protesting, cursing, flinging empty threats at Freeling, who laughed at him. Everyone began laughing except the bouncer, Philips, and Lena, who from her expression didn't quite seem to know what was going on. The bouncer gave Jeptha's gun to the bartender, who shoved it under the bar.

"Did you have to make him look so foolish?" Emerald asked. "Embarrass him so?"

"Are you blind in *both* eyes?" rasped Freeling. "He was going to shoot me!"

"He'd never, he was only threatening you—"

"With his finger on the trigger?"

At a signal from the bartender he got up and walked over to the bar and relieved the man, accepting his apron and pouring out a refill for a patron. Philips emptied his glass and Lena refilled it for him. He noticed she was eyeing Emerald, now sitting alone, waiting for the bartender to come back from the bathroom so Freeling could return. He, meanwhile, had turned to polishing glasses. The bouncer had left his station at the end of the

228

bar and was talking to the other bouncer at the back of the room.

The door burst wide, slamming against the wall. It was Jeptha, his face flushed, eyes wild, another gun in his hand. The reaction to his first appearance was repeated in sequence, at least on the part of the patrons looking on. But the bouncer was caught well out of position. Jeptha took quick advantage of this, rushing quickly down the bar, confronting Freeling.

He fired at him point-blank.

But not before Freeling fired first. As Jeptha had made his way down the bar, Freeling had reached under it. Philips, looking on, couldn't see what he was reaching for, but didn't have to. He never did see Jeptha's confiscated gun in his hand. Freeling fired through the front of the bar, the bullet angling slightly upward, slamming Jeptha in the chest. Almost simultaneously his slug flew straight into Freeling's open mouth, smashing through his skull. The bullet struck the mirror behind him, etching a star.

Freeling lay stretched out behind the bar, Jeptha lay stretched in front of it. The smoke from their weapons lifted slowly to the ceiling, spreading, thinning. The initial silence settling over the scene was shattered by a horrendous scream rising from Emerald's throat. Her chair toppled as she jumped up and ran to Jeptha. The bartender, meanwhile, had come back in and was kneeling out of sight behind the bar, examining Freeling. He rose shaking his head.

"My God," muttered Philips and bolted his whiskey. "What a lovely place to bring the wife and wee ones on a quiet Sunday evening."

"They're both dead," said Lena.

He said nothing, only looked long and hard at her. She interrupted his newfound fascination with her face.

"Does this mean I'm out of a job, do you think?" she asked.

21

Jeptha Hunnicutt was buried beside his mother. His sister, his father, Lincoln Rhilander, Dr. Gogarty, and a minister who quoted Ecclesiastes were the only ones present at his funeral. Jubal and Lorna were doing their utmost to console each other, but the tragedy was still too fresh. They had just buried Hannah, and now they only had each other.

Lorna emerged from the tragedy with bitterness towards Delise Giradoux, whom she saw as responsible for Jeptha's death. Lincoln sat with her in the kitchen two days after the funeral. Jubal had resumed working on the barn an hour after it to keep busy. Lincoln did not think the blame should be laid on Emerald. He couldn't see what Lorna could gain through hatred.

Harvey Philips described to her what had happened in lurid detail. Up until then, for the first few days after Jeptha was killed, all she knew was that it had happened at the Two Mile Ranch. It was Harvey who told her that Emerald was there and had seen it all.

Lincoln stirred his coffee and pretended to be absorbed in the circling on its surface. "Hating can wear you out," he said. "Is it really worth it?"

"I'll get even with her if it takes the rest of my life."

"You going to shoot her?" He looked startled.

"I don't want to talk about it anymore."

It was useless and so. unlike her it surprised him. He could only hope that like the pain of loss, the effort at hating would diminish as time went on. But at the moment she wasn't about to listen to advice from him or anyone. Nor was Jubal, though he didn't hate. He didn't know Emerald Giradoux, apart from hearing her name. He was simply too grief-stricken over Jeptha's death to think about anything else. Father and daughter imbued Lincoln with a feeling of abject helplessness. He couldn't say anything or do anything that helped either of them. Sympathy went unheeded, unacknowledged.

"I wonder where she's gone?" Lorna asked the wall behind him.

"You're not going looking for her. It's a waste of time if you are, I hear she's left town."

"And gone where?" she asked.

"Search me."

"Can you find out?"

"I probably can, but I won't." His expression assumed stubborn defiance.

"Thanks."

"Darling . . ."

He paused and shook his head, then got up.

"Where are you going?" she asked.

"I have to go back to the fort."

"Must you?"

Work was piling up, paperwork he'd been bombarded with before Rudy came, work he'd happily taken over. But Rudy was gone. Lincoln had sent off an eight-page summary of the operation confident that Headquarters, C. C. Augur's successor, wouldn't blame him for Crazy Horse's getting away. They'd been lucky to catch up with him and they had succeeded in chasing him north, where he wouldn't be bothering anybody until spring.

His two-page report on Rudy had taken him most of one entire day to compose. He'd rewritten it at least a dozen times. He took pains not to make judgements or presumptions, other than speculating that Rudy may have killed himself while still not in complete possession of his faculties. He hated the phrase but he couldn't think of any other way to describe the poor man's presumed state of mind, and they would want his personal opinion. Better to give it to them than having them asking for it.

He was at his desk the next morning, recently reunited with it, as it were, immersed in drudgery, plowing through supply manifests, signing letters and directives, his mind as much on his work as thoughts of Lorna permitted. Through the window he could see his newly assigned striker leaning against the hitch rack talking to another private. Rudy had taken over his old striker with the office. Terrence Mellon had been killed in the hillside meeting with Crazy Horse. Lincoln's striker now was Enos Bibby, an Iowa farm boy. It was easy to see he was fresh off the farm from a hundred yards away. You could *see* the wisps of straw in his hair, the calico shirt above the bib Levis, despite his wearing a uniform. Only he didn't wear it as much as he posed as a pole on which it hung. His homely face was spattered with freckles, he smiled toothily and gulped when he talked, and his Adam's apple, the size of a turkey's egg, rode tirelessly up and down his throat.

Enos and his friend stopped talking when a lone rider came dusting into the fort, drummed across the parade ground, and reined up outside. Two stripes rode his sleeve; over his shoulder was slung a dust-caked dispatch case. He handed a letter, a pad, and pencil to Enos. Hooking his left hand around the pencil, he signed the pad. He brought in the letter and handed it over, saluting smartly. Lincoln returned the gesture without looking up. Enos went back out. By now the dispatch rider was well away from the fort, heading for his next drop.

Lincoln read the upper left hand corner of the chocolate brown envelope.

E.C. Gillette, Major General Commanding Department of the Platte, Headquarters, Omaha, Nebraska

Your report on the recent operation against Crazy Horse, the Sioux and Cheyenne, received, read, discussed, and accepted. You and your men are to be commended for the success of your efforts. Limited though they were, you did as well as anyone could expect under such difficult circumstances.

Your deposition on . . .

Deposition? What the hell was he talking about? He went on . . .

deposition on the unfortunate death of Colonel R. W. Schwimmer also received, read, and discussed. Please be advised that a court of inquiry is to be convened on the fourteenth of this month instant to be held here. Your presence and that of Lieutenant Mario Anthony Consolo, Private Charles Ellis Baldwin, and Private Cuthbert Bizlowski will be required. Please arrange for an experienced officer to replace you temporarily in command. At this time it is impossible to say how long the investigation will last.

"Son of a blue-balled bastard!"

This was followed by an even more eloquent and imaginatively worded opinion of the message and its demand. He exploded, jumping up, gripping the edge of the desk with both hands, tipping it over, scattering papers in every direction, shattering the inkwell. Next he snatched up his chair and hurled it through the window. Then jerked out a file drawer and threw it at the door. He was gasping, sweating, and still cursing when he finally got hold of his physical monster and quieted it. He sat down slowly on the bottom drawer of the overturned desk and cast about, looking for the letter. But it was lost among the scattered papers, folders, reports, and envelopes and other things stacked on his desktop.

Enos had set the chair back up outside and was examining it for damage. Lincoln came out.

"Sir?" asked the striker in a tone that strongly hinted concern over his superior's mental state.

"Put that back inside, then go find Lieutenant Consolo. Whatever he's doing, tell him I said drop it and get over here fast as he can."

"Yes, sir."

Lincoln didn't bother to return his salute. The S.O.P. mark of deference paid to superiors by their subordinates in the service was the last thing on his mind at the

A. R. Riefe

moment. Mario Consolo showed up minutes later. He was in his undershirt with his suspenders down, his face covered with lather, razor in hand.

"Lincoln—"

"Come inside."

Consolo took one look around and managed to look slightly frightened and surprised at the same time. "What the hell?"

Enos stood in the doorway, his Adam's apple climbing and descending. He moved his hands about and shifted his feet, not knowing what to do next, what the colonel would do or want of him. Lincoln was picking up papers and throwing them down, looking for the letter from General Gillette. He found it, unballed it, and shoved it at Consolo.

"Read this."

A low, worrisome whistle was Consolo's first reaction. "Oh boy."

" 'Oh boy' is right."

They had moved back outside. Enos set about straightening up the office without being told to.

"What exactly did you say in your report?" Consolo asked.

"Deposition, he calls it." Lincoln sniffed disapprovingly and shook his head. "Stupid me, I thought it was a report when I sent it in. I described what happened, what else would I tell him? I did add that I thought, I mean it was strictly my opinion, that when Rudy killed himself he wasn't himself."

"Did you say he was crazy?"

"I said he wasn't in total possession of his faculties."

"That's a nice way of saying it," said Consolo. "Still, why would they want to open his grave and dig him up, do you think? I mean that literally . . ."

"I know what you mean. I think it's her."

"His wife?"

Lincoln nodded. "I think she's off center. I know she must be bitter and wants somebody to blame. Who better than me?"

Consolo offered him a cigarette from a pack of Richmond Straights. Lincoln declined. Consolo wiped what

234

remained of the lather from his chin, lit up, and puffed thoughtfully.

"She did try to rape you," he said.

"It's not funny, Mario. But that could be what decided her to turn her guns on me."

"Slow down, Lincoln, you don't know if she did. It's possible she's got nothing to do with this. I wonder if your old and dear friend is poking his nose in—"

"Grenville Dodge?"

"He and Schwimmer were friends. He handpicked him to replace you. It's possible he heard about General Augur's arrangement with you two and disapproved and . . ."

"What, blames me for Rudy killing himself? That's a bit of a stretch. Besides, I can't believe Dodge wants to involve himself. He's probably two thousand miles from Omaha and busy as hell with the U.P. I don't know, maybe I'm overreacting. Maybe Gillette just wants every stone turned over before closing the file. After all, it's not every day a post commander kills himself."

"Maybe the War Department's prodding him for an investigation," said Consolo.

"That's possible. Get ahold of Baldwin and Bizlowski and cut travel orders for the four of us. We'll leave for Omaha tomorrow morning."

"It says the inquiry's scheduled for the fourteenth. That's six days."

"I know," said Rhilander, "but the quicker we get there, the quicker we'll be able to see General Gillette. If we're lucky there won't be any need for a court of inquiry. We can sit down and answer all his questions in an hour. I can't imagine he's got it in his head to put on a spectacle. Not with Mona still in mourning. But the quicker we get there, the sooner we'll find out what's on his mind."

He stood with Lorna on the platform. The 8:04 from Laramie was three minutes late. It had just come into sight a mile up the tracks, carrying its dirty gray plume of cinder-studded smoke toward them, hooting its whistle

A. R. Riefe

faintly. Consolo and the two privates stood to one side talking. Lincoln took Lorna in his arms and kissed her.

"Why can't I go with you? You may need me. If Mona's involved I could help. I was there when he came back, remember?" She searched his eyes pleadingly.

"I know. I appreciate it, darling, but I can't take you. It wouldn't look right, you sitting by my side. Besides, we don't even know what they'll be after."

"All the more reason—"

He stopped her with a gentle forefinger to her lips. "It could be a week, maybe more. You shouldn't leave Jubal. He needs you, Lorna. You need each other."

"I need you," she murmured. "Oh, go if you have to, only get back fast. We have a date, remember?"

"How could I forget?"

She broke from him and looked away. "Only not a gown and church and all the trappings."

"Every bride's entitled to the trappings," he said smiling.

"I wouldn't feel right so soon after Jep. I'd rather just take Daddy and Major Philips or somebody you know to the minister's house, and have him perform the ceremony in his living room. The wedding doesn't mean beans, anyway, it's the marriage that counts."

He held her again and kissed her. "And we'll have an absolutely stupendous one."

"Just happy will do, Colonel."

At the sound of his rank his face darkened slightly. "I hope you realize you're marrying the U.S. Army. It won't be a wifely lot anybody in his right mind would recommend. We'll have to live at the fort."

"I know, and I don't mind. Mona and Rudy's place was kind of cute."

"It was a dump, all the houses are."

"We'll fix ours up, you'll see. You'll be amazed what a little paint and curtains and a few other inexpensive things can do."

The train was pulling in loudly. Passengers began descending the steps of all six cars; Cheyenne passengers waited impatiently to board. The express car ramp was thrown down and crates and packages and mail sacks carried aboard.

"Take care of yourself," said Lorna. "And darling, please try to hang onto your famous temper." Consolo and the others came over. "Take care of him, Mario."

"You bet."

They kissed one last time. Her hand slipped free of his. Her smile gave way to disappointment. Moments later he sat in the window above her, looking down, waving. She despised his having to go when her heart was down and only he could pick it up.

The train was pulling out. Lorna blew him a last kiss, he returned it. Consolo was sitting beside him, the two privates in the seat behind them. None of the three had anyone seeing them off.

"Did you say something?" Consolo asked.

"Nothing important."

"She's beautiful, Lincoln. You're a lucky man."

"The luckiest. Only one regret."

"What?"

"I wish *she* were luckier," said Rhilander.

"She's marrying you, isn't she?" He laughed.

"She's marrying Fort D. A. Russell and everything that goes with being an Army wife. You know what the biggest problem is for married couples in the service? It's that *it* always comes first. It's like newlyweds being saddled with a demanding and domineering maiden aunt. Their life isn't their own. It's what she wants it to be, what she thinks is best for them, which is really what's best for her."

"Say it," said Consolo.

"Say what?"

"What you're obviously leading up to. You're thinking of quitting."

"It's crossed my mind. Gillette sent it across with his damn-fool letter. I'm like a hundred thousand others, Mario. When I joined, it was with my eyes open. I knew what the drawbacks would be, I knew I'd have to sacrifice my privacy and a hundred other things. I was going to be a patriot who put his love for country first. Only now I've met her it's all changed."

"A woman can do that."

"She's not choosing the Army, she's being drafted," said Rhilander. "And submitting to it out of love for me. How do you think that makes me feel? I think about Harvey and Andrea Philips."

"Andrea Philips was too spoiled to even try to adjust," said Consolo. "Don't compare Lorna to that one."

"You miss the point. Andrea may have been that and worse, but do you honestly blame her for leaving? Why should she be forced to adjust to the life?"

"Are you quitting?" Consolo asked pointedly.

"No," Rhilander replied.

"But you're thinking about it."

"I don't know . . ."

"Want to know what I think?" Consolo asked.

"No."

Consolo laughed and slapped Lincoln's knee. And the train rolled on toward Omaha and Major General E. C. Gillette with his waiting questions. Lincoln folded his arms across his chest, turned his glance toward the moving territory, closed his eyes, and went to sleep.

22

A brass chandelier hung from the ceiling, surrounded by molding of a Greek key design. The walls glared white. A table nearly as long as the bar at the late O. K. Freeling's Two Mile Ranch paralleled the back wall, and a small square table stood in front of it. A fly arrived and began circling the chandelier. Its buzzing was soft as it flew around, then it spun off, heading for the nearest window. It settled on a pane and strode slowly up it, looking for a way out, finding none, taking off and returning to the chandelier, where it perched waiting for the inquiry to adjourn, the intruders to leave.

At the small table sat a private scribbling with a pen that seemed to be giving him trouble. Again and again he would jerk his hand to loosen the ink adhering to the nib or wipe the point on the edge of his inkwell. The questions had been written down beforehand; all that was required of him were the answers and whatever offhand remarks were made, but his uncooperative pen was not making his task easier. Taking such a dull job so seriously, and the ability to write quickly were the major requirements, thought Lincoln watching. And he was serious; so solemn was his expression he looked like he was taking down the ten commandments.

Behind the long table, Major General Edwin Carver Gillette filled a bow-backed Windsor chair. Lincoln had tried to meet with him four days earlier upon arriving, but was told the general was away and would not be back until today. Here he was, a large, broad-shouldered man, clean-shaven at the front of his face but sporting luxurious sideburns. His well-shaped features made a handsome collection and his smile was benevolent; he was every child's jolly, indulgent uncle, but for his eyes. They were the pale blue of a summer sky under assault by a scorching sun. Ten feet to his left sat Major Arthur John Jacob Wells, representing the judge-advocate-general's office. He was in his sixties, ten years older than Gillette, all eyebrows—fierce-looking, wild eyebrows—and soft, sluggish-looking jowls. He smoked a pipe with a large bowl, although he had not yet filled it. He was only playing with it, tapping the bowl against his palm, sucking the stem clear, sliding the stem up the side of his nose to polish it. Before him on the table lay his bulging pouch. If he was listening to the proceedings, neither his eyes or his manner showed it.

To Gillette's right sat a captain, a scrawny individual who looked like a boy playing soldier in his father's uniform, lacking only a wooden sword and a folded newspaper cocked hat. If ferrets wore small scraggly beards and pinch glasses with black ribbons, a ferret the captain would have been. His eyes were beady, his nose slender and turned up at the tip, revealing wet, red nostrils, and his cheeks were pinched. The cuffs of his jacket crawled halfway up his hands when he propped his ferret face on his upraised palms and stared under his lids at Consolo, seated in the witness chair, responding to his questions. Gillett had introduced the ferret as Captain Stephen DeGuisse, appointed by him to conduct the investigation into "the unfortunate death of Colonel Schwimmer." Outranked by his two associates, the captain was nevertheless in nominal charge of the proceedings.

Privates Baldwin and Bizlowski had already testified and been dismissed. It was hot and stuffy in the room. Lincoln wished somebody would open a window. From the sweat pouring down Major Wells's face, he too should have wished it, but was obviously too involved with his pipe to think about it. He rapped it on the table. Consolo stopped talking in mid-answer. Everyone stiffened, Captain DeGuisse looked up at the offender. The major mumbled apology, and Consolo resumed.

"We left him with his wife and son. Privates Baldwin and Bizlowski returned to their quarters, I went to headquarters to report to the acting CO, Major Philips."

"Retaining possession of Colonel Schwimmer's service revolver."

"Yes, sir."

DeGuisse covered his profile with his hand and mumbled something to Gillette. The general nodded.

"Thank you, Lieutenant," he said affably. "You've been very helpful, we appreciate it. Would you take a seat in the rear, please? Colonel Rhilander?"

"Yes, sir."

Consolo had gotten up. He turned and smiling thinly at Lincoln, who took his place.

"Colonel Rhilander," said DeGuisse, "just a few questions. As you heard me tell the lieutenant, none of you are on trial here. We call it a court of inquiry, but it's not really a court. We just want to get to the bottom of this tragic business for the record, if we can. And we're asking you to help."

"If I can."

"Good. With what the lieutenant and his men have told us, we pretty much know everything from when the battle ended back to Fort Russell. We can call that the second half. Let's turn our attention to the first half. Let's go back to shortly after General Dodge appointed Colonel Schwimmer to replace you. No need to go into your reaction to that or his to you. Suppose we begin with your visit here. You came to petition General Augur to restore your command, is that right?"

"I did."

"He responded by creating a dual command. You were to continue in charge of field operations, Colonel Schwimmer would continue in charge at the fort. A proposal that the colonel agreed to. Now, when your orders came down to take charge of the expedition to locate and deal with Crazy Horse, the colonel asked to go along."

"Yes."

"How did you react to that?"

"I tried to talk him out of it."

"But he insisted on going. Still, you could have refused him."

"I thought about it. I decided that even though I could, it would be better if I didn't."

"Why is that?"

"We had to work together. It was a fragile arrangement."

"Awkward."

"Yes. I couldn't see starting out by pulling my field rank on him. He didn't have to go along with General Augur's proposal, but he did. I was grateful. He'd extended himself for me, I did the same for him. That's really all."

"So he went along. Were you with him, I mean in his immediate company, when the Indians attacked Fort Fetterman?"

"I was."

"How did he behave?"

Major Wells was filling his pipe, thumbing tobacco into the bowl, tampit down, making it into something like a religious rite.

"Fine," said Lincoln. "Nothing unusual."

"Nothing unusual. He didn't panic."

"No."

"No signs of it."

"No."

"And were you together at any time during the subsequent battle on the hillside?"

"We rode up together, but the battle didn't start, it exploded. Suddenly it was all noise and confusion. We got separated and I didn't see him for the next hour, not until Mario—Lieutenant Consolo found him sitting in the ravine."

"Terror-stricken."

"Yes."

"You assigned the lieutenant to take him back to Fort Russell when he calmed down and was fit to travel."

"I did."

CHEYENNE

"I'm curious, why Russell?"

Major Wells had finished his preparations and was lighting up with great ceremony.

"I saw no point in sending him back to Fetterman," said Lincoln, "when he'd eventually be going back to Russell."

"You sent him straight back to his wife and son after he'd undergone an ordeal it would be fair to say it would take the strongest individual weeks, perhaps months, to recover from."

"I thought being with his family would be best for him. They could help him more than any of us."

"I see."

Lincoln mentally brought his guard up a notch higher. Bizlowski and Baldwin were done, as was Consolo. The captain was now concentrating all his guns on him. He was looking for somebody to blame. He'd found him. Let him try, reflected Lincoln grimly, let him fall on his ferret face. I'll even give him a shove.

The fly took off and landed on the table two inches from DeGuisse's cuff. Unnoticed by the captain, and perhaps resenting it, it flew off, landing on the molding directly above the general's head. DeGuisse went on.

"You've said you didn't see the colonel during the battle, you had no idea where he'd gotten to until the lieutenant found him after. You were busy giving orders, I'm sure, fashioning strategy, responding to officers and men, the usual. But considering the colonel's total lack of experience, wouldn't it have been wise if you could have kept an eye on him? Just one. Or assigned somebody to do so?"

"If I were to do that for him, why not for the dozen or so junior officers and enlisted men also seeing action for the first time? It can't be done. He was armed, intelligent, and I'm sure he knew what he was up against. He'd been forewarned by the attack on Fort Fetterman. I didn't think I should hold his hand, I didn't think he'd want me to."

"Nobody asked you to hold his hand," snapped DeGuisse irritably. But he quickly resumed his syrupy tone. "You're

243

A. R. Riefe

obviously intelligent yourself, Colonel. I can imagine you're wondering where all this is leading. So why beat around the bush, eh? Your command was taken from you and given to him. You tried to get it back, General Augur gave you half a loaf, but you didn't see it as better than none. You let an untested man go into what you had to know would be a helluva bloody battle."

"You son of a bitch," said Lincoln quietly.

DeGuisse leered. "I beg your pardon—"

"Colonel—" began the general.

"Sir, with all respect, I refuse to sit here and let this pasty-faced, armchair two-bar accuse me of deliberately, intentionally taking a man into battle, hoping he'd be killed so I'd be rid of him."

"I've heard no such accusation," said Gillette, hardening his icy eyes.

"Sir—"

Wells had stopped puffing and was staring at Lincoln. The fly came down, lighting on the corner of the table and looking his way.

"General," said DeGuisse, holding a hand up, interrupting. "Sir, inasmuch as the colonel has seen fit to open up this particular tin of beans, perhaps we should pursue it."

"You," said Lincoln. "To your heart's content. I've said all I'm going to."

"Colonel," said the captain. "This court has formally requested your cooperation. It's within my authority to make that request a demand."

"Go ahead, I'm done."

"Gentlemen, gentlemen," sighed the general.

DeGuisse was suddenly scowling. "Careful, Private, don't push me."

"That's Colonel, Captain."

"That's Private, Colonel, that's what you can be broken down to if you persist in defying me." He turned to Gillette. "Sir, what I said I stand by. This man had the authority to refuse the colonel's request to go along. He did not. He took him into battle and what happened? The only thing that could happen, given the circumstances and the colonel's inexperience. You didn't kill him, so nobody's accusing you of murder. But I would call it premeditated devising of a situation that could only lead"—his voice rose, becoming shrill—"inevitably to the calamitous result we've seen. Unavoidable! Inescapable! It couldn't have turned out any other way!"

Lincoln jumped up cursing, rushing at DeGuisse, grabbing him by the neck. Consolo came running up, grabbing him around the chest, pulling him off. Gillette was on his feet roaring, and the major's pipe had fallen from his mouth. The captain massaged his throat gingerly, grimacing, twisting his neck. His pain gave way to a triumphant smirk. Gillette, meanwhile, had summoned the two guards from outside, ordering them to stand on either side of the witness. Consolo had cajoled and physically moved Lincoln back to his seat. The room settled down, the fly shifted its six feet and continued watching.

"One more outburst or one move from that chair and I'll have you locked up in shackles!" said Gillette. "And see you curb your foul mouth. As for you, Captain, you've made a goddamn serious allegation here and a pretty goddamn flimsy one as far as I can see. You'd better be able to back it up with something more than your goddamn suspicions!"

"Sir, we do have Mrs. Schwimmer's deposition."

Again Lincoln was on his feet. "General, General, I want her brought in. I want her to testify. She knows how insistent he was that he go. She tried to talk him out of it. Ask her, she'll tell you."

Gillette scowled. "Didn't I just finish telling you to stay put? We got her deposition. It's here someplace . . ." He searched among the papers in the folder in front of him. "Here. And this'll have to do. She's a civilian, she can't testify at a military hearing with no civilians involved. You should know that. But her story's all here. I think, I haven't had a chance to read it."

"I have!" DeGuisse stood up. He was in the spotlight of his glory and savoring every second of it. "General, with your permission I'll read aloud from my copy."

Gillette signaled him to go ahead.

245

"Sir," cut in Lincoln, "may I see a copy?"

The general handed his copy to the secretary, who passed it to Lincoln. DeGuisse sat silent and leering while he scanned it. He hurried down the first page, pausing at the paragraph at the bottom that continued on the second of the two pages. In it Mona claimed that she had approached him and asked him (she used the word beseeched) to dissuade Rudy from going along. And that his response was that he'd tried, that Rudy wouldn't listen, was determined to go, adding that there was nothing further he could do. It was Rudy's decision.

"Sir," said Lincoln. "Can I read this last paragraph aloud?"

Again Gillette flung his hand, signaling permission.

Lincoln read. He was not even halfway through the passage before DeGuisse was on his feet beaming victoriously, gesticulating.

"You hear that, sir? She confirms it. Exactly what I said. This man wanted the colonel—"

"It's a damn lie!" snapped Lincoln. DeGuisse stopped and gaped. Lincoln softened his tone. "Sir, she never came near me, we never discussed it. I'll take an oath on it. But if she *had* come to me, I would have ordered him to stay. It was, at least in part, because she did not that I let him come. As I said before, I was thinking down the road. I didn't want to do anything that might jeopardize the arrangement, certainly not so soon after he agreed to try it. But General, what she says here is a goddamn lie, every syllable! Just as false as the allegation that I encouraged him to come along, hoping he'd be killed."

Gillette knit his brows and shook his head. "I haven't heard anybody accuse you of encouraging him."

"Letting him, then. I'd like to say one last thing. I came here with Lieutenant Consolo with every intention of cooperating. I have no reason not to. I've told you the truth, exactly what happened from my point of view. Perhaps it's true that it was wrong of me to let him come. It sure looks it, but that's hindsight.

"So he came and hid in the ravine and that probably saved his life, there on the hill at any rate. As I said before, I don't know, I was nowhere near him. When the shock wore off, what he'd done mortified him. Suddenly every eye he looked into accused him of cowardice. He couldn't face his wife and son, knowing the story would be all over the fort an hour after he got back. He killed himself. But if anybody here thinks I wanted him dead just so I could get back my command, they're crazy. I may be a hothead, but I'm not an animal, and not a fool.

"On the other hand, let's say I'm guilty of everything the captain is accusing me of. What would possibly lead me to believe he wouldn't be replaced? He had agreed to share command with me. *How could I be sure the next man would?* Why would he? I wouldn't if I were him.

"When he first showed up to replace me, I resented him so I couldn't stand the sight of him. But as the shock of what had happened gradually began to wear off and we got to know each other, the chill began to fade. I began to realize that he hadn't asked for the job, Dodge had shoved it on him. From then on, things happened that drew us closer and closer. By the time we set out for Fetterman we were friends."

DeGuisse laughed, Lincoln bristled.

"Friends," he repeated. "When he killed himself I lost a friend."

"General," piped DeGuisse. "If I may go on . . ."

"No, Stephen," Gillette said firmly.

"Sir?"

The general looked stern, the major looked surprised, the captain looked flabbergasted. Consolo started to laugh at the back of the room, then stopped it with his hand.

"This horse is dead," said Gillette. "No need for more beating. Thank you, Colonel Rhilander."

With this Major General Edwin Carver Gillette waved to Lincoln, accorded him a grin, and got up from his seat. Lincoln turned to Consolo. The lieutenant raised his fist. Lincoln frowned and shook his head. Everyone started for the door. When it swung open, the first one out was the fly.

23

"Why would she do such a thing?" Consolo asked, when he was done slapping Lincoln on the back and congratulating him. They stood outside the inquiry room door. Men of all ranks moved up and down the corridor.

"Remember the other day?" said Lincoln. "When I gave you Gillette's letter to read? I said I thought she was a little off balance. Who knows, maybe pushing it off on somebody else helped lighten her load. I'll tell you one thing, Mario, Christopher Augur and Gillette sure have helped restore my respect for generals that Dodge took away. Let's go see when the next train back to Cheyenne comes in."

"Six oh five tonight."

Lincoln checked his watch. "It's five after three."

"Pardon me, sir."

A sergeant in full dress, the scarlet trim on his uniform, the plume and cording of his helmet, off and sitting on his forearm, indicating he was an artillery man, had clomped to a halt beside them. He saluted stiffly.

"General Gillette's compliments, sir, and would you join him in his office in one hour, sir?"

"Four o'clock—"

"Four, sir, down the corridor, turn left and right."

"General Augur's old office," said Lincoln.

"Yes sir, thank you, sir."

With another salute, snapped off so sharply he risked dislocating his wrist, he was gone.

"He probably wants to congratulate you and say goodbye," said Consolo.

"An hour from now? Oh well, maybe he's busy. Let's go find Baldwin and Bizlowski. We all need a drink."

It was two minutes before four. Lincoln turned the corner and spied the general's office. He took two strides toward the door; it opened and out came a parade of men in civilian clothes talking animatedly, laughing, moving past him without noticing him. The door had been left open; he knocked and went in. Gillette was standing behind the desk, his jacket off and draped on the chair behind him. The sergeant who had delivered the general's request nodded and withdrew, closing the door. In the office were three photographers; from the look of things they were prepared to begin shooting. Their cameras sat atop tripods, behind them two light reflectors were directed at the general, and in their hands each held a flash powder holder in readiness.

"Come around here, Lincoln," said the general.

Lincoln complied. To his surprise the general threw his arm around him.

"Say cheese!" snapped one of the photographers.

Gillette beamed and tightened his grip on Lincoln's shoulders. The magnesium oxide powder exploded, smoke rose, and a faint acrid odor filled the room.

"One more, gentlemen," barked a photographer.

The sequence was run through again, then the photographers filed out the door with their equipment. Lincoln blinked his eyes, ridding them of the effects of the flashing.

"That didn't hurt a bit, did it now?" Gillette clapped him on the shoulder and laughed. "Have a chair."

"What's going on?"

"All done. Except for the reporters, they'll want to talk to you later. You may not realize it, but you're a celebrity. The Department of the Platte's champion against the hostiles. Have a look."

Turning in his chair, he pulled down a map of the

western territories. It stretched from Chicago and the
Mississippi to the east, to the coast to the west, to Mexico and Canada. The Department of the Missouri perched
above the Department of Texas. Above Missouri sat the
Department of the Platte; above it, the Department of
Dakota. He indicated St. Paul, Minnesota.

"Headquarters, Department of Dakota. General George
Simpson, commanding. Old friend. Ever meet him?"

"No, sir. General—"

"Good man, brilliant, but the personification of the
armchair general. Locked to his cushion. Has been for
years. Never mind him. Over here—" He moved his
finger westward, stopping at the Powder River just below
the Montana border. "Now if they stray into George's
territory, we'll be out of luck. Timing's vital. Right now
they're here, somewhere just below the border. And
you, Lincoln—may I call you Lincoln?—you're going
back up there after them."

"Next spring."

Gillette sobered. "No . . ." It came out more apologetic than anything else. "Right away, Lincoln, as soon
as you can assemble a decent-sized body of men, big
enough to match Crazy Horse's, which our scouts tell us
is currently around two thousand able-bodied. Yes, sir,
back you go to follow up the advantage you created when
you routed him on that hill overlooking Cow Creek."

"General, may I say something?"

"Please do. Forgive my prattling on so, I'm just so
goddamn enthusiastic. Speak."

"Today is October first. It'd take at least three weeks
to assemble that big a force and get up there. Winter
comes early that far north, and in plain English, sir, it's a
rattling bitch. Two years ago General Dodge tried winter
fighting, and not even that far north, down here in Nebraska. The 11th Cavalry refused to ride, the weather
was so severe. He had to arrest their officers and replace
them. Before he even saw an Indian, just getting over
here, thirteen men froze to death."

"Was he successful? Did he rid the territory of Indians?
He did."

"That's not the point."

"It is to me," snapped Gillette. The icy eyes suddenly looked so hard they seemed about to shatter. "The way I see it, if a bunch of naked savages can stand the cold, properly dressed members of the finest army in the world ought to be able to."

Lincoln's attention had begun to wander, finding and fastening on an irksome conclusion. Gillette had not dragged him all the way here to question him about Rudy's suicide; that was only a device to summon him. He'd gone through the motions, the questions had all been asked and answered, and they were satisfied. The general was. He'd let him off the hook and into his debt, to drop this harebrained scheme into his lap.

"General, when spring comes we can go back up, find Crazy Horse, and finish him. My pleasure, sir."

"No no no no. This campaign has to be underway as soon as possible. I mean yesterday. I know the winter can be harsh—"

"I said, a rattling bitch."

"Hey, you may not be up there long enough to even get into it," said Gillette airily. "You could catch up with the bugger in a week. And be back before the end of the month all wrapped up."

"Sir . . ."

"It's all decided. And I've decided you're the man for the job. The other fellows are either too old or too young and inexperienced. Besides, I've already announced it to the newspapers."

"You what?" Lincoln gaped.

"Can you imagine what I'd look like if I had to retract it?" He shuddered. "I know how it'd look to those flat-asses back at the War Department. They'd say I was indecisive. Look, son, you can handle it—the weather, I mean. Good God, when has weather ever been a factor in formulating military strategy? How many battles in how many wars have been fought in bitter cold, in torrents? I've already contacted the other post commanders in Wyoming Territory. This'll be classified as a follow-up operation, an all-out effort to complete what you so ably initiated at Cow Creek."

"Sir . . ."

"Don't misunderstand, I'm not criticizing you for Cow Creek. I know you didn't have enough horses to follow them, that you had to come back, but this time—"

"There's not going to be any 'this time,' sir."

The icy eyes hardened. Gillette narrowed them, setting them gleaming evilly. He set his jaw. "You're going, that's an order."

"Sir . . ."

"In case it's slipped your mind, only an hour ago I saved your hide and your leaf. I pulled a peck of grief off your back. Thanks to me, you walked out of that room completely exonerated. Clean as a —"

"I never should have walked in."

"See here!" burst Gillette.

"May I have a pencil and paper?"

Gillette jerked back his head and saucered his eyes in confusion. "Eh?"

"A pencil and a piece of notepaper. Better yet, your pen there."

He began scribbling. He handed the paper to the general.

"I'll save you the trouble of reading it. It's my resignation. You'll notice it's effective today, October one."

"You cowardly son of a bitch!" snapped Gillette.

"You conniving, dirty-dealing son of a bitch!"

Gillette began roaring, Lincoln turned about and whipped the door wide. A wall of faces blocked his way—the reporters, each with his pencil and pad out. They were grinning; they'd overheard every word. At sight of them Gillette stopped shouting. The reporters gave way, and Lincoln rushed down the hall, sprinting away from the crowd.

24

Twice Lieutenant Colonel Lincoln Rhilander had let loose the leash of his temper and cursed a major general. The first time brought him a long succession of headaches; the second time, oddly enough, brought him quite the opposite.

In less than thirty seconds, fifteen years had come to an end. On the return trip to Cheyenne, after telling Mario what had happened and listening to his astonished reaction, Lincoln went looking for an empty seat so that he might sit in privacy and reflect on what he'd done. He sat eyeing the distant horizon joining the blue heavens to the yellow earth and thinking, inviting not the slightest twinge of regret for his actions. Even before Omaha his world had shifted; Lorna had shifted it for him. All this did was complete the changeover from the Army to her. She'd be ecstatic when he told her what he'd done. And no doubt immensely relieved at not having to move to Russell.

The window through which he viewed Nebraska provided him a looking glass as well. Within hours after he arrived he'd be out of his uniform and into mufti for the first time in fifteen years. Everything he wore down to his Jefferson boots and underclothing measured exactly to conform to dress regulations. Army time was measured in the same precise manner. Army rules, regulations, laws and the characteristic bindings of the military reminded him of the Lilliputians holding Gulliver captive.

All of these realizations flocked to mind, mixed about, and evaporated, leaving him with a single thought: it was over. Mario Consolo had told him he wasn't surprised at it, but his expression clashed with his words. Everyone else back at Russell would be astonished.

He slept in his seat. The train got into Cheyenne at noon the next day. He wearily descended the vestibule steps into the milling crowd. He stood with Mario and their two companions on the platform.

"You fellows go back and report in," he said. "Tell Harvey I'll be there shortly, but don't tell him what happened to me. I've something I have to do."

Consolo grinned. "Give her my best."

Rather than return to the fort for his horse, Lincoln rented one in town and set out for Bear Creek. His thoughts went back to Gillette. The general was impetuous, but he was not a fool; he'd seen the reporters filling the doorway. If he tried to sidestep the truth with some bull tale, they'd roast him.

He'd probably tell them the truth (since they already knew it) and follow up by playing up to his common sense and down to his ego. He'd point out that Colonel Rhilander had valid grounds for objecting to the assignment. It was too close to winter to go hunting Crazy Horse or anybody else up north; he'd acknowledge that he was deferring to the colonel's judgment in the matter. That the colonel had resigned his commission over the matter could be explained away. He could tell them he'd gotten out the door before he could stop him.

He got the feeling that Gillette had a good working relationship with the press, and as long as he kept his door open to them and fed them a steady stream of copy for their editors, they'd play along and protect his image.

The general had made a bad tactical mistake, jumping the gun with the reporters and photographers, but to his credit he realized it and faced it. Now all he had to do was cover it up, and with their cooperation he'd do exactly that.

Lincoln found Lorna putting up curtains in the parlor.

CHEYENNE

While he'd been away she'd worked magic, transforming bare walls, ceiling and floor into home. She dropped everything to rush to his arms. Jubal came in greeting him loudly. He sat them down and told them what had happened. Lorna was, as he expected, relieved that he'd quit, happy, and proud of him for not knuckling under to Gillette's demands. Jubal was amazed.

"You resigned?" he murmured.

"I quit," said Lincoln. "There's a difference. Resigning is something you consider, weigh the consequences of, go about clearheaded and intelligently. I just stood up and jumped overboard."

"I don't blame you!" burst Lorna.

He grinned. "I didn't think for a second you would."

It was good to be home. Having told them what had happened, he dropped the subject. They talked about the wedding. It didn't interest Jubal, he excused himself and went back to work. They set the date for the following Saturday. The ceremony would take place in the parlor.

Lorna found only one small dark cloud in the gloriously radiant sky of her wedding day; with Mona Schwimmer back in Bluffs there was no one to act as her maid of honor. She knew none of the other wives at the fort and no one in Cheyenne. Lincoln came to her rescue, pressing a willing Molly Harrigan into service. Harvey Philips, appointed temporary post commander by General Gillette (a move that immediately inspired Philips to renounce the bottle in favor of the wagon) was the best man. Mario, Cicero Pinchot, and Dr. Gogarty were also present. The parlor came to life when Molly hung a paper wedding bell from the ceiling and stretched streamers to the corners. Then the room was brightened with bouquets of scarlet and lavender beebalms, six different colors of tall gilias, wild pinks, morning glories, and delicate columbines that resembled miniature bridal bouquets. And from her own window box she brought golden mums.

It was a joyful occasion. That Hannah and Jeptha could not be there to share in Lorna's happiness saddened Jubal, but he concealed his regret with a smile, swelled with fatherly pride, and filled the parlor with music from his harmonium.

The ceremony was brief, the response to "you may kiss the bride" prolonged and heart-stirring, and Mario filled everyone's glasses for the toast to the happy couple while Jubal, having successfully essayed Mendelssohn's "Wedding March," played the "Recessional." The celebration exploded in merriment.

It was nearly midnight when the last guests departed. Jubal went to bed. Husband and wife went to paradise.

Cheyenne had been heaved up by the Union Pacific, nurtured by necessity, exploited by greed and opportunism, invaded by a roistering, rollicking, rascally horde. A French writer, Louis Laurent Simonin, visited the town shortly after the railroad reached there. He described the men he found: "How rough and crude in appearance they are . . . with their long hair . . . their ill-kept beards, their clothing of nondescript color, their great leather boots engulfing their pantaloons. How wild and lawless they are, how defiantly uncivilized. But what virile characters, proud, fearless! What savage dignity, what resourcefulness, what remarkable adaptability! No one complains here."

Over the winter of 1868 the flotsam of railroad-construction days began drifting away; respectability arrived in the person of homemakers, hardworking businessmen, and clergymen. Three churches—Methodist, Episcopal, and Roman Catholic—were established even before the rails moved over Sherman Hill. A two-room schoolhouse opened shortly after Christmas, costing $2,235, of which $1,335 was raised by private subscription. For the balance of $900, the town issued bonds bearing five per cent interest per month, a commentary on its determination to gain respectability. By February the town had 114 children enrolled in the school, with a daily attendance of 86. By that time the population had settled at around six thousand. Maintenance of law and order was a major problem both before and after the arrival of the rails, for despite the influx of decent citizens, no existing brothels, gambling houses, or saloons closed their doors. The majority of men strapped on a gun before venturing into the streets; five killings a week, accidental or deliberate, was a consistent average.

But in spite of continuing to harbor its share of society's dregs, lawlessness and violence were clearly on the wane. Cheyenne was no Abilene or Dodge City; it was not prey to invasions of wild Texas drovers, professional gunslingers, and criminals on the run.

Laramie County had been created by the Dakota Legislature the previous January with Fort Sanders as the county seat. At that time, all of Wyoming comprised just one county of Dakota Territory. But in an October election, a full set of county officials was named, and 1,645 voters indicated a preference for Cheyenne as county seat rather than Fort Sanders, which received 439 votes. Cheyenne was finally classified as a city. Luke Murrin was elected mayor.

One of the most pressing problems facing the city government was the danger of fire. The Cheyenne *Leader* described the situation accurately: "A ruinous fire is the danger we, in this town of tinder like tenements, live under at all times." Mayor Murrin named a fire warden. His duties included the inspection of chimneys, flues, and stovepipes. Despite his best efforts, dozens of buildings burned down. Usually only one building went at a time, until early on the morning of October 8, 1868, when a half block was destroyed with more than $50,000 damage.

An ordinance authorized a volunteer hook-and-ladder company. Red flannel shirts, ornamented belts, and blue cloth caps arrived, after which the hook-and-ladder boys received plenty of exercise. In December a steam fire engine was purchased.

With the coming of March, Jubal began to count the days until planting time, despite the heavy snows blanketing the area. On the tenth of March, Eli Leimkuhler, whose cattle ranch occupied the land north of the Hunnicutt property, died. He had taken ill with pneumonia, his condition had worsened, and nothing Dr. Gogarty could do was able to forestall the inevitable. Three days after his funeral his widow sold the property and moved back East.

The buyer was a newcomer to the area, an Austrian nobleman, Count Heinrich Leo Thun-Martenitz Weigans, a less than shining light of the house of Hapsburg. Heinrich had not come to America to seek his fortune. That, he brought with him, an amount rumored to be close to half a million in gold ducats, each ducat worth two American greenbacks. He came to immerse himself in the Wild West. Sitting in the family castle outside Vienna he had read everything about the territories he could get his soft, well-manicured hands on. The day after his twenty-first birthday, he packed thirty trunks and his fortune, and fled his royal responsibilities and his homeland for distant climes.

He was a small man, standing less than five foot five, handsome, with curly black hair and snapping black eyes, a trim figure in his gray and white officer's uniform of the Gyulai Regiment, his gold chin strap anchoring a tall pillbox cap displaying a gold eagle at the front. He was handsome as well in his custom-tailored suits, cloaks, and forty pairs of handmade boots. He was a profligate and a wastrel, the despair of his doting mama, a flagrant embarrassment to his disgusted and frustrated father, the envy of his peers, and pillared and adored by ladies of all ages. He was also the life of every party, enormously good-hearted, eminently likable, blessed with a marvelous sense of humor and an attractive personality. Had he been a beggar in rags, he would have attracted friends.

He arrived in Cheyenne with his bride of two weeks. She was an American, the daughter of a French trapper and Teton Sioux squaw. Emerald Giradoux was back to establish herself as mistress of the Weigans's H&W Ranch—and Lincoln and Lorna Rhilander's next-door neighbor.

25

Rumors over Heinrich Weigans's wealth were super-ceded by those concerning how he and Emerald met. One story said she picked him up at a faro table in a saloon in Denver. Another said the Duke of Jarlsberg, in America on a buffalo hunt, introduced them. A third story, and the one most people subscribed to—probably because it sounded the most romantic of the three—was that the count had walked into a hotel in Lincoln, Nebraska, spied her coming down the stairs, drank in her beauty, approached her, doffed his hat, and proposed. It was said that she had thought it over a good five seconds, long enough to estimate the number of trunks accompanying him, and accepted.

He had bought her a ten thousand dollar white silk wedding gown intricately embroidered with gold thread and decorated with seven thousand pearls. Lincoln brought all these rumors back from town. Mere mention of Emerald's name visibly flushed Lorna's cheeks and raised her voice in anger.

They sat at the kitchen table. In the other room Jubal was playing an intricate melody that sounded much too intricate for his skills.

"Calm down, sweetheart," said Lincoln quietly.

"Our next-door neighbor, do you believe it?"

" 'Next door' is at least three miles from here."

"I don't care if it's fifty! She's back."

"And rich as Croesus. Can I ask you a question? Are

you upset because she's back or because she hit it lucky?"

"You know perfectly well why I'm upset. Jep's dead because of her. Why did her husband buy Leimkuhler's place? I'll tell you why, because she told him to. She knows we're down here."

"That's absurd," said Lincoln.

"Is it?"

"He bought it because it's a great spread and it was available. I hear he paid a fortune, almost twice what it's worth."

"You see? He could have bought land anywhere, could have staked out public land as we did, only she just had to have Leimkuhler's."

"Why don't you get in the buggy, go on up there, introduce yourself, and run her off?" Lincoln asked.

"It's not funny!"

"It's pathetic. For God's sake, Lorna, put it behind you."

"How can I? Poor Jeb . . ." She shook her head.

"Is spitting out hatred against her going to do him any good? Or her any harm? Bring you any satisfaction? Look at you, my God, you look like you could tear her eyes out. She's not to blame, she didn't kill him. I'm sure his showing up at the Two Mile Ranch that night was as big a surprise to her as it was to Freeling."

"I'll get even with her. I don't know how, but I will."

"Good, do that." He got up.

"Where are you going?" she asked.

"Nowhere. Into the other room. I'm sick of hearing about it."

She held out her hand. "Come here, sit. I won't talk about her anymore, I promise."

"Thanks," he said tightly.

"I just don't see how you can defend her."

"I'm not!" He rose from his chair again.

"Okay. Okay. The coffee's freshly made. Want some?"

They had coffee. Jubal played on. Outside the sun was out and the snow was beginning to melt. The drift by the door dazzled the eye as it shrank. It was the last week of March. April would bring warming showers and wildflowers, and new grass would break the earth. Planting would begin.

Jubal's announced schedule for planting may have sounded overly optimistic in March, with two feet of snow blanketing the ground, but on the tenth of May the same ground welcomed his seed sets. He invited Lorna to ceremoniously plant the first set. He and Lincoln, working ten-hour days, finished planting the first acre and more than nearly fifty additional ones before the month's end. The set fragments were planted in rows two feet apart, with the sets themselves separated by a distance varying from eight to ten inches. Trenches were dug six inches deep, the sets placed, covered, and left to the sun and rain, nothing more—apart from weeding when the weeds came up, and hilling soil around the mature plants come July.

While Jubal and Lincoln worked, so did their neighbors. The critical times for every cattle rancher occurred twice a year, at the spring and fall roundups. In spring the men traditionally rode out to harvest the cattle when the grass first turned green. In Texas this was generally sometime in April. In Wyoming and the other northern territories the grass did not turn until middle or late May. The purpose of the roundup in the south was to brand new calves and gather the mature beef for sale. But in the north, few if any cattle were brought in. Instead, cattlemen concentrated on branding and returning strays that had wandered from their home ranches.

His neighbors' wandering strays posed no problem for Jubal during the winter months, or even in the spring up to the planting. But when the shoots appeared and foliage developed, the strays became a nuisance. They ate the foliage or trampled it. The expense of fencing his entire property was not one Jubal was prepared to incur so early in the game, certainly not before pocketing the profits from his first harvest. And profit there would be. He found he had no need to approach prospective buyers. They came to him, beginning with the Army, closely followed by the Union Pacific. What he could not sell in

Wyoming could be shipped to eastern cities. So the pot of gold waited at the rainbow's end. Now all he had to do was reach it.

Unfortunately, by the middle of June it became apparent that if a fence were not put up along the northern boundary and at least a partial one along the eastern side, possibly as much as one third of his sets would fail to produce. His neighbors' cattle doted on the extensive buffalo grass, but they were not particular; almost anything that grew green appealed to them, and they speedily developed a fondness for potato leaves. Deprived of their vegetation, the maturing tubers would die and rot in the ground.

The money Jubal had brought from Pennsylvania was almost all gone, the bulk paid out to the Davisranch sawmill. Lincoln offered him two thousand dollars, nearly half of his savings; Lorna persuaded her father to accept it. It would be used to erect a fence. For his part Lincoln had only one reservation about spending the money for such an addition.

"Not counting posts, we'll have to figure on at least a hundred thousand board feet of fencing."

They stood at the corner of the front yard where the planting began. Jubal was kneeling, aimlessly hilling up a set; as far as the eye could see stretched orderly rows.

"Back in Pennsylvania a fellow I knew raised draft horses and found he had to put up a fence. Not as big as we'll need, but good-sized. He stretched wire between the posts, stapling it to them. Upper and lower strands. Stapled it so if there was a break, only the strand between two posts would be parted; it wouldn't affect the wire left and right."

"I don't know where we'll get wire around here, Jubal."

"The railroad uses it. I saw some at the sawmill. Plenty strong. You can get it plain or galvanized. Galvanized is a luxury we can't afford, even with your generosity. Wire generally comes in hundred-pound bundles. Costs about a dollar a bundle."

"We'll need men to string it. We can hire them in town. If we can't, I'll speak to Harvey Philips at the fort.

There must be fellows who'd be willing to pick up a few extra dollars when they're off duty."

"What's the matter, son?"

"I still think it's much too big a project."

"It is, but—"

"We'll need literally miles of wire. Hundreds, thousands of posts."

"What else can we do?" Jubal asked.

"Talk to your neighbors," said Lorna, coming up behind them. She had on her apron. Her sleeves were rolled up, her hands red from scrubbing washing on the board. "Tell them to keep their cattle home."

"Talk to the rocks," said Lincoln. "Tell them to rise up out of the ground and form a wall."

Jubal snickered, Lorna glared.

"Practically the entire territory is waiting money in hand for your crop to come in," she said to Jubal.

"Our neighbors don't care about that," said Lincoln.

She pointedly ignored him. "It represents a tremendous contribution to the economy of the territory. It should be protected, not trampled. It's in everybody's interest to protect it."

"Not theirs," said Lincoln. "Jubal, instead of a fence, I think the money would be better spent hiring men to patrol the boundaries."

"That'd cost a fortune," interposed Lorna. "We'd need fifty men."

"Let me check over to the sawmill," said Jubal. "See what sort of deal I can make. Tell you one thing, Mr. Bragg, the superintendent, hasn't got a better customer in the area."

Jubal checked that very day. Posts and wire were purchased and men hired to string the fence. This was not a welcome sight to his neighbors. There was something menacing about a long stretch of wire fence. It looked unfriendly and silently demanded that one stay on one's own side. Jubal's fence was not in harmony with the land. To cattlemen brought up on the open range, it was an insult. It was like Jubal saying, "I can't trust you to control your livestock, so I'll do it for you."

He, Lincoln, and Lorna didn't see it that way and could not understand why the ranchers resented it. At no expense to themselves it would help keep their beef home. Their lands were not overgrazed, so there was no need for their cattle to wander in search of grass. Nevertheless, to the cattlemen, posts and wire were like a red rag to a bull.

A week after the work had begun along the northern boundary, with the H&W Ranch beyond it, Lincoln got up early, dressed for the day, and saddled his horse. There was still more than an hour to go before dawn. He left Lorna and Jubal sleeping and rode north. The full moon painted the twelve-foot-wide break between the neat green rows. Here and there he could see paths of destruction where cattle had wandered through. The center third, more than a mile of fence, had been completed late the previous afternoon. He was within a quarter mile of it when he spotted figures moving about directly ahead. Within an eighth of a mile he pulled up, dismounted, checked his rifle, and proceeded on foot. He moved carefully, ducking low.

Presently he heard a telltale sound that stiffened him, the unmistakable sharp twang of wire cut, the tension broken, the loose ends flinging away singing. He hurried his step. He descried three men working, their horses standing idly by. He made his way back to the break and bellied down, his weapon in front of him, his finger on the trigger. Squirming forward he moved to about forty feet from where they stood. He jumped to his feet. "Hold it! One move and I'll kill you."

They froze, dropping their cutters, raising their hands, exchanging surprised looks. He came up to them. They had already cut the fence between at least 30 posts left and right. The severed strands lay on the ground. None of them said a word, but all eyed him malevolently and with growing fear in their eyes.

"You—" He motioned with the rifle to the man closest to him. "Toss your six-gun into the potatoes behind me. The three of you. Let's see who can throw the farthest." He aimed at the first man's face. "Do it!"

They threw their guns. Again he addressed them, injecting menace into his tone. "Pick up your cutters."

"Huh?"

"You heard. Pick 'em up. Cut a foot and a half off the loose end of the top strand there and join the ends of the bottom one. Taut as you can. Move!"

He put them to work, collected and emptied their guns, and one by one smashed the cylinders with his rifle butt. They groused and grumbled and worked on. He moved up the line, keeping them in plain sight. Twenty yards from them he found where Jubal's men had been working the previous day: posts, post-hole diggers, and half a dozen bundles of wire. He carried one bundle back to where the men were working, ordering them to cut their ties from it. It was seven in the morning by the time they repaired the damage they had inflicted. He assembled them.

"I should ride you down to Cheyenne and turn you over to the law, but I can't be bothered. Only if this happens again, if so much as one strand is cut, I'll know who did it: Red, Ugly, Shorty. Now get on your horses and get out of here."

"You ruined our weapons!"

"They can be fixed. If you want them back, send your boss down for them."

"Jesus—"

"Embarrassing, isn't it?"

"You go to hell, sodbuster."

Lincoln fired between two of them. They blanched, stiffened, mounted their horses, fled.

Jubal and Lorna were up and at work by the time he got back. He took them into the kitchen and told them what he'd found. They sat at the table. Lorna refilled his cup from the coffeepot.

"When I woke up, I had the funniest feeling," said Lincoln. "I thought to myself that wire's standing up there unprotected; sooner or later somebody's bound to cut it." He eyed Jubal. "We'd be kidding ourselves not to expect it. It was the dumbest luck in the world I actually caught them in the act."

"What do we do now?" Lorna murmured. "I think . . . Does anybody want to know what I think?"

"Of course," said Jubal smiling at her, winking at Lincoln.

Her head down, plunged into considering what she was about to say, she failed to see him.

"I think we should meet with Weigans, with all three ranchers," she said. "Air our differences and find solutions we can agree on. If they don't want the fence, we'll take it down, but only on condition they start controlling their herds."

Lincoln was eyeing her in manifest disbelief. "Are you saying you really want to sit down and discuss it with your friend Emerald?"

"With her husband."

"I doubt if it'll do any good. As I see it, things are well past the talking stage."

"If that's true, we're done for. Can't we at least try? I want to. I'm going up there right now."

"I wouldn't, sweetheart. You won't be in the same room sixty seconds with that woman before you'll be at each other's throats. If it'll make you happy, Jubal and I'll go up. Okay, Jubal? We'll talk to her husband."

"I'll come, too," said Lorna.

"No."

He could tell when her mind was made up and locked. But over the next hour she evidently changed it, and when he and Jubal rode out, she stayed behind.

They spotted Jubal's three-man crew at work in the distance to the east. They rode through the north gate onto H&W property. They were about fifty yards in when two men came barreling up, guns out. Neither was any of the three Lincoln had encountered earlier.

"We want to see Mr. Weigans," he said.

"Who be ya? Whatta ya want?" snarled the taller, older of the two.

"He just told you," interposed Jubal.

"His Lordship don't wanna see ya," said the other, waving his gun.

"We're your neighbors," explained Lincoln.

"We know who ya be, sodbuster," said the first man. "And he don't wanna see ya, so turn 'round and get the hell outta here."

Two riders, a man and woman, came into view to the west. Perceiving the confrontation, they came over at a trot. Lincoln had never seen Emerald Giradoux-Weigans before; he knew her only by reputation. Her beauty, he was quick to note, was not at all exaggerated. Nor were her husband's good looks. He was attired in a custom-tailored cowboy outfit between a Navaho hat with turquoise and leather band and expensive, elaborately stitched, fancifully designed inlaid and overlaid boots, complete with handmade silver-plated spurs with oversize rowels and jinglebobs. Lincoln introduced Jubal and himself.

"We'd appreciate a few minutes of your time," he concluded.

"Of course. Forgive me, gentlemen, may I present my wife, Countess Weigans? Please, come up to the house, I am at your service."

"Your Lordship," began the taller man.

"It is all right, Walter," said Weigans.

Emerald, Lincoln noted, said nothing.

They sat in the elaborately furnished and decorated parlor. It made Lorna's parlor look desperately drab by comparison; still, there was something overly ornate and artificial about this room, and for all its richness and color it was cold. The uniformed maid brought coffee and a platter of small jam cakes. Emerald excused herself to go upstairs and change. Lincoln watched Jubal follow her up with admiring eyes. Lincoln told Weigans what had happened earlier. He studied the man's eyes, hoping they would betray guilt, shame, something. They showed only surprise shadowed with disappointment. His reaction was genuine. He obviously knew nothing about his ranch hands' activities, and learning about them now was slowly firing his anger.

"Disgraceful!" he burst. "I assure you both I would have no part of such heinous doings. Why would I? I have nothing against you. What you do with your land is your business. I will question my men. The ones responsible will be discharged. Who could have put them up to such a thing?"

He shook his head in disgust and turned away. His eyes strayed to the empty stairs for a barely perceptible moment before he turned back and with an apologetic smile. "I am very sorry this happened. And embarrassed. I shall, of course, make restitution. If you'll be so kind as to submit a bill——"

"That's all right," said Lincoln. "The damage has been repaired. It was no big expense."

"Good." Weigans shook his head and sighed. "Such a pity that you even *have* to put up a barrier between neighbors."

Jubal explained the reason for it.

"I see," said Weigans. "Well, for now on my men will see to it that none of our cattle wander onto your property."

"The fence'll take care of that," Jubal said airily. "Providing it's left as is."

"It will be, it will be. My word as a gentleman. Alas, I cannot speak for Herr Knox to the south of you or Herr Bazarian to the east. But having met them, I can't believe either would encourage their men to ignore the wandering of their cattle."

"It's not deliberate," said Lincoln. "It's . . . well, pretty much just neglect. Knox and Bazarian may feel exactly as you do, but not their men. And to cowhands and cattlemen in these parts, fencing is about as welcome as green flies in August."

"Mmmm."

Weigans appeared to have plunged into thought. Jubal interrupted him.

"We just wanted you to know what happened, Your Lordship," he said.

His expression as he said the last two words very nearly started Lincoln laughing. They sounded so self-conscious, so unlike him to even consider saying.

"Heinrich, please. This is America, not my homeland. Here titles are meaningless, a pompous affectation. And formality is for men of the cloth, *nicht wahr*? That's just one thing I find absolutely delightful here. I mean in America every man is a lord. So do please call me Heinrich, better yet Henry."

"How do you like Wyoming?" asked Jubal.

"*Wunderbar!* I kick myself for waiting this long to come. Of course, one cannot travel very far on an empty purse. I had to wait for my ship to come in. But now I'm here, I am in love with your country, with Wyoming, with my wife. Is she not magnificent? And no empty-headed beauty. You should see the way she runs this place. She handles all the finances and pays the bills. Money bores me sick." He laughed. "I like only to spend it."

They spent the next hour with "Henry." He showed them about the house. He showed them his collections of sabers and hunting rifles and shotguns. He showed them his uniforms and was deeply impressed when Jubal told him that Lincoln was formerly commandant at Fort Russell. He reminded Lincoln of Louis Schwimmer, a wide-eyed boy with an insatiable curiosity about the Army, the Indians, Lincoln, the U.P., and Cheyenne.

"I am in the process of becoming a U.S. citizen, you know," he announced proudly. "It will be a few months before my test, but I will pass. Being married to a citizen helps, of course."

It was eleven o'clock by the ornate Second Empire clock guarded by three naked seraphims which decorated the imported Travertine marble fireplace mantel. Jubal and Lincoln thanked Henry for his hospitality and rode off. The two ranch hands who had stopped them earlier glared as they galloped by, but said nothing. Jubal didn't even bother to look their way.

"Fine figure of a woman, that wife of his," he murmured. "You do know who she is?"

"I know. She was with that Freeling fellow at that whorehouse bar the night Jeptha was killed."

"That's her."

"See here, she didn't have anything to do with it. I know Lorna's got it in for her, but she was just an innocent bystander. Your friend Major Philips said she was."

"But if she hadn't twisted Jeptha around her finger, he wouldn't have gone there."

"It takes two," muttered Jubal.

Lincoln couldn't believe his ears.

"I'd be pretty stupid to go to my grave carrying bitterness in my gut for her," Jubal went on. He paused. He caught on. "Say, you don't think it was her put the men up to cutting the fence?"

"I don't know, the idea seemed to cross Henry's mind."

"I can't believe she'd do such a rotten thing."

Lincoln was surprised that Jubal seemed to want to defend her. It was almost like Emerald had cast her spell on him, too.

26

The fence was completed to the north and half-finished to the east, but it was to remain half a fence for some time. There was no more money to buy posts, wire, and labor until the first harvest was sold in September.

By July, Jubal estimated his loss for the season at between twenty-five and thirty percent of the crop by harvest time. And in the middle of the month, a bad situation took an abrupt turn for the ugly.

After he and Lincoln had called on Henry Weigans, they had also spoken to Carleton Knox and Mark Bazarian. Both cattlement were cold and inhospitable to the point of rudeness. Both denied any knowledge of the fence cutting, leaving Jubal no choice but to let the matter go at that.

There was no further damage to the fence. Worse and more dangerous harassment was in store. One night while Lincoln and Lorna slept in each other's arms and Jubal snored away the hours of a long, arduous day, the three were awakened by shouting. Lincoln sniffed, a disagreeable, familiar odor stinging his nostrils. Slipping through the lingering veil of sleep and reaching his ears came a low roaring sound punctuated with crackling. Eerie shadows flung themselves through the bedroom window. Lorna snapped upright beside him.

"The barn!"

Lincoln jumped from bed and pulled on his pants and boots. He met Jubal at the back door, red-faced, wild-eyed, and cursing with shotgun in hand. Outside, the barn was ablaze, huge pennons of flame leaping for the stars, driving sparks upward. Smoke billowed and the wind seized it, pushing it toward the house. The house itself was in no danger, situated a hundred feet from the barn. But the barn, it appeared, was doomed. Lincoln ran for the well. Jubal called after him.

"Don't bother, she's too far gone! At least they let the horses and the cow out, damn them! The cowardly scum!"

There was neither sight nor sound of the arsonists. The black skeleton of the barn stood stark and defenseless in the roaring furnace. Beams tumbled, supporting studs snapped and fell into the growing heap of blackened rubble.

The fire crackled and raged. Long tongues ran up the still standing corners to meet the glowing mass within. The blaze was so bright and powerful that it began to swallow up the smoke rising from it.

Lorna and Lincoln looked over at Jubal. He appeared mesmerized by the sight. His eyes took in the ghastly destruction, and his brain spun forth memory of all the hours and labor of erecting the barn. It took minutes to destroy it all.

Gradually the glare of the flames sank into a glowing pile, which diminished, shrinking into itself, and flattening into extinction. In its stead wisps of smoke rose straight upward into the night, the breeze resting for the moment as if it too were absorbed in witnessing the end of the destruction.

Presently, all that was left was the flat, black heap of ashes, silence and desolation.

The horses and the cow had not strayed far. Jubal collected them. When he brought them into the yard, Lincoln took his horse from him and swung up onto his back.

"Where do you think you're going?" Lorna snapped.

"What do you think?" He gestured for Jubal to hand up his shotgun.

"No!" she exclaimed. "No guns. No shooting."

"If you don't mind, I'd like to be able to protect

myself," he said dryly. "In case somebody else decides to shoot."

He rode away with the shotgun in his right hand. He knew he'd never catch up with whoever it was, but hoped to find something to indicate where they'd come from. As he rode around the property border, he thought about the fire and realized he should have seen it coming. He half wondered why it hadn't happened long before this.

He'd heard the talk in town lately, the rapidly growing resentment, the threats. Perhaps Knox and Bazarian had joined forces to harass them so that eventually they'd give up and leave. They obviously didn't know Jubal Hunnicutt. Nothing would drive him off his land.

And what about Henry Weigans? More to the point, what about Emerald? She had a reputation for ruthlessness few men he knew could equal. Had she despatched Henry's cowhands on tonight's mission? Since he and Jubal visited, had she talked Henry into seeing the situation her way? Was she conspiring with Knox and Bazarian without her husband's knowledge?

Even likelier was that she secretly coveted Jubal's property, particularly the creek—the best source of water in the area—that he shared with Carleton Knox. Avarice in inexhaustible supply was not a quality of character she took pains to conceal. For the Emeralds of the world, no ranch, not even Richard King's 146,000-acre Santa Gertrudis in Texas, was big enough.

Jubal demanded and got a meeting with his neighbors. Henry Weigans hosted the gathering. Emerald was not at home when the five men sat down in the parlor. It had been three days since the barn was destroyed, ample time to dull the cutting edge of Jubal's anger, but his resentment smoldered, threatening to burst forth in accusation any moment. Seeing this within seconds after he and Lincoln walked into the room, Weigans appointed himself peacemaker.

Carleton, C.W., Knox was a huge, hairy Texan in his late sixties who had been a cattleman all his life. He had never had neighbors who were homesteaders or farmers, and he bluntly proclaimed they had no more right to the land than the "stinkin' savages."

Mark Bazarian, a recent arrival from Kentucky, was even more vehement in his vexation against Jubal's "trespassing." He was a tall, ungainly, homely individual with the dark hair and skin of his Armenian forebears. He had a minor speech impediment, a lisp of sorts that, when he got angry and raised his voice, became more pronounced and consequently made him more self-conscious over it. His argumentative nature and his rudeness led Lincoln to believe that bile flowed in the man's veins. He'd never seen so much hatred stuffed into a single body before.

"We don't know who burned down your barn and we don't care," said Bazarian. "If your house is next to go, that'll be too damned bad. Only don't go blaming me or Carl for your problems. Or Heinrich here."

Knox nodded assertively. "When you put up that fence, brother, you declared war. On the three of us. On every cattleman!"

"Here here, gentlemen," interposed Weigans soothingly. "Let us *be* gentlemen. Not snap at each other. As I see it, Herr Hunnicutt and Herr Rhilander have every right to fence their property and do as they wish with it. It was originally public land like ours, was it not? Where in the laws governing public lands does it say you can't fence, can't plant potatoes . . . ?"

"It's the goddamn unwritten law!" snapped Bazarian. "Erecting a fence, I mean. Who gives a damn about his stupid spuds?"

"Unwritten law for you," snapped Lincoln. "Not us."

Knox held up a letter. "This here says it's written now. Good as. We've formed us a cattlemen's association. Just held our first meeting. Boys come from all over. And one of the first statues we voted on, and unanimously, was to outlaw fences. No fences on no property in the territory."

"Which means," added Bazarian leering. "Your fence has to come down."

"Like hell!" burst Lincoln.

"Simmer down, soldier boy—"

Lincoln jumped up. He stood glaring and seething.

"Who the hell are you calling soldier boy, you god-damned clown!"

"Now now now," burst Weigans. "Please control yourselves."

Knox ignored him. He was on his feet. He tossed the letter at Jubal, who made no move to catch it, letting it sail to the floor.

"Read it yourself," rasped Knox. "Or don't, whatever you please. Only as far as I'm concerned this here meeting's over. You coming, Mark?"

"You bet. We got nothing more to say, Heinrich."

"Please sit down," pleaded Weigans.

Knox shook his head. "It's all in the letter. Every cattleman's rights. Let me give a piece of free advice, Hunnicutt. If you're smart, you'll pack up and get out. While you still can."

"Don't threaten me, Texas," rasped Jubal. "If either of you or your men give us any more trouble, I'll make you wish—"

"Go to hell, sodbuster!" burst Bazarian.

The two of them went stomping out. Weigans threw up his hands, then spotted the paper on the floor and retrieved it. Lincoln read over his shoulder.

"It says no fences, all right," he said to Jubal.

"I don't care what it says. You heard him, Cattlemen's Association. Organized, I'm sure, for the sole and express purpose of driving us out. Well it's not going to work—"

Weigans drew a breath in sharply. He had squeezed a monocle into one eye to read.

"I count nearly thirty signatures at the bottom," he said.

"I don't see yours," said Lincoln.

"I wasn't invited. I see others weren't either. Lots of names are missing."

"Don't you want to read it?" Lincoln asked Jubal.

"Waste of eyesight. Whatever they decide, it's not legal. They won't find a judge in the territory who'll back them up."

"I don't know about that," said Weigans, asking with his eyes what Lincoln thought.

"They *are* the majority, Jubal," said Lincoln. "And do have the power. They can write chapter and verse. The Union Pacific did."

"Give that here."

Jubal read the letter to himself. In it the undersigned specified not only that no fences could be erected on property, but that existing ones must be taken down. It said also that cattle ranchers' water rights were to be respected over those of any and all other property owners, that cattle were free to graze wherever they wandered, and if any cattle were shot, the owner of the land on which they were found would be subject to arrest and a fine equal to the amount of the value of the animal.

"They must have been drunk out of their minds when they got this up," growled Jubal.

He tore the letter to shreds, placing them in an ashtray.

"I don't know what to say," said Weigans. "They refuse to even discuss matters. It looks like from now on things can only . . ."

"Get bloody." Jubal nodded. "If they want a fight, I'll be happy to accommodate them."

"No no no," interrupted Weigans.

"We can't fight them, Jubal," said Lincoln. "They'd wipe us out in a week. I'll be damned if I'll put Lorna's life in danger."

"You don't have any say in it, son. They're the ones kicking over the kettle. We either stand up for our rights or run away. I'm going to hire a dozen men in town to ride the boundaries."

"And what'll you pay them with?"

"They'll be paid. In September."

Lincoln shook his head. "That's six, maybe eight weeks from now. You seriously expect men to work for nothing until harvest time? There may not even be a harvest."

"You would not have to patrol your fence up here," said Weigans.

"Henry," said Jubal, laying a friendly hand on his shoulder, "you're a good soul and a fair one, but you can't control your men. What owner can? They're free-lancers, they do as they please. Hell, it was your men cut our fence."

"We don't know that, Jubal," said Lincoln.

"Jesus Christ, of course it was! I'm not blaming you, Henry, but you know it's true. In your heart you do. The same goes for Knox and Bazarian; they're a couple loud-mouths who can't stand the sight of me, but neither one is the sort who'd burn down his neighbor's barn or shoot at him. It's their goddamned men. And yours."

"I will talk to my men."

"You already did, and it didn't work. They respect you, but they don't give you loyalty. In their minds, your land and your beef are theirs."

"He's right, Henry," said Lincoln. "But Jubal, you're wrong about hiring men now and paying them later. I still have some money in the bank in Cheyenne. We can afford to hire a couple men until the harvest. Only then what? We dig up the crop, you count your money, and next spring the whole merry-go-round starts all over again."

Jubal brightened. His eyes narrowed, he smirked mischievously. "Maybe not."

"You have an idea?" Weigans asked.

Jubal nodded at the torn pieces of paper in the ashtray.

"They think they can write the book, right? Let's see if they can. Let's see if we can find us a judge who'll give us a court order that'll stop them in their tracks." He placed an arm around their shoulders. "My friends, I'm the legal owner of a parcel of what was formerly public land. I have rights, I'm entitled to the full protection of the law. Not their law, territorial law."

He took down his arms and began pacing, generating more and more enthusiasm for what he was saying with every step. "The only law that counts. And can't be superseded by their pipe dreams. Lincoln, we're going down to Cheyenne. I want to have a talk with Lawyer Pinchot. I want to hire him."

Weigans wished them luck with all his customary sincerity. Emerald arrived home as they rode away. She looked, thought Lincoln, more beautiful than ever. Jubal seemed to think so. He tipped his hat, accorded her a radiant smile and addressed her as "Your Ladyship" in passing.

She was impressed.

27

His hand glided along her thigh. She gasped and seized his head, bringing it down and sealing his mouth with a passionate kiss. When their lips parted he kissed her eyes and down her face. There were no words to express their feelings. They were locked in the glow of gratification, clinging to the warmth. She stroked his cheek. He propped on his elbows and gazed down at her in the darkness. She could hear his quiet, measured breathing, feel his breath on her cheek like a feather.

When he stood shaving before the mirror, she reveled in the sight of his muscular upper body, his broad shoulders and back, the powerful cords of his neck. She could see the three faint scars: on his right shoulder, one grazing his rib cage on the right, and the other on the small of his back near his left side. These were the trophies of his valor in battle. As curious as she was, she'd never felt compelled to ask about his experiences. That life had ended when he came back from Omaha.

But she wondered about the scars on his conscience—the needless deaths at the railhead, Rudy's suicide. He never talked about either, but he'd never forget them.

"What are you thinking about?" he whispered.

"You, the Army . . ."

"My God, how my lovemaking must inspire you . . . What army? Where?"

She kissed him into silence.

*　　*　　*

279

Knox's and Bazarian's threats proved to be as empty as the Cattlemen's Association's arbitrary claims to rights over the homesteaders. Attorney Cicero Sebastian Pinchot obtained an injunction from Judge Arthur Shankland in Laramie, the same judge the Hunnicutts had met enroute to Cheyenne. The injunction rendered unbinding the association's so-called statues, and made Knox, Bazarian, and Henry Weigans responsible for the extent of their cattle's grazing. Henceforth they and all other ranchers in Laramie County would be duty-bound to keep their livestock on their property. If their cattle wandered onto homesteaders' property and inflicted damage, they'd be held liable.

The half fence on Jubal's land remained in place. July gave way to August, and a benevolent sun and sufficient rain nurtured the plants. The tubers below ground grew large and in late September the crop was dug up.

It brought nearly five thousand dollars in the marketplace. What Jubal kept for seed for the following year's planting was stored in his cellar. The largest potato in the crop, weighing better than seven pounds, was proudly displayed on a side table in the parlor. Lorna refurbished the parlor and all three bedrooms. The parlor ended up much less flamboyant and more tastefully decorated than the Weigan's.

Jubal was elated with the success of his first crop. He had planted only a little over fifty acres of his one hundred sixty, leaving wide swaths between the outer edges of the crop and the boundaries of the property. Cattle had damaged the plants, but it was not as bad as he'd anticipated. In the spring, with the help of his six new hired hands, he planned to sow at least one hundred acres.

The barn had been rebuilt and another, larger one put up close by it. A bunkhouse was built and furnished for the hired hands. During the winter postholes were dug in the frozen ground, and the fence completed on three sides of the property.

But in spite of Judge Shankland's injunction, and the protection it afforded him, Jubal knew that trouble would erupt again. Where his foes would strike and how bloody the encounter would turn out to be, remained to be seen. It was a worry Jubal would carry in his breast from harvest to spring, notwithstanding Pinchot's repeated assurances that Knox and Bazarian would cause him no further trouble.

It upset Jubal for another reason. He wanted to live in harmony with his neighbors, as he had back in Pennsylvania. No matter how far apart ranches and farmhouses may be, a sense of community should exist. But in this instance the atmosphere was anti-social to a point of being almost warlike, with winter providing a lull between the battles.

Jubal called on his lawyer in Pinchot's office shortly after the onset of the new year. The two were joined by Aloysius Gogarty, who, along with Pinchot, had enjoyed Christmas dinner at the house.

"Those two would be idiots to cause you any further trouble," remarked Pinchot. He sat at his desk basking in the warm winter sun slanting through his fanlight window, critically eyeing Dr. Gogarty sipping bourbon and trying his utmost to maintain some semblance of sobriety. "Haven't you had enough for one day, Aloysius?"

"Impossible, Counselor." Gogarty covered a cough with the back of his hand. "Don't you know an alcoholic can never get enough? His legs are hollow, his belly unfillable—"

"If you call yourself an alcoholic, you damned well must be," rasped Pinchot.

Jubal suppressed a grin.

"I just did call myself," said Gogarty slurringly. "Weren't you listening?"

Pinchot snorted derisively. "As I was saying, Jubal, the two of them are marked men. And *their* men know they are. If anybody does anything to you, they'll be the first to be suspected. They'll be guilty until proven innocent."

"Don't listen to him, Jubal," averred Gogarty. "He's talking through his fur hat. Nobody's ever proved Knox or Bazarian or anyone connected with them burned down your barn." He paused, coughed, and excused himself.

"Oh, I know what it looks like, but I remember you saying yourself Lincoln thought it was Heinrich Weigans's boys. It had to be them damaged your north fence.

"What you're going to have to look out for is outsiders, hired guns from up around Casper or over near Green River. If they hit you and put you out of business, there's no way in heaven you'll be able to lay it at the Association's door. Disagree with that if you can, Counselor."

"I most certainly do," said Pinchot. "It's ridiculous. Why should outsiders pick on him? Why single out his place to attack? You overlook the fact that the law is in place."

"What law is that?" sputtered Gogarty in sudden exasperation. "It's no law, it's an injunction, a piece of string holding them in check. That's all it is."

"When the legislature meets, it'll be enacted into law," responded Pinchot defensively.

"Balderdash! The cattlemen are in the majority. They've got the money to fight it and the clout to kill it." The doctor nodded sharply, agreeing with himself.

Lincoln and Lorna arrived. They had come into town with Jubal to shop. Lorna's arms were filled with purchases. Lincoln was sweating from the weight of a copper plunge bath he'd been carrying over his head like a canoe through the streets. He set it down.

The three of them left Gogarty hacking and sipping, Pinchot reproving him for his drinking and reproving himself for contributing the bourbon. It had started snowing about ten that morning, great, fat flakes drifting quietly down, settling in the frozen, deeply rutted quagmires of the streets. The day had dawned windy, dull and cold with two thirds of the sky hidden by a lowering dark cloud. Outside of town the wind was more bitter. It whirled the falling snow about, sending it laterally at their faces as they drove back. It pelted their exposed cheeks and built up on the horse's crest like a white boa, stretching from her ears almost down to her withers.

By the time they came within sight of the house looming in shadow, the snowfall had become so thick the blanket on the ground appeared to have accumulated several inches before their eyes. Lincoln got down and opened the gate; Jubal drove around the house into the backyard. Almost the instant he pulled the horse to a stop, it magically stopped snowing. In moments the sun came out, but it shone feebly as if the storm had drawn the power of its rays. Jubal and Lorna took the groceries and other purchases into the house while Lincoln tended to the horse.

In their absence the fire in the Globe Sunshine stove had reduced itself to glowing ashes. Jubal set about resurrecting it. Lorna put away the groceries and got out the utensils and ingredients she needed to bake bread.

She was breaking the tie string on a new sack of flour when Lincoln came to the kitchen door.

"Jubal," he called past her into the parlor. "You'd better come."

Lorna stared at him quizzically. He looked very disturbed.

"What is it?" she asked.

"Nothing. Stay here, sweetheart. Jubal!"

"Coming, coming, let a man get his boots back on, can't you?"

"Hurry up."

She set her hands against his chest. "Lincoln . . ."

She got her coat back on and tied a scarf around her head. Her sheep-skin-lined boots stood by the sink. She getured for him to hand them to her.

A lit lantern hung from a peg just inside the barn door, sending a weak, weary glow over the interior. The horses stood quietly in their stalls. Wisps of hay littered the floor under the edge of the loft. On the floor, looking as if he'd been thrown down from the loft, lay a man, his face down and buried in the crook of one arm.

He had been shot twice in the back. Two dark splotches the size and shape of silver dollars stained his coat. His right arm was stretched out, his fingers curled as if he'd been clutching for something when death seized him. But there was nothing on the floor within reach. Lincoln knelt and turned him over.

It was Henry Weigans.

28

A pistol lay about six feet from the body. Jubal inspected it while Lincoln examined the corpse. Lorna stood watching fascinated.

"This thing's fully loaded," said Jubal. "Look at the scrollwork on the grip, and it's silver."

Lorna sensed that the grisly discovery had dazed her father, and now he was concentrating all his attention on the little weapon not out of curiosity, but to enable him to ignore the dead man. Lincoln rose from where he'd been kneeling.

"What the devil is he doing here?" he asked mystified.

"Good question," said a voice behind them.

They turned. There stood Carleton Knox with three of his men. They were bundled up to their eyes against the cold. Knox undid the scarf from around his face. He was unarmed, but his men wore guns.

"What happened? You two good neighbors have yourselves a falling-out?" he asked.

"What are you doing here?" snapped Lorna. "What do you want?"

"That doesn't answer my question, little girl. Speak up, Hunnicutt. Are you going to tell me finding him dead in your barn is as much a surprise to you as us?"

"I'm not telling you anything, Knox." Jubal softened his tone. "To be perfectly honest, I don't know anything. None of us do. We just got back from Cheyenne."

"I know," said Knox. "Saw you passing my window.

CHEYENNE

We followed you up. I wanted a word with you about this phony injunction. Looks like I came at the wrong time."

"Amen to that," said one of his men.

"None of us killed him," said Lincoln.

Knox nodded. "You mean somebody else did and dragged the body in here to incriminate you." He shrugged. "Sounds fair. Maybe they did. That's for a judge to decide, not me. Say, it's as freezing in here as it is outside. Can we go into your house and talk?"

"Not now," said Jubal without looking at him.

He had shoved the pistol into his belt and was staring down at the body.

"See here!" snapped Knox.

"You! See here," Jubal added softly. "Are you blind? At the moment I'm not interested in talking about that stupid injunction."

"Stupid is right. It'll never become law."

"Why don't you just get out of here?" said Lincoln tightly.

"Will do. We got to do our duties as good citizens, go into town and report a murder, right, boys?"

His men snickered and shared his offensive grin.

Aloysius Gogarty teetered slightly as he straightened, having finished examining the body. It had been brought into the house and laid on the bed in the guest room. Lincoln stood in the doorway watching Gogarty.

"How long has he been dead?" he asked.

"Hard to tell. Impossible in this weather. Could be two hours, could be ten."

"Are you saying he could have been killed sometime last night and dumped in the barn at seven-thirty this morning?" Lincoln asked. "That's impossible. He wasn't here when I came in to get the horse around nine."

"If you say so."

"If he was, would I have left him here?"

"I don't know, I'm just playing devil's advocate. But I'm not the one you and Jubal have to prove anything to." He scratched his chin thoughtfully. "He's thawed out some since you brought him in here, but out in the

285

barn he was damn near frozen stiff. When the body freezes, everything stops. Temperature drops like a shot."

Lincoln stepped into the room. Through the window he could see the barn. Both doors were wide open. Somebody had extinguished the lantern. Sheriff Ben Swaggart and three of his deputies had arrived with Gogarty, and were inside looking for clues to the tragedy. The deputies were; Swaggart and Jubal stood in the doorway talking. His attention momentarily diverted from Gogarty, concentrating on them instead. Lincoln wondered what they were saying to each other. Swaggart didn't seem to be accusing or Jubal defending himself, he decided.

He didn't like the sheriff; he had no reason to dislike him, but unsavory rumors about him clung to his coattails. Part of his job was to collect petty fines and levy big ones. Everybody in town knew that the worst crimes, excepting outright murder, generally saw the culprit go free. Laws governing operation of the saloons, brothels, and gambling parlors were systematically bent and broken. Swaggart knew the art of bribery and practiced it to perfection. Unfortunately for Cheyenne, nobody else wanted the sheriff's job.

Swaggart didn't command Lincoln's—or anyone's—respect. He was just the mayor's loudmouth toady. Most of the law and order in force came as a result of groups of vigilantes, to whom he gave free license. In a sense they did his job for him, leaving him to his bribe collecting. He wore two six-guns. He also wore thick spectacles, and it was claimed that he couldn't hit the side of a barn if he'd been standing inside it. As befitting his name, he swaggered about town, exuding an air of authority and command he had neither the heart nor guts to enforce. He talked a courageous game, but his conduct and his actions spoke infinitely louder.

He was a clown, but a dangerous one when crossed.

Lorna joined them in the guest room, drying her hands on a finger towel as she entered. She had been listening. "If you can't set the time of his death, if that's supposed to deny any of us an albi—" she began.

"I'm sorry," interrupted Gogarty. "Believe me, I wasn't even thinking of that."

She went on. "My father was with us every hour for the past three days, apart from when he stopped in at Mr. Pinchot's office this noon."

Gogarty shifted his head and put on an expression that said that this particular intelligence did not impress him.

"Did you two sleep eight hours last night?" he asked.

Lincoln exchanged glances with her. "Close to it," he said.

"Well, Mrs. Rhilander, if you want to get technical, and there are those who will, it would have been possible for Jubal to leave the house after you two fell asleep and come back before you woke up. Understand, I'm not accusing him—"

"It sounds like it to me!" burst Lorna.

"I'm not."

"All he's saying is anybody can do anything while others in the same house are asleep," said Lincoln. "He's right." He turned back to Gogarty. "Are you sure you can't fix the time of death any better than from two to ten hours?"

"I'm sorry. I'm being honest with you, Colonel. I'm telling you what I'll be telling the coroner's jury at the inquest. Which is unavoidable as far as I can see."

He replaced the sheet over the dead man's face, put his stethoscope in his valise, and snapped it shut. Case closed, reflected Lincoln. Gogarty looked, he thought, like God's wrath: steeped in stale liquor fumes and gradually disintegrating in both body and spirit.

"Anybody break the good news to the poor man's missus?" Gogarty asked.

"I'm sure Knox beat a trail up there fast as he could travel after he left here," said Lorna.

They drifted into the parlor. Gogarty was preparing to resume talking when the kitchen door opened and Jubal filed in with the others. His cheeks were ashen. Lorna ran to him. One of the deputies carried a deerskin jacket with blood stains on the lower right sleeve. Swaggart took it from him.

"We found this in the hayloft. It's your father's, he don't deny it."

"Hell!" snapped Jubal. "I haven't seen the damn thing in ages. I hung it up in one of the stalls last summer and left it there. Is that supposed to prove I killed him? That's stupid. Why would I? We got along, we were friends; if I wanted to shoot somebody it'd be Knox or Bazarian, not him."

"Nobody's accusing you," murmured Swaggart.

He was enjoying the limelight, decided Lincoln, with all eyes on him.

"You damn well better not!" burst Jubal.

"Look at it from my point of view, brother. Man's body was found in your barn, this is your jacket with blood on it. Hidden away—"

"It wasn't! It was hanging in plain sight. Somebody moved it up to the loft and still hung it in plain sight. On purpose, can't you see that? Whoever killed him brought him here. Knox and his boys showed up Johnny on the spot, perfect timing. Talk to him, why—"

"Easy, Jubal," interrupted Gogarty. "It does sound pretty farfetched to me," he said to the sheriff. "If Jubal here shot him, why didn't he hide the body? Why leave it in plain sight?"

Swaggart eyed Gogarty with a long and jaundiced look. "Do me a favor, brother Gogarty, let me do my job. I can only go by what I see. Haven't found the murder weapon yet, but it's got to be around." He glanced at the deputy standing nearest him. "Homer, you stay here and look further. The barn, the house—"

"Now wait a minute!" burst Lorna. "Nobody is going poking around my house!"

"What good will it do if you do find a gun?" Gogarty asked. "And you're bound to. Everybody's got guns."

"If it's been fired recent—" said Swaggart.

"What would that prove?" Lincoln cut in.

"Maybe nothing, maybe the case. Be that as it may, I'm gonna have to take you in, brother Hunnicutt."

Jubal exploded. Swinging his arms, he cast about wildly, threatening to throw himself through the nearest window and run for it.

"Calm down!" snapped Lincoln. "We'll get Cicero Pinchot on it right away. I'm coming in with him," he added to Swaggart.

"I'm not setting foot out of this house!" roared Jubal. "Not going to any damn jail. I'll kill the first man lays a hand on me!"

"Now now now," purred Swaggart. "Be smart, come along quietlike. If you got nothing to hide, you got nothing to worry about. Give us a chance."

"To string me up!"

"Please, just come along. Don't make me have to hogtie you."

Lorna moved to Jubal. "Do as he says, Daddy."

He gaped in surprise at her.

"If this doesn't beat all," he murmured. "First Fletcher, now this. It's crazy, I'd no more harm Henry than I would any of you."

"Nobody can prove you did," said Lincoln. "Cicero'll take care of everything."

A buggy had pulled up outside. The driver was helping a woman down. Emerald stormed in, stopping just long enough to glare about her at the array of faces before launching a search of the premises. Before Lorna could block the way, she pushed open the guest room door. She froze, her hands flying to her mouth; she screamed and rushed to the bed, then tore the sheet from the dead man's face and began carrying on hysterically, throwing herself across the corpse and beating the bed with her fists.

Lincoln and Gogarty went to her. They pulled her to her feet and talked soothingly to her. Gogarty gave her his handkerchief as she leaned her tear-stained face against his chest. She got control. They brought her back into the parlor. She noticed Swaggart holding Jubal's arm with one hand, his other cupping his handcuffs. He seemed to be debating whether to snap them on or not.

"You did it!" she shrilled. "You killed him!"

She threw herself at Jubal, pounding his face and chest.

Again Lincoln and Gogarty pulled her off. To Lorna's surprise it was Swaggart who rescued Jubal from her fury.

"We don't know that, ma'am," he exclaimed. "We purely don't. He denies he did, and like the doctor says, it doesn't make much sense to kill a man and leave his body in plain sight in your own barn. We're just taking him in while we sort out the pieces and put 'em together. I swear to you, the killer will be brought to justice. Brother Gogarty, if you'll be so kind as to see to the corpse. Homer, start looking. Brother Hunnicutt, come along."

◄29►

Jubal was locked in one of the two cells in the Thomas
Avenue jail, a log cabin which had been converted
into Cheyenne's jail by Mayor Luke Murrin only two
months earlier. The interior had been divided into the
two individual cells, a single large holding pen and a
hole-in-the-wall office with a small rolltop desk, a bow-
back chair, two stools, a badly dented filing cabinet, gun
rack, and Peoria Fire Insurance Company calendar.

Whenever the holding pen became too crowded, a
semi-official mob would march the prisoners to the edge
of town, one at a time. There a spokesman would ask
each where he wanted to go. When the prisoner responded, he was faced in the direction of his choice and
admonished to march. And he did. If he was slow in
starting, the sting of a whip or the sound of bullets hitting
the ground at his heels hurried him along.

Lincoln left Jubal at the door in Swaggart's custody
and went to find Pinchot. A deputy sat dozing in the
sheriff's chair, his rifle across his lap. Swaggart woke him
after locking Jubal up. The deputy looked as if he'd slept
the night in the gutter, displaying a week-old beard,
bloodshot eyes, a dirty, sweat-stained face and neck,
liquor-fouled breath, and a monumental hangover. Swaggart eyed the holding pen.

"Whole new bunch, Ben," said his deputy.

"I can see. Which is better than you can. Brother, you

291

sure are determined to drink yourself to death. Shame on you, what we got here?"

"Disturbin' the peace, trespassin', 'sault and battery, the usual."

"Mmmm. Well, it's 'bout full as it can get. Time to dispense justice. Okay, boys, listen up. Quiet down, goddamn it. Today's fine is set at six bucks. Any of you got six bucks on him, you're free to go. Anybody? Raise your hands. Six bucks and you're out. One, two, three, four. Come on, you got to have at least six bucks. Any of you carrying a wad, you can pay for your friends. Charge 'em twenty percent interest. Work it out 'mongst yourselves, there you go. Deputy, open up, let the lucky ones out."

A groan went up from the unlucky ones. They were so tightly jammed in that everyone was forced to stand, even those who looked unable to. Jubal sat on his cot, his eyes on the floor, ignoring the goings-on. Six men were let out, paid their fines, and left. Swaggart came over to Jubal's cell. He stood looking down at him, his expression sympathetic.

"Sorry about this, brother Hunnicutt," he said quietly. "You must be feeling pretty down. I'd sure be, murder being a capital offense."

Jubal snapped his head up. "What murder? Are you crazy?"

Swaggart shrugged. "Hey, it's not up to me to decide your fate. Up to judge and jury of your peers, but you must admit it doesn't look too good."

"You brought me in for questioning, so you said. Let's get to it, shall we?"

Swaggart looked perplexed. "Questioning? You're mixed up, you're under arrest for cold-blooded murder."

"I'm not under arrest. You said—"

"What the hell are you talking about, man? If I brought you in just to question you, I'd sit you down over by the desk. I wouldn't lock you up, would I? 'Course not."

"You double-crossing son of a bitch!"

"Hey hey, easy." Swaggart looked both ways, then back at his office in the corner. The deputy slumped on a

stool dozing. "Don't go losing your temper on me. I
don't make the law, I just enforces it. You say you didn't
kill him? You swear you didn't? That's good enough for
me. May not be for the judge, but I believe you. And I'd
like to help you if you let me."

"Help me?"

"Last fall you made yourself a bundle of money ped-
dling your potatoes, isn't that so? Ten, twelve thousand
dollars." Jubal stared at him. "Listen to me, you listening?" Swaggart drew a long breath and again looked both
ways and back to his sleeping deputy. "I'm not greedy,
anybody in town'll tell you Ben Swaggart is a fair man."
He cleared his throat. "How much you give me to open
this door and turn the other way whilst you walk?"

"You scum—"

"Now now now, is that any way to talk to the man who
can give you your freedom? Freedom, brother. I'm talking right now. I open this door and you leave. Only keep
walking right down to the train. Get on, go to Oregon,
Arizona." He bent closer, his forehead touching the bars.
"You give me two thousand bucks cash money and you're
free. When that son-in-law of yours shows up with Cicero
Pinchot, you tell Pinchot you won't be needing him after
all, and send the colonel to the bank or back to the
house, to wherever you keep your money. Tell him to get
two thousand—"

The outer door opened. Swaggart stopped talking and
straightened. He cleared his throat again and turned. It
was Emerald Weigans, a wholly different Emerald Weigans
from the one who'd come sweeping into the house to
discover her husband's body and gone to pieces on the
spot. Gone were the tears and tear stains, gone the
hysterics, the wild accusations; she appeared as placid
and as controlled as always. She smiled and nodded
greeting to Jubal.

"Sheriff."

"Yes, ma'am? Something I can do for you?"

"Open the door and let Mr. Hunnicutt out."

"What?"

She smiled at Jubal again, then took Swaggart aside

out of Jubal's hearing. Swaggart's face proceeded to undergo a profound change as she talked close to his ear. Amazement supplanted his jaunty expression; it in turn gave way to an uncomfortable look that, by the time she resumed speaking aloud, threatened to yield to one of desperation.

"It's as simple as that, Sheriff. I made a terrible, a very cruel mistake in accusing him. I was in shock. *Oui*, I did not know what I was doing. Now that I have thought it over it is obviously *impossible*. There is no way he could have killed my poor Heinie. Heinie was with me this morning. We had breakfast together. He did not leave the house until after ten. I remember seeing the time on the mantel clock. The Rhilanders and Mr. Hunnicutt were here in town at that time. Mr. Hunnicutt was with his lawyer, *n'est-ce pas*? And Dr. Gogarty. No question about it: Heinie was killed while all three were in town, and his body was carried down to the barn. *Absolument*."

Jubal had gotten to his feet and stood gripping the bars, his eyes snapping from one to the other. Swaggart rubbed his chin. He looked nervous.

"I don't know, ma'am. It coulda been he wasn't shot till they come home early this afternoon."

"*Impossible*. What did they do, come home and find Heinie standing there? I tell you he did not go there. He was killed elsewhere and his body brought there. Heinie was already dead at least two hours by the time Dr. Gogarty got to Mr. Hunnicutt's. He told me. And they sent for him at once. No, Sheriff, the timing of it absolves Mr. Hunnicutt completely."

"But—"

She patted Swaggart's cheek with one gloved hand. "Let him out."

"I don't know—"

"Do it!" she snapped. "Don't argue. And resume your investigation. You could start by questioning our hired hands. I understand, too, that Monsieur Knox popped up at a most convenient time, barely moments after Colonel Rhilander discovered Heinie."

Jubal stood outside on the sidewalk with her. He took

a deep breath. He felt like he'd been behind bars for ages. He felt relieved beyond description, and he owed it all to Emerald.

He shook his rescuer's hand. "I don't know what to say. I feel like you saved me from the hangman. Weigans, you're an angel."

"There is nothing to say. I could hardly stand by and watch such a gross miscarriage of justice. He intended to railroad you. Nobody alive wants poor Heinie's killer arrested more than I, *naturellement*, but I refuse to see an innocent man made to suffer. Heinie was very fond of you, Mr. Hunnicutt."

"I liked him. He was honest and fair. What happened was a terrible thing."

"He respected you, Jubal, your courage, your gumption. The way you stood up to Knox and Bazarian." She fastened her lovely eyes on his and held them. "There's something else I've wanted to say to you for a long time. About Jeptha. I was there when he was killed. I saw it all. It happened so suddenly there was nothing anyone could do. A terrible tragedy. *Horrible*. He was a fine young man. His death shocked and saddened me. It is still on my conscience and will always be."

"You had nothing to do with killing him."

"No, but if we had never met, he would not have shown up that night. I'm so sorry."

Lincoln and Pinchot came hurrying up.

"What the devil?" began Lincoln.

Jubal explained, adding, "Mrs. Weigans, Emerald, rescued me."

"Nonsense, it was all too ridiculous. Swaggart is an idiot." She squeezed Jubal's hand; his eyes danced. "If you'll excuse me, I must be going. I must see to the funeral arrangements."

She beamed and walked off, her skirts rustling under her long cape, her parasol spinning slowly over her shoulder.

"Beautiful woman that," murmured Pinchot.

Jubal nodded. "And smart. She sure saved my bacon, God bless her."

A. R. Riefe

"I wonder why?" mused Lincoln aloud.

Pinchot snorted. "Isn't it obvious? She could see he had nothing to do with it even if Swaggart can't. And he wouldn't get far if she refuses to accuse you, Jubal."

Lincoln sniffed. He seemed very reluctant to accord her even a little credit. "I wonder who did kill Henry?" he asked rhetorically. "Could she have? Even indirectly? Ordered one of their hands to do the deed and dump his body in the barn?"

"Frame me, then step in and clear me before Swaggart can get his hooks in any deeper?" Jubal waved away the thought. "You're not making sense."

"It wouldn't be the first time money's bought murder," Lincoln went on.

"Pretty serious accusation," observed Pinchot.

"Come now, Cicero, you know her reputation as well as I do. Am I really exaggerating? Now that I think about it, I wouldn't put it past her. Those two bullets in his back make her the wealthiest widow in the county."

"Let's just drop it, Lincoln," said Jubal tightly. "She saved my neck. I owe her and if you don't mind I'd rather not have to hear her slandered."

"Who's slandering? Just thinking out loud. Something, gentlemen, is rotten in the territory of Wyoming."

She vanished from their sight around the corner.

"Yes, sir," said Pinchot. "One beautiful woman."

In mid-January a thaw set in. It lasted nearly a week, then overnight the temperature plunged and a bitter cold wind came howling out of the Laramies. Freezing rain fell, icy tears lamenting the absence of the sun. They struck the empty trenches lining Jubal's potato fields, hammered the fence posts, and drummed the roofs of the barns and house as if to pound the nails more securely in place. At Fort Russell they assaulted the gilded knob at the top of the flagpole, setting it gleaming like the golden egg of the tale. They tested the rebuilt roof of headquarters porch, and thrashed a disgruntled and discouraged Corporal Salme, marching up and down the parade ground dragging a twenty-eight-pound cannon ball attached to his leg by a two-foot chain, his punishment for insulting Lieutenant Colonel Harvey Philips, his commanding officer, during inspection.

The rain clattered down like spilled dried peas upon Molly Hannigan's barren window box. In town it attacked saloon and school, brothel and church without distinction. It clacked upon the tin roof of the courthouse in Paxton Street, beat upon the wooden shake roof of the U.P. platform at the depot, and thumped and pummeled the canvas roof of Young's Bath House on Crow Creek. It fell in the frozen streets and dark, narrow alleys, down wells, down chimneys, and onto the gleaming tracks that led east to Egbert and west to Boire. Upon the forlorn little cemetery south of town it fell, upon the frozen graves of Hannah Hunnicutt and her son Jeptha. Upon the sunken eternal bed of Oscar Freeling and that of an unnamed drifter, whose knife wound was beyond Dr. Gogarty's ability to heal, and the final resting places of other souls who had come west with high hopes, seen Cheyenne, and died.

It rained for a day and a half, and when it stopped the temperature dropped lower. When the sun came out, all of Cheyenne and the area surrounding assumed the look of a frontier fairyland clad in crystal, dazzling the eye and enchanting the heart.

Heinrich Weigans's killer was never found. Two weeks after the shooting, deprived of his prime and only suspect, Sheriff Swaggart dropped the investigation, deciding—Jubal commented—that time without profit was time ill spent. It was not the first unsolved murder in Wyoming's brief, turbulent history, and it would not be the last.

Lorna echoed Lincoln's suspicions of Emerald. Unarguably Heinrich's conspicuously and briefly grieving widow had much to gain from his demise. He left her everything—his fortune, his ranch, the reflected glow of his title. Her hired hands had always called her countess; now that the count was dead she strongly hinted that everyone else do so.

"She murdered him," averred Lorna flatly.

"I wouldn't go repeating that outside these walls," said Jubal. "It could get you in a peck of trouble."

"How can you be so gullible! You're infuriating!"

"I'm not gullible, I just don't go around accusing people just because I don't like them." Jubal sat fiddling with his harmonium. "Besides, Henry and her business is no business of ours."

"How can you say that after what she did to poor Jep?"

Jubal looked up. His expression was suddenly hard, accusing. "What Jeptha did to himself, you mean."

"That's a fine thing to say!"

"It may not be fine, but it's the God's truth. Why don't you be honest with yourself, you've just got it in for the woman. I should think you might show a little appreciation for what she did for this family. I sure appreciate her."

"Stuff! Swaggart couldn't accuse you and he knew it. He'd have *had* to let you go with no evidence, no witnesses, no gun—"

"That's not the point, Lorna. She came forward. She didn't have to, but she had the decency to, and I'm grateful, I respect her."

"Good—"

Lincoln came in and the discussion ended. From the looks on both their faces, they were relieved.

Winter was a time for rest and reflection for Jubal, as it is for most farmers. Conversely, for Jubal's neighbors it was a time of ceaseless activity. The storm had taken its toll on their herds. One of Mark Bazarian's men was found frozen to death in his saddle, man and horse. Three of Carleton Knox's men were suffering frostbite, and it was rumored that he had lost eleven head, including four calves. Cattlemen throughout the territory viewed the winter months with dread. Blizzards and ice storms invariably victimized the weaker cattle. Calves born the previous spring were particularly vulnerable, especially those that wandered away from their mothers and got lost. The farmers' relief and the cattlemen's difficulty only intensified the latter's resentment toward the former. Members of the Cattlemen's Association were unanimously determined to break the lock of Judge Shankland's injunction and restore the status quo. The cattlemen wanted the federal government to do more for them than hamstring the invading homesteaders with regulations that restricted their activities and rights. They fired a number of resolutions off to Washington, urging the government to prevent the Indians from stealing their stock, offer long-term grazing leases on lands owned by the government, and secure to cattle ranchers priority over all available water.

It was rumored in town that some canny stockmen were filing homestead claims on the banks of streams, and were paying their ranch hands to file fraudulent claims along the same waterways with an eye to absolute control over the range. Carleton Knox may have wanted to control Bear Creek in such a manner, but he was too late. Jubal had already registered his property, his side of the creek and his right to a share of the water that ran through it.

Winter blustered its way through the months, retiring in early April. In April the Cattlemen's Association's efforts met with success. Judge Shankland's infamous injunction, the farmers' only protection, was declared invalid, overruled by Dakota Judge Ara Bartlett. The year before, Laramie County had been formally created by the Dakota Legislature and Cheyenne classified as a city. At that time a full slate of county officials had been named, but the legislature had yet to convene for the first time, so the Dakota officials still controlled Wyoming's destiny. And Judge Bartlett controlled the territory's practicing jurists, among them Judge Shankland. It was to Judge Bartlett that the Cattlemen's Association took their grievances, and in April he decided in the ranchers' favor. Mark Bazarian and Carleton Knox celebrated the good news. Jubal Hunnicutt took stock of the suddenly altered situation and pondered his future. Lincoln suggested they join with other homesteaders and form their own association, then go over Bartlett's head to the legislature in Yankton. Lorna had a better idea.

"It stands to reason that no matter what approach you take, you won't get them to overrule him," she said. "If by some miracle you do, the Association will only go back to work and get them to reverse themselves. Why get into a tug-of-war?"

"Are you saying we should wait for the Wyoming legislature?" Jubal asked. "I don't know, those boys may not get together until next fall."

"They'll still be closer to the problem and more concerned with it than the Dakota legislature," interposed Lincoln.

"I'm not talking about territorial legislatures," said Lorna. "I think we should appeal directly to the federal government, the Department of the Interior. We're so new here lots of laws have yet to be written. If we explain the situation to the Secretary of Interior . . ."

"Orville Browning," said Lincoln.

"Whoever. Tell him what's happening to the public lands out here and persuade him it's in the government's best interests to bring order to the situation before it gets any worse, maybe he'll do something."

"You mean go all the way to Washington?" murmured Jubal. "That's a long way. To come back with your hat empty."

"Ever the optimist," said Lincoln, grinning.

"I don't see as we have any choice," said Lorna. "One thing's sure. If the government takes action, the ranchers will have to respect them. If they flout them, they'll run the risk of the Army stepping in to settle things. I doubt people like Bazarian and Knox want it to come to that. I think they'd be willing to make concessions rather than take on the government."

"I wonder," said Lincoln.

"What?"

"If Browning or anybody else back there really cares about the problems in the territories. When you think how they've bungled and neglected the Indian problem."

"We're not Indians," said Lorna. "I think we should approach him. I think he's the only one we can."

"Orville Browning," mused Jubal aloud. "I've heard the name."

"He took over for James Harlan two years ago," explained Lincoln. "I don't know anything about him, but . . ."

Jubal frowned skeptically. "How do you know you can even get in to talk to the man?"

"I can get to talk to Edwin Stanton, the Secretary of War," rejoined Lincoln. "Don't look at me that way. I resigned from the Army, I wasn't kicked out in disgrace. I know a few people in Washington who might be willing to lend a hand. I think we should leave as soon as possible."

Jubal shrugged, then shook his head. "You go, son, if

you think you can do any good. Lorna and I'll sit by the windows with shotguns and watch for trouble."

He smiled as he said it, but it was clearly with deliberate effort. Judge Bartlett's decision had stunned him, and he could not hide his concern for the future.

"I'll go with you," said Lorna.

"Sweetheart—"

"Don't argue. I'll start packing."

·◄31►·

On Pennsylvania Avenue, nearly midway between the Capitol and the White House, rose the six-story Post Office Building. A few blocks northwest of it stood the General Land Office, headquarters of the Department of the Interior, boasting an impressive Doric portico and dark-paneled walls within. On the second floor was the office of the Secretary of the Interior, a lofty-ceilinged mausoleum redolent of old leather and bureacratic stuffiness, its sill to ceiling windows looking out upon 18th Street.

The Rhilanders had arrived at the Union House Hotel, exhausted from the tedious and arduous train ride, the final leg of which had brought them in from Clark, Virginia. In all, since departing Cheyenne, they had covered 1,650 miles in fifty hours, changing trains in Omaha and Chicago enroute.

The nation's capital was not an impressive sight at two o'clock of a rainy night. It was muddy. But when the visitors arose from their bed eleven hours later, the sun was out and the mud spattering everywhere was already baked to the hardness of kiln-fired brick.

They were to wait nine days to see Secretary of the Interior Browning. In fairness, he was a busy man. According to his secretary, a young man with a flair for flamboyant attire that seemed very much at odds with the dignity of his job, Browning worked twelve hours a day six days a week. When the visitors from distant Chey-

303

enne did get in to see Browning, they'd be alloted the customary half hour to voice their complaints. Lorna pointedly wondered how the young man could assume they had come to complain. His response, accompanied by a bored smile, was the assertion that everybody complained to the Secretary.

The nine-day wait was not wasted. Lincoln prepared for the meeting by calling on a number of old Army friends, officers he'd known in the war who had remained in the regular Army after Appomattox and ended up being posted to Washington. Unfortunately, he was to discover that the people in the War Department had about as much influence with the people in the Department of the Interior as Sitting Bull had with President Andrew Johnson. They might well have been two arms of government in two different countries. Lincoln's friends in high places were understanding and sympathetic when he told them his reason for coming, but not one had ever even seen Orville Browning.

In inquiring about town Lincoln did manage to learn a few things about the secretary. Browning had obtained his appointment by virtue of his close friendship with his predecessor, James Harlan, who, when he retired for reasons of health, recommended his replacement to the president. Browning was considered by many to be both intelligent and fair-minded, but he was unfamiliar with the problems of the West and too busy to study them. He left Indian affairs to the Department of Indian Affairs, squabbles over public lands to the people downstairs in the General Land Office. He was not afraid to make a decision, but if he didn't know the particulars of what he was faced with and did not have the time to study said particulars, he would push the problem onto someone else. He didn't discover this escape hatch; it was the backbone of the bureaucracy long before he arrived on the scene (along with interminable delay in rendering decisions).

This worried Lorna when Lincoln told her about it. They were sitting at dinner in Grovers Restaurant across the street from their hotel. She made a face and shook her head wearily. "He'll plead ignorance and turn us down. Or pass us on to somebody. They'll pass us on to somebody else. We could be here till next year. In the meantime—"

Lincoln had stopped a forkful of lettuce halfway to his mouth. He scoffed: "Don't jump the gun. Let's just take it as it comes. Everybody says he's reasonable and bright."

"Only he has no time."

"Sweetheart, give the man a chance."

"Will he give us?"

"We're not asking for the moon, all we want is fair play. When we sit down with him tomorrow, we'll just trot out all the facts. If he's half as good as everybody says, the least he'll do is get somebody to check into what's going on. Not just in Wyoming, all over. The situation's the same all over. He may already know all about it."

He covered her hand with his comfortingly. He ran his fingers soothingly over the space between her thumb and forefinger. She turned her hand to clasp his. His warmth raced through her, and an identical look of yearning came into their eyes. It was so marvelous, she thought, and so simple. The mere touch of his hand aroused her anytime, anyplace, and in a wink nothing else meant a thing. She had been famished when they sat down; now, barely halfway through her meal she was no longer hungry.

He left money by his plate and they left the restaurant.

They slipped naked beneath the sheet. She trembled as his arms slipped around her; she swallowed to keep from crying aloud with joy. She ran a hand through his hair and brought his head down, resting his cheek on her breast. His warm breath rhythmically caressing her nakedness made her gasp.

He raised his head and kissed her.

He made love to her thighs with his hands, his lips, his tongue. He set fire to her body, and the small mound of hair between her legs glistened. But he did not touch her there, and she did not touch him. That would come later. For now his mouth and tongue loved her thighs, her

305

fingers slipped through his hair, down his cheek, caressing his throat, tenderly stroking his shoulders and upper arms.

His mouth wandered from her inner thighs up to her heaving breasts, pausing there, kissing and laving them with his tongue. Then he began to tenderly fondle them. He made love to her earlobe as if it were a pearl to be worshiped for its beauty. She felt his breath against it before his lips touched and the tip of his tongue kissed it. It came alive, sending warmth shafting down her neck and down to her breasts, where his hands continued their tender assault.

For an hour he made love to her so without touching her sex, without bringing his throbbing hardness close to her body. Every moment of hand and fingers, of lips, tongue, mouth was slow and deliberate and gentle, gentle . . .

Again and again, like a flat stone sent skipping across a tranquil pond, he brought her to climax. The peaks were not high, the valleys did not plunge as deeply as in complete, unrestrained orgasm, but these neverless thrilled and transported her. It was as if an incalculable number of orgasms lay dormant inside her, simmering with expectancy, aching to explode, needing only his touch to trigger them. Like living things they waited, locked inside her, and only he could release them. And when at last the skipping stone sank she rose upward, positioned herself astride him, settled her lips down upon his enormous shaft and took him driving hard up into her. Her mind swung dizzily, swirling, reeling, and she nearly fainted with joy.

•⊰32⊱•

Orville Browning looked right for his role: weary, beleaguered, a relentlessly harassed and overworked individual cornered by droves of complainers who, failing to get his help for whatever reason, took their frustration out on him personally. The well of his patience had to be dry, decided Lorna as his secretary ushered Lincoln and her into the office, and his job had to upset his digestion, his ability to fall asleep, and other normal functions. But the prestige of the title Secretary of the Interior evidently offset all the detrimental aspects, for here he was under siege in the arena of another day.

He was prematurely bald, alarmingly underweight, carrying no more than one hundred fifty pounds on a frame that raised the top of his head a good six feet, two inches above his heels when he stood up, smiled thinly, and shook their hands in greeting. He was not handsome, not homely; he had the look of one whose face seen in a crowd is quickly forgotten. Ordinary eyes, not piercing, not deep-set or soulful, an ordinary aqualine nose, lips neither fat and full or pencil thin, a clean-shaven jaw quite like any other, not generously large or pugnacious or narrow or slack. He only had one notable feature: his hands. They were artistically slender, never still, alabaster white with meticulously manicured nails. Every so often he would close the fingers of his left hand and set it against his cheek, framing it with his index finger. This was his pose of thought, and when Lorna saw it she knew he was listening and absorbing Lincoln's explanation of the situation.

On the side walls hung two huge portraits: President Andrew Johnson and President Lincoln gazed critically at each other. Behind the Secretary a large map of North America dominated the space between two windows looking out on 18th Street. Wyoming appeared no larger than a playing card.

"I can certainly see that you people have your problems," said Browning. "I sympathize with you. Indeed I do. Something has to be done."

He went on to explain that like organic acts for other territories, Wyoming's was rooted in the Ordinance of 1787, which, in providing a government for the Ohio country, set a pattern to be followed, with minor changes, time after time. Wyoming had been given a simple government designed to serve a small population temporarily.

"Until conditions warrant statehood. But bless my soul, that doesn't mean you're to be powerless to protect yourselves and your property. Most of the land out there is still public, under the jurisdiction of the federal government."

Lorna nearly sighed out with relief. "Yes."

"This squabbling isn't doing anybody any good."

The door opened and his secretary entered.

"Excuse me, sir, a messenger just arrived from the White House. There's to be a cabinet meeting in twenty minutes."

"Twenty minutes?"

"Yes, sir, I was told to say it's very urgent."

"It must be."

"I sent Bernstein to get your driver. He should be here any minute."

Browning was on his feet. The news clearly disturbed him. He suddenly was acting like a man about to be called on the carpet and discharged, but watching him, Lorna recalled that the problem of the moment wasn't his but the president's. Johnson's attempt to carry out Abraham Lincoln's policies of reconstruction and reconciliation had brought him into bitter conflict with the Radical Republicans in Congress. Indeed, impeachment proceedings had already been instituted; he was charged with usurpation of the law, corrupt use of the veto power, influence at elections, and misdemeanors. The proceedings promised a long and drawn-out process, and the chances of conviction almost nil, but the tempest was disruptive, and business as usual in the government no longer possible.

"I'm so sorry," said Browning. "We'll have to reschedule you for another time, I'm afraid." He looked past them at Adam. "You'll see to it like a good fellow."

"When?" asked Lincoln.

Browning looked flustered. "I . . . have no idea. Adam?"

"As soon as possible."

"Tomorrow, next week? When?" exclaimed Lincoln.

Lorna's hand found his forearm. He was losing his temper. Adam looked sheepish as he shrugged.

"I'll have to check the appointment schedule. Sir—"

"Coming."

Browning had collected himself. He started for the door.

"Sir," said Lincoln to him. "Let us go with you. Let me. I'll ride over, we can talk further . . ."

"No. I mean, I'm sorry. There's no time." Browning glanced at his secretary. "Twenty minutes, you said?"

"Closer to fifteen now, sir." Adam moved to the window and looked down into the street. "Ah, your carriage is here."

Browning escaped before Lincoln could appeal further. The secretary looked sympathetic.

"Let me check the book for you."

He rescheduled them for six days later, a Tuesday afternoon.

"If there's a cancellation before then, I'll be in touch. I *am* sorry."

Isn't everybody, mused Lorna.

33

They returned to see Orville Browning the following Monday morning. During the interim both waxed optimistic. There were bright spots. In the short time they'd had with him, he had shown concern. And he'd hinted that he might be able to do something. But when they met with him on Monday he quickly destroyed their hopes.

"The problems between cattlemen and homesteaders out West are not unique to Wyoming, you know."

We know.

"What is eventually done for one territory will be done for all."

Eventually?

"For now, at least until the president appoints a governor, I'm afraid the best you can do is try to make peace with your neighbors. I realize that won't be easy, but is it really impossible?"

Really impossible.

"Cattle rancher and farmer are both relative newcomers to the territory, both settling in, sending down your roots. The natural resources are bountiful, there's plenty of just about everything for everyone. It's actually like a banquet where only half the guests show up. Those that do can gorge themselves."

"Let me get this straight," said Lincoln coldly. "What it comes down to is Wyoming's the orphan in the family, at best a stepchild. Until we become a state, we homesteaders don't have a nickel's worth of rights."

"No say in our destiny," said Lorna. "None."

"Bless my soul, if you'll forgive me that's a bit of an exaggeration. My dear Mrs. Rhilander, try and understand, the country's so vast, so many areas yet to be explored even, so few people out there."

"With no political power, too little to make any impact."

Lincoln raised a reproving finger. "We're still Americans. Citizens. Tell me, sir, what's the difference between a man who breaks down his neighbor's fence and damages his property here in Washington and the same thing back home? Are we a special category of citizens, second-class? Third? Citizens in name only?"

"I'm sorry, Mr. Rhilander, Mrs. Rhilander. Believe me, if it were in my power I'd stand up in Congress and argue for the laws you need and when they're enacted send you marshals to see that they're enforced. But I'm not a Congressman, I only work for the Congress and the president. I can only do what they tell me to. Until the president appoints a governor—"

"When will that be?" Lorna asked.

"Soon, I hear. Possibly as early as this fall. Not only a governor but a secretary for Wyoming. Of course, Congress will have to confirm—"

Lincoln stood up.

"Thank you, sir."

"Now now, you mustn't be upset with me. Try and understand my position. I'll be candid, my hands are tied. Once they're untied, and they will be—"

Lincoln nodded. "Eventually."

"Perhaps sooner than you think."

"Perhaps," said Lorna, "after enough blood is spilt, enough people are killed, even women and children, so that the situation begins to embarrass you people."

Browning stared at her. He didn't know what to say, having run out of "I'm sorrys."

Again they thanked him and left.

"Jubal was righter than he knew," muttered Lincoln as they started down the stairs. "It definitely was a long way to come to go home with our hat empty."

They left for home on the 8:10 next morning.

34

Aloysius Gogarty was upset. Up and down the station platform he strode, three steps one way, three the other, alternately clasping his hands behind his back and flinging them angrily in the air. It was ten minutes to midnight, the train had pulled into Cheyenne and was now pulled out. Above the rattle and roar and loud bay of the whistle Gogarty vented his ire.

"He said he'd be on it. You didn't see him? Of course you didn't, you'd have already said. What the devil happened?" He paused to cough, fisting his mouth, excusing himself to Lorna. "Dear Cicero, he's a boon companion and a true friend, but about as reliable as a bitch in heat, excuse the expression. Had to go over to Kimball to see a client, swore up and down he'd be—oh well, you already know." He looked from one to the other and shook his head slowly. "I take it from your faces you've come back empty-handed. Either that or you're exhausted."

"Little of each," said Lorna. "Empty-handed for sure. The mills of the gods grind slowly, the mills of the bureacracy not at all."

"I like that." His face darkened. "But it's a damned shame. If the ranchers get wind of it they'll probably raise hell, knowing the government's not interested in keeping 'em in line. I hope it doesn't turn into a shooting war. I really don't need the business."

By now the platform was all but deserted. Behind it the lights of Cheyenne shone feebly. Not a scream was heard, not a shot, not at the moment. If was, for some inexplicable reason, as quiet and as civilized as Washington, mused Lorna. Was the place actually settling into some semblance of sobriety and dignity?

"Have you seen Daddy?" she asked.

"Day before yesterday. I only see him when he comes to town. You folks are quite a ways out, you know. He's fine. Got his men back with him. The ground's pretty well thawed out, I expect they'll be starting planting soon. Damn Cicero, I could have been home asleep." He scowled. "Hope nothing's happened. Still, what could in Kimball? Place is like a grave." He had stopped his pacing. He looked about. "Well, no sense hanging around here. Good night and again, I'm sorry you didn't have better luck."

"Try no luck at all," said Lincoln grimly. "Good night."

They hired a driver and buggy, piling their luggage in the back and setting out for the house. There was no moon, no stars, nothing but nearly pitch black from the top of heaven to the ground under the wheels once they got out of sight of the lights of the town. They were tired and discouraged; neither spoke. The driver hardly stopped; he regaled them with stories of recent incidents in town, each one grislier than the last. Spying the house ahead at last, Lorna quietly thanked the Lord. The buggy splashed across the creek and pulled up at the door. The driver helped Lincoln unload, he was paid and off he trundled.

The house was in darkness.

"Anybody home, I wonder?" Lincoln asked.

"It's past one. Daddy's asleep. I do hate to wake him."

Lincoln pounded the door. "Me too."

Jubal came to the door in his nightshirt carrying a lantern, holding it up, squinting at their faces, beaming. "Well, well, well, the two prodigals return at last. Back with empty hat in hand . . ."

"May we come in?" Lorna asked and threw her arms around him.

Lincoln stayed in the parlor to answer Jubal's barrage of questions while she retreated to the kitchen. She called back to Jubal.

"Daddy, where's the bathtub?"

"In my room. It's—"

"I'll get it for you," offered Lincoln.

"I can," she said. "I'm no invalid."

Both heard her start for the bedroom.

"Wait," called Jubal.

She did not. She opened the door and raised her lamp. The woman in the bed sat up startled, blinking, rubbing her eyes, realizing she was exposing herself and covering her breasts.

Lorna gawked. "You!"

She came out slamming the door, confronting Jubal and Lincoln approaching from the parlor. She glared viciously at her father.

"What's *she* doing here? In my mother's bed!"

"*My* bed, little girl. The countess is my guest."

He lowered his eyes, avoiding hers.

"Get her out of here!"

Jubal raised his eyes; the sheepishness had fled, displaced by sudden anger. They stood jaw to jaw, sparks flying. Lincoln raised an ineffectual hand, lowered it, and sighed.

"Now, you listen to me," growled Jubal.

"Out!"

"Lower your voice!"

"Will both of you calm down?" pleaded Lincoln.

"Stay out of this!" She whirled back to Jubal. "Will you throw her out or do I?"

"She stays. This is my house, you and nobody else gives the orders!"

"Get your coat on, Lincoln. We're leaving."

"It's one-thirty in the morning."

"We'll get a hotel room in town. Go out and hitch up the buggy."

"Lorna," burst Jubal, "you're being ridiculous. Her Ladyship is here and she stays. She's . . . moving in."

"What!"

"We're going to be married."

"Are you insane!"

The door opened. Emerald stood in Jubal's robe; she looked uncomfortable, embarrassed.

"Next Saturday, here . . ." He slipped his arm around Emerald's waist. "So you'd better get used to the idea of seeing her around."

Lorna relaxed slowly, her eyes continuing to burn into his.

"Wonderful," she said quietly. "Congratulations to you both, I hope you'll be very happy. Come, Lincoln, I'll go out back with you. We'll bring the luggage on through." She picked up a suitcase, started back, paused, and turned back to Jubal. "We'll be by tomorrow to collect the rest of our things."

"Please don't do this," murmured Emerald. "Please. I'll get dressed, I'll leave—"

"No!" bellowed Jubal. "She's the one that's leaving."

"You bet I am!"

"Get out, then! And don't come back. Your things'll be delivered to you in town."

With this he laid his hand on Emerald's shoulder, hugged her to him, and started her back into the room.

"I'm sorry," she murmured.

"No reason to be sorry, my dear. No reason in the world."

35

Cicero Sebastian Pinchot did not return from Kimball for two more days. When he did come home, Aloysius Gogarty speedily handed his head to him for worrying him sick. Emerald Giradoux moved in with Jubal. Lincoln and Lorna took a room at the Cheyenne House in town. For the remainder of the week, Lorna carried on like a madwoman.

"He's out of his head! Stark, staring mad! How he can blithely ignore that she killed Jep. Don't say she didn't. Don't you dare! Not to me. How could he marry that slut! A woman half his age. A witch! Oh, you know why, it's plain as day. She wants his land. It's certainly not him she wants. Wants his land for her damned cattle!"

"You don't know that—"

"Don't argue with me!"

"I'm not," said Lincoln. "You've been carrying on like this for three days. Are you going to keep it up for the rest of your life?"

"Doesn't it grind you? Doesn't it chew you up? Talk about leading a lamb to the slaughter . . ."

"Lorna, he likes her, he's always admired her. He's alone and so is she. If they love each other—"

"Love! Must you be so insufferably dense! You're always on her side."

"I'm not," he rejoined. "I'm not on anybody's."

"You don't care about him?"

"I do, but—"

"Never mind. He can't marry her. He'd be better off six feet under!"

"He's certainly planning to marry her. Tomorrow. It's coming awfully fast. If you're going to talk him out of it, you'd better get busy. You could start by talking to him period."

"No!" she snapped. "He made it very clear."

"Lorna, will you stop being such a fool? There's got to be an end to it if I have to tie you together! You're going to talk to each other like human beings!"

He softened his tone and finally, after three days of trying, talked her into meeting with Jubal. As he saw it, they were equally guilty for the falling-out and equally responsible for putting their relationship back together.

"It's got nothing to do with her or me, it's strictly you two. I'll go up and speak to him first thing in the morning. If you meet him halfway, he'll come the other half."

"He won't, he's the stubbornest human on the face of the earth."

"Maybe the second stubbornest."

The next day was Jubal and Emerald's wedding day. Lincoln got to the house shortly after eight. The parlor was decorated with Lorna's paper wedding bell back in its place in the center of the ceiling. New streamers and fresh flowers had been prepared for the great event. Jubal was shaving, the bride-to-be was back up at her house getting ready.

"Lorna wants to talk."

Jubal stood at the mirror in his long johns, reeking of lilac and scraping away at his chin.

"Good. She can start by apologizing to my wife."

"Jubal, don't you think it's time you sat down and started behaving like normal people?"

"If she apologizes to Delise I'll forget the whole thing. Not that she ever will."

Jubal refused to budge from his demand. There was no meeting, no ceasefire, no armistice. That afternoon the widow Weigans became Mrs. Jubal Hunnicutt. The same minister who had married Lorna to Lincoln performed the ceremony. The Rhilanders were not invited. Lorna remarked that she would prefer going to a full-scale massacre, adding that the word seemed appropriate to the occasion.

Although Lincoln avoiding saying so, he saw advantages to Jubal's marrying Henry's widow. For one thing, now that their respective properties were joined, Carleton Knox and Mark Bazarian would probably be a bit more attentive as to where their cattle grazed. Emerald, after all, was one of them. Did she plan to talk Jubal out of raising potatoes and into raising beef cattle? Who could say what she planned. But Lincoln doubted if Jubal would go along with that idea.

One thing was certain: Lincoln's own days as a potato farmer were over. Looking back on the previous summer, he had to confess that he hadn't been exactly enchanted with farming, not compared to Jubal, who saw it as something like a divine authorization. He had protested when Jubal insisted on repaying his two thousand dollars after the harvest. When he'd offered him the money he hadn't thought of it as a loan, but Jubal did, and pestered him until he accepted the money. To what use he'd put it he had yet to decide. He returned it to the bank.

Lorna's fury diminished after the wedding. She did not approach Jubal olive branch in hand, but there were no more long diatribes on the subject for Lincoln's defenseless ears. She rarely mentioned her father's name. It saddened her to do so, and Lincoln saw nothing he could say or do to ease her resentment.

She could not take to living in town; she hated the noise, the crowds, the incessant turmoil. They decided to buy property. Under the Homestead Act of 1862, like Jubal and thousands of others, they were entitled to purchase land at ten dollars per 160 acres. They selected the best parcel of land still available in the area: the acreage west of Jubal's land. They would hire men to build a house, a barn, a silo, but before the first nail was driven, a decision had to be made as to what use the land would be put to, if not farming or raising beef.

One afternoon Lincoln bumped into Mario Consolo on

CHEYENNE

17th Street. He invited him to join him in a drink at
Berryman's, around the corner. Mario told him all about
Fort Russell: Molly Hannigan had remarried, Harvey
Philips was considering the idea, B Company barracks
had burned down and was being rebuilt, the sutler had
been shot by an irate private whom he'd cheated in a
transaction. Lincoln told him about the Hunnicutt feud
and about buying the property. They sat sipping the
house bourbon, disregarding its arrogant foulness, enjoying their accidental reunion.

"So what will you do with your land?" Mario asked.

"We haven't decided."

"What about sheep?"

"Sheep? Nobody raises sheep around here."

Mario sipped and grinned. "They ought to, the grass is
ideal for sheep. I know all about them. My father raised
millions of them back in Michigan."

"Are they a lot of trouble."

"To raise? No trouble. Lots easier than cattle. They
cost less to keep, you need fewer men to care for them,
and they're more profitable than cattle. That's not all. I
don't have to tell you the winters around here can get
pretty harsh. Sheep can stand severe cold and heavy
snows better than cattle. Your initial investment would
be about half of what you'd have to pay out for the same
number of cattle. You just turn them loose, they get fat,
you shear them, peddle the wool, it grows back, and you
shear them again. When you get tired of shearing, you
send them to slaughter and start over with their young."

"You make it sound as easy as a rocking chair."

"It practically is. And brace yourself, Lincoln, because
this is the gospel according to Consolo. Cross my heart,
one man, just one, can handle how many sheep do you
think?"

"I have no idea."

"Three thousand," said Consolo.

Over the next two hours Lincoln got a crash course in
sheep and sheep raising. Mario had an answer for his
every question. By the time their conversation wound
down, they had nearly finished the bottle.

319

A. R. Riefe

"Shall we get another one?" Lincoln asked.

"Not me, Colonel. Besides, there isn't much more to tell you, except the most important thing."

"What?"

"If you do decide to go into sheep raising, I'd like to get in on it." He straightened in his chair and cleared his throat. "I neglected to mention it, but I'm getting out of the Army. Next Saturday. Enough is enough."

"Not because I—"

"No, no, no. Simply put, it's just the end of the line. I haven't decided where I'll go or what I'll do, but if you decide—"

"Would you consider working for me?" Lincoln cut in.

"I'll think about it, I really will."

They shook hands. Lincoln awarded what remained in the bottle to his guest, thanked him for "the fascinating conversation and one I intend to sleep on," said good-bye, and went back to the hotel.

Husband and wife sat up half the night talking about sheep. Lorna liked the idea. Lincoln's enthusiasm was so infectious she could not wait to get started. They were so carried away that neither gave even passing thought to what the impact of their decision might have on others. It hadn't occurred to Mario Consolo to warn Lincoln.

But this was understandable. After all, the cattle raised in Michigan were more than a hundred miles from the sheep ranches.

Not next-door neighbors.

36

The house was built, the Rhilanders moved in. A barn, a silo, and pens were begun, and the new enterprise launched without delay. A trained sheep dog was purchased, two experienced herders hired—along with Mario (who was given a quarter share in the projected profits), and four thousand Saxon Merino sheep ordered from a dealer in Nebraska.

But even before the first bleat echoed across the rolling land that led westward to the mountains, the Rhilanders' rancher neighbors heard of their plans and voiced disapproval. When Lincoln and Lorna came back from Cheyenne late one afternoon a week before their flock was due to arrive, they found a crudely lettered note fastened to the front door.

"This land is cattle land. No woollymonsters is allowed. Graze them somewheres else. Not here. This is fair warning. Graze them on this land and they'll be killed, every stinking one!"

The claim that any man's land had to be devoted to a use ordained by his neighbors was claptrap, of course. The problem was that in most cases cattlemen had reached the grasslands first giving them the right to dictate how the land should be used. And now they anticipated the invasion of the "hoofed locusts" with rising anger. Among cowhands it was known that everything in front of a sheep was eaten, and everything behind died.

In California it was discovered that where too many

sheep were crowded together or held too long, they ate the grass down to the roots, and cut and trampled what was left with their sharp, cloven hoofs. In dry areas ground laid bare by sheep would fail to put forth new growth until next year's rains. Nothing infuriated a cattle owner more than a flock of sheep enroute to mountain pasture lingering on low-lying range, which the cattleman regarded as his, then moving on to higher ground where the cattle would not follow, leaving the ground "sheeped."

Cattlemen all over the West were convinced that sheep tainted the land and fouled the water holes, leaving behind a smell that made cattle refuse to eat or drink.

Shortly before the Rhilanders' sheep were to arrive, an incident took place in Cheyenne that neither Lincoln nor Lorna heard about until two days later. Sheriff Ben Swaggart was shot and killed in the street. No one knew who did it; no fewer than a hundred men were suspect. Mayor Luke Murrin quickly appointed Swaggart's successor, pinning the badge on the dirty shirt of the drunken Depty Hugh Eccols.

Eccols's appointment was looked upon as a joke in poor taste by the townspeople, but almost from the moment he took office a remarkable change came over the man. The star on his chest infused him with, of all things, a sense of responsibility. He swore off liquor, he bathed, he shaved, he discarded his ragged wardrobe and bought new clothes. He renounced slouching and shuffling in favor of good posture and a normal step. He took the job seriously, he looked and acted like a sheriff and made it plain to everyone that he intended to be sheriff to all the people. He would respect the law, would adhere to it, would neither flout nor bend it like his predecessor. He promptly arrested the first four people who offered him bribes, effectively terminating the practice and sending a clear message throughout the community that he intended to be an honest sheriff. Before his first week on the job was completed, the decent people of Cheyenne were unanimously hailing the mayor's shrewdness in appointing him. Others grumbled, worried, and curbed their restless behavior.

CHEYENNE

To think that two ounces of tin star could effect such a remarkable transformation in such a sorry excuse for a man was inconceivable, but such was the case.

The day before delivery of the flock, Lincoln, Lorna, Mario, and the two newly hired herders, Eric Wedman, a rangy, shambling Oklahoman with ten years experience as a sheepman, and George Meadows, recommended by Mario as a monk in Levis, a man who had come east from California. It was agreed that the flock's grazing would be restricted to the mountain pastures where there would be plenty of available water. The last thing Lincoln wanted was a showdown with his neighbors. Their reaction to his decision to raise sheep surprised him, but not much. It stood to reason that if they resented Jubal's potatoes, they'd probably resent anything he and Lorna elected to do with their property. If he planted a hundred acres of peach trees they'd object. He did not want a confrontation, but he'd never backed away from one in his life.

"If things get too rough, I know where we can get help," said Mario. "So do you."

Lincoln shook his head. The five of them had assembled in the parlor. Lorna was serving coffee.

"I'd rather not ask Harvey," said Lincoln.

"Come on," retorted Mario. "You're in no position to be proud. It's the Army's job to protect us civilians. I'm surprised you don't know that, Colonel. All we'd have to do is whistle."

"I don't know, Mario. The Army's supposed to protect the settlers, but against the Indians, not against each other."

"Why don't we let old Harvey be the judge of whether he should help protect us or not?"

"You're making it sound like we're in for an all-out war," interposed Lorna.

"I've seen it before," said Wedman solemnly. "When the grass runs out, the tempers get short. I remember once down to Red Hook in injun territory, fellas kilt near two thousand sheep. With sticks of dynamite. Chased that sheepman back down to Texas, stony broke and

A. R. Riefe

wiser, you bet. I seen cattle stampeded through a flock, tramplin' 'em and scatterin' 'em in every direction."

"I've seen rim-rocking," said George Meadows, "up near Rifle, Colorado. More than three thousand sheep stampeded over a bluff, falling like hail two hundred feet down into a dry streambed."

Lincoln slapped his knees and stood up, raising everybody's eyes with him.

"I don't see the situation as threatening imminent bloodshed. There will be ill feeling—the note on the door already confirmed that. But if the flock is herded through the cattle's range to the mountains, and if the sheep keep their distance from the cattle, the ranchers will have nothing to complain about. And as time goes on, hopefully they'll get used to our woollymonsters."

If they had the common sense God gave a normal man, they would.

The flock arrived, escorted from the railhead by Wedman, George Meadows, and the sheepdog, a two-year-old, rough-haired collie named Flag. A wooden trough four feet deep welcomed them. It was filled with sheep dip that ensured the sheep could barely touch bottom passing through it. One by one the animals were forced into the trough at one end, swam or scrambled the fifteen feet to the other, and climbed up a sloping, cleated ramp.

After they had dried off, a Double-L mark was applied to their freshly clipped fleece with a wooden stamp dipped in a bucket of red paint. To make double sure his ownership was clear, the sheep were earmarked with a combination of cuts and notches. At Mario's suggestion, a slightly different mark would be used each year so that they could tell the age of the sheep when it came time to separate them for market.

After dipping, the lambs were docked, relieved of all but one or two inches of their tails for sanitary and reproductive reasons. A red-hot iron was used, which severed the tail and cauterized the wound.

One final operation was performed before taking the flock to pasture: castrating most of the males. This pro-

CHEYENNE

duced a better quality mutton and guaranteed improvement of the breed by ensuring that the ewes would be bred only with prize rams. The operation was a supreme test of Wedman's and Meadow's devotion to their calling. Instead of castrating the sheep with a single swipe with a knife, they removed the testicles by a much more practical method, one popular among sheepmen in Europe for centuries. While the animal was being held by all four legs in a sort of elevated sitting position, one or the other herder would kneel and extract the testicles with his teeth. Not only was this technique more precise and less bloody than a knife, but it was the most dependable way to remove the connecting cords.

Out of curiosity Lorna watched the first castration. She went back to the house very quickly.

Early the next morning Lincoln accompanied Mario, Wedman, Meadows, and Flag in escorting the sheep across the open range to the mountains to pasture. There were no incidents enroute; Knox's and Weigans's cattle were seen scattered about grazing, but no cowhands.

The sheep were put out to pasture until nightfall. The meadow grass was abundant and there was water from no less than three sources close by. Most important, from Lincoln's point of view, cattle did not range into the mountains.

"If your friends want to cause any trouble, they'll have to climb up here," said Mario. "It doesn't seem likely they'll bother."

The sun was going down under a slender purple wedge of cloud, and the air was still, as if with expectancy. It was noticeably cooler up here, the grass greener than that on the level ground beyond the foothills below, which was fully exposed throughout the day to the sun. Wedman was at the far end of the pasture with the dog, keeping the sheep from straying; they were already beginning to settle down for the night. George Meadows had started a fire and was sitting reading his Bible, his lips forming each word. Lincoln got up from the rock he'd been sitting on.

"You were right about one thing," he said to Mario. "They certainly do smell."

"Stink. You get used to it."

"Do you suppose I'll ever learn to castrate a lamb with my teeth?"

Mario chuckled. "I never did. You going to stay the night?"

"I'd rather not leave Lorna alone. At least until the neighbors make their play, if they're going to."

"I really don't think they will, Lincoln."

"Not up here, maybe, but they could pester us around the place. You coming back with me?"

"No. I'd like to stay at least tonight and tomorrow."

"Will they need you?"

Before Mario could answer, a wolf howled in the distance. Mario tightened his hand around his rifle on his lap.

"They may."

Meadows had stopped his reading. He called over. "That's the second time I heard him. He's about two miles away, he's getting closer. Wonder if he's alone or with the pack?"

Lincoln mounted his horse and rode back.

Mario came riding in shortly after eight the next morning. It was raining lightly, but the sky was breaking, indicating it would probably let up soon. Lorna and Lincoln met him out front. He had ridden at a gallop, so his horse was blowing hard. Lincoln took one look at Mario's face and read it correctly.

"What happened?"

Mario dug in his pocket, bringing out his knotted neckerchief. They went inside. He untied it to reveal what looked like table salt.

"I think it's arsenic," he said grimly.

Lorna sucked in a breath sharply. Lincoln glowered. Mario went on.

"I don't know what arsenic tastes like, but if you burn it, it burns with a blue flame and smells like garlic. Somebody scattered it along the edge of the pasture during the night. The sheep started grazing at sunup. I'm afraid—"

"How many?" Lorna asked.

"About thirty—"

"My God!"

"We moved them right away, of course. Higher up. Good spot, better than the first one. We took turns guarding them last night. George says when he was standing guard he heard horses at a distance and spotted two or three men riding off."

"Knox's men!" burst Lincoln.

"He said they were heading north. He just got a fleeting glimpse of them. Wouldn't have gotten that except he heard them."

"They came from the Weigans," said Lorna to Lincoln.

Mario nodded. "George woke me this morning. A couple sheep had already died. He and Eric moved the whole flock out of there, but not before the others died. Thirty's bad, Lincoln, but it could have been a lot worse. After they pulled out I examined the grass, found this." He shook his head discouragedly. "Here we're looking out for wolves and coyotes and all the while two-legged skunks are sneaking around salting the grass with this stuff. Those people just don't believe in live and let live, do they? I never saw anything like this back in Michigan."

A man on a big bay stallion was riding toward the front gate. He reined up. They met him at the front door. It had stopped raining; the water dripped from the porch roof. The sun had come out. He introduced himself, removing his hat and revolving it slowly in front of him.

"Mr. Rhilander, Mrs., my name's Polk, I work for your father, ma'am. I'm afraid I got some bad news."

She gasped, her fingers going to her throat. "What's the matter?"

"He's sick in bed. Took sick late yesterday."

"With what?"

Polk scratched his head and studied his hat in his hands. "Don't know."

"When exactly?"

"Must have been sometime last night."

He shrugged. He was about fifty, with a handsome and honest face, a massive chest, and the beginning of a bulge encircling his waist. He seemed a gentle man, uncomfortable in the role of bearer of bad news. He resumed turning his hat in his grasp.

"She, the countess, went off. To Hot Springs up to Dakota Territory, so they say—"

"Deserted him!" burst Lorna. "Left him sick, helpless!"

"No no, she went before he took sick. She left right after supper. He was okay then. He woke up in the middle of the night sick. He's in a real bad way. The maid, Maria's, taking care of him best she can, I reckon."

"Get my horse," she said to Lincoln.

"I'm coming, too."

He started around back, Mario a step behind him. Lincoln talked to him over his shoulder.

"Wait here for me, we'll go back out to where the sheep are when I get back. George's seeing those men riding toward the H&W cinches it. Knox and Bazarian weren't in on it, they weren't before. It's all come from Weigans's place. Lorna's been right all along, Emerald's the instigator. Cutting Jubal's fence, burning the barn, stirring up the Cattlemen's Association."

"But she married Hunnicutt—"

"You know of a better way to get control of somebody?"

Mario helped saddle the two horses. Lincoln mounted and led Lorna's horse.

"You stay here," he said to Mario.

"Right. Everything's okay out there for the moment. The sheep are safe. What'll we do with the dead ones, leave 'em for the buzzards?"

"Later . . ."

Lorna cried out at first sight of Jubal as they entered the room. He looked dead. His skin showed an ominous bluish tinge; it was moist, clammy looking, his features sunken. He struggled to breathe, getting barely enough oxygen to sustain him. The maid was nowhere to be seen. Lorna set a hand against Jubal's forehead.

"Not very hot, but that doesn't mean anything." She

pulled up a chair and checked his pulse. "It's so feeble you can hardly feel it. Get Dr. Gogarty!"

"He's coming, he's coming." Lincoln set his hands on her shoulders comfortingly.

"Where the devil is the maid? Mariaaaaaa!"

When they came in, Polk had excused himself to go talk to the other hired hands and send a man down to Cheyenne after Gogarty. Now Polk reappeared. He came hesitantly into the room. He had overheard Lorna.

"Boys say Maria's left, bag and baggage," he murmured. "Must have been while I was over getting you."

Lorna sat staring down at her father, cupping her hand over his, suffering, frightened, dreading that his next breath would be his last. Lincoln brought a glass of water and damp cloth, laying the cloth across Jubal's forehead. Lorna moistened his lips with the water. For nearly two hours she did not move from her chair, watching, waiting in a quiet frenzy, at the mercy of her nerves, beset and bullied by her fears. Jubal did not stir, did not open his eyes.

Gogarty arrived. He came rushing in, stopped in the bedroom doorway, surveyed Jubal, crossed himself mumbling something, and ordered Lorna out of the room. She demurred, but he nearly shoved her out. She and Lincoln stood at the closed door listening, neither speaking, waiting. She clenched and unclenched her fists, staring at the knob as if fighting to keep from throwing the door open.

Five minutes passed; the door slowly opened. She held her breath. Gogarty had taken off his jacket and unbuttoned his vest. His ancient order of Hibernia pin glinted in the sunlight coming through the front window. His stethoscope hung around his neck. He looked deeply distressed.

"Heat some water," he said. "Not boiling, just warm. I'm going to have to pump him out. It's a little late, but—"

"What is it?" she burst.

"Poison."

"My God! The bitch!"

A. R. Riefe

"Take it easy," said Gogarty. "Get the water. Lincoln, you can help me here."

She flew off to the kitchen. Gogarty pulled Lincoln into the room and lowered his voice.

"He's in very rough shape."

"Poison? Are you sure?"

"Definitely. It looks like arsenic. I'll flush out his stomach, give him a dose of castor oil, then a solution of ammonia and iron perchloride. Drain off the precipitate, suspend what's left in water, and try to get it down him." He paused and glanced back at Jubal. "I can't imagine he'll put up much resistance."

"What are his chances?" Lincoln asked.

"You tell me. We'll know better in a few hours. I only wish I could have gotten to him earlier."

"It's too late," said Lincoln resignedly.

Gogarty seemed to have suddenly plunged into his thoughts, giving no indication that he even heard. He looked up and about him.

"Where the hell's that water?"

"Coming!" Lorna called from the kitchen.

Gogarty did all he could for his patient. Now the three of them were doing the only thing left to do. They sat in the parlor waiting, Lorna forbidden by Gogarty to sit by Jubal's bed.

"Staring at him won't help either of you. He's made it this far. Now we leave him alone and give his system a chance to come back."

"Arsenic," said Lorna quietly. "The murdering bitch!"

"You're assuming it was Emerald," said Lincoln.

She jerked her head up and scowled so at him he pulled back instinctively.

"You think it was the maid? That's idiotic. Go down to Cheyenne. Right now. Get hold of Sheriff Eccols. Sign a complaint or whatever. I want a warrant sworn out for her arrest. Attempted murder."

"Amen," said Gogarty.

She went on through his interruption. "She wanted to turn this land back to cattle, take down the fences, restore the grass, double the size of the H&W. He refused, they argued, she decided she couldn't budge him—"

"And got rid of him," interposed Gogarty.

"When he wakes up," she went on. "The first question I ask is, did you two argue about the property."

Gogarty shook his head. "I don't understand. Not what you're saying about her, that's probably exactly how it was. What I don't get is why arsenic?"

"You mean why didn't she pay one of her men to shoot him like she did Heinrich?"

"It could be she messed up. When somebody tries to get rid of somebody with arsenic, they generally do it gradually, in small doses. The shape he's in it looks like he swallowed half a can. Off course, it could be he only ingested a little bit and suffered a particularly violent reaction. People do vary."

Lorna had stopped pacing. She narrowed her eyes. "I don't care if she gave him two grains or two thousand, it's still murder."

"Attempted," corrected Lincoln.

"She's dead! I'll personally spring the trap on the gallows."

"How long does arsenic take to work?" Lincoln asked.

"Anywhere from a few minutes to eight or ten hours," said Gogarty. "If he ingested it on a full stomach, which he did from what we got out of him, if say he ate at six o'clock, it probably hit him around two or three in the morning."

"That's how she planned it," said Lorna. "So she'd be miles away."

"On the way to Hot Springs in Dakota Territory," said Lincoln.

"That's the last place she'd head for," she said. "That's just to throw us off the track."

"I'll tell you something," said Gogarty. "If you can find that maid of hers, she's bound to know something."

"Where can she be?" said Lorna.

Gogarty shrugged. "Jubal probably woke her up with his thrashing and carrying on; my guess is she took one look, panicked, and ran. But if you can find her, if you hire Cicero to prosecute and he gets her up on the witness stand, she'll be the one to put the noose around the Giradoux woman's neck."

"To save her own," added Lorna.

"Exactly."

Lorna had resumed fuming. "The heartless bitch. She got away with murdering the count and who knows how many others, but this time we've got her."

Gogarty smiled thinly. "If you can find her, bring her back."

She ignored this. "Lincoln—"

"I'm going, I'm going."

37

That night and throughout the following day, Jubal's condition showed no change. The thread of his life stretched taut and vulnerable under the menacing blade. The waiting and watching was gradually becoming intolerable for Lorna. Still she kept her vigil. Sheriff Eccols, meanwhile, issued a warrant for the absent Emerald's arrest. Two deputies were dispatched to Hot Springs on the assumption that if she had gone there, even if she'd since left, someone might know where she'd gone. A search was also launched for the maid, Maria.

Jubal began mumbling incoherently in his sleep. Clutching at straws, Lorna thought this a good sign. Gogarty thought it neither good nor bad. Once Lorna thought she heard her mother's name, but could not be sure. The only certainty was that the demons that had captured Jubal's system were now in possession of his mind. Gogarty came every morning. He was also asking about town if anyone knew of a trained nurse anywhere in the area. Meanwhile, Lorna filled the role. Gogarty ordered Jubal covered with blankets to keep him perspiring. In the absence of any other safe, mild stimulant he administered injections of brandy. Lorna took Jubal's temperature every half hour and kept a written record. The pain in Jubal's stomach was persisting; it could be seen by his expression. He also had cramps in the calves of both legs. Gogarty eased his discomfort with periodic injections of morphia. The bluish tinge of Jubal's skin, caused by a

333

reduction of hemoglobin in the capillaries, seemed to be gradually fading. But this was the only good sign.

Three days after Jubal was stricken, to Lorna's and Lincoln's astonishment Emerald returned, walking in the front door carrying her valise.

"Jubal, I'm home. Jubal?"

Lincoln and Lorna were in the bedroom. Emerald came to the door, pulling off her gloves.

"What . . . ?" She eyed them, eyed Jubal and started. "What's the matter with him?"

"As if you didn't know!" shrilled Lorna and sprang at her.

Lincoln had to pull her off. Emerald shrank back against the wall, finding her lip with the back of her hand to see if it was bleeding.

"Murderer!" screamed Lorna.

They began yelling curses and threats at each other. The bedroom window was open at the top. Two hired hands heard and came running in, eyes questioning. Emerald was seized and taken out kicking and screaming. They had to tie her hand and foot before they could get her into her buggy. Throughout the struggle Jubal never so much as opened his eyes.

Emerald was taken down to Cheyenne and locked up. Apprised of the charge against her, she hired a lawyer. James Madison Bloodworth was reputedly the ablest and most successful trial lawyer west of Chicago. The Rhilanders hired Cicero Sebastian Pinchot to oppose him. The contrast between the two men was little short of remarkable. Pinchot was astute and eminently capable, but he was untested in the arena of two-fisted legal squabbling. His experience was pretty much restricted to paper cases: disputes over wills, deeds, agreements, contracts, licenses, and the like. He was a less than imposing presence regaling a jury, an aging and weary backwoods stump lawyer.

By contrast James Madison Bloodworth was the sort of individual who could enter a courtroom and stop all conversation immediately without even opening his mouth. He dressed like a self-indulgent nobleman, almost foppishly, being partial to expensive foulard ties that stood out like gonfalons, custom-tailored suits and cloaks. Surmounting this sartorial ostentation was a flowing snow-white mane that he wore at shoulder length. He delighted in flinging his head histrionically, sweeping his hair like a white flag of surrender, setting female hearts aflutter and impressing men easily impressed by obvious devices for commanding attention. Bloodworth was also gifted with a profile that rivalled Apollo's, a voice extraordinarily rich and deep, and a superb command of the language. It was said that he could play a jury with the ease and excellence of a virtuoso. Brilliant, articulate, shrewd, and perceptive, he was capable of reading the presiding judge's mind, his opponent's, the witnesses', as easily as lesser mortals read their morning newspapers.

His client was a beautiful and wealthy woman, and within hours after his arrival in Cheyenne, Bloodworth heard her story, took stock of the situation, and resolved to make the best of what she had to offer: her seductive appearance (there would be no women on the jury) and a flair for the dramatic second only to his own. He came in on the noon train. By five o'clock he was painting his client to the press and the public at large as a fiercely loyal and adoring wife, as shocked by what had happened in her absence as anyone, completely misunderstood by her accusers, an innocent victim.

The trial was to be held in the courthouse on Paxton Street, formerly a gambling saloon whose owner had defaulted on his mortgage held by the bank and fled the county. The bar and the mirror overlooking it still remained, but the stock of liquor, gaming tables, and piano had all been taken away.

The nature of the case, the beautiful defendant, Bloodworth's involvement, and Jubal's precarious condition fascinated the locals. It promised to be a sensational trial; suddenly little Cheyenne found itself on the front pages of big city newspapers across the nation. Aloysius Gogarty remarked that if tickets were sold to the trial, standing room would likely go for fifty dollars a head.

Judge Aaron Slye Turnbull, formerly of Denver, was selected to preside. Turnbull was in his late sixties and looked ten years older. He was almost completely bald, no more than twenty or so sorry looking hairs clinging to life on his pate. Gogarty saw a value to the prosecution in this.

"Wait'll he gets a look at Bloodworth's mop. He'll turn bilious with envy and hate the son of a bitch," he observed.

It was rumored that despite his age and his fifty-four years of marriage, the judge retained a young man's eye for the ladies. How Emerald would impress him remained to be seen. He had a violent temper; it was said that he'd once hurled his gavel at a defense attorney, knocking him cold and giving him a concussion. He was also not above reviling those who crossed or upset him, and had once ordered an entire jury off the case and out of the building for incurring his displeasure. As some fancy themselves little tin gods, Turnbull fancied Turnbull a little tin god-judge.

The jury comprised twelve reasonably decent, law-abiding citizens, among them two ministers, a school-teacher, one of Cheyenne's four overworked blacksmiths, and men from various other callings, including two bar-tenders and an itinerant faro dealer.

Sheriff Eccols's men were still searching for Maria. Emerald, meanwhile, had been freed on bail at the request of her lawyer. Jubal remained unconscious. He neither gained nor slipped back. Dr. Gogarty spared Lorna any false optimism.

"It can last a day, a week, years. It can last—"

"Until he dies."

"There have been cases—"

"There's nothing more you can do."

"Nothing more."

The courtroom was so crowded the standees at the rear and along the sides of the double row of seats were packed as tightly as the branches of a besom. Lorna remained at Jubal's bedside. Lincoln sat with Gogarty two rows behind Cicero Pinchot at the prosecution's table. Judge Turnbull, bent and shrunken, head lowered, gleaming pate focused on the crowd, looked as if he'd just made it to the top of a wall, enabling him to peer over it. He hammered for silence and instructed the bailiff to read the charge.

Bloodworth called Gogarty as his first witness. He established that in the doctor's professional opinion, it was entirely conceivable that the poison could have been given to Jubal hours after Emerald had departed. Cicero Pinchot had no questions for his friend, and Gogarty was thanked and dismissed by the judge. Bloodworth then summoned his client to the stand. He had dressed her skillfully for her role.

She had on a depressingly plain black dress, no makeup, her hair was pulled up and pinned in a crown that gave her a look that suggested she spent most of her waking hours in church.

At Bloodworth's request she related her part in the events of the tragic evening. She had gone to Hot Springs by stagecoach from Laramie, boarding at Horse Creek. In Hot Springs she stayed at the home of an old and dear friend, helping her get ready for her wedding. She left for home the day after the wedding. Before she left home she and Jubal had had supper together. She did not prepare the meal, not even the coffee. She and Jubal had sat outside talking while Maria readied everything. She called them in and served.

"Unless the prosecution objects, Your Honor, I'll pass over what the meal consisted of," said Bloodworth.

"No objection," muttered Pinchot.

"Appreciate it, old boy," rejoined Bloodworth in a syrupy tone. "Mrs. Hunnicutt, to your best recollection, did your husband eat everything set before him?"

"We both did."

"He took dessert."

"Yes."

"Did he drink his coffee?"

"He did. I did not. I do not drink coffee. As I recall, I did not drink anything, not even water."

"And before and during the meal, did you at any time go into the kitchen? For any reason?"

"No sir," she rejoined.

"You never got up from the table."

A. R. Riefe

"No."

"Did he?" Bloodworth asked.

"I must think, please."

"Take your time."

She thought, straining melodramatically. "No."

"Then would I be correct if I say never to your recollection were you out of each other's sight from the time you came into the house, sat down to eat, and finished?"

"No."

"You are very sure."

"*Absolument.*"

"The maid prepared the food and served it."

"Yes."

"And you left before or after your husband started on his coffee?"

"Before. He never drank it with his meal. He always waited until later."

"Mrs. Hunnicutt, did you put arsenic in your husband's food, in his coffee, in anything he ate or drank?"

"I did not. I swear by the saints. When I came back and found out what had happened, I was astounded. And so shocked I thought my heart would stop. And terribly worried about poor Jubal. I saw him lying there, naturally I wanted to go to him, but his daughter blocked my way. She attacked me, accused me. Her husband and some of the men overpowered me, tied me. I was taken to Cheyenne and locked up."

"Accused of attempted murder."

"It's ridiculous! I love my husband. To think I would harm him in any way is absolute nonsense."

"Nevertheless, he *was* poisoned."

"Not by me."

"But since that tragic night, since you arrived back, I'm sure you've thought about it."

"I've had nothing to do but think about it. They won't even let me see him. Me, his wife!"

" 'They,' meaning his daughter and her husband."

"Who else? She despises me. Why, as God is my witness, I don't know. I can't understand it, neither can her father. We've talked about it many times. It is like a

338

stone on his heart. Before he and I were married, his daughter and her husband lived with him. She was dead against our getting married."

"Your Honor," interrupted Pinchot. "I object. This is irrelevant—"

"Overruled. Go on, my dear."

"Jubal and his daughter argued terribly; he finally had no choice but to ask both to leave. She hasn't even spoken to him since. Heaven only knows why she's so bitter."

"One more question, Mrs. Hunnicutt. You say you've had nothing to do but think about what happened. You say you're innocent. Based on what you've told us, your account of your conduct, your movements, the timing, I accept that. Tell me, who do you think did it?"

"Objection, Your Honor," rasped Pinchot. "The question calls for a conclusion by the witness. Her opinion, and that's all it is, has no value."

"Overruled. I'm curious to hear her opinion. And I do know, Counselor, that's all it is. Proceed."

"Mrs. Hunnicutt?"

Emerald sighed melodramatically and shook her head. "I do hate to accuse, but this is so serious. Poor, poor Jubal may die. Whatever could have possessed her? Oh, they've had words, more than once, but to dislike someone, to argue, is a far cry from wanting to kill them. But I've thought and thought about it and I keep coming back to the same conclusion. The only conclusion. Jubal certainly didn't accidentally poison himself. It had to be Maria."

"Your maid."

"Yes yes, *incroyable*—"

"Your Honor," continued Bloodworth, "I would like to point out that the maid, Maria Esposito, fled the premises and has yet to be found. I'll point out further that the defendant here returned to her home voluntarily and with absolutely no inkling of what had happened. Thank you, Mrs. Hunnicutt. That will be all, and please, try to calm yourself. This nightmare will soon be over, the truth will prove your innocence."

A. R. Riefe

The gavel came down hard enough to shatter it.

"Save the speech till the windup, friend."

"I'm sorry, Your Honor, I apologize."

"Your witness, friend Pinchot."

Bloodworth retired to his seat glowing with victory. Pinchot approached Emerald.

"Mrs. Hunnicutt, or should I say Countess Weigans? And how many were there before the count, five, six?"

"Objection, Your Honor, the prosecution is attempting to smear the lady's reputation. How many times she's been married is irrelevant and immaterial."

"How many, dear?" asked Turnbull, leering lecherously.

"Only twice, Your Honor," said Emerald, smiling demurely.

"Twice," repeated Pinchot. He picked a sheaf of papers up from his table, waving them.

"Six registered marriages, Your Honor. Six registered, God knows how many phony ones."

"Objection! He's smearing the defendant, Your Honor. Have you no decency, sir!"

"Let's get off this and back onto the case," said Turnbull wearily.

"You've said that during supper neither you or your husband left the table at any time."

"We did not."

"Did he ever turn his head? I mean, you're obviously an attractive woman, but at any time during the meal was he able to tear his eyes from you?"

"Objection!"

"Oh shut up, friend!" snapped Turnbull. "And you, Pinchot, could you frame your questions a little less sarcastically?" He smiled at Emerald. "Answer him, my dear."

"He may have looked away, I cannot say I remember."

"He may have looked away. Giving you a chance to drop something into his coffee."

"Objection!"

"Like sugar. Now you've claimed, so very reluctantly, that Maria Esposito was the only one in a position to poison your husband."

"I feel so badly for her, poor soul. She must have been, how do you say it, temporarily deranged?"

"That's how you say it."

"Now she's run off and no one can find her," added Emerald in a worried tone.

"So it appears, and that makes her guilty, right?"

"Well . . ."

"You, on the other hand, came back, and that exonerates you. It proves you're innocent. Who but an innocent would come back and walk into a buzzsaw? Unwittingly. Unless of course, you actually did the deed and got the brilliant idea that nobody could possibly believe you guilty if you did return."

"Objection!"

"Sustained. Friend, if you're going to accuse the lady, I suggest you get up some proof."

"Mrs. Hunnicutt, or do you prefer Countess?" Pinchot eyed her archly.

"Mrs. Hunnicutt," she replied, looking through him.

"Your previous husband, the one before Mr. Hunnicutt, was shot and killed, was he not?"

"Yes."

"His killer was never found." Pinchot paused to consult the papers in his hand. "Your second husband, a Mr. Weir, also suffered an untimely demise at the hands of a person or persons unknown."

"Yes."

"You divorced your third husband, your fourth was killed in a bar fight. Four, five, six months later you married his killer, a Mr.—would you help me?"

"Colclaw."

"Right."

"Objection!" Bloodworth was on his feet gesticulating, bellowing.

"Sustained. Is any of this leading anywhere? You keep slipping off the track." Judge Turnbull hefted his gavel, then shored up his chin with it.

"Your Honor," said Pinchot. "I'm merely trying to prove that the lady's past history in matters matrimonial is anything but praiseworthy. Practically every time she hits town some poor fellow winds up cashing in."

"He is right, Your Honor," said Emerald. "I confess I don't know why it is, but I am dangerous to men. Men fight over me, they have dueled, they have died, and I do nothing to provoke any of it. I swear by the saints, all I want out of life is happiness, security, and perhaps love; what every woman wants. When I married Jubal I hoped and prayed I would get all three. And I did. He is a wonderful husband, a prince, a saint. I love him with all my heart and being." She brought out a handkerchief and touched her nose and daubed at the corner of her eye. "If he dies—" Her voice broke.

"Now now, my dear," said Turnbull. "Don't upset yourself. Any further questions?"

"Just one, Your Honor," said Pinchot. "Mrs. Hunnicutt, keeping in mind that you're under oath, tell us, can you prove that Maria Esposito attempted to murder your husband? Or merely that you suspect she did."

"I *know* she did. And I'm to blame."

A rumble passed through the spectators. As one they leaned forward.

"I don't follow you," said Pinchot.

"Jubal suspected she intended to harm him. He warned me against her. I pooh-poohed it, I told him she was a hothead, but that was all. I never dreamed . . . Please understand, she is an excellent maid, a superb worker, *merveilleuse*, but . . ."

"Thank you, that'll be all," snapped Pinchot.

"You're excused, my dear," said Turnbull. "Bloodworth, your next witness?"

"We have no more witnesses, Your Honor. We stand or we fall on my client's testimony and the failure of the prosecution to unearth one iota of evidence against her. You've seen for yourself, Your Honor, she has been a rock—"

Gavel down.

"Counselor?" said the judge, beady-eying Pinchot.

"One last witness, Your Honor. I call Maria Adeline Jacqueline Roberta Esposito to the stand."

CHEYENNE

A roar of surprise erupted. Turnbull banged his gavel to restore order, yelling for it. Bloodworth reacted amazed. Emerald reacted as if suddenly stricken. Lincoln and Gogarty exchanged astonished looks.

"What the hell . . . ?" began the doctor.

A woman seated in the center of the spectators had risen from her chair. She threw back the scarf covering her head, revealing her face. Turnbull called her forward. The crowd resumed babbling as she took the witness chair, then quieted. The bailiff held the Bible for her.

"Doyouswearthatthetestimonyyou'reabouttogive isthetruththewholetruthandnothingbutthetruthso helpyouGod?"

"I swear by Holy Saint Vincent."

"Swear by God."

"By Saint Vincent!"

"Your Honor . . ."

"Let it go, let it go. You may sit down, my dear. You are Maria Esposito?"

"Yes, Your Honor."

"You're supposed to be long gone."

She explained that she had gone to Albino, had heard about her mistress being accused and jailed, and had returned to Cheyenne that morning, walking into Cicero Pinchot's office.

Lincoln studied her as she sat clutching her handbag and enlightening her listeners. She had not changed a hair since the last time he'd seen her: in Weigans's parlor the morning he and Jubal had visited Henry to complain about the damage to the fence. It would be generous, he thought, to describe Maria as drab, but homely would be more truthful. The dullness, the emptiness, the unhappiness of her existence was mirrored in her face, and her eyes and voice carried bitterness. He watched her thick lips move and her glance dart to the right at Emerald seated beside Bloodworth at his table. Clearly the woman was a neurotic in a class with Mona Schwimmer, Lincoln decided. Pinchot must think her an emotional tinderbox;

343

his tone in speaking to her was like that of a doctor addressing an unstable patient.

"You ran away," he began.

"I got up at six, made breakfast, called him. He didn't answer. I knocked on the bedroom door, no answer. I called, opened the door, there he was dead. He looked dead, his face all blue. I couldn't look. I left. Oh blessed Saint Vincent, what a sight he was, he was dead, dead . . ."

"All right, all right," said Pinchot soothingly.

She shot out her arm, pointing accusingly. "She did it! She murdered him. Her!"

Turnbull rapped his gavel.

"Hold it! The jury will disregard that last. Woman, get hold of yourself. Don't talk, just answer the questions."

"I worked myself to death for her. Up at the old house, down at the new one. I do everything, you know, cook, wash, clean, she doesn't lift a finger. Now she accuses me! She dares! Me, faithful as an old dog I am, sticking by her. This is the thanks I get!"

The gavel pounded, Turnbull fumed and sputtered, Bloodworth shot to his feet objecting, Pinchot tried to get a word in, but she babbled on, oblivious to them all. "Arsenic? There was arsenic up at the old place. We got in six sacks for the rats in the big barn. There was a plague of rats. You dare accuse me, you Jezebel! Harlot! Oh, I left, but when I heard they'd arrested her I knew they wouldn't accuse me. I was afraid before, that's why I left. He didn't *die*, I could see, somebody'd done something to him. Her. Who else! She killed His Lordship, you know. Cameron did, the big one who smelled like the barn and was always sweating. He's gone now. She hired him, he shot His Lordship, and dumped his body in Hunnicutt's barn."

"Objection! Objection! Objection!" roared Bloodworth. "She's raving, listen to her. She's a lunatic!"

"Lunatic? Stupid man, what do you know? They killed him, her and Cameron. Murderer! Murderer! He was a good man, a gentleman, polite, such fine table manners, and always immaculate."

"Quiet!" Turnbull banged away without stopping.

"Counselor, shut her up! Bailiff, get a gag, get rope . . . Order, order in the court. Order in the goddamn court!"

"She's the one, she killed Mr. Hunnicutt. Not me. He was kind to me. She lies and lies; look at her, she's a devil, she has a map of all the land and it's marked and she has it all hers, not theirs, not Knox's, hers, hers!"

The uproar was swelling, she was out of control, standing, pointing at Emerald, glaring at the judge; Pinchot got hold of her, sitting her slowly down.

"I'm holding you in contempt!" boomed Turnbull. "Contempt, you hear?"

"As if I'd harm a hair on his head . . ."

Turnbull was on his feet, holding his gavel like a hatchet, as if threatening to strike her if she didn't stop.

"Off the stand. Get her off!"

Pinchot got her out of the chair and back to his table; she was beginning to quiet down. He sat her down and talked soothingly to her. She dug out a hanky and began sniffling into it.

"Jesus Christ, what a spectacle!" rasped Turnbull. "Shut her up and keep her shut up. Damnation! Any more witnesses? No more. Summations. Bloodworth."

"Your Honor," said Bloodworth, rising again and casting what was designed to be a sympathetic glance at Maria. "There's nothing to say. This case speaks for itself and most eloquently. The defense rests."

"Pinchot."

"The prosecution rests," mumbled Pinchot discouragedly. He sat slumped in his chair, staring into space and shaking his head, a comforting hand on Maria's back.

"Gentlemen of the jury," said Turnbull. "You've heard the witnesses, you will now consult among yourselves and determine your verdict."

The jury foreman stood up. "No need, Your Honor, we find the defendant not guilty—"

"Not guilty!"

Maria had shot to her feet. She looked stunned. Color rose in her cheeks as if blood was rapidly being pumped into them. She glared fiercely at the foreman, at the judge, at Emerald seated to her left less than ten feet away. Emerald and Bloodworth were both standing; she was embracing him, then she turned and smiled triumphantly at her accuser.

Maria roared like an animal. She was purple with rage, like dynamite threatening to detonate. She quickly drew a pistol from her bag and fired squarely at Emerald's chest. She turned slowly and aimed at the judge; he ducked and two shots sped through the space where his head had been; she turned, aiming at the foreman, firing, missing.

The judge, the jury, the crowd had watched her kill Emerald in awestruck silence, but when she shifted her aim toward Turnbull everyone came alive. With more than three hundred people crammed into such close confines, there was nowhere to move but down. The seated spectators dropped to the floor as one; those standing at the sides and in the rear were so tightly packed they could not budge. All they could do was stare white-faced with fear. Everyone else went down except Cicero Pinchot. He stood unflinching not two feet from her, calmly surveying her, extending his hand, asking for the weapon.

She seemed to consider handing it over. Then changed her mind, shook her head, thrust the barrel in her mouth, and fired.

38

Lincoln sat with Lorna in the bedroom watching Gogarty fuss over the still unconscious Jubal. Lincoln had finished telling her about the bizarre and abrupt end to the trial.

"One thing I don't understand," he said. "How did she get the gun into the courtroom? Everybody was supposed to be searched at the door. Aloysius and I were."

"The boys at the door slipped up," said Gogarty, looking back at them. "Either that or she hid it on her and sneaked it back into her bag during the trial."

"She certainly came prepared," said Lorna.

Jubal stirred. She jumped up.

"Is he?" she began.

"Nothing," said Gogarty. "Still, look at his face, his cheeks. I do believe there's faint pink."

Jubal remained unconscious for the next five days. On the morning of the sixth day, a Saturday, he came out of it. He was utterly drained but able to smile feebly when he recognized Lorna and Lincoln. From then on he improved by the hour. Her first question put to him was the one she had held in mind all along. Did he and Emerald argue about the property? She couldn't believe she heard right when he said no.

"She wanted to change over to cattle. We talked about it, but we didn't argue. I suggested she change the H&W over to crops, and that's where we left it."

"So why in God's name did she try to kill you?"

347

"Old habits are hard to break," interposed Lincoln. "She sure was something different. I've seen rapacious people, the greediest of the greedy in my time, but she was queen of the pack."

Within a week Jubal was able to get out of bed and supervise the last of the planting. As his wife's only surviving relative, he inherited her wealth, the money Henry Weigans had brought with him from his homeland. The crop turned out even better than the previous year's; the farm thrived and Jubal bought additional land.

Lincoln and Lorna's flocks also thrived. Other settlers turned their efforts to sheep raising and in time—in a very long time—the cattlemen grudgingly came to accept the presence of the wooly monsters in what had been their exclusive domain. Their prejudices died slowly, but they died. With Mario's help Lincoln and other sheepmen set out to educate their neighbors. They convinced them that sheep and cattle can exist side by side without harm to either. Lincoln fenced his property, dug irrigation ditches and wells, put up a windmill to pump water, set aside land to raise fodder crops for winter feeding, and turned to running a stock farm rather than a ranch.

Jubal's farm prospered as did the cattle ranch and the fortune he'd inherited from his wife. It did take nearly twenty years before the die-hards among the cattlemen came to accept sheepmen and sodbusters in their midst, but accept them they did.

Fort D.A. Russell was rebuilt of brick in 1880, and the parade ground and many of the buildings are still in use at Warren Air Force Base.

Cheyenne became the chief city and the capital of Wyoming, which itself became a state in 1890. Cheyenne prospered from the beginning, thanks largely to the presence of the Union Pacific and later other railroads, and to the extensive railroad shops of the U.P. situated there. Today it boasts a population of nearly fifty thousand, making it second in size only to Caspar in the state.

CHEYENNE

And now for what comes next
Thou waitest in thine invulnerable West,
Blazoning more large thy living-lettered text,
"Chance and the tools to those who use them best."

—Charles Leonard Moore, "To America"

Read all the titles in
THE INDIAN HERITAGE SERIES
by Paul Lederer